INDIGO ROAD

Reed Bunzel

coffeetownpress

Kenmore, WA

A Coffee Town Press book published by Epicenter Press

Epicenter Press
6524 NE 181st St.
Suite 2
Kenmore, WA 98028

For more information go to:
www.Camelpress.com
www.Coffeetownpress.com
www.Epicenterpress.com
Author's website: www.reedbunzel.com

This is a work of fiction. Names, characters, places, brands, media, and incidents are the product of the author's imagination or are used fictitiously.

Indigo Road
2023 © Reed Bunzel

ISBN: 9781684922048 (trade paper)
ISBN: 9781684922055 (ebook)

LOC: 2022946248

Printed in the United States of America

For Jennifer – Love you three.

Chapter 1

Lengthening shadows of slash pines and swamp chestnuts reached across the blacktop, as if grasping at the last filaments of daylight Willis Ronson would see before returning to his cell at the county jail.

There would be no bond this time. No leniency from the judge who first time around had set bail at twenty grand and then released him into the custody of his fuming wife. No more oyster roasts or shrimp boils, no whisky and billiards at the corner tavern. No slap-and-tickle with said wife on Sunday mornings before she headed off to church, or on Tuesday afternoons if her boss gave her a few hours off from her job adjusting the hems of other women's dresses.

The sinking knowledge of this fast-approaching deprivation was etched deep in his face as he stared at the sunbaked road stretching out before him. Sitting upright in the back seat, one hand cuffed to the steel support of the head rest in front of him. Not saying a damned word, at the advice of his court-appointed public defender, who had insisted on coming along for the ride and was positioned directly in front of him. Not something she did for all her bond-skippers, but she didn't trust Ronson to keep his mouth shut.

Nor Jack Connor's pledge not to try to get him talking on the ride home.

"It's going to be a good, long time before you get to see any of this again," was how Connor put it, talking over his shoulder to his prisoner. Or, in the eyes of the state of South Carolina, his apprehended ward. "You have anything to say for yourself before we get you checked into Leeds?"

Leeds being the colloquial term for the Sheriff Al Cannon Detention Center, located on Leeds Avenue in North Charleston.

"Don't listen to him," the lawyer warned Ronson, not for the first time. Her name was Cherine Dupree, no more than three years out of law school. Black skin that spoke to her coastal Gullah heritage, wire-rim glasses and double gold posts in the lobe of each ear. An angel's face, fresh and naïve and searching for the good in everybody, no matter what he or she had done.

Allegedly.

"I'm just keepin' to myself and enjoyin' the peace and quiet of nature," Willis Ronson lied. No expression on his pale white face, barely blinking his red eyes that were puffy from a long liaison with a bottle the night before, even though he'd insisted it was just a bout of the flu that was causing him to spit up bile. "Soaking in all the green and blue out there."

"Cuz you know what it's like *in there*," Connor reminded him.

He knew Ronson had done two stretches before, and now here he was again, looking at five to ten for attempted theft of copper wire from a power company transformer station. Came *this close* to getting the life shocked out of him, after taking a massive set of bolt cutters to cables that could have been carrying thousands of live volts. Typical Carolina redneck whose brain stem got separated from common sense at an early age, and who had rapidly descended into high crimes and misdemeanors from that moment onward.

"Why do you think I done what I done, and split?

Ronson's attorney glanced at her client over her shoulder, said, "Willis, please…I told you not to—"

She never got to finish her words. At that moment a bullet tore through the rear window of the Jeep Cherokee, shattering it in a cascade of diamonds before it bit into the windshield just below the rear-view mirror. A web of cracks spread instantly across the glass, leaving a hole the size of a wolf spider in the center.

Half a second later bullet number two entered the vehicle through the opening created by the first. It struck Ronson in the back of the neck, taking out his cerebellum and altering the trajectory of the slug just enough for it to become embedded in the side support pillar between the front and rear door. If that shot hadn't killed him, the next surely did, as it penetrated his skull and rattled around the cranium a short while before exiting through his left eye and coming to stop in the head rest in front of him. Death had been instantaneous and his body had been blown forward and down, so rounds four and five missed him completely.

Instead, Cherine Dupree screamed as the first of those next two rounds plunged directly into her shoulder. The next one slammed through her seat back, its path diverted only slightly by a metallic lumbar support that redirected it into her lower torso. The bullet came to rest precariously close to her L5 vertebrae, which later would cause her team of surgeons considerable worry and grief.

The average human reaction time from the moment of stimulus to the transmission of a signal through the spinal cord to the muscles—resulting in spontaneous nerve contraction—is less than a quarter of a second. Connor's was a bit faster than average, but not quick enough to cause him to do anything but spin the wheel reflexively to the right just after the windshield was cratered. He'd barely seen the vehicle racing up behind him, only a blur of motion in his side-view mirror a fraction of a second before the shooting erupted and his sensory system kicked in.

This action came far too late to save the life of Willis Ronson, whose range of motion was limited by the high-tensile steel chain of the handcuffs. By the time the fifth bullet had penetrated Cherine's back, Connor had wrenched the wheel back again to the left. Too fast and too far, because at that point the Cherokee was riding on two tires, and a moment later it was rolling side-over-side into a deep run-off ditch that paralleled the narrow county road. Each fragmented second that came next seemed to be marked by more gunshots, although no one but the man holding the weapon in the pick-up twenty yards back was keeping count.

One of those subsequent rounds struck Ronson a third time, a wasted chunk of lead since he was already bleeding out. The final shot managed to graze the back of Connor's right hand, carving a furrow in the compass rose that had been tattooed there a few years back. The impact caused him to release his grip on the wheel, and a moment later his arms and legs were flailing around inside the vehicle like the limbs of an untethered crash test dummy.

At some point every airbag in the vehicle deployed. At least half of the fourteen bones in Cherine Dupree's face were fractured by the sudden blast, while Connor endured a similar assault to his mandible and maxilla, as well as a roundhouse punch to his left ear. Because Willis Ronson was riding in the backseat, he was spared any such injuries which, because he was already deceased, would have been postmortem and therefore inconsequential.

The SUV continued in a forward, yawing motion for a few more seconds before it came to rest upside down in a trickle of brackish water left over from a flash thunderstorm the evening before. The trunk of a blackjack oak absorbed most of the impact, the force of which drove the six-cylinder engine rearward through the firewall and into young attorney's legs, snapping them like saplings. Her injuries, combined with the blood loss from her gunshot wounds, caused her to slip into hypovolemic shock and black out.

So did Connor, momentarily, until he blinked his eyes open and tried to regain his bearings. First thing he realized was he was hanging from his three-point seatbelt which, along with the water trickling through the shattered side window across the ripped headliner, told him the car was upside down. His head throbbed from what sure as hell felt like a skull fracture of great magnitude, probably a concussion. His jaw and nose seemed as if they'd just gone ten rounds in the ring, his ribcage punched as if he'd been gored by a bull running through the streets of Pamplona. His hand stung like a sonofabitch where the bullet had slashed his skin, and his ankle screamed from momentarily being twisted backwards.

His mind reflexively jumped back to the desert outside Kirkuk, that blistering day when a burning sun was hanging in a dusty sky as white as linen, sand biting at his parched lips like mites. He was at the wheel of a Humvee, bouncing over crumbled bricks and stone in a blown-out neighborhood northwest of the city, when a suicidal zealot cuffed to the wheel of a van packed with explosives came racing out from behind a mound of rubble that at one time had been a market. The blast had blown Connor up and outward, causing him to cartwheel through the air before he came to rest in a field of rocks, wondering if he was dead or still in the living hell known as war.

He'd lost a good friend that day, a young Texas all-state quarterback named Danny Benson who had been riding shotgun in the passenger seat next to him when the bomb detonated. Poor kid never had a chance. Several others had lost toes and fingers, and one took a piece of hot shrapnel in an eye that would never again see the beauty of a new morning, or the rosy hue of his girlfriend's shy blush.

Eddie James, who had drawn gunner duty, was blown into the air, his arm severed at the elbow by the force of the initial blast. He came to rest on what was left of the front passenger door that had done nothing to protect Private Benson, and opened a bloody fissure in the side of his head. It was a miracle he was alive.

All this swept through Connor's brain in a microsecond, caused him to glance over at Cherine Dupree, who also was hanging upside down. Either dead or unconscious, he couldn't be sure. Blood was everywhere, no way to know if it belonged to him, or her, or Willis Ronson in the backseat. Who likewise was hanging from his three-point restraint and the handcuffs, although he most definitely was no longer among the living.

A faint moan bubbled from Cherine's lips, indicating that she was breathing—but for how long? There was nothing Connor could do to help her unless he freed himself from his own safety belt, so he wriggled his feet around until he was able to brace them against the steering wheel. He then used his good hand to probe for the latch between his seat and the center console. He pressed the button and immediately dropped to the mangled ceiling, which was sticky with blood and covered with fragments of tempered glass. His ribs cursed with pain—although nothing like that day in Kirkuk—but he knew Cherine Dupree was in far worse condition.

He managed to position himself partly beneath her, pushing up on the shoulder that wasn't bleeding to give her just enough slack so he could click her belt latch. When he did, she tumbled down on top of him, momentarily pinning him against the roof. He felt, rather than heard, a low gasp seep from her lungs and, for a second, he wondered if it might have been her last. He felt her wrist for a pulse, found something that seemed no more than a quiver.

Alive, but losing a lot of blood.

It was then that he heard a voice. Or was it his own mind starting to grow numb, a deceased relative calling to him from across the great divide? No, that would hardly be possible, since most of his known family was a full time zone away, and none of them—not even the dead—wanted anything to do with him. Plus, he was quite sure he was only bleeding from superficial wounds and, at least in his mind, he hadn't really been shot.

A second later Connor heard the voice again. Muffled and tentative, and a little guttural. It also meant there had to be at least two voices, because human conversation generally required more than one person. Logic that was spot on, because he then heard a response that was a bit louder, more decisive. In charge.

"Hold your fire."

It sure didn't sound like some good Samaritan who had witnessed the crash and pulled to the side of the road to check for casualties and assist the injured.

Hold your fire. Which meant guns, and fingers on triggers.

All of which Connor took to mean these were the same bastards who had raced up behind them and laid siege on his Jeep, killed Willis Ronson, and critically wounded Cherine Dupree. And in the process had run them all off the road.

Now it seemed they were moving through the brackish run-off ditch, coming to finish them off.

Chapter 2

As a state-licensed bond-runner, Connor had considerable latitude when tracking down bail skips. One perk of his job was the pistol he kept in his glove compartment, which he'd made sure was loaded before setting out in pursuit of Willis Ronson. While he didn't care much for guns, they'd been a fact of life and death from the moment he'd hit boot camp, and had saved his life on more than one occasion. Even so, following his discharge from the army, he'd done his best to distance himself from them as best he could. Too many of his brothers in arms had turned their weapons against their wives or girlfriends, or themselves. The seduction of the trigger was incredibly strong, and the result so incredibly permanent.

As someone once said, *the problem with temptation is that you may not get another chance.*

Today, however, he needed the SIG Sauer P365 he'd picked up several months ago at Pawn-O-Rama in North Charleston. Problem was, the entire dashboard on the passenger side had been driven inward from the impact with the tree, coming dangerously close to crushing Cherine Dupree's chest. Connor knew the glove box was there, somewhere, tangled in the deflated airbag, and after a few desperate seconds his probing fingers eventually managed to pry it loose. All while the voices outside the car inched closer and closer.

The micro-compact 9mm pistol dropped to the ceiling and Connor grabbed it, the quick motion sending a spear of pain through the bones of his right hand. He winced, then twisted his body back to where he could get a good look—and a clean shot—at whoever was approaching.

"You think that's him, hanging there?" the first voice asked. Tentative and anxious, close enough to see inside the vehicle. Just a few yards away now, on Connor's side of the Jeep.

"Looks like," the leader replied. "Take it slow and easy."

"What about the others?"

"Can't see 'em."

"I know I had to've hit 'em—"

"I said, hold your fire."

Just then another voice called out, this one louder but at a much greater distance. Most likely up on the shoulder of the road. "Everyone all right down there?"

"Fuck," the leader cursed. Hushed and pissed at the same time, close enough for Connor to hear the phlegm in his lungs. Then he ordered, "Stand down."

"But—"

"Be cool. No shooting."

Connor heard a grunt of discontent; then the leader called out, "Looks real bad. Can you call nine-one-one?"

"Ten-four," the guy up at the road responded.

There was a short silence, no more than a few seconds. Then the closer, more tentative voice whispered, "What now?"

"Now we get the fuck out of here."

"But—"

"Move out. Back to the truck. And hide the fucking gun."

"But the others…they may be alive—"

"We'll deal with them later," the leader said. "Let's go."

The two men then seemed to move back toward the road, their retreating voices replaced by the steady rhythm of blood pulsing through Connor's brain.

Connor refused medical help. Despite the pounding in his skull and the stabbing pain in his joints and chest, he insisted he was fine.

The cops and EMTs on the scene overruled him. Possible concussion and broken ribs, bruises and contusions just about everywhere. Signs of mental confusion and disorientation. Forty minutes later the ER doctor at the hospital in Kingstree concurred, and ordered him to spend the night for observation. More than a simple precaution, considering the magnitude of the accident and the condition of the other two passengers in the vehicle. One dead, one critical.

Connor argued that he felt better than fine, and Clooney—his chocolate lab rescue who right now was patiently waiting for him in his corner of the bar—needed to be fed and walked. Not necessarily in that order.

"Call someone," the humorless doctor said, handing him a phone.

His skull felt as if it had been used as a soccer ball and his memory was cloudy. Without access to his digitized contacts, it took him a few minutes to remember the number for Julie, his ace bartender who had agreed to single-handedly navigate the Sunday crowd at the bar. She gave him a load of shit for not showing up on time, until Connor explained that he was in the hospital out in the middle of bum-fuck nowhere.

"What the hell happened—?"

"Accident," he explained, not wanting to get into it. "I'll fill you in whenever they let me out of here."

"You sure do know how to step in shit, Jack," she said. "You want me to keep Clooney for the night?"

"If you could, I'd owe you big time," he replied.

"Don't make promises you can't keep," Julie told him.

Connor handed the phone back, and the doctor and attending nurse left him alone in the ER examining room. His thoughts bounced around, from Iraq to the shoot-out to his weeks in rehab, then back to Iraq. Eventually his mind drifted to The Sandbar down in Folly, just a few steps from the beach at *The Edge of America*, as the locals called it. His home now for almost two years, slinging drinks never being something he'd pictured himself doing and now couldn't see himself doing anything else but. The bounty hunting thing was just a side hack he did a couple days a month, to shake things up a bit and because he was good at it. Right now, he couldn't think of anywhere he'd rather be than behind the counter, mixing a gin and tonic or showing off the stupid magic tricks he'd learned at the VA rehab joint in Georgia.

He glanced around at his confines, listened for noises out in the hallway. Quiet for a weeknight in Kingstree, which was widely known as the slick underbelly of meth in this part of the state, and all the petty crime that went with it. Connor wondered if that's what Willis Ronson had gotten himself into, why his body was now lying in a cold, steel drawer somewhere nearby. He'd had no idea why the dumbass had skipped out, just that he didn't show for his preliminary hearing and Citadel Security Bail Bonds was out twenty grand if his ass wasn't hauled back to Leeds. A dozen phone calls and some mental triangulation had led him to Ronson's hideout, a cheap motel room that was littered with tequila bottles and fast-food containers.

What really irritated him was that no one would tell him a damned thing about Cherine Dupree. He'd seen the EMTs wheel her into the back of an ambulance, strapped securely onto a gurney with her face exposed. He figured that meant she was alive, at least at that point. But that was hours ago, and all anyone was telling him now was squat. Notification of family, HIPPA laws, patient privacy—the whole package of bureaucratic BS.

Twice he'd felt like walking out against medical advice, but there were multiple problems with that ill-conceived notion. First, the clothes he'd been wearing had been soaked with blood and noxious run-off sludge, and the very efficient nurse who had tended to him in the emergency room had removed and bagged them. Before he'd landed behind the counter at The Sandbar, mixing pina coladas and daiquiris, he'd cleaned death and decomp scenes for a company called Palmetto BioClean. It was a gig that caused him to be familiar with all the hazards that coursed through human veins and arteries, such things as HIV, herpes, hepatitis, hantavirus. All the H factors, plus dozens more.

Besides, he wouldn't make it ten yards down the hallway with the last shred of his dignity hanging out the back of the cheap cotton gown he was wearing.

Assuming he was able to run the gauntlet and engineer a clean getaway, he would have to pass through the lobby to the parking lot. What then? His car had been pulverized, and he'd solemnly watched as it had been winched out of the runoff ditch and loaded onto the bed of a flatbed. He didn't know where his phone and wallet were, and he couldn't exactly summon an Uber to a hospital parking lot at one in the morning to drive his bare ass back to Charleston.

The third hurdle to his escape plan—and notably, the most difficult—was the cop who had shown up about three minutes ago and had taken up residence at his bedside. Against the doctor's recommendation, but Nelson Burdette—special investigator for the State Law Enforcement Division, aka SLED—did not appear to believe in the word "no." Getting ahead of the gunmen who had unloaded an unknown number of rounds into a vehicle traveling on a county road in the state of South Carolina was of the *utmost* importance.

"Emphasis on '*ut*,'" he explained to the ER doc, clearly finding no humor in his words.

Burdette was a large man, maybe two-twenty and an inch or so over six feet. Salt-and-pepper hair, ruddy skin, weary eyes—details Connor attributed to the wear and tear of a cop job, which he figured could suck the life out of just about anyone.

"There's a killer out there, maybe more than one, and every passing second means someone else could get hurt," the SLED cop further explained, emphasizing the immediacy of the moment.

His plea prompted more discussion, and more discord. Eventually Burdette got his way, as experience most likely dictated he would. "Just your patient and me," he told the doctor and a nurse, who had joined forces in protest of his demands.

They left, not without a lot of grumbling and mumbling, and once they were gone, the investigator placed a digital recording device on the overbed table. He punched a red button, recited his and Connor's name, and gave the date and time. Then he scooted his chair forward until his knees were almost touching the bed railing, and said, "I want to talk about what happened out there, if you're up for it."

Connor was propped up in his bed, a white sheet loosely tucked under his chin. A length of sterile gauze was wrapped around his skull, and an IV of saline solution was dripping into a port in his arm. A monitor clamped to his finger indicated that his blood oxygen and heart rate were within normal range for someone who had just survived a fatal accident. Same with the pressure cuff squeezing his arm.

"Out where?" he asked.

"Where you were shot at and run off the road," Burdette replied. "Indigo Road."

"I need to get home to my dog," Connor said. "He's hungry and he hasn't had a chance to do his stuff since I left." Figuring the SLED cop wouldn't have any way of knowing that he'd already lined up Julie to help out.

"I'll try to keep my questions brief," Investigator Burdette said. "But it doesn't look like you're going anywhere tonight."

"His name is Clooney."

"What?"

"My dog. That's his name."

"As in the actor?"

Connor dipped his head in a nod, and he had to admit—only to himself—that the movement hurt. *A lot.* "I picked him up at the side of the road during the hurricane," he explained. "Poor thing was drenched to the bone, had his name on his collar along with a note asking whoever found him to take care of him."

"People," Burdette replied, shaking his head, as if that one word said it all. "Now, let's start from the top, beginning with why you were out there on that barren stretch of highway with that punk loser cuffed to the headrest."

"Just doing my job," Connor said. "I'm a bond runner."

"You have a license to do that?"

"In my wallet, wherever that is."

"And you carry a gun?" Burdette pressed him.

"A SIG P365. But I'm sure you already know that, too."

The SLED investigator nodded once. "You have any problem if we test your hands for GSR, Mr. Connor?"

"They already did that at the scene." Connor had little patience for police, not since they had gotten the death of his niece so fucking wrong way back when. Almost ten years ago now. "You really think I shot Ronson and his lawyer?"

"In fact, I don't," Burdette said. "I just need to rule things out, for the record."

Connor lifted his good shoulder in a slight shrug. "Test away," he replied, drawing his hands out from under the sheet and holding them out in front of him. One of them was bandaged to the first knuckle, and he wiggled his fingertips.

"No need, if it was already done. And don't be a wise ass. You came just a few inches from dying out on that stretch of road, and I'm hoping you can help me figure out who was responsible. And why."

Connor took a deep breath, realized Burdette was right: he needed to lose the attitude. He knew he could be a bit of a hothead, and this state cop was just trying to do his job. Which he probably was damned efficient at, since it looked as if he'd been doing it his entire adult life.

He raised his good hand, palm outward in a peace gesture, said, "Guess I'm still rattled, maybe in a bit of shock. You have any word on Miss Dupree? Nobody's telling me squat."

"All I can tell you is she's in surgery," Burdette told him. "Critical multiple injuries."

"At least she's alive."

"Hope she stays that way, too. I need to talk to her."

"You're all heart," Connor said. He stared at the white dry-erase board affixed to the wall beyond the foot of his bed, covered with black and red ink scribbled by the nurses. "She shouldn't have been there, you know? I tried to talk her out of it, but she insisted on coming along."

"She was the punk's lawyer, right?" the SLED cop asked. "Ronson."

Willis Ronson may have been just as Burdette said, but he was a dead punk. Not even cold yet. And while the guy didn't deserve any respect for his crimes, alleged or not, if Iraq had taught Connor one thing, it was that death was neither black nor white, male nor female. Rich nor poor. The living, breathing soul of a human being took on many shades, many forms, and he'd come to learn that a life was a life no matter what side of the line it was on. His platoon's mission had been to root out the vicious insurgents who hadn't gotten the message to greet the American soldiers with armloads of flowers and open arms. Connor had jumped into the fight with all the fervor and zeal that the recruitment posters intended, but the moment he'd shot a young kid in a blown-out grocery store—saw the look of agony and fear on the boy's face as Connor waited for his heart to stop beating—he was reminded that all that separated the two of them was fate. Fate that had placed him at the business end of an M4, in the middle of a battle of disconsonant faiths that had been ensnared in conflict for eons.

All of which caused him to think then, and now: who really were the insurgents in that wasted neighborhood in the scorched Iraqi desert?

Truth is what you make it.

"Court-appointed attorney," Connor said, blinking himself back to the here and now.

"And she was just along for the ride?"

"She felt responsible for her client. Something about keeping Ronson from saying anything that could and would be used against him in the courtroom."

Burdette nodded and stared at the red light on the recording device. Was he considering his next question, or just framing his thoughts? After a few seconds of silence he finally asked, "How do you think Ronson felt about her being black?"

"I wouldn't know, and it's too late to ask him," Connor said. "And I don't see what it has to do with whoever opened fire on us out there."

"We live in a mighty screwed-up world right now, and people are losing their minds over the smallest things. Someone could have seen a black woman riding in a car with two white men. Or maybe Ronson flipped someone off when you weren't looking, or you cut in front of another vehicle."

Connor felt his blood begin to simmer, just as he had years ago in Lansing when the knee-jerk cops investigating his niece's death took a sudden and quick detour toward the usual local suspects, and ignored the facts. "This wasn't a case of road rage," he said. "Nor a hate crime. It was deliberate and premeditated."

"We'll get to that," Burdette replied. "Right now, let's go back to the beginning."

"Which is where?"

"Wherever you picked him up."

Finally: a question that made some sort of investigative sense, rather than a total waste of Connor's time. "The Sunrise Motel, outskirts of Andrews," he said.

"Did you find that odd?"

"I find it odd any time a grown man jumps bail when he knows he's probably going to get caught. But yeah, that motel didn't quite fit what I expected. Fifteen, maybe twenty units facing a gravel parking lot, old farts sitting in plastic Walmart chairs drinking beers and smoking, dropping dead butts into coffee cans. I'm sure you know the kind of place."

Burdette nodded; he knew. "How'd you know he was there?"

"Something his wife told me."

"She ratted out her own husband?"

"Not directly," Connor replied. "She said he'd used his credit card at a Waffle House and a Walgreens up there. And a Circle K. I checked 'em out on Google maps, found a motel right in the middle of them."

"Smart thinking," Burdette conceded. "So, walk me through how his lawyer ended up in the car with you."

"I called her to let her know I had a solid lead on her client's whereabouts, and I should have him back in jail by dinnertime."

"Do you do that with all your jumpers?" Burdette wanted to know. "Give their lawyers a courtesy call?"

The ER examining room felt just as confining as an official interrogation room, the only real difference being the absence of a one-way mirror. "She'd been helpful during my search, without violating any attorney-client stuff. I felt she deserved a heads-up."

"Instead, she asked to go along." It was a statement, not a question.

Connor winced from a sudden, sharp spasm in his chest, and tried to reposition himself to make it go away. Eventually it did. "A little more forceful than that, and I had no reason to refuse," he said. "As I'm sure you know, Ronson was an ex-felon, so he couldn't own a gun. And the crime he was wanted for was non-violent. There was no reason to believe he would put up a fight, and he didn't."

Since receiving his license, Connor had tracked down and returned a couple dozen bail skips to jail. Only one of them had given him any trouble, a wife-beater named Lyle Hicks who had greeted him from the entrance flap of his survivalist tent in the mountains, with a gun and a promise to kill him and the goddamned bitch. It was the only time he'd ever had to call for police back-up, and things had not gone well for the guy.

"And Ronson didn't put up a struggle?"

"Drink yourself stupid with tequila, you don't have much fight in you," Connor said. "The guy was totally crocked."

"And then you cuffed him and put him in your car?"

Connor talked Burdette through the motions, from locking Ronson's wrist to the passenger seat headrest, to making sure he was thoroughly hydrated, to assuring Cherine Dupree that he wouldn't ask her client any questions. Even though he did anyway.

"After that we pulled out of the lot and headed back toward Charleston," he concluded with a weary sigh.

"And at no point did you encounter another vehicle, or interact with anyone in such a manner that would have caused them to pull a gun?" the SLED cop pressed.

"No road rage, like I already said," Connor replied. "Whoever it was came up from behind real fast—no warning at all—and just started unloading."

The questioning went on another fifteen minutes. How the shooting unfolded, the vehicle rollover, the voices he'd heard. The commands to "stand down" and "hold your fire" and "put away the fucking gun."

Connor's stamina and the ER doc's patience wore out about the same time. "Time for my patient to get some rest," the doctor said when he finally pushed his way back inside the room.

"A man was killed in cold blood, and his lawyer is undergoing life-threatening surgery," Burdette reminded him. "Mr. Connor's memory is my best chance at nailing these bastards before the trail grows cold. That's my job."

"And mine is to keep him alive," the doctor replied. "Right now, that means making sure he gets the rest he needs. Visiting hours ended long ago. No more questions tonight."

The seasoned SLED investigator knew enough to choose his battles wisely, burn no bridges on the field of conflict. Every one of his questions—and Connor's answers—had led to more questions, but the longer he stayed here asking them, the less time he had to process the facts, pound the pavement. And get some much-needed rest of his own.

"All right…I have enough for now," he conceded as he clicked the power button off and slipped the recorder back into his pocket. He rose from his chair and turned to leave, then pivoted back to Connor. "Get some rest," he told him. "Like the man said, I'll be back."

"I can hardly wait," he replied, already picturing Clooney waiting for him in his corner of the darkened bar, while Julie closed up and prepared to head home for the night.

Chapter 3

Connor was held in the ER until the following morning.

It was a quiet night for emergencies. No ODs or shootings or other car accidents, so he was allowed to remain in the examining room rather than go through the admissions process. His condition was listed as good, but if he suddenly developed any internal bleeding or his vitals began to tank, it was the best place in the small hospital for him to be. A mild sedative and some Tylenol dropped him into a deep and relatively pain-free sleep, and there was no point in moving him to another unit unless the place suddenly got crazy busy. Which, this being Kingstree, could happen at any second.

But it didn't. Next morning, after a muffin and yogurt and a dish of tasteless fruit cocktail, Connor proclaimed himself fit to be released. A new doctor, much prettier and younger than last night's version, concurred with his self-assessment after sufficient probing and questioning. Yes, he hurt just about everywhere, but it was mostly just bruises from the airbags and high-speed rollover, plus the groove sliced across his right metacarpals by the wayward bullet. Blood pressure, pulse, and oxygen levels were normal, and he was experiencing no light-headedness or dizziness. Plus, he'd voided, which seemed to be a serious qualification for discharge.

So to speak.

Connor's only challenge was how to get home to Folly. He had no car, his phone was busted, and calling a taxi or ride share turned out to be an exercise in futility. No one wanted to drive more than seventy miles down to Charleston without a guaranteed return fare, or the upfront cash payment for a round-trip.

His problem was solved when Jordan James pushed his way into the ER a little past ten. By now Connor was seated in a chair in the hallway—no need to take up a bed—and James' abrupt entry was accompanied by a pair of nurses double-teaming him for gaining entry without permission. No one but immediate family was allowed past the door, and he was in violation of a half-dozen hospital rules. As was his custom he waved them off, mansplaining that Jack Connor was not only a son to him, but an American war hero who should be treated with unconditional respect and dignity.

"Your service to our country is most appreciated," one of the nurses said to Connor. Male, muscles pushing the seams of his scrubs to the limits. Thinning hair that was mostly gray, tattoo of a trident visible on his neck. He shifted his gaze to Mr. James, a no-nonsense, take-no-prisoners look in his eyes that said, *don't push it*. "And you, sir, need to get your pompous ass and attitude out of here now, before I'm forced to call security."

As the seventh-richest man in the city of Charleston, Jordan James was accustomed to being treated with respect and deference. Maybe even fear. In return, he had developed an imperious and self-absorbed demeanor that was all about image, and very little substance. He reigned over a growing commercial empire that included several hundred apartment units, a chain of pawn shops, two branches of an FDIC-insured bank, liquor stores, laundromats, and a biohazard clean-up company. As well as Citadel Security Bail Bonds, the company that periodically hired Connor to track down clients who had gone AWOL. One direct call could have the mayor of Charleston on the line, and a quick hold would get him the governor. The president of the United States might take appreciably longer, but eventually that call would come, as well.

But this was Williamsburg County—part of Boondocks, South Carolina—where his wealth and power had no measure, and thus no consequence. He was just another bonehead who had barged into the emergency room with the arrogant assumption that no one would dare kick him out.

"I'm here to take Mr. Connor home," he explained.

The two nurses regarded him with similar looks of uncertainty and disdain, then glanced at Connor. "Do you know this man?" asked the woman, whose name was Gloria.

"I do," Connor replied. "Please forgive him his poor people skills."

"My what?" James shot an annoyed look from Connor to the nurses, then to several other members of the ER staff who had heard the commotion and had gathered to watch. "I have more people skills in my right pinkie than most folks will ever have in their lives. I've even met the Pope—"

"Please, sir," Connor interrupted him. As was typical, he detected a hint of juniper berries on his employer's breath, and was trying to prevent a small flap from becoming a major fracas that might lead to a sobriety test. "My head hurts and my ears are ringing."

Jordan James caught himself then, raised both hands in a gesture of apology, while not actually having to utter the words *I'm sorry*. "*Mea culpa*," he said instead. "As you can see, I get very…spirited…when I see my son, here, in distress."

"Seriously, is this man your father?" the male nurse inquired.

"It's a long story," Connor replied. "But it works for me."

A hushed conference among the nursing team followed, after which the one named Gloria said, "Mr. Connor has already been discharged, which means he's free to leave with anyone he chooses. Unfortunately, his clothing was destroyed in the accident, and we don't have anything other than the gown he's wearing."

"I stopped at Target on the way up," Jordan James replied, holding up a red-and-white bag no one seemed to have noticed until now. He turned to Connor and said, "You can change in the men's room."

Ten minutes later Connor was sitting at the curb in the requisite wheelchair, an orderly chewing his ear off about an awesome multi-car pile-up at a NASCAR race he'd watched over the weekend. It was the last thing Connor wanted to hear, much less talk about, but it was easy to tune him out until Jordan James pulled up in his Bentley. Specifically, a Continental W-12, midnight blue lacquer and chrome accents, all gleaming in the morning sun.

"Sweet ride," the orderly said as he opened the passenger door. "What kind of mileage does something like this get?"

"About ten per fill-up," Connor told him. "And don't worry, I'm good from here."

"You sure?"

He held up his hand, tightly bandaged from where the bullet had grazed him. "Just a flesh wound," he replied as he slid into the car, glacier white hand-stitched hides and matching convertible top. Handcrafted walnut dash and veneer, diamond-milled tech finish, walnut burl fold-down trays in back.

"Then you're good to go," the orderly told him, giving an informal salute as he turned and wheeled the chair back inside.

As soon as the young man had disappeared through the sliding glass doors, Connor slipped back out of the car and walked around to the driver's side. "Out," he said.

"What the hell are you doing?" James asked.

"We're switching places."

"No way—you're in no condition to be driving."

"Pot, meet kettle."

"What the fuck does that mean?" James asked.

"It means it's ninety minutes to Charleston," Connor replied. "Half of it's a major speed trap. You think you can walk a straight line if you get pulled over?"

"You let me worry about that. I know people."

"This isn't Charleston, sir. If they haul you off to jail up here, you're screwed."

"I'd be out in an hour," James insisted with his typical confidence.

"And I'd be stranded by the side of the road," Connor said, laying it out for him.

Jordan James sat there behind the wheel, the six-liter W-12 purring under the hood while he considered what his honorary son was telling him. The engine seemed anxious to get going, the transmission just a gentle nudge short of laying down whatever rubber a three-ton automobile can burn.

Eventually he said, "You think you're up for it? After what happened yesterday?"

"Fall off a bicycle, the best thing to do is get back on."

"I've got to warn you, this baby doesn't handle like a regular car," James said, lovingly massaging the leather wheel.

"Out. Now."

They rode in silence for the first few miles. The jeans and T-shirt Jordan James had picked up were a little loose, the shoes a little tight. He'd forgotten to buy underwear, which felt a bit odd. And scratchy. But it was better than the hospital-issue cotton gown and padded booties, which Connor had wadded up and stuffed in the rest room trash.

Despite his honorary position within the James household, stemming from the semi-heroic act of saving James' son in Iraq, Connor had little in common with the man. And thus, by extension, little to share. Likewise, James made no attempt at small talk, no discussion of the weather, no Wall

Street news playing on the radio. No update on how Eddie was convalescing at home. Not even a mention of the Braves' chances of making it all the way to the World Series.

Instead, he punched a chrome button in the polished dash and a burled walnut panel dropped down over his knees. Inside the glove box was a small mini-bar, complete with a pint bottle of Beefeater, a silver pump-top atomizer, and a hand-cut crystal glass held in place by a strip of Velcro. There also was a small thermos he had thoughtfully filled with ice before setting out, from which he dispensed a handful of cubes into a silver-plated shaker.

Sixty seconds later James was reclining in his seat, his martini placed on the table in front of him. He was dressed in a seersucker suit and light blue button-down shirt, white linen cap on his head. His cheeks were puffy and crisscrossed with a roadmap of red corpuscles that all seemed to lead to liver disease. He peered out the side window at the commercial blight that seemed to flank every suburban byway in America: fast food joints, auto parts stores, gas stations, dollar stores.

Once they were beyond the suburban canker, cruising by farms and fields rather than gravel lots filled with cars, he hoisted his glass and took a sip. Encouraged by the taste and the inviting effect of the gin, he took another. Then he glanced over at Connor, sitting beside him with one hand draped over the wheel as if he were driving a fifty-eight pick-up rather than a Bentley Continental, and said, "Can you tell me what the hell happened?"

"Sir?" Connor replied.

"You almost got yourself killed, Jack. Seeing you in that wheelchair back in the ER, well, it brought me back to what happened to Eddie all over again. I did not offer you the job at Citadel to go through this sort of shit again."

"I don't know how it happened, Mr. James. Everything was going fine one second, and then it all just seemed to go sideways."

"Sideways," Jordan James repeated. "What does that mean?"

"It means someone was out to kill Willis Ronson," Connor replied.

"And who the fuck is he?"

"The bail skip I was bringing back. He didn't show in court the week before last, and your bond company was looking to kiss twenty grand good-bye."

James set his glass back on the Velcro glove box lid. He chewed on his lower lip while he thought this through, and finally said, "Not worth it."

"What's not worth it?" Connor asked him.

"Dying. Not you, not Eddie. Christ, not even Shirl."

Shirl was James' first ex-wife and mother of their only son and with whom, in fact, he had a reasonably passable relationship. "What about Ronson?" Connor asked.

"He's deceased, which means the court will drop the case against him. And I won't have to forfeit the bail." Willis Ronson clearly was just a name to him, a line item, and he'd already earned two grand by charging a ten percent bond fee to assure the guy showed up in court.

"Still, someone wanted him dead," Connor mentioned again.

"And succeeded. Look, Jack…I've known you what, six years now?"

Connor tried to steer the Bentley around a pothole, but the luxury British suspension managed to slosh a few drops of martini from the cut crystal glass onto the fold-down glove box table. "About that," he replied, thinking *more like seven*.

"Thing is, since then I've come to know you pretty well. Starting with what you did out there in the desert, keeping my boy alive, going that extra mile when life and death were hanging in the balance. You're a good man, with a good soul. A no-nonsense thinker and a true American hero, like I said back there at the hospital."

"I appreciate the sentiment, Mr. James, but you're overlooking a few things. Like the drinking and the blackouts. The VA doctors, the meetings, the relapses, and all the tremors and horrors that sometimes show up in the dark of night."

"Don't sell yourself short, son. I've heard Eddie's screams. I know there's a nest of vipers writhing around deep inside his brain. They're the invisible spawn of the reality he brought home from that Goddamned desert, and it gnaws at him morning, noon, and night. War is the dark underworld of human want and greed, and as long as it's a part of our existence, we all will suffer from it in one form or another."

Connor stole a glance past James at the martini glass, sitting on the fold-down tray like an idol to be worshipped in an ancient temple. Wondering, *how many of those have you had today*? "Are you trying to tell me something?" he asked.

"I'm trying to point out that, despite all that darkness that traveled home with you from Iraq, you stand by principle. You have this overpowering thirst to seek out truth and justice."

"What about to the American way?"

"You joke, but it's a damned fine question," James said. "And since you made a vague reference to the mythical Superman, let me remind you that the man of steel had a big issue with kryptonite. And you do, too."

"Is that a fact."

Jordan James plucked the glass from its Velcro coaster and brought it to his lips, took a long, slow sip. "The fact is, you're brave and confident and persistent, almost to the point of being fearless. But you also have this reckless streak that keeps placing you in harm's way."

"What happened yesterday had nothing to do with any of that," Connor assured him. "Like I said, it was a textbook collar of a bail jumper. Willis Ronson had no history of violence, and I had no reason to think his detention would be anything but routine. And it wasn't."

"Until it was. And that's not really the point."

Then please get to it, Connor thought.

As if reading his mind, James, said, "I assume you've already spoken with the police about what happened?"

Connor felt the same skewers of pain in his chest as before, probably the sprained ribs waking up from the painkillers. Probably not such a good idea for him to have taken the wheel, although the martini glass in James' hand strongly suggested the lesser of two evils.

"Both at the scene, and an investigator from SLED last night," he confirmed. "Why?"

"Because I know you. And I know you can't leave well enough alone."

"You're asking me to ignore what happened?"

"I'm saying that a man died yesterday, and his attorney is in grave condition in the hospital." James knocked back the rest of his cocktail, then set the empty glass back on its Velcro pad. "I spoke with a doctor friend who said her chances for survival are questionable. And even though you keep telling yourself that everything you did was routine and by the book, I know that inwardly you're blaming yourself for everything that happened."

"Since when did you gain access to my head?" Connor asked him.

"This isn't about me," Jordan James told him. "It's about your word, not your head."

"My word? What about it?"

"I want you to look me in the eye right now—just briefly, so we don't veer into the trees—and tell me in no uncertain terms that you will not take matters into your own hands."

"What the hell are you talking about?"

James eyed the gin and vermouth bottles longingly, but closed the glove box before temptation could get the better of him. "I want you to promise that you're going to let the police do what they're paid to do, and you're going to stay out of it."

"It never crossed my mind to do anything but," Connor assured him.

Chapter 4

Ninety minutes later Connor was home in Folly.

He pulled the Bentley into a small gravel lot that had enough space for about four cars, plus a couple more between the wood pilings that supported the main level one floor up. Located across the shore road from the beach, The Sandbar had been built high enough so any tidal flood from a hurricane would spill across the road and wash underneath it. A set of stairs led up from the parking lot, while a ramp with several switchbacks provided disabled customers access to the drinking deck. At this hour it was closed off with a sign that indicated it opened at five o'clock, at which point customers would be competing to get in as if it were Black Friday. Connor had been told countless times he was missing out on beaucoup bucks by not letting folks start partying before noon, but he felt that sticking to evening hours gave the place a certain cachet and elevated it above the other beer joints in town.

Jordan James, who actually owned the place, agreed.

Despite outward appearances, the place was a no-frills hole-in-the-wall with a long wood counter that seated a dozen customers on stools polished by years of backsides. Plastic tables with matching chairs were arranged along all three sides of the deck rail, and a hot dog cart and popcorn machine were set in a corner as far away from the weather as possible. So was an antique jukebox, with a collection of well-worn forty-fives that dated back half a century or more. The roof consisted of a Dacron spinnaker fastened tightly to aluminum support stanchions, strands of party lights and colorful paper lanterns slung between them.

Connor's apartment was in a small attic constructed above the rest rooms, just enough space for a guy to escape from the hubbub of a tourist town, and the greater world at large. Bed, couch, stove, and fridge. Wall-mounted TV, and a view out across the street to the ocean beyond. Not a bad set-up, but a bit of a hike for someone who'd been seriously banged-up in a fatal rollover crash less than twenty-four hours ago.

"You sure you're good to make it all the way up there?" Mr. James asked, glancing up at all the steps.

"The doctors said nothing's broken," Connor assured him. "You okay to make it home?"

"Never better, unless you want to make me one for the road."

"Not one of your finer ideas, sir," Connor said.

Jordan James nodded but didn't seem convinced, then climbed out and walked around the car to the driver's side. "Wisdom prevails over impulse," he observed as he climbed behind the wheel. "I'll take a rain check."

Connor waited until he made sure his boss had successfully backed the Bentley out of the tight lot and was heading back toward the main drag. Only when he was convinced both car and driver would make it safely back to Charleston did he begin the long slog up the stairs, the alternating stabs of pain in his Achilles tendon and his knee ligaments causing him to wince with every step. He paused for a second when he reached the drinking deck, where he found a note taped to the heavy plywood cover locked to the bar that secured the booze from all manner of elements. Which, since The Sandbar was an open-air drinking establishment at the Edge of America, included all-night revelers and drunkards and aspiring sinners in search of one last beer.

The note was scribbled in Julie's chicken scratch and read:

If you see this, you made it back. Hope you're doing better. I'll bring Clooney when I come in at four.

One more flight of steps took him to the small landing outside his front door. He fumbled in his pockets for his keys, then let himself in. He'd managed almost no sleep for more than twenty-four hours, and the second thing he did when he pushed his way inside was collapse on the bed.

The first thing was to change out of the scratchy jeans and pull on a pair of briefs.

Two hours later a car horn woke him up. Specifically, a red Ford Edge that had rolled into the gravel lot down below, courtesy of Citadel Security Bail Bonds. The delivery was arranged by a tag team that included Bucky

Foster, who managed the business and occasionally hired Connor to track down the latest client who'd failed to show at an arraignment or court hearing.

"You are one lucky sonofabitch," he told Connor as he handed over the keys to his new company car. "Willis Ronson and that lawyer of his, not so much."

"I never saw it coming," Connor told him, half-asleep. "Happened so friggin' fast."

"Don't beat yourself up over it. It is what it is."

"What it was, was my job to get him back to jail in one piece. I fucked up."

"He's the one made the choice to skip out," Foster assured him. "Actions come with consequences." He glanced up at the drinking deck, almost longingly, and added, "You actually live here?"

"Someone's got to do it. You want to come up for a cold one?"

Foster appeared to consider it for a second, then shook his head and said, "No, I gotta get back to the office. Monday mornings are always heavy in bond court, and the afternoons get busy."

"Whoever said crime doesn't pay was wrong," Connor replied. "Anyway, thanks for delivering the car. And for what it's worth, I'm sorry how yesterday went down."

"What's done is done," Bucky Foster replied. "That's what I meant earlier about being one lucky bastard. That could be you instead of Willis Ronson lying in a drawer right now. I guess it just wasn't your time."

Connor's commanding officer in Iraq had told him the same thing after his Humvee had been blown to bits. *It just wasn't your time.* He'd spent ten days in a hospital bed in Kuwait recovering from a broken arm and two pierced ear drums, giving him plenty of time to ponder those five words. Made him wonder if Danny Benson had been walking around with an invisible time stamp on his forehead from the moment he'd left the womb, some kind of counter that was ticking down to that very moment when the suicide bomb detonated. Was that how it worked? Was everyone destined to die at a preordained moment, and when the numbers clicked to zero, your time on earth was up?

"Guess not," Connor said now, as he had then. "But someone punched that guy's ticket, and almost got his lawyer and me while they were at it."

"SLED's already on it," Bucky said. "Some investigator talked to me this morning, and I know he had a word with you last night."

"Nelson Burdette," Connor replied. "Yeah, he dropped by the ER."

"Well, not for nothing, but the guy seemed to be on top of it. Mr. James is right."

"About what?"

Bucky Foster leveled him with a steady glare that probably was meant as a warning, but only served to highlight the wrinkles in his brow. "About you sitting this one out."

"Are you benching me?"

"Like you said, someone wanted Willis Ronson dead. Punched his ticket, like you also said. You were there; you're a witness. Leave this to the pros."

"I *am* a pro," Connor reminded him. "Fully licensed in the state of South Carolina. But I get what you're saying, so if it makes you feel better, I'll tell you the same thing I told Mr. James."

"And what's that?" Bucky asked him.

"I have no interest in tempting fate, running down the clock to see if it's my time yet."

Connor spent the afternoon getting a copy of his license at the DMV, then signed a contract for a new phone with the same number. A two year-deal that included all contacts and photos downloaded from the cloud, guaranteed upgrade at the end of twenty-fours months. Plus, a shitload of free apps and functions he knew he'd never use. He had just hiked back upstairs to start prepping for the evening's rush when his new device rang.

He connected the call and said "Jack Connor," his standard response since it was a work device as well as personal.

"You goddamned sonofabitch," a voice screeched into his ear. "You got him killed."

"Who is this?" Connor replied, thinking the caller sounded more like a howler monkey than a human. Anger and hysteria—combined with substances and stress—often worked that way.

"Will didn't deserve to die," the voice said. A woman, and now there was sobbing as well as rage. "How could you have let this happen, after all you promised?"

Connor shifted the phone to his other ear, the one without the bandage. "Mrs. Ronson?" he replied. "Look, ma'am. I can't tell you how sorry I am about what happened to your husband, but I had nothing to do with it. He was just in the wrong place at the—"

"Don't feed me that bullshit, you bastard, cuz I ain't hungry," she wailed. "You said you were going to bring him back, and now he's dead. I trusted you."

"Yes, you did," he conceded. "But what you didn't do was tell me there were people who wanted him dead."

"You're blaming *me*?" she screamed at him. "He was in *your car*. You were supposed to bring him back to jail. *Safely*."

It was clear that Mrs. Ronson was on a grief-induced tear, one with which he could fully empathize. Connor had spoken with her on two prior occasions, the first when he had called to discuss her husband's failure to appear at his preliminary hearing, and inquire whether she might know where he was. No, she most certainly did not, she had told him; never wanted to see or hear from the two-timing lout again. The second time was when she'd called him with the info on the Waffle House and Circle K, suspected he might be holed up somewhere nearby. A suspicion that had turned out to be true.

"Someone was watching us," Connor said in an even voice. It was the only explanation for how—no more than twenty minutes after driving out of the parking lot—a vehicle had raced up behind his Jeep and someone inside opened fire. "You didn't mention that part."

"How could I mention something I didn't know crap about?" she snapped at him.

Good question, if she were being totally honest. A trait he'd long ago learned could be in short supply when a person had run afoul with the law. "Yet they were there, pouring bullets into my car," he said. "Any idea who it could've been?"

She actually took a moment to answer, and she notched her voice down a bit. "No. Will didn't have a lot of friends, and I can't think of anyone who wanted him dead."

"Well, someone did," Connor replied. Thinking *at least two people*, since that's how many voices he'd heard approaching through the run-off ditch when he was squatting on the ceiling of his upside-down vehicle.

"Well, it's your fault, and you gotta make this right," she said.

"I've already talked to the cops," he told her, doubting that bit of knowledge would in any way ease her grief or her agitation.

It didn't. "Screw the bastards," she fumed. "All I've ever known from them is a load of grief and misery. Same as Will. You got him killed, it's up to you to find the fuckers did this. It's the least you can goddamned do."

Chapter 5

Connor had worked as an *ad hoc* private investigator from the moment Jordan James had hired him to track down a valuable painting several years back. That case had led him to do an undercover job for the former governor of South Carolina, leading to a progression of events that eventually resulted in his takedown of one of the largest drug dealers in the southeastern US.

When he finally agreed—after considerable hesitation—to work freelance gigs for James' bail bonds company, he applied for his beginner PI ticket. The governing body in South Carolina for such things is the State Law Enforcement Division, which now was looking into Willis Ronson's murder, and was the number one reason why Connor wanted to avoid a direct collision with Nelson Burdette. Full cooperation with every aspect of the investigation was in his own best interest, meaning it was critical for him to fly as low under the radar as possible. Ground-level low. Interfering with the legitimate function of any state agency was grounds for review and potential reprimand, a rebuke that would carry serious penalties if it in any way involved the obstruction of SLED activities.

The ER doc in Kingstree had offered Connor a prescription for pain meds, which he declined out of principle. He'd personally witnessed the speed with which they dragged a person under their destructive spell, offering temptation for a quick and easy release from a full spectrum of physical and psychological miseries. Connor had lost a number of buddies, either accidentally or intentionally, to the mind-numbing deliverance and escape they provided. And then were mercilessly snatched away in an instant.

Instead, he popped a couple of doctor-recommended extra-strength Acetaminophen, then retreated to the top step of the stairs outside his door, overlooking the dunes and the beach and the glimmering ocean beyond. His watch told him he had about a half hour before Julie arrived and the evening's work began, so he didn't have much time. He inhaled a wisp of sea breeze, then opened the flap of a manila envelope he'd plucked off his kitchen table, and pulled out a dozen sheets of paper fastened by a paper clip.

Several of them were Willis Ronson's arrest record; the rest were his own scribbled notes from his attempt to narrow down the bail skip's whereabouts. When Ronson had not shown up for his initial court appearance, the bailiff had notified Bucky Foster who, in turn, had called Connor. Unless and until the jumper was hauled in, Citadel Security Bail Bonds was on the hook for the full twenty grand that the judge had set.

He reviewed the rap sheet first. Ronson—age thirty-six—had been arrested five times, beginning at eighteen when he'd boosted a neighbor's car so he could drive to a music festival in Tennessee. An hour later an alert trooper on the interstate caught him doing ninety, and a judge handed down a sentence of two years' probation. He was arrested again a year later for breaking and entering, got two years mandatory in Bennettsville because of his probation violation. Sentence reduced to fourteen months upon the recommendation of the parole board and several unspecified outside parties. He'd managed to remain clean for a couple years after that, then was arrested for public intoxication, which earned him another conviction and a sentence of time served.

Arrest number four brought him one-to-three years for breaking into a pawn shop and attempting to retrieve a ring he had hawked there a couple weeks earlier. A ring that actually belonged to his wife Donna who, upon finding it missing, extracted a tearful confession from him as to its whereabouts. She'd promised him in no uncertain terms that he'd land in deep shit if the coveted piece of jewelry didn't show up back in her box by the next morning, and his bungled attempt to comply with her demand had landed him at Tyger River, a medium security facility outside the town of Enoree.

His fifth and final brush with the law had come just six weeks ago, when a patrol officer in North Charleston spotted what he thought was suspicious activity inside a secure electric transformer station. A white man, early thirties, dressed in jeans and a plaid flannel shirt was using a pair of bolt-cutters to slice through a tangle of heavy gauge copper wires, some of which he had already piled in a heap near a freshly cut hole in the fencing. The cop had called for back-up, then continued to film the activity with his body cam until help arrived. Ronson had made a run for it, got as far as the razor wire coiled along the top when he realized the drawn guns meant business.

Via a video hook-up at the county jail, the judge had set bail at twenty grand, ten percent of which Donna Ronson had posted that same afternoon in order to bond her husband out. He was out in time for dinner, which he was forced to eat at a local fast-food joint because his wife had locked the doors and said she never wanted to see his sorry ass again.

Connor felt just as puzzled by this last arrest as he was the first time he'd read the report. Of all the crimes that could be committed across Charleston County, why risk your life stealing copper wire from an electrical complex? Coming in contact with the thousands of volts surging through those lines was enough to knock the life out of anyone, which suggested Ronson either had a guardian angel looking out for him that morning, or he'd received advanced notice of a power reduction and had taken advantage of it.

Or he was just one lucky, but seriously stupid, sonofabitch

However it had gone down, the attempt to steal copper was perplexing. Sure, it was a valuable commodity, but it wasn't exactly a rare element. Mines churned out plenty of the stuff every year, and there was no shortage on the market. Even with the price at a near-record high—Connor had checked—it amounted to just a fraction of what a few ounces of gold or platinum would fetch. Willis Ronson would have had to fill the bed of a pick-up truck with wire in order to get the same return as when he'd pawned his wife's ring. Why bother?

He set the rap sheet aside and focused on his notes. When Bucky Foster had assigned him the task of hauling Ronson's ass back to jail, he'd conducted a thorough search through all the databases available to the public, plus some to which access was highly restricted. Connor had tackled the simple stuff first, found the guy was born in Lancaster, not far from the North Carolina line. Graduated from high school, no indication of athletics or anything else that made him stand out. Got a steady job at a paint store and then, for reasons unspecified, he'd tried to steal the neighbor's car.

After his stint in Bennettsville he moved to Florence, where he found gainful employment with a landscaping business that was willing to hire a former inmate. He mowed lawns and groomed hedges for a few years, then fell in with a loosely knit biker group composed of self-proclaimed road warriors whose collective goal was to rule all the blacktop in the county. It was during this time that he'd met his future wife Donna, who had worked as a seamstress and had sewn the Thunder Dogs' patches on their denim jackets. The alcohol-induced altercation mentioned in his record happened at a bar just a few miles down the road in Timmonsville, during which Ronson tipped over a row of a rival gang's motorcycles. His actions put an end to any leadership aspirations he might have had, and he was forced to abide by the judge's order that he leave the area and never ride with more than one other biker at a time.

Willis and Donna moved to Charleston soon thereafter and got married. She found work in a custom tailoring shop, and he got a job as a line chef for a catering company. The money was poor, and at the end of one particularly meager month he pilfered her ring from the hand-carved jewelry box on her dresser and hawked it. After getting caught trying to get it back, his attorney convinced him to plead down to an unspecified lesser charge, a decision that landed him his residential stint at Tyger River. The sentence subsequently was reduced to six months because of overcrowding and good behavior.

By that time their marriage was beyond strained. Donna Ronson hadn't acknowledged any marital issues when Connor had spoken with her the week before, but he suspected she had not been entirely faithful during the time of her husband's incarceration. She hadn't exactly come out and said "a woman has needs," but it was close.

In any event, they had been unofficially separated for a couple weeks when Willis was pulled down from the razor wire surrounding the high-voltage transformer compound. "We'd been trying to work things out, but, well you know," was how she'd described it.

Mrs. Ronson had gone on to explain that at the time of his arrest he'd been bunking in temporarily with a guy named Joey Barber. Nicknamed Scissors, because of his last name. When Connor had started his search he'd paid the guy a visit, but Barber insisted he didn't know a damned thing about where Ronson might be. Connor didn't believe him, strictly on principle, and now that the bail skip was dead, it was time for another chat.

Same thing with two other known associates who had turned up in the non-public databases. One was a house painter named Scott Strickland who lived in North Charleston, and apparently had graduated from high school in the same class as Ronson up in Lancaster. Connor assumed their paths also might have crossed at the store where Willis had worked years ago, but he had no proof of this. And Strickland had denied any contact with him the first—and only—time they'd spoken on the phone.

The other acquaintance was the leader of a weekly post-prison reform group Ronson had been mandated to attend as a condition of his parole from Tyger River. Ed Wheeler had been a hard-time recidivist halfway through a sentence of ten-to-twenty at Broadview when he'd proclaimed his discovery of Jesus Christ the Almighty. Seemed the good Lord had forgiven him all his sins, including his most recent felony conviction for involuntary manslaughter, and his sudden and unequivocal rebirth had convinced a parole board that he had found guidance through the Heavenly Father. Satisfied that he was a changed man with a profound message to share, they recommended his release into the community, with ten years' supervision by the correctional system. He would be allowed to remain free as long as he kept himself squeaky-clean, and pledged to fulfill a purpose-driven life by enlightening his fellow felons about the blinding light of God.

Wheeler was number three on Connor's list of things to do in the morning.

He also needed to reach out to Donna Ronson, an exercise he figured probably bordered on futility, considering their conversation of yesterday. He couldn't tell if she'd called him when she was under the influence of grief and anger, or maybe whacked out on booze or pills. Maybe even something stronger. Even though she and her husband had been sleeping under separate roofs for the past few weeks, she had stepped forward and bonded him out following his alleged copper theft. Was that move borne out of sincere hope to rekindle their crumbling marriage, or a calculated gesture to use in family court when they finally appeared before a judge?

Connor set the last page of notes aside and spent a minute watching a volleyball game unfolding on the beach. High-altitude contrails appeared like jedi light sabers in the sky, jets heading northward to Philly and New York, south to Miami or maybe the islands beyond. Closer in, a sailing yacht was inching its way along the line of the horizon, maybe heading up to the Chesapeake for the summer, possibly as far as the Vineyard or Nantucket.

His ribs groaned as he pushed himself up from his postage-stamp landing. Tylenol had its limitations, and his injuries were pressing the outer periphery. He rotated his shoulders to flex away what aches he could, noticed that a smear of blood had seeped through the bandage on his hand. He'd picked up a box of gauze and a spool of tape at the pharmacy on his way home from the DMV and could deal with it later, if needed.

At that moment a vintage red VW Beetle swerved into the parking lot beneath and squeezed into a space below, dodging the ground level pilings. He recognized he car as belonging to Julie, and sure enough—a few seconds later—he heard her car door slam, followed by the scampering of paws racing up the wheelchair ramp. Clooney veered around the last switchback and lunged toward the gate, Connor getting there at the exact same moment as his best friend.

"Hey, big guy…how you doin' today?" he said, crouching down to look at him nose-to-nose, at the same time rubbing the aging lab's ears.

"That you, Jack?" The question came from Julie, who had decided to take the stairs.

"Home from the trenches," he replied. "Thanks for taking the old boy for the night."

"The pleasure was all mine," she said as she trudged into view. "You didn't tell me how much he snores."

"That's not all he does when he's sleeping," he told her, getting to his feet.

"Yeah, you didn't mention that, either." Wrinkling her nose as she said it.

"That would be bad marketing. Anyway, I can't thank you enough for taking care of him last night."

"Fact is, the old boy's a real gem. And you look like you went through a meat grinder."

"It's not as bad as it looks," Connor assured her.

"Looked pretty damned awful to me," Julie said as she set her backpack down next to the bar. "It was all over the news today. You didn't tell me your perp died."

"Not part of the plan," he replied. "I never saw those guys coming."

"The news said the Jeep was pretty much tin-canned," she went on. "Hard to believe you actually walked away from it."

"I'm still waiting for something to snap or pop. Come on…we can't just stand here all night. We have a bar to run."

"Slave driver."

They had just unlocked the plywood bar cover and stashed it in closet when a black GMS Yukon pulled to an angle in the lot down below and lurched to a stop. Connor and Julie exchanged wary glances, and then the SLED investigator from last night climbed out. He flexed his shoulders and slowly surveyed the small patch of gravel, then nudged the door closed with his hip. Nelson Burdette, Connor remembered now as the guy shaded his eyes with his hand and looked up at the drinking deck.

"That you up there, Connor?" he called out.

"You found me."

"Permission to come aboard?"

"Permission granted."

Julie leaned close to his ear and said, "Cops?"

"State, not local."

"Christ…not this shit again."

She was referring to a time last summer when a customer had been shot in the bar, right over there where a slight stain of blood had stubbornly refused to be cleaned out. Jordan James had talked about replacing a few composite planks, but the blemish had become part of local legend, which translated to profits. At the time of the killing, the police had made the place their second home until the case eventually came to a grisly close.

Burdette chose the stairs, and when he came into view, he had already soaked his long-sleeved cotton shirt. A fresh one, blue with thin white stripes, collar unbuttoned at the neck. Wire-rimmed shades hid his eyes from the glaring sun slipping toward the trees in the west.

"Quite a spot you've got here," he said as he entered the bar. "Now I see why they call it the Edge of America."

"Welcome to The Sandbar," Connor greeted him. He picked up Clooney's empty water dish, ducked through an opening under the long wood counter, and filled it up. Clooney waited until he ducked back out and set it down, then eagerly attacked it with a tongue that looked like a side of pastrami.

"I saw your vehicle downstairs, figured you'd be up here."

Julie cocked her eyes and made a motion with her head, indicating she was going to leave the two of them alone. Find something else to do, like slice mangoes or limes. Anything other than deal with the police.

"I've only had it for a few hours," Connor said. "How'd you know it was mine?"

"Two plus two. Anyway, I just came here to return a few items from yesterday." The SLED investigator set the leather case on the counter and reached into it. Out came Connor's wallet, followed by his cell phone, the thin glass screen shattered beyond repair.

"Looks about the way I feel," he said.

"You can always donate it for parts." Burdette's hand went back into the valise, emerged with Connor's micro-compact SIG Sauer P365. "Found this on the floor—excuse me, the ceiling—of your Jeep," he said. "Fully loaded."

"And licensed," Connor assured him. "My line of work carries a few risks."

"I know. I checked." The SLED cop paused, as if thinking back to their conversation last night. "Were you seriously considering shooting it out with those fuckers?"

"Whatever I had to do. But then the other guy showed up, called nine-one-one before I had to take action. You going to give it back to me, or is this just show and tell?"

"On account of it wasn't fired and wasn't used in the commission of a crime, it's not evidence," Burdette said as he set the gun on the bar beside the wallet.

"Greatly appreciated," Connor thanked him. "Is that all you stopped by for?"

"Pretty much. Except I also wanted to let you know I just came from MUSC, where Ms. Dupree was transported last night for emergency surgery."

MUSC was the Medical University of South Carolina, just about the best hospital in the state for patients dealing with severe trauma. "How's she doing?" Connor asked.

"As good as could be expected," Burdette told him. "Critical but stable after multiple procedures to repair all sorts of damage. Doctors can't say when I'll be able to talk to her, but they're guardedly optimistic."

Connor's mind had kept flashing back to the young public defender dangling upside-down from her seatbelt, blood trickling from her mouth and an almost lifeless look in her eyes. He did a quick fast-forward to when he'd released her buckle and she had tumbled down on top of him with what he'd feared was her last breath. Just before he'd heard the voices approaching out in the runoff ditch, talking about finishing them all off.

And at that moment a mental conversation began in his head, one he sincerely hoped Burdette didn't sense and couldn't hear. A one-sided dialogue that went something like, *I'm coming for you, you sonsofbitches. If it's the last thing I do.*

Not realizing for a moment just how close to the truth that line of thinking might take him.

Chapter 6

Next morning Connor drove to MUSC and inquired about Cherine Dupree's condition. As expected, the university had a policy about only immediate family being allowed into the intensive care unit to visit a patient. Thus, the attending nurses refused to let Connor in, nor would they even confirm that Cherine Dupree had been admitted to the hospital. HIPPA laws and patient confidentiality being what they were.

He said he understood the need for her privacy, and only wanted to look through the glass at her. Just a peek to confirm in his own mind that she was alive and breathing.

"And who are you?" the nurse manager asked him, after refusing him entry to the floor. "A brother from a different mother?"

He grinned at that, said, "I was in the car with her."

"You…what?"

"I was driving. I'm the reason she's here in the first place."

"O.M.G.," she said, pronouncing the letters rather than the words they stood for. "Dr. Guerrero said you probably saved her life, getting her out of her restraints the way you did."

"All I was thinking was she could be dying," Connor replied.

"Well, that might have been the outcome if not for you." The nurse seemed to weigh pros against cons for a second, then said, "Follow me. I'll let you have a peek, but only for a second."

He didn't say a word as he trailed behind her through a locked door and down a long corridor. They finally stopped outside a room with the number "6" stenciled on the wall, and a white board that read "C. Dupree." Beneath that was the notation "No Visitors—Medical Personnel Only."

Connor stood at the glass, gazing past his own reflection at the young attorney lying in the murky darkness. Wires and tubes fed in and out of her arms, and the glow of monitors just out of the line of sight cast an eerie glow on the ceiling. Ms. Dupree's entire head appeared to be encased in bandages, leaving only her eyes visible, while a machine seemed to be pumping air through a plastic tube inserted down her throat. The dreaded ventilator that had made so much news during the pandemic. He couldn't see the numbers and data read-outs on the screens above her head, but she appeared much more stable than the last time he'd seen her.

Which wasn't saying much.

"What are her chances?" he asked the nurse, who had not left his side.

"Can't say," she replied.

"Can't or won't?"

"Both," she said. "And I meant it when I said only a second."

Connor had driven to the hospital first thing after stumbling out of bed and walking Clooney. No breakfast or coffee, both of which he now found at a Starbucks located adjacent to the main medical building. He took them to go, then walked the two blocks back to the garage where he'd parked his new company car. He sat behind the wheel while he hurriedly downed a raspberry scone, then pulled out of his parking space and fought the traffic out to North Charleston.

Joey Barber's address was a couple blocks off Dorchester Road, a tired neighborhood of small brick houses, chain link fences, and crumbling sidewalks. Mature oaks and gum trees, mangled satellite dishes, garbage cans sitting inside pre-fab carports defined the yards. Pick-ups and old sedans were parked at the edge of the pavement, while brown lawns were dotted with rusty swing sets and tricycles and dog chains tethered to stakes. Grass unmown, hedges untrimmed.

Last time Connor was here, Barber's truck had been parked in the driveway, but now it was gone. In its place were three overstuffed garbage bins waiting to be picked up on trash day. A mound of furniture and household goods was piled at the curb, inviting the neighborhood pickers to help themselves before the town trash collectors loaded it up and carted it away. A sign that read "For Rent…call Gator" was fastened to the rusty fence, and seemed to tell the whole story.

Connor climbed out of his red Ford and stood at the edge of the yard in the growing heat, eyeballing the house. Just a week ago the carport at the side of the house had been clogged with auto parts and cinder blocks and old lumber, but now it was empty. Same with the yard, which had featured a ring of old beach chairs around a cinder block fire pit. All gone.

He navigated his way around the rubbish heap and wandered up the walk to the front door. He knocked, waited, then knocked again. No answer. He retreated back down the steps and worked his way past an overgrown azalea bush to the front window so he could take a look through the grimy glass. In the event a nosey neighbor happened to wander by, he was just a prospective tenant taking a look at his potential new home.

The living room was empty, except for a couple of boxes and an ancient floor lamp that for some reason hadn't made it out to the curb with the rest of the unwanted junk. A quick peek through the kitchen door around back also produced a whole lot of nothing. Lots of dust and dirt, but not much else. Just like Willis Ronson before him, Joey Barber had split, and didn't seem to be coming back any time soon.

Connor snapped a quick photo of the "For Rent" sign, including the phone number listed at the bottom, then got back into his car, where the AC greeted him with a blast of welcome Arctic air.

Scott Strickland lived in a single-story brick house in an area known as Park Circle, just a stone's throw from the Norfolk Southern railroad tracks.

The appearance of the neighborhood suggested that a lot of these places had been built not long after the war, most of them designed around the same set of blueprints. Pretty much identical, too, except for the mature plantings around the foundation and roofs that appeared in need of repair. The Strickland residence had a stained concrete walkway that led from the front door but ended about two-thirds of the way to the street, as if it had seen no reason to go any farther and had just given up. An older Ram dually with faded black paint and a busted headlight was parked in the driveway, telling Connor that someone probably was home. A plastic tricycle with a big front wheel and a tire swing drooping from a tree limb suggested the presence of kids or grandchildren.

He knocked, and a woman in a flannel robe opened the front door about six inches and peered out at him with weary eyes. Dishwater blond hair was tied up on top of her head, and mascara had dried under her eyes. Thin lips, small nose, pale cheeks that looked like they rarely made it past the front stoop into the sunshine. A dog was barking somewhere in the bowels of the house, which smelled as if something had recently burned on the stove. The weathered screen door that separated them was no match for a housefly that ducked around a frayed piece of netting and buzzed inside.

"We sent the check on Friday," she said as she peered out at the puck-up. "That makes us up to date, 'cept for last month."

Connor hesitated a second, realized the woman—*Mrs. Strickland?*—probably thought he was there to repossess the truck. Or possibly something else. "No, ma'am," he told her. "I mean, that's not why I'm here."

"It ain't?" The wail of a crying child joined the barking dog somewhere in the far reaches of the house. "Then what do you want?"

"I'm looking for Scott Strickland."

Because of the heat, Connor was wearing a T-shirt, which revealed two full sleeves of body art. The woman's eyes fixed on a menacing dragon wrapped around his arm, and then she said, "He done sumppin' wrong?"

"No ma'am.

"Then who's asking?"

"My name's Jack Connor. Tell your husband I'm here to talk about a friend of his, name of Willis Ronson."

"He ain't my husband," the woman said. The chorus of dog and baby in the background was now joined by the cursing of an adult, one who didn't seem too happy about something. "What's that no-good scumbag gone and done this time?"

"I'd prefer to discuss it with Mr. Strickland," Connor replied. "I just have a couple questions and then I'll be gone."

"Who you with?" she asked. "I mean, all that ink, no way you're a cop."

Connor dug a business card out of his wallet, and the woman who was not Mrs. Strickland opened the screen an inch to take it. "I work for Citadel Secure Bail Bonds," he explained. "Like I said, it's just a couple questions."

At that moment the door swung open wide and a man in baggy briefs and a sweat-stained T-shirt glared at him through the screen. "Whatever you're selling, we ain't buying," he snapped. "Get off my doorstep or I'll spray your ass with lead."

"Mr. Strickland?" Connor asked, not moving an inch.

Scott Strickland leveled his eyes at him, then let them drift to the tattoos covering his arms. "You hear what I just told you?"

"Yessir. You threatened to shoot me, but I don't see a gun."

The man reached for something in the darkness, produced a rifle not unlike the one Connor's uncle used on his autumn deer hunting excursions to the Upper Peninsula in Michigan. "You mean this?"

"Looks like a Remington bolt action seven hundred," Connor said. "Damned fine piece. And you're in deep shit just holding it."

"What the fuck?" Scott Strickland fumed.

"It's that felony you've got on your record. State law says you're allowed to live in a house where a firearm is present, but that gun must be in the control of a person, or people, who can legally possess it. That excludes you."

"I knew you was fucking cop—"

"That's what I thought," said the woman who was not his wife. "He gave me this."

Strickland examined the card, then flicked it to the ground. "Bounty hunter?" he asked.

"Bond runner, actually. I'm not here to give you trouble, sir. I just want a word with you about Ronson Willis."

"Wait," Strickland said. "I know you. You're the guy called me on the phone, trying to find that dumb fuck. Well, I'll tell you again what I told you then. I don't know where he is."

"The morgue," Connor replied.

"Say again?"

"He was shot, yesterday. It was in the news."

"I don't watch that lamestream shit." Strickland set the Remington against the wall, then stepped into the light and studied Connor's tattoos. "I gotta say, you got some mighty fine artwork there."

"Picked it up here and there, mostly when I was in the Army. How 'bout you?"

"Got a couple, but they're mostly prison shit." Strickland leveled him with his dark, penetrating glare, then said, "You got questions about Ronson, come on in."

Connor eyed the rifle propped against the wall, then stepped into the living room. The woman closed the door behind them, letting the screen slam against the weathered frame. Strickland waved him toward a chair, old paisley upholstery that had more stains than pattern, ragged fringe along the bottom. It reminded Connor of his own house when he was a kid, furnished from the pages of Sears and Montgomery Ward.

"Ellie, get the man some coffee," Strickland said.

Finally, a name. *Ellie.* "I'll only be a minute," Connor told them both as he sat down.

"Small cup, then. How do you take it?"

"Black. And seriously, I don't want to put you to any trouble."

"Nonsense," Ellie said as she disappeared into the kitchen.

As soon as she was gone, but probably not out of earshot, Strickland plopped himself into a chair across a wooden cocktail table from Connor and said, "She don't look like much, and can't cook worth shit. But Christ, that woman knows her way around the bedroom. You said Ronson was killed?"

"Two shots to the back," Connor confirmed.

"How did that go down?"

Connor had driven out here to Strickland's house to ask questions, not answer them, but he spent the next thirty seconds giving a thumbnail version of the shooting as it had unfolded inside the Jeep Cherokee. "Never had a chance," he summarized when he was finished.

"Damn," Strickland said. "Sure seems like someone was gunning for him. Any idea who?"

Connor drew his eyes around the room, from the dusty drapes covering the window to the floral wallpaper that was starting to peel at the seams. Not much on the walls except a metal sign from an old Flying A gas station and a black and white photo of a country music star he recognized but couldn't name. No books, just a few ceramic knickknacks and a flatscreen television on a stand.

"That's why I wanted to talk to you," he explained.

"Hold it right there. If you think I had anything to do—"

"No, I don't," Connor said, cutting him off. Truth was, at this point in an investigation anyone and everyone was a person of interest, but he didn't want to start off on that footing with Scott Strickland. Nor was he officially investigating anything. Either of those things could change, but for now he simply wanted to know whatever the man might be able to provide. Even if it seemed like nothing, it eventually could be something. "We're just talking here."

Strickland said nothing for a second, then settled back in his own chair. "Okay, man…I just wanted to get that straight. And I don't really know why you're here, because me and him, we weren't friends."

"You knew each other up in Lancaster," Connor reminded him. "High school, and after."

"It's a small town. Everyone knows everyone."

"He worked in a paint store, and you're a painter. He moves to Charleston, and here you are."

"Things happen," Strickland said. "No connection."

"You never ran into him, not once?"

"Charleston's a city, but it's kinda like a small town. So yeah, we ran into each other once or twice. But never more than to just say 'hi.'"

Connor always considered himself a good judge of people. He had a strong bullshit meter, and a solid sense of when they weren't being honest. Or simply were leaving out pertinent facts. Some things add up, some don't. Which was why he knew the cops in Lansing had nailed the wrong guy for shooting his five-year-old niece. Same principle here: if Scott Strickland wasn't lying through his teeth, the truth was getting hung up in them somehow.

He decided to change tactics by ramping things up with a lie of his own. "That's not what his wife tells me," he said.

"She…what?" Anger smoldering in his eyes again.

"She makes it sound like you guys hung out from time to time."

"Fucking twat don't know what she's talking about."

"Okay, okay…maybe I misunderstood what she was saying," Connor said, raising his hands in a peace offering. No need to set the guy off on a fit of rage. "But when you ran into him, like you say, do you remember where it might've been?"

"What's it matter?" Strickland said. "Poor bastard's dead."

"And someone made him that way. Almost killed me and his lawyer, too."

"Yeah, yeah…I get that." The heat in his eyes seemed to settle down a notch, and he said, "Can I be honest with you, no blowback?"

"I sure hope so," Connor replied.

Scott Strickland fell silent as he appeared to be mulling something over. Then he said, "The place we bumped into each other…well, it was the gun range. But like I said, only once or twice."

Finally, something that made sense. Both he and Ronson were felons, and coming into contact with firearms was a violation of federal and state law. Target practice was definitely something that could get them both busted back to prison.

"Which one?" he asked.

"Which one what?"

"The gun range. I promise I'll keep your name out of it."

This required another moment of deliberation before Strickland said, "Top Shot Sports and Armory, out in West Ashley."

Chapter 7

Next on Connor's list was the Universal Church of Spiritual Resurrection, located on Wappoo Road a few blocks off Old Savannah Highway. As with most establishments in the area, it had been reborn from various previous lives as a laundromat, wholesale furniture outlet, exotic pet store, and hibachi bar and grill.

Then the good reverend Ed Wheeler had found it, or it had found him, and it became home to a congregation composed of delinquents, outcasts, and felons. In other words, the usual spectrum of Saturday night sinners who sought Sunday morning repentance.

Connor had been here before, a lean-to annex behind a storefront sanctuary. Mostly cinder blocks and dry rot trim that seemed to provide a steady diet to termites and other insects, fogged glass windows covered with bars designed to keep the bad guys out, rather than in. The born-again pastor and ecclesiastic had welcomed Connor into his temple with impassioned grace and abiding acceptance, but had proved to be of little help in locating Willis Ronson. Yes, the guy had attended meetings. No, his interest had not seemed genuine, and admittedly he only was there because the court said he had to be. No, Wheeler didn't think the group meetings had done him a bit of good, and he wasn't surprised to learn that he'd been arrested again. Jesus loves everyone, but He can only help those who choose to help themselves.

After leaving the Strickland residence up in North Charleston, Connor had called ahead to verify that Wheeler was in the house. He was, and when Connor pulled his car into a space beside an overflowing dumpster in the alley out back, he found the minister sitting on a picnic table, whittling a piece of wood with a pocketknife. Connor slid out from behind the wheel and closed the door, wondered if the blade was a subtle threat, or just an idle pastime the guy had picked up at Broadview, shaving toothbrushes into prison shanks. Either way, he chose to ignore it as he approached the redeemed felon for whom God had provided unyielding faith and a resounding conviction far different from that which any jury had handed down in a court of law.

Wheeler kept cutting as Connor approached, eventually setting the knife down so he could use his hand to shield his eyes from the sun. He slid off the table, clenched his fingers for a pious fist-bump, and said, "Peace be with you, brother Jack."

"Back at you," Connor replied. He couldn't remember the last time he'd been in an actual church, and this one didn't count since it was just the rear gravel lot of a building that bordered the rear gravel lot of another building. Lily's funeral; that was it. So many years ago that his memory of the event had all but faded, except for a five-year-old life cut short because of a lottery ticket and a quart of ice cream.

The storefront pastor made room for Connor to sit beside him on the table, leaving a good twelve inches between them as an unspoken boundary. "I don't know what more I can tell you than the last time you were here," he said. "Nothing has changed."

"Except Ronson is dead," Connor replied.

Wheeler nodded at the grim reminder, tilting his head up at the sky as he closed his eyes. Communing with the Lord, or just paying a silent tribute to a member of his flock? "Like I told you before, Mr. Willis was very much a private person. Didn't let go of himself too easily."

One of the things Connor had not yet grown accustomed to in the South was how people were raised to attach a common prefix—usually Mr. or Miss—to a person's given name. Mostly it was a sign of respect, but often deference, in the case of class or employment. Mr. Jack, Mr. Jordan, Mr. Willis. Or in the case of Wheeler, he supposed, Mr. Ed.

"He never spoke in your meetings?" he asked.

"Only when spoken to, if I tried to drag him into the conversation. Most of the time he would just sit there, hands in his lap, staring at the floor. Fact is, if it weren't for the parole board, he wouldn't have been there at all."

"Did you ever see him talking to anyone outside of your group sessions?" Connor asked. "Before or afterwards?"

"You asked me that before." Wheeler picked up his knife and the chunk of wood and started carving again. "Like I said, he was pretty much a loner."

"Did he usually drive himself, or did someone drop him off and pick him up?"

"Mostly came and went by himself, but a few times a woman gave him a ride."

Connor figured that would have been Donna Ronson, who previously told him she made it her mission to ensure that Willis stuck to the provisions of his parole. No guns, no public drinking establishments, no backsliding. And mandatory attendance at the post-prison reform meetings twice a week. Religiously.

"Did you ever talk to him in private, when no one else was around?" he asked.

"At the very beginning, when he needed my approval to enroll in the program," Wheeler said. "He made a point of letting me know that he didn't want to be a part of it, and wouldn't give it a second thought if he wasn't being forced to. Quoted that old saying about not wanting to belong to a club that would have him as a member."

"What did you say to that?" Connor asked.

"I reminded him of a passage from Luke, chapter eleven, where Jesus tells us, 'Keep on seeking, and you will find. Keep on knocking, and the door will be opened to you. Everyone who asks, receives. Everyone who seeks, finds. And to everyone who knocks, the door will be opened.' Thing is, Willis Ronson had an answer for everything, and all he said was, 'Bullshit. I knock and I knock, and all I get is a fucking door slammed in my face.' Pardon my French."

"French is my second language," Connor replied. "Did he ever talk about his time in prison? Anyone he met in there?"

Wheeler took a minute to shave a long curl of wood from the block, which he then flicked to the ground. "Not really. Mostly I got the feeling he hated it about as much as the rest of us. Too much time to think, reflect, hate, curse, blame. And dodge the bullshit comes at you twenty-four seven. Where'd you finally find him, if you don't mind my asking?"

The question caught Connor off-guard, but he figured there was no reason to hold back. Give a little, get a little. Maybe, if Wheeler had anything of substance to give.

"Holed up in a motel outside a hick-ass town in the middle of nowhere," he said.

"This town have a name?"

"Andrews. Did Ronson ever mention it?"

Pastor Wheeler gave the question some serious thought, but eventually came up empty. "Don't ring a bell, but then again, he didn't talk much. Did you ask him about it when you caught up with his sorry ass?"

"His lawyer told him not to talk," Connor explained.

"The colored chick who got shot, same time he did," Wheeler said. Not a question; he already seemed to know the details. "That must've been some fucking drive-by."

"A lot happened in a short period of time," Connor conceded. He knew he needed to steer the conversation back on track, so he said, "If Ronson showed up at your meetings under duress, only as a condition to being paroled, do you have any idea why he would have risked going back to Leeds by jumping bail?"

Pastor Wheeler stopped his carving, stabbed the point of the knife into the wooded picnic table. "Mr. Willis knew he was looking at some serious time for doing what he did, and I could tell he was scared shitless about going back in," he said. "I did my best to talk to him about that, help him conquer his fear. I explained that Isaiah tells us 'Despair not, for I have redeemed you; I have summoned you by name; you are mine.' And in Deuteronomy we're told, 'Lord your God goes with you; he will never leave you nor forsake you.' But I could tell he wasn't listening. Fact is, I don't think he'd ever listened to anyone his entire life. Especially the Lord."

"When was the last time he attended one of your meetings?" Connor asked.

"That would've been a day or two before he got himself arrested for spoolin' up that wire," Wheeler replied. "I mean, that was some dumbass cracker idea. Where'd he think he was going to sell it, anyway?"

Connor had been thinking the same thing ever since Bucky Foster tasked him with going after Ronson. Not just the shit-for-brains idiocy of stealing wire from a live electric transformer station, where thousands of volts could fry your ass, but trying to dispose of it afterward. Sure, there were scrap yards that would pay good money for things like steel and tin, but hardy worth it for a load of wire boosted from a Dominion Energy yard that any recycler would recognize from watching the news.

Maybe money had gotten tight, living on his own, and Ronson needed a few hundred bucks to tide him over. Maybe he'd found himself in a financial scrape that he had to pay his way out of. Street debt carried a high vig, and the rapidly compounding interest usually required an extra-legal means of staying ahead of the enforcers.

"Maybe he wasn't," Connor said to Wheeler. The aroma of smoking barbecue from a joint down the street invaded his nose, reminding him that he'd only eaten a pastry for breakfast and might be due for an early lunch. "Maybe he had other plans for that copper."

"Something like that would require advance planning," Wheeler pointed out. "I didn't get the sense that Mr. Willis did much of that."

No, but someone else might have, Connor thought as he hoisted himself off the picnic table. "Thanks for all your help, Reverend," he said. "You still have my card?"

"In my office, what there is of it," Wheeler told him. "Listen, if you ever feel the need to confess your sins to the Lord, you come on by, you hear?"

"This'll be the first place I come," Connor assured him.

Willis Ronson's last known gainful employment had been at a vehicle wrap shop on the other side of Charleston, but the gun range Scott Strickland had mentioned was closer. So was the rib joint that had gotten Connor craving barbecue, so he stopped off for a quick bite before heading up Sam Rittenburg Avenue, where Top Shot Sports and Armory was located.

He found it at the far end of a strip mall that also housed a mattress store, a small fitness club, and a Dollar General. It was a nondescript building, muted beige stucco, with a sign in the tinted window that advertised "Group and Private Training." The front door featured a decal of rifle crosshairs, and block lettering on the wall beside it read: "Schedule your next event here: Birthdays - Bachelors/Bridal Party - Team Building – Catering – Family Fun. Inquire within."

Connor parked a few doors down and cut the engine. A digital readout on the instrument panel told him the outside temperature was in the upper eighties; another steamy lowcountry summer was on its way. He got confirmation of this as soon as he opened the door and felt as if he'd just passed the gates of Hell.

As he pushed his way inside, he was struck by how the place didn't look like any gun range he'd ever seen. Certainly not the one he'd gone to after he'd bought his SIG Sauer P365 and needed to refresh his boot camp shooting skills. That place had been all business, gray walls racked with pistols and rifles, new and used, some for sale and some just to be fired on the premises.

By contrast, Top Shot had the ambiance of a corner coffee shop, where one might be just as inclined to order a Smith and Wesson as a chai latte with nutmeg. The design palette was woodsy green and earth tones, glossy epoxy floor covered with natural jute rugs. The walls were hung with photos of bears and deer and ducks that were meant to be appreciated as targets, not as nature prints. An L-shaped glass counter held an array of new rifles and handguns, from AR-15s and Brownings on one side of the room to ever-popular Glocks and Rugers, and even Connor's own micro-compact SIG, on the other. Every one of them glistening and new, nothing used. Clean and spotless, first class all the way.

In other words, not the sort of place he would picture Willis Ronson frequenting.

A signal connected to the front entry must have rung through to the back, because ten seconds after Connor walked in, a clerk emerged through a door designated "Range." The unmistakable sound of a pistol being fired followed him out, indicating that was where the action went down.

"Afternoon, sir," the man said as he removed a pair of what appeared to be noise-cancelling headphones, and slipped behind the gun counter. "What can I do you for today?"

"Quite a set-up you've got here," Connor replied. "Don't know if I should sign up for some time on your tactical range or order a vodka martini with a twist."

The clerk didn't seem to have a sense of humor, because he came back with, "Mixing alcohol with guns isn't a good combination for safety."

"I suppose not," Connor said. "And you do have a good selection of firearms here."

"You an owner, or looking to buy?" the guy behind the counter asked him.

"Owner. That one there, in fact." He pointed at the SIG P365 SAS under the glass, less than six inches long and just over a pound fully loaded.

"That's a truly fine handgun," the clerk said. "Carbon steel barrel, stainless steel frame with flush-mounted FT bullseye fiber-tritium night sight. Are you military?"

"Was. Tenth mountain division, Ft. Drum. One tour in Iraq."

"We honor your service, sir. In fact, there's a ten percent discount on all products and range time for current military and veterans."

"Good to know," Connor said. "But today I'm here for something else."

He immediately sensed a hitch in the clerk's demeanor, a subtle shift in attitude from warm and affable to wary and suspicious. "And what would that be?" he asked.

Connor already had Willis Ronson's photo dialed up on his phone, and he held it out for the clerk to see. "This man comes in here from time to time. You recognize him?" Phrasing it in such a way that his patronage at Top Shot Sports and Armory was already known and documented, not leaving room for an outright denial.

"You said you were former Army. Does that make you a cop?"

"Not then or now." Connor was ready with a business card, which he handed over. "Bond runner, with Citadel Secure Bail Bonds. The person in the photo is Willis Ronson, deceased."

"No shit," the clerk said. "I mean, I'm sorry to hear that. And yeah, I know him. Knew, I guess. How'd he die?"

"Two bullets to the back. Day before yesterday. Maybe you saw it on the news."

"I try not to watch it, what with everything in the world going to hell. Mind if I see that picture again?"

Connor brought it back up on his phone and held it out for the guy to get a better look. "Anything you can tell me would be a help," he said.

"There ain't a whole lot, since I only saw him once or twice," the clerk said. "You might want to talk to Tony. He's the owner—Tony Young—but he's at lunch."

"I'll do that," Connor replied. "But right now, anything you can tell me about Mr. Ronson would be useful."

"Yeah, well…if memory serves, he had this thing for Glocks. Didn't own one, but was really into shooting them. Not too good at it, to be honest, usually hit way outside center mass."

"He ever talk about why he was shooting? Self-defense, neighborhood crime? Sport?"

"Like I said, I only saw him a couple, three times. Not enough to chat him up. And he pretty much kept to himself. The kind of loner you end up hearing about on the news."

"If you watch it."

"Right. What's all this about, anyway?"

Connor hesitated, considered how he was going to frame his answer.

Since Willis Ronson was dead there were no real privacy issues to deal with. He'd been caught in the act of pilfering wire from the electric company, skipped out on his bail, and holed up in a dingy motel room with empty Cuervo bottles scattered around the floor. A felony conviction had followed him when he was paroled, and the law stated he was to have no contact with firearms. Ever. So why was he paying good money to shoot handguns at Top Shot Sports, if he could never own one again?

"Did Ronson ever meet up with anyone here, maybe talk to other customers?" he asked, dodging the question.

"Not that I ever noticed. Part of the loner thing, I guess. But again, you might want to talk to Tony."

"Were you aware he had a felony on his record?"

"Whoa," the clerk said, raising his hands defensively. "Not our job to run a background check on every customer who comes through that door."

"Course not," Connor replied. "I've got no beef with you. I mention it only because he's supposed to stay away from guns, yet here he was."

"You thinking someone he might've met here coulda been the one who shot him?" the guy asked.

"One of a thousand scenarios," Connor said with a noncommittal shrug. "You've got my number there, so if you think of anything that might help, give me a call?"

"Sure." He glanced at Connor's business card, then stuffed it into his pocket. "Since you tracked this Willis Ronson here, you think the cops might could do the same?"

Connor doubted Nelson Burdette would know enough to talk to Scott Strickland but, even if he did, Strickland likely wouldn't give up much to a SLED investigator. Not if it might bump him back to prison. He also wondered if some other kind of enterprise was being conducted here besides selling and shooting guns.

"Probably not," he replied. "And like you said, it's not up to you to vet everyone who comes in and asks to shoot."

Chapter 8

Lowcountry Vinyl and Tint was a local business that wrapped commercial box trucks and panel vans in custom logos and artwork.

Since it was the last place Willis Ronson had held a job, Connor had already talked to the owner, about a week or so ago. Alex Reeves was a self-professed motorhead who tore car engines apart and put them back together when he had a little free time, which seemed not to be very often, since every work bay in his shop held a truck or car that was in the process of being wrapped.

"Looks like business is booming," Connor commented as he followed him from the lobby into the back of the garage.

"There's two box trucks for a local plumbing company over there, and a tour bus in back getting a full wrap," Reeves explained as he waved Connor into the shop. "Plus, we're putting some black chrome stripes on that orange Mustang by the door, and that ninety-nine Corvette's being prepped for a full color change. Taking her from white to matte black."

"What's that sort of thing cost?"

"It's all based on time and materials," Reeves told him. He was wearing a green and yellow shirt, same colors as the sign out front and the baseball cap on his head. About six feet, day-old stubble on his chin, broad nose, and dark, beady eyes. "But if you've got something old you want looking new again, bring it by and we'll price it out."

"All I've got right now is a company car, but I'll give it some thought," Connor said as he watched a guy heat a sheet of vinyl with a blowtorch and then gently smooth it to the contour of a fender. "Meanwhile, I just wanted to circle back to you about Willis Ronson."

"What about him? I told you all I know last time you were here."

"I know you did, but there's been a development," Connor said. "Mind if we step over there where we can talk?"

Over there was a corner of the massive garage area where no one was working. Unassembled pieces of scaffolding were propped up against a wall, and a pitted chrome bumper that looked as if it came from an old muscle car lay on the concrete floor. A garbage can stuffed with scraps of vinyl was being used to prop the door open, mostly to encourage air flow.

"The acoustics in this place are for shit," Reeves said when they'd moved out of earshot of the other employees. "We should be good here. What's up?"

"What's up, is things have changed a bit since we last talked."

"Changed how?"

"Ronson's dead."

Reeves looked genuinely stunned at the news, blinked his eyes in disbelief as he said, "Holy shit…for real?"

"As real as it gets."

"Sonofabitch…I mean, *damn*. For all his problems, Ronson was a good guy. Troubled dude, his mind scattered all over the place. But…what the hell happened?"

"Cops are trying to figure that out," Connor told him, not wanting to go into details. That was up to Nelson Burdette, if he ever circled by to question Alex Reeves. "All I can tell you is he was ambushed. Shot in the back."

"That is so fucked up," Reeves said. He massaged his forehead with his fingertips, stared up at the exposed ceiling as he inhaled a deep breath. "How—?"

"Someone opened fire on him, and he died instantly."

"You were able to locate him, then?"

"He was in my custody when it happened," Connor explained, leaving it there. "Reason I'm here is that this whole thing has turned into a murder investigation."

"Damn," Reeves said again. "Like I said before, the guy was a bit odd. Kept to himself, but he was a good worker. Appreciated that I gave him a chance, since a lot of places won't hire felons."

"Do you remember why he quit?"

Reeves gave the question serious thought, eventually shook his head. "It didn't seem like anything was bothering him, but you never could really tell with that guy. Then one day he just didn't come in, and he didn't come in the next day. Eventually I got a text asking me to send his final check to the address we had on file."

Connor remembered it was the house where he lived with Joey Barber, but by then he'd already split. "When was this, again?"

"Five, maybe six weeks ago," Reeves told him. "Before he got busted for that copper thing. Just doesn't make sense, like I told you before. None of it. And now he's dead."

Connor's eyes were drawn to a pair of doors that had been removed from some kind of high-end sportscar, and had been sanded down to bare metal. "Those last few days before he quit…do you remember anything odd about his behavior?" he asked.

"Nothing unusual, not for Willis. He smoked too much, took too many breaks because of it. No booze, though, not on the job. Or drugs, at least as far as I know. Plus, he almost never talked on the phone, like some of the other guys. Always focused on his work when he was laying vinyl."

"Did he ever get chummy with any of your customers?"

Reeves shook his head as he checked his watch. Time was money. "Wasn't the chummy type," he replied. "Like I said, he was pretty much a lone wolf. But you know, there was this one time he bolted when a cop showed up."

"Bolted, as in took off?"

"Went out the back door, there," he said, nodding toward an emergency exit at the rear of the garage. "Definitely got spooked by something."

"Do you remember when this was?" Connor asked.

"About a week before he quit," Reeves told him. "Funny thing, the cop was here to ask about getting his wife's car wrapped, an old Subaru that had baked too long in the sun. Never followed through."

"Do you think Ronson recognized him?"

"Don't know, and afterwards he didn't want to talk about it. Maybe it was just because the guy was a cop. You think it had something to do with who shot him?"

"Everything does, until it doesn't," Connor told him. "Any chance you wrote down the guy's name?"

Reeves looked doubtful, as if record-keeping was a chore that always fell to the bottom of his list. If he even had a list at all. "I may have put something in a file, in case he came back," he said. "I'll take a look and let you know if I find anything."

It wasn't much, but it was the best commitment Connor would get. "Good enough," he replied. "Meanwhile, if anything else comes to mind, give me a call?"

"You got it, man."

"You still have the card I gave you last time?"

"Top drawer in my desk," Reeves assured him.

Connor returned home to The Sandbar from a late-afternoon beach walk with Clooney to find SLED investigator Nelson Burdette camped out on a plastic chair on the drinking deck. The guy was wearing khakis, blue shirt with a starched collar, brown lace-up shoes. Feet up on the rail, soaking in rays, visor shielding his eyes from the sun.

"A man could get used to this," he said, barely moving his head to acknowledge Connor's presence. "You ever think of opening earlier in the day?"

"You ever pay attention to signs?" Connor shot back, annoyed that Burdette had assumed he could bypass the locked gate and make himself at home. He gently rubbed Clooney behind the ears, letting him know that while this interloper was not the enemy, his status as friend might be in question.

"Your car was in the driveway, just like last time," Burdette said. "I didn't think you'd mind."

The polite thing would be to offer him a beer, or a soda. Even a glass of water. Connor did none of those things. Not even sit down in another chair to join him. Instead he asked, "What brings you all the way to Folly at the end of what I assume has been a busy day?"

"Answers to a few questions," was the reply.

"Well, ask away," Connor said as he shoved his hands into his pockets. "I want these scumbags, whoever they are, behind bars as much as you do."

Burdette said nothing for a minute, just watched a surfer in the distance navigate a wave that couldn't be more than four feet high. Eventually he adjusted his chair so he could look Connor square in the eye, rather than twist his neck to face him.

"The other night when we talked, you said you suspected Willis Ronson was at the Sunrise Motel because his wife had tipped you off to the Waffle House and Walgreens."

"And a Circle K," Connor added.

"Right." Burdette rocked a bit in his chair, as if his entire body were nodding. He tipped his head back and stared at a lone cloud loping by on the horizon, then asked, "When you arrived to pick Ronson up, did you go directly to his room, or to the office?"

"The office," Connor replied, suspecting where Burdette was going with his questions. "I had good reason to believe he was there, but I had no idea which room he was in. And I didn't want to call ahead and ask the manager, just in case he decided to tip Ronson off."

"And the manager told you which room he was in?"

"Room eighteen, down near the end. And if I might ask, is there a point to this?"

"There is, which I'll get to."

"When?"

Burdette narrowed his eyes and said, "Are you in a hurry to get somewhere?"

"I have a bar to run, and the limes and mangoes don't slice themselves."

"And I'm conducting a murder investigation, one in which you got shot."

Connor took in a deep breath, let it out slowly. "Look, detective—"

"Investigator," Burdette corrected him.

"All right. Investigator. I've already told you all I remember, and I've cooperated with everything you've requested. If there's a point to why you're squatting here on my deck, grilling me, please get to it."

Burdette wrestled a small notebook out of a pocket, leafed through the pages until he found what he was looking for. "You're right about the Waffle House across the street," he finally said. "Thing is, they have all-night surveillance. One of the cameras is outside the front door, and has a full view of the motel in the distance."

"Good to know," Connor replied.

"Indeed it is. Because that video shows two things you didn't mention before, not that you would have known them."

"What two things?"

At that point Clooney edged toward Burdette, leading with his nose. *Not the crotch*, Connor silently warned him. The SLED investigator gave the dog a wary look, then tentatively held out a hand to let him sniff it. He did, and then lowered himself to the floor with an ungainly thud.

"First, were you aware you were being followed?" Burdette asked.

Connor lifted a shoulder in a slight shrug, said, "If I'd known that, I wouldn't have let them come up behind me and start firing."

"I'm talking before that," Burdette replied, shaking his head. "When you were driving up to Andrews."

"What are you talking about?"

"The waffle cam clearly shows your Jeep pull into the parking lot, near the office. You sit there about a minute, then someone gets out and goes inside. That would be you. But it's a wide-angle lens, and another vehicle—a pick-up truck—drives up at the far edge of the video. Sits there, maybe with its engine going, then slips into a parking space in front of another room. A minute later you come out of the office, get back in your Jeep, and park directly in front of room eighteen."

"Pretty much as I remember it," Connor agreed. "Except I don't remember seeing this truck you're talking about."

"You weren't looking for it," Burdette said.

No, but I should have been, he thought, mentally kicking himself. "Go on. You said there were two things."

"I did." He consulted his notes again, then glanced back at Connor. "The surveillance tape shows you and Miss Dupree, his attorney, get out of your car. You knock on the door. No one answers. You use a key I presume you got from the office, and you both go inside."

"Again, pretty much how it went down."

"You were inside just over five minutes, and when you came back out you had Willis Ronson in cuffs. All three of you approached your vehicle, and then you opened the right rear door and locked him inside. Thirty seconds later you left."

Connor shot him a glance that meant, *is there a point to this*?

As if reading his mind, Burdette said, "What happens next, is the truck that followed you to the motel stays where it is for a few seconds, then pulls out and appears to follow you again."

"The truck that ambushed us."

"Possibly. Unfortunately, we don't have a plate and the video is a bit grainy. Anyway, that's when we normally would stop watching, but this is anything but normal. A couple minutes later another vehicle shows up, this one a sedan, American-made. Chevy or Buick, dark blue or gray, four doors. Someone gets out and goes into Ronson's room, which you left unlocked."

"It was full of bottles and trash and stink," Connor explained. "We got what we wanted."

"I know. But this other person—can't tell if it's a man or a woman—stays in there another five, maybe six minutes, before coming back out. Looks angry, kicking at the ground. Like he was looking for something and didn't find it." Burdette let the last words hang there, waiting for Connor to pick up on it.

He didn't.

"Do you know anything about that?"

"About what?" Connor asked.

"Whatever the guy—or gal—might have been looking for."

"The room was a mess, so it could be just about anything. And like I said, I have to get to work. If you have a real question, how 'bout being direct about it?"

The two men locked eyes for a moment, then Burdette said, "Look, Connor. You're not a suspect or a person of interest. But whoever went into that room after you took Ronson out of it was looking for something specific. I just want to know if you have any idea what it was. Is that direct enough?"

"It is, and I don't," Connor told him. "But if that guy—or gal—didn't find it, it's probably still out there somewhere. And pretty damned important to someone."

"Enough to kill for?" Burdette asked, letting his question hang there.

Chapter 9

That night a storm swept through the lowcountry.

Fortunately, it held off until after last call and the bar was locked up tight. Sharp blasts of lightning flashed through his attic window, followed almost instantly by deep bursts of thunder that echoed through palmettos trees and reverberated off the sand. The wind rattled the spinnaker roof, and torrents of water poured from the corners onto the composite decking.

Connor lay in the dark trying to tune out the tempest as it unleashed its fury. As often happened on such nights his mind carried him back to the desert, the unsettling blasts of RPGs and mortar shells recoiling off the inside of his skull, each sudden burst compounding the flashbacks of death and blood and loss. Despite the cool June evening, his skin erupted in a cold sweat that he carried into his dreams, in which he repeatedly experienced the worst possible destruction ever conceived by the human mind.

At some point Clooney let out a pitiful yelp from where he was lying on the floor at the foot of the bed. He, too, hated nights like this, for reasons and irrationalities that came from his own genetic memory. Connor jolted upright at the noise, then slipped out of bed, dragging the comforter with him. He spread it out on the cold floor, then lay down and curled up with him, wrapping his arms around the dog's chest until they both stopped shaking.

Eventually the cacophony faded into the distance and the weather passed. Connor no longer was taking fire in the ruins of a pulverized marketplace, where he had just taken the life of a kid who, had he been born in Michigan instead of Kirkuk, might have been preparing to take a date to the senior prom. Same age, same wide-eyed look of innocence mixed with anger that these foreigners had invaded his country, leveled his neighborhood and maybe killed his family.

A little past six the phone rang, a sweet Jamaican drum riff he'd recorded back when he'd played congas in a reggae band just a few blocks from The Sandbar. Connor grabbed it from the nightstand, saw it was a local number he didn't recognize. Almost didn't answer, knowing that good news usually slept in, but he hit the "answer" button anyway.

"I owe you an apology," a voice said into his ear.

It took him a moment to place it, as he sat down on the edge of the bed. Then he replied, "Good morning, Mrs. Ronson."

"I'm sorry. Sorry for calling you so early, and for the terrible things I'm sure I said to you yesterday. That wasn't me. I mean, it was, but I was just so…well, I hope you understand. My mind was just…well, it was all over the place, and I wasn't myself. I'd just been to the morgue to identify Will's body, and I needed to blame someone."

"Forget it, Mrs. Ronson." The first hint of dawn was just beginning to seep through the cracks in the plantation blinds, but the room was mostly dark. "You'd just lost your husband, and you were angry and scared."

"Doesn't make what I said to you right," she said. "Look…I'm sure I woke you up just now, but I've been thinking about this for most of the night. I'd really like to make it up to you."

Connor wondered if Donna Ronson had started in early, maybe a swig of the hair of whatever dog had bitten her. "That's really not necessary," he told her, closing his eyes, thinking maybe he'd be able to drift back to sleep as soon as this call ended.

"It is to me," she pressed. "Like I said, I know it's early, but I'm hoping I can buy you a cup of coffee. Not now, of course. Nothing's open. But maybe later, when you have a chance to really wake up."

He glanced at the watch on his wrist. Yep, it really was as early as the clock on the nightstand was telling him. "Thank you, Mrs. Ronson, but I really don't think—"

"Please, Mr. Connor. You're the only connection I have to my husband…late husband now, I guess. I treated you wrong yesterday, and it's the least I can do. Especially considering how I lied to you."

Those last few words grabbed his attention. Was the woman astute enough to know they would instantly suck him in, or was she misleading him now, just to get him to agree to meet?

"Lied about what?" he asked.

"Not on the phone," she said. "Coffee?"

How could he say "no"?

Any chance of sleeping in was gone.

How had Mrs. Ronson lied? Overtly? Falsehood by omission? Little white lie or a major fabrication? Had it contributed to her husband's death, or was it totally unrelated to his no-show in court? Or just a slick contrivance designed to get him to meet up with her.

Connor's normal routine was to get in a three-mile run that would take him along the sand of Folly Beach, but not this morning. Not since the accident. He'd overdone it yesterday, too much time behind the wheel, ignoring the stabbing pain in his ribs and the throbbing in his ankle and his head. He'd removed the bandage from his hand last night after closing up the bar, found that several stitches had pulled out. He couldn't find any antiseptic in his bathroom, so he soaked the wound in well gin from the bar before using strips of adhesive tape to pull the edges of the wound together. Then he'd rewrapped the whole thing with new, sterile gauze and hoped it wouldn't become infected.

Despite the coffee Mrs. Ronson had promised him, he took Clooney for a walk down to Gilbert's, a breakfast joint half a block up the street. Everything was wet from the soaker the night before, and there was a fresh crispness to the air that always seemed to follow the tail end of a spring storm. Both man and beast walked slowly, each for their own reasons, and when they finally returned home—coffee and a biscuit sandwich in one hand, leash in the other—Connor set out a bowl of kibble. Clooney downed it all with the trademark gusto of a chocolate lab, then gave a side-eye glance at whatever smelled so good in the grease-soaked bag from Gilbert's.

Thirty minutes later Connor was riding the elevator up to the ICU at the Medical University downtown. A phone call on the drive up had told him nothing, and he was determined to find out how Cherine Dupree had fared overnight. He fidgeted in a chair out in the waiting room, leafing through well-thumbed magazines and checking news on his phone until a nurse pushed her way through the automated double doors. She was clutching a tablet device in her hand and seemed to be headed toward some other part of the floor. An appointment, maybe a meeting.

He jumped to his feet and said, "Excuse me, ma'am. I was hoping you could help me with something."

She clearly was in a hurry, as if she had somewhere to be. "And what might that be?" she asked.

Connor tried to get a good look at her ID badge, but all he could make out was the name Brenda. "I'm hoping you could tell me about the condition of a patient in the ICU is doing," he said.

"And who might you be?" she asked.

"Jack Connor. I'm not a family member, and I understand your privacy policies and HIPPA rules and all that. It's just that no one would tell me over the phone—"

"You said Connor?" she interrupted him.

"That's right. The patient's name is Cherine Dupree, and we were both involved in a car accident. I just want to find out how she's doing."

The nurse named Brenda no longer seemed to be in such a hurry. In fact, Connor sensed a wave of relief wash across her face. "You're the one who let her down from her belt," she said. "She was asking about you."

"She was?"

"In the middle of the night. I wasn't on duty, and no one who was seemed to know where to find you."

"That means she's okay?" Connor asked.

"Well, 'okay' is hardly the word I'd use. I really can't share any specifics about a patient's health because…well, you know. But if you're willing to wait a bit, I'm sure I can find someone who can bring you back to look in on her."

Five minutes later Connor was peering through the same window into the same dark room as yesterday. Cherine hadn't seemed to have moved an inch, nor had the wires and tubes leading in and out of her extremities. The thick glass prevented him from hearing the monitors, which he figured were positioned so no one on this side of it could read her vital signs.

"Any change in her condition?" he asked the nurse who had brought him into the ICU.

Her name was Luna, a few years older than Connor, and considerably more hair. Latina, eyes the color of coffee, full lips painted with gloss that matched. "No, sir. Not much. Except she's woken up a time or two."

"I take it that's a good thing?"

"Very good."

"I was told she asked about me?"

"Don't get excited," Luna replied with a grin. "She wasn't trying to arrange a date."

Connor felt his skin go warm, and he tried not to blush. "I was just hoping she might be awake so I could have a word."

"Only medical personnel and family are allowed in at the moment. Sorry."

"What are the doctors saying?"

"It's day to day," Luna said. "She's lucky to be with us."

Donna Ronson had suggested they meet at a local coffee joint on James Island. No franchise dark roast, no cup sizes with Italian names. It was just a couple miles across the Ashley River from the hospital, not too far from the house she had shared with her husband until he'd moved out. Connor wondered if that was what she had lied to him about, and he figured he was about to find out.

She was waiting in her car, a blue Chrysler van at least ten years old with a few chips and scrapes that cars and people both acquire with the march of time. A window placard for one of the popular ride-share companies indicated she augmented her seamstress salary as a parttime driver. Connor suspected she'd taken a day or two off from work in order to deal with her husband's death, but bosses could be hard-edged about things that cut into company time.

Connor had met with her once before, their initial contact coming after Willis Ronson had skipped bail and he'd been trying to ascertain the man's whereabouts. The spouse was always the first person of interest, whether it's a murder case or a no-show, and Donna Ronson had done a good job convincing Connor that she was concerned about her husband's disappearance. She also was pretty damned pissed that she'd been foolish enough to post his bond with her previously pawned ring, eight hundred from savings, and the balance on her Mastercard. Soon to be maxed out.

Connor found a shady place to park under a magnolia tree and got out. She appeared to recognize him—maybe it was the tattoos and shaved head—and met him halfway across the parking lot. She had a dark intensity in her eyes and, when she raised her hand in a half-hearted greeting, it seemed as if she might slap him in the face. But he was wrong about that, because she just flung her arms around him and gripped him tightly as she sobbed into his shoulder.

She held him that way longer than felt comfortable, then let go and faded back. "I…I am so, so sorry, Mr. Connor. I'm just…I am such a Goddamned mess. Excuse me. I just don't know what's come over me."

He touched a hand to her shoulder, and she stopped. "There's nothing to apologize for, Mrs. Ronson. This has to be a devastating time for you."

Tears were trickling down both her cheeks, and she used a bare arm to try to rub them away. She was wearing a yellow blouse and pale blue jeans, no jewelry, no make-up. Dark shades. Still in shock and appearing to be at a complete loss as to what to do next.

"Please…call me Donna," she sniffed.

"Only if you call me Jack."

She nodded at that but said nothing as she dragged a tissue out of a small clutch purse. She dabbed her nose with it, then said, "Let's get some coffee. Tea. Whatever you want."

The coffee joint had four outdoor self-serve tables that were spaced far apart, as if they were left over from days of social distancing. Because it was past breakfast and not yet noon, all of them were vacant and clean.

"I'll go inside and order, while you stake out a place out here," Connor suggested.

"I look that bad?"

"Not at all," he lied. "But it's a beautiful morning and the sun might do you good."

She nodded again and handed him a ten from her purse. "I invited you, so I'm paying," she said. "No argument."

Five minutes later Connor returned with a cloud caramel macchiato and cranberry scone for her, and a medium Somali roast and muffin for him. Donna Ronson had selected a round table in the shade of a large crepe myrtle that was just beginning to explode with crimson buds. A nearby planter was thick with sweet-smelling alyssum and gardenias, which had attracted some bees, and a pair of mourning doves pecked at the pavement for crumbs left over from the earlier crush of customers. He sat across from her as she arranged her food and drink, then rearranged it again, as if not knowing how to begin, or what to say.

"Looks like you injured your hand," she finally observed. Awkward and stiff, saying anything just to say something.

"Bullet grazed me in the accident," he replied. "Nothing serious."

"You were lucky."

The implied message was that Will Ronson had not been lucky, and there was no turning back the clock. No alternate reality, no do-overs. Not for him, not for his widow. She was clearly in shock, telling herself over and over that she was going to wake up from this horrible dream and everything would soon return to normal. Whatever *that* was. Meanwhile, the sub-atomic collision of grief and anger was probably releasing highly charged particles of pent-up confusion.

"That was Will's problem," she went on. "Luck, I mean. Everything that man touched seemed to go to shit."

Connor eyed his muffin, left it on the paper plate where it was. "He met you, didn't he?" he reminded her.

His words brought a smile to her face, if only for a second. "He always said that the day he met me was the brightest spot in his entire life," she told him. "Thing is, the next morning it snapped shut again when he was riding his Harley too fast around a turn and hit a raccoon. Totaled his bike, put him in the hospital for nearly a week."

Connor nodded, thought back to what Burdette had told him yesterday about the truck that had tailed him out to the motel in Andrews. Not to mention the person who had tossed the room after he'd driven off with Ronson cuffed to the headrest in front of him.

He took a sip of coffee and said, "We were followed."

"That's what the cop told me," she replied. "The one from SLED. Said a truck probably tailed you from that motel, and someone started shooting."

"Right," Connor agreed. "But what I mean is, we were followed out there to the motel. That means someone was watching me before I got there, knew I was going to pick up your husband. And I led them right to him."

Donna Ronson glanced down at the scone sitting on a napkin in front of her. "That's why I wanted to talk to you," she said. "Whatever I said yesterday, it's not your fault. What happened to Will, I mean."

"Water under the bridge," he insisted. "But when you called me earlier, you said you lied about something?"

"Well, more like I wasn't totally up-front about everything, the first time we talked."

He took a sip of his coffee and let her words hang there. Meeting here was her idea, her show.

"The night he moved out, we had a big fight," she finally said.

Connor remembered those well. His own marriage, years ago to his local sweetheart, had ended almost before it had a chance to begin. All because of the arrogance of youth, and the unwillingness to compromise. Along with all the empty screaming and closed minds that prevented any sort of concession or understanding.

"It happens," he replied.

"Yeah, well, it wasn't our first one," Mrs. Ronson went on. "Plenty of others, in fact, usually on account of his drinking, Or gambling, although he wasn't into that too much anymore, except for scratch-offs. Shit, did that man ever spend a ton on those fuckers. Anyway, the night he left, it was because I found out he'd been…well, reconnecting with someone from his past."

"By reconnecting, I assume you mean a woman?"

"Yes, a woman." She picked up her coffee drink but just stared at it, then set both elbows on the table and looked at him through her sunglasses. "Bastard was cheating on me."

This was the last thing Connor expected her to be telling him. He had no idea what issues might have plagued their marriage, or why she was so certain—*confident*—she was right. Or why she felt it was any business of his.

Which was what he tried to tell her, as delicately as he could. "A grieving mind can play all sorts of tricks on you," he said.

"Just hear me out," she replied, her voice trembling. She had placed her clutch purse on the chair to her left, and now she opened it and removed two sheets of paper that were stapled together and folded, then folded again. Connor could see it was a print-out of some sort, but didn't want to appear too inquisitive. "This is a record of his phone calls. I don't think he knew I was smart enough to figure out how to get them."

"When did you get this?" Connor asked her.

"The night he left. We never had a computer—no need—so I used my neighbor's Mac. Figured out how to pull up our Verizon account and damn, there it was."

"And you didn't think this was important to mention when I was looking for him?"

"That's what I'm trying to tell you, about not being totally honest. If I'd said something, Will might still be alive."

"Maybe, maybe not. You can't torture yourself over what-ifs."

"Easy for you to say." She wiped the back of her hand across her nose, said, "Anyway, this print-out shows every phone call from the last month, right up to that final night. See that one, right there?"

She pointed at the last conversation on the print-out, which she had circled in red. The call had come in a few minutes past seven on a Friday morning from an area code Connor didn't recognize, and lasted about four minutes.

"It was an incoming call, and you can see there were nine others from the same number over those last two weeks."

"All incoming?"

"No, Will made three of them. See?" She pointed to all the other calls, highlighted in yellow.

"Any idea who he was talking to?" he asked her.

Mrs. Ronson wrinkled her nose as if the wind had suddenly brought a foul odor her way. "Oh, yeah. I know her. Never met the sleaze, but her name is Liz Morgan." She pronounced it as if it were a highly contagious disease.

"And your husband had a history with this Morgan woman?" Connor asked.

"That's a polite word for it," she said. "But yeah, they met when he was in prison the first time, up in Bennettsville. She wrote to him, some sort of sicko inmate pen pal thing, and then when he got out, they carried on for a while. He called it quits when he moved to Florence, about the same time we hooked up. Or at least that's what he told me."

"How do you know it's her number?"

"Because I fucking called it." She must have realized she was getting overly heated about the whole thing, because she made a motion to zip her lips. "Sorry. It just goes up my ass sideways, just thinking about that whore."

"She told you her name?"

"I got her voicemail. 'Hello, you've reached Liz Morgan. You know what to do.'" Putting a nasal inflection to her voice. "Yeah, I knew what to do, all right."

This was getting way too deep into Ronson marriage dynamics than Connor wanted to go, or needed to know. "Why do you think she had something to do with your late husband's disappearance?" he asked.

"You didn't know Will," she said as she finally took a big bite of her scone. "Thing is, Mr. Connor…Jack…I think that slut was trying to wriggle her way back into his life, and she's the one wound up getting him killed."

"If *p* does not necessarily mean *q*," Connor said, reciting one of the few things he remembered from high school back in Lansing.

"What the hell does that mean?"

"Cause and effect," he tried to explain. "One suspicious phone call does not make her a killer. Not even nine of them."

She shook her head rapidly and said, "You don't understand. If that woman told my husband to jump, he'd ask her which bridge. I'm telling you, she got him killed."

"Do you have any proof?"

"I don't need proof…I have this." She tapped a finger to the side of her head, which Connor didn't take as much reassurance. "Look…I probably shouldn't have called you, if you're not interested in getting to the bottom of this."

Getting to the bottom of this was Burdette's job, and Connor had already overstepped that boundary by a mile. "Have you told the detective from SLED about any of this?" he asked.

"That douchebag doesn't listen," she snapped. By the way her voice was getting all brusque and huffy, Connor figured she probably thought he was a douchebag, too. "He's rude and offensive, just like all cops."

"Do you have any idea where this Liz Morgan might be?"

"No, I don't, and I damned sure don't care. But whatever she's up to, I hope she gets what she has coming to her."

Whoever wrote *hell hath no fury like a woman scorned* was a master of understatement. Connor intuitively knew he was making a mistake, but something Donna Ronson had said about Liz Morgan struck a distant chord, one that was off-key and too dissonant to decipher at the moment. He suspected that would come later, when he was lying in bed late at night with the anxieties of the entire world boiling in his mind.

"How 'bout you text me her number, and I'll see what I can find?" he suggested.

Chapter 10

Twenty minutes later Connor was cruising north on Route 41 through the Francis Marion National Forest.

The vast tract of second- and third-growth woodlands was named for the legendary patriot who had terrorized the British redcoats during the American Revolution. The Swamp Fox, as he was known through filtered American folklore, possessed a remarkable knowledge of the mucky terrain, which helped him guide his men through the woods and fens, enabling them to sneak in and out of British camps and cause maximum mayhem. A determined nationalist who fought ruthlessly to gain independence from the tyranny of King George, Marion later became known for his inhumane treatment of slaves as well as his brutal abuse of the Cherokee tribes—savagery that shattered the mythic patina of his guerilla tactics, and caused more than a few contemporary historians to reconsider his proud legacy.

As Connor drove, he mentally replayed everything Donna Ronson had told him, wondered how much of her story about Liz Morgan was based on fact. The needle hovered ten miles above the posted limit most of the way, two lanes of monotony that took him past malnourished pines and tupelos that seemed to be facing a mid-life crisis, and power poles that were falling prey to age. Tires whined on pavement that was damp from an earlier shower, an earthy petrichor coming off the wetlands stretching toward the tree line in the distance.

A few miles past the four-corner junction that marked the entire presence of Jamestown, Connor hung a left onto a strip of blacktop that his phone's GPS told him would take him toward SC-521. A faded sign on a crooked post told him it was Indigo Road, the same stretch of highway along which he'd been driving Sunday afternoon when, a moment too late, he'd noticed the truck racing up from behind and unloading an explosion of gunfire into his Jeep Cherokee.

The scene of the crash was not hard to find. The pavement held scars from where the mangled vehicle had been winched through the ditch and up onto the back of a flatbed truck, shedding fragments of plastic and diamonds of glass. Bushes were flattened and trees snapped, while tire tracks along the muddy shoulder indicated where emergency vehicles had parked or made three-point turns.

Connor inched past the scene and pulled to the side of the road. A dark wall of clouds was lumbering in from the west, the tops towering high into the sky, the bottoms dark and menacing. A thunderstorm was building quickly, and he figured he had no more than twenty minutes before it arrived. He opened the door and got out, rolled his shoulders to relieve the stiffness that always settled in after a long drive. The result of broken bones and gunshot wounds he'd collected over the years.

The road ran in a straight line in both directions, no curves to navigate. No skid marks, no streaks of rubber on the pavement that had been chewed up by thousands of tires and the passing of the seasons. Connor recalled that he hadn't had time to hit the brakes before the steering wheel got away from him, and the Jeep began its roll. It all came back to him now, almost frame by frame as he recalled how the car had crossed into the oncoming lane that fortunately was devoid of traffic, then plunged through a skirt of dense scrub and vines before finally coming to a stop in a thicket of broken saplings.

He inched his way down the side of the runoff ditch, which was about five feet deep and had about a half foot of water in it. Probably from the recent showers that had dampened the area, and the approaching clouds would add significantly to that amount when they broke open. He dug a heel into the muddy bank, made a quick hop across the foul sludge that was brown from iron that had leeched out of the soil, combined with bluish swirls of oil. A long gouge was hacked into the opposite side of the ditch, cut when the Jeep's front bumper had come into contact with the earth. This must have been where it had flipped upside-down, before coming to a rest against the oak tree a few yards further down the culvert.

Despite the rough furrow that had been carved by the tumbling vehicle, it took Connor a few minutes to scrape his way through the thick underbrush to where it had come to rest. Scraps of shattered safety glass and plastic trim were strewn everywhere. He thought back to how he'd released himself from his seat belt, then did the same for Cherine Dupree. Crouched on the upturned ceiling, listening to the voices of two men approaching, preparing to finish what they'd started.

A distant flash of lightning suggested the dark clouds were gaining speed. Connor counted sixteen seconds until the resulting thunderclap hit his ears: just over three miles away. Given the wind that now was picking up and rustling the branches overhead, he figured he had six or seven minutes until it arrived. Ten at the outside.

He started to pick his way back through the dense brush, tangled thick with briars and thorns, when a speck of yellow caught his eye. More like brownish mustard, the fancy kind whose name he couldn't immediately remember. He hunched over and took a closer look, saw it actually was a scrap of fabric that had been speared by the sharp thorns of Carolina creeper stitched into the underbrush.

Dijon: that was the color. With a black logo embroidered in the middle of it: ⊨

Another spear of lightning and a round of thunder just four seconds later warned Connor the deluge was about to hit. He plucked the fragment of cloth from the pricker and tucked it into his pocket, then scrambled through the ditch and up to the road just as the first fat drops began to plop on the pavement. He hurried back to where he'd parked his car, barely pulled the door closed when a wall of rain began to hammer the roof, sending a sheet of water down the windshield.

The storm reduced visibility to just a few feet beyond the hood. Connor kept the speedometer to around twenty for the next ten minutes, until the rain eventually let up and the continual booming of thunder began to retreat behind him as the clouds tracked toward the coast.

The diversion to the crash site only took Connor a few miles out of his way, and thirty minutes later he was driving past the roadside blight of convenience stores and gas pumps that announced the outskirts of Andrews. He had passed through here just about seventy-two hours ago, Willis Ronson in the back seat, and he figured he'd never have reason to be back this way anytime soon. But Burdette's mention of the "waffle cam" had set his mind on replay, and he wanted to see the scene again in order to process the order of things.

The Sunrise Motel was marked by a rusted sign atop twin white poles, the words painted and—at some point in history—illuminated with orange and red neon. A yellowing marquee with movable black letters beneath it advertised "Daily, Weekly Rates," "HBO Cable WiFi," and "Kitchen Units." Nothing seemed to have changed since Sunday, except maybe the assortment of cars parked in front of the rooms. And the puddles that had formed when the rain had moved through just a short while ago.

Connor pulled into the lot and slid the transmission into "park." He glanced across the highway at the Waffle House, spotted where the camera was located just below the eaves at the entrance. Capturing whatever went down in the restaurant's parking lot and, by chance, the comings and goings in front of the motel. Just as Burdette had described.

It had not occurred to him when he'd driven out here on Sunday that he was cruising into an ambush. No reason to think that, since Ronson hadn't skipped out on charges of a violent nature. In fact, the man had no record of assault of any kind, other than tipping over a row of motorcycles. Aside from his one-time affiliation with a wannabe biker gang, he'd shown no tendencies toward bar fights, no disturbances of the peace. When Connor knocked on his motel room door and shook him out of his tequila-infused stupor, he'd accepted the inevitable and held out his wrists for the cuffs. No attempt to flee or resist in any way.

Which again begged the question: who the hell had wanted him dead?

The same desk clerk was sitting in the office today as on Sunday. He had a distant, hazy look in his eyes and didn't seem to recognize Connor right away. Mid-twenties, round face, short hair with a flat top. Jeans and an Insane Clown Posse T-shirt. His pupils appeared slightly dilated, and he seemed to have a permanent yawn that was opening and closing his mouth. He was staring at his phone, probably thumbing his way through a video game or a private stash of porn.

He looked up as the door closed with the tinkle of a bell. "Help you?" he asked, putting the phone down.

Connor wasted no time, just showed him a digital photo of Ronson. "I was here three days ago, looking for this guy," he said. "Remember?"

"Room sixteen. No, eighteen, right?"

"That's right. You said the guy paid cash."

"I guess."

"That's what you said," Connor assured him.

"Then yeah, that's what he did. That a crime?"

"Except he didn't really, did he?"

A confused look crossed the guy's face as he tried to figure out what Connor was saying. "Didn't what?" he asked.

"Someone else paid for the room."

The desk clerk massaged his forehead as if some real difficult mental work was being attempted in the prefrontal cortex behind it. "I really don't recall," he said.

Connor dug his wallet out of his pocket, slipped him two twenties. "This help your memory?" he asked.

"It might. What was the question again?"

"Did someone else pay for the guy's room?"

"Come to think of it, yeah."

Acting on a hunch, Connor said, "Man or woman?"

That brought another look of doubt. The clerk appeared to reach way back into the past as he nervously wrung his fingers. Eventually his eyes brightened and he said, "Definitely a she."

This made sense, considering the scenario that was forming in Connor's head. "Can you describe her?"

The bright look instantly gave way to a frown as the clerk said, "Shit, man. I dunno. Dark hair, dressed nice. I mean, like gray pants, crisp creases, or whatever you call 'em, like they just got ironed. Pleats. Shirt with little ruffles on it. Glasses, too, I think. Yeah, glasses."

"Did she come in here with Ronson?"

"Who?"

Connor showed him the digital photo again. "Did they come in together to register?"

"Yeah, I think." The guy would be a terrible witness to bring to the stand. "Now that I think of it, I know they did. Peeled the money right out of her wallet."

"This woman, did she fill out a registration card?"

The desk clerk gave a quick shake of his head, said, "We don't do that. Most of our guests have this thing about privacy, you know?"

"What about a license plate?"

"Nope."

"Nope, she didn't have one, or you didn't see it?"

"Didn't see it."

"You remember what kind of car she drove?" Connor pressed, taking one last stab at it.

"Yeah. A Chevrolet, named for a beach, I think."

"Malibu?"

"That's a lake, not a beach," the desk clerk said. "Hey…you following up on that cop was here yesterday?"

Meaning Nelson Burdette. "Did he ask you about this woman in the car?"

"No, nothing like that. He wanted to know more about the guy in room eighteen, whether we had security cameras. Any vehicles that came and went, that sort of thing. And he mentioned you."

"What did he say about me?"

"Stuff like what you was asking about, who you was with. And whether it looked to me like you were here to arrest that guy, or maybe you were working with him."

Connor thought on that for a second or two, let it slide. Burdette would say he was just covering all bases, everyone's a suspect until they aren't. Typical cop stuff. "Have you rented out that room since Sunday?" he asked.

"The cops sealed it," the clerk said. Detached and apathetic, no skin off his nose whether it was generating cash flow or not. He just worked there nine to five, or whenever.

Two more twenties unsealed the room, as long as Connor was quick and careful to tape it back up again.

"They spent a long time in there, so I doubt you'll find anything," the guy told him.

Three days ago, Connor had knocked on the same door, found Willis Ronson sprawled on his back across the unmade queen mattress. The paisley earth-tone bedspread and tissue-thin sheets had slid to the floor, and Ronson was clutching a bottle of tequila in his hand, even though he was passed out. How he kept the thing from rolling out of his grasp was a mystery.

The intervening days and nights hadn't changed things much. Empty cans and cigarette boxes were scattered everywhere, and packaging from Waffle House and a Carl's Jr. down the street indicated where he'd been getting most of his nourishment. Since no vehicle had been parked out front, Connor assumed Ronson didn't have a set of wheels, even though his wife had said he'd taken his Ford F-150 with him when he moved out.

His backpack lay open—and empty—in a corner of the room. Connor had allowed Ronson to go through it quickly to gather up anything that might be important, but he ended up taking nothing. It would all end up in a property locker at the jail, anyway. That meant Burdette's team had probably cleaned it out and tossed it aside. Or the desk clerk had been inside the room and had done the same thing.

Connor lowered himself to his hands and knees, checked between the mattress and box spring. Nothing. Same with under the bed. He pawed through the trash on the floor, eyeballed crumpled receipts that corresponded with the food wrappers. Seemed everything he'd eaten had come from a place within walking distance, starting ten days ago—eight days before Connor showed up and put him in cuffs. The same day the desk clerk had said Ronson had checked in, with a smartly dressed woman driving a Chevy. All of which meant he probably hadn't ventured further than a few hundred yards from the motel since he'd arrived.

He was just getting ready to leave when he noticed a scrap of paper beneath the HVAC air handler built into the wall below the front window. He plucked it out from where a puff of cold must have blown it, saw it came from a Pizza Hut on County Line Road in Andrews the night Ronson had arrived. Nothing odd about that, if he'd driven out here in his own truck. He could have gone trolling for dinner, settled on pizza and brought it back to the room. Ate it while guzzling his Jose Cuervo, watching NASCAR or *Ninja Warriors* on TV.

Only problem with that scenario—aside from the absence of a set of wheels—was the pizza itself: Ronson had ordered a large hand-tossed pie, half meat-lover and half mushroom.

Who did that, unless you were ordering for two?

And *mushroom*?

Connor considered himself the least sexist guy he knew, but he also knew there wasn't a man in this universe who would order mushrooms on half a pizza, not if it was just for himself. Which meant one thing: Ronson's dinner date that first night had been a woman and, stretching that thread of logic just a bit further, it suggested her name may have been Liz Morgan.

He was late getting back to the bar, something he knew Julie would needle him about for the rest of the night. To even things out, and since it was the middle of the week, not quite summer, and business was slow, he let her go home a little after ten. He issued last call half an hour later, drawing grumbles from a couple of locals who appeared in the midst of a perpetual pub crawl.

After collecting the receipts and cash he lumbered upstairs, Clooney trailing a couple steps behind him. Man and dog both were tired, and Connor knew he should just throw himself on the bed and go for as many hours of sleep as the night would give him. Before he did that, however, he had one more thing he needed to do. Something that had bugged him from his meeting with Donna Ronson, and had bothered him the rest of the day.

Because of his bond-running gig, he had access to every online search service Citadel Secure Bail Bonds subscribed to. That meant he was able to trace Liz Morgan's school transcripts, arrests, vital records. Residential addresses past and present, employment history. Licenses and insurance, even bank accounts and credit cards, up to a point. Plus Social Security, if he'd had her number. Likewise her fingerprints, which he could run through IAFIS. Again, if he had them.

Everywhere he looked, he found nothing. The woman was a ghost.

Connor exhausted his resources around the same time he ran out of patience. He sat back and checked the clock on the wall: thirty minutes, way more than he'd counted on. His note pad was almost empty, except for the name he'd scribbled at the top—Liz Morgan—and the phone number Donna Ronson had texted him. Other than that, *nada*.

Her cell phone had a Georgia area code, but it had been activated too recently to show up on any database. Public records revealed there were hundreds of people in the U.S. named Liz Morgan, a number that grew exponentially when the search was widened to Elizabeth Morgan. None of them, however, seemed to be associated with the number on Mrs. Ronson's printout, which told Connor it probably belonged to a burner. Furthermore, no one with either name—Liz Morgan or Elizabeth Morgan—lived within the area code, and there were only three such persons in the entire state of Georgia. Two under the age of eighteen, one in her late-eighties. No birth certificates or driver's license or home address. No jobs or schools given.

Similar story in South Carolina.

Whoever this Liz Morgan was, whoever had been pen pals with Willis Ronson while he was doing time at Bennettsville, her name wasn't Liz Morgan. And if she actually existed, he had no idea where she might be, or how he might find her.

Chapter 11

Next morning, not even the sound of clanging tanks and weight belts at the dive shop next door awakened him.

It was the first full night's sleep he'd gotten since he'd begun his search for Ronson, and he would have gotten even more if his phone hadn't started up with the same reggae drum beat. It was from a local 843 number, not one he recognized but, because it was local, he needed to pick up. Even if it turned out to be a computer trying to sell him an extended warranty for a car he no longer had.

The call turned out to be from the nurse's station in the Intensive Care Unit. The woman on the other end identified herself as Amber Elliott, the critical care physician who was on duty that morning. That sent a winter chill through every nerve ending, and he said, "Is this about Cherine Dupree?"

"In fact, it is," the doctor said.

"Is everything all right?"

"Yes, considering," Dr. Elliott told him. "That's why I'm calling. Her condition has improved slightly, and when I saw her a few minutes ago, she asked about you."

"She's going to be okay?"

"Well, her vitals are within an acceptable range, although her injuries remain of great concern. You could say I'm cautiously optimistic."

"Can she talk?" Connor asked.

"Short sentences. But she's very tired, and in a good deal of pain."

"Would it be possible for me to visit her?"

"Well, Mr. Connor. That's why I'm calling. Ms. Dupree isn't allowed to have a phone at this time, but she's been asking to see you. Whenever it's convenient."

He checked the bedside clock, then said, "I'm heading out to take my dog for a walk, but I can be there in an hour. Does that work?"

"Perfectly," Dr. Elliott replied. "I'll let Ms. Dupree know."

Cherine was awake but sedated when Connor was allowed in to see her. The overhead lighting was on, but dimmed to a low level, causing her dark face to appear as just a shadow of the woman who had been riding beside him on Sunday. Her skull was wrapped in a thick layer of gauze, and a neck brace kept her from being able to turn her head. Her right arm was in a cast, as was her left leg. Several tubes snaked under the layers of blankets that were keeping her warm, and a corresponding set of wires led to a monitor on a stand at the head of the bed. The same monitor he hadn't been able to see when he'd looked in on her earlier.

The nurse who brought him into the ICU confirmed what Dr. Elliott had said: her condition had improved, although her injuries remained serious and she was anything but out of the woods. The ventilator tube that had been inserted down her esophagus had been removed, but her throat was sore and it was painful for her to speak.

"Please don't ask her a lot," the nurse said. His name badge identified him as Glenn Landis, RN, and he reminded Connor of one of the Army medics who had attended to him in Kuwait following the Humvee explosion. "You have five minutes."

Connor barely knew Cherine Dupree. He'd only talked to her on the phone twice prior to Sunday's excursion to Andrews, and both times she'd seemed guarded when they spoke. Reserved and wary of conversation in case she revealed too much. Maybe in her mind he represented the blue side of the law, the full power of the police establishment behind him and, by extension, as close to being a cop as one could get without actually carrying a badge.

"Cherine?" he asked from the foot of the bed.

Her eyes blinked open, and she said, "Good guess."

"Heard you called in sick," he replied. Going for lame humor, because what else was there?

"Your fault," she managed to say through the cuts and bruises that were her mouth.

"I know, and I'm sorry. I had no idea."

Cherine fixed him with her eyes, then closed them in a slow blink. When they opened again, she said, "Willis Ronson's dead."

Connor nodded and relied, "He never had a chance."

She closed her eyes again, which he figured may have been her way to nod. "Thank you."

"For what?"

"Saving my life."

"I don't know what you've been told, but I hardly deserve your gratitude, considering—" Connor glanced around the sterile room "—well, considering all this."

"Whatever. I owe you."

He didn't like the hero role, a persona he'd never been able to shake as long as Jordan James was stitched into the seams of his world. Yes, he had saved Eddie James's life that horrific day in the desert but, in Connor's mind, he should have seen the suicide van approaching long before he let it get close enough to do any damage. Just as he should have been aware of the pick-up truck racing up behind him Sunday evening, long before the bullets started flying.

What valor was there in saving a life when you put it in jeopardy in the first place?

"All I want is for you to get better and get out of here," he told her.

"Working on it." She seemed to wince, then said, "You just missed the cop."

"Let me guess: Nelson Burdette from SLED?"

Cherine tried to nod, but the bandages and neck brace wouldn't allow it.

"He talked to me, too," Connor said. "Not a bad guy, really. Just doing his job."

She fell silent a moment, rolled her eyes up to look at the ceiling. "Hope they catch the bastards," she said.

At that point the door opened and a woman poked her head inside. She was tall, close to six feet, broad shoulders that filled the turquoise long-sleeve T-shirt tucked into a pair of chinos. White, blondish hair cut just below her ears, eyes that normally would have been blue but now were streaked with red. Cheeks that bore the tracks of dried tears. She was holding a vase of flowers that looked as if it had come from the hospital gift shop.

She shot a confused glance from Cherine to Connor, then said, "Who are you?"

"His name's Connor," Cherine explained. "He saved my life."

"Not exactly," Connor replied.

The tall woman cocked her head, and then a blaze of recognition flashed in her eyes. "Wait a sec…you're the guy who was driving the car."

"Guilty as charged."

The woman flung her arms around him, taking care not to spill water from the vase. She squeezed him hard, then stepped back. "Cher would have died out there if it weren't for you," she told him.

"She never would have been there if not for me," Connor countered. Wondering who was this woman who was tall enough to play point guard for the WNBA.

"My name's Claire," she explained, as if reading his mind. Then she held up her left hand, displaying a simple gold band on her ring finger. She drew an invisible line between her and Cherine, and added, "Just in case she didn't tell you."

No, Cherine hadn't. In fact, they'd spoken very little about anything other than Willis Ronson on the ride out to Andrews, mostly how the judge was certain to keep him locked up until trial. Which probably wouldn't be for months and months. When he hadn't shown up for his preliminary hearing, she had insisted that her client had probably just made a simple error, entered the wrong date for the court appearance into his phone. Something like that. Everything could be cleared up quickly if he—the judge—would just give her forty-eight hours to get him into the courtroom. But rules were rules, and the judge showed no compassion or leniency. Mrs. Ronson was out the two grand in cash and plastic she'd posted to bond him out, and he was looking at a long time back at Leeds, then upstate again for a long stretch. A bench warrant for his arrest was issued on the spot.

Which had set all this in motion.

"Pleased to meet you," Connor said. "I'm sure you already know it, but you're married to one very strong woman."

"So is she," Claire replied with a broad smile. Then to Cherine she added, "I knew how you love peonies. Where would you like me to put them?"

Connor was good at picking up cues, and he read this one correctly. "Time for me to go," he announced as he backed toward the door. "I'll show myself out."

• • •

Later that evening—the bedside clock said it was well past midnight—Connor awoke to the sound of muffled footfalls on the landing outside his apartment door. Clooney evidently heard them, too, since he let out a startled *woof* as he practically levitated from his usual position at the foot of the bed.

Connor was on his feet in an instant and grabbed a robe he kept on a hook by the door. Raccoons and possums down at the street always seemed to be attacking the trash bins, which he tethered shut with bungee cords. When that didn't work, he built an enclosure with a hinged lid to keep them out, but they still managed to finesse their way inside. One evening he'd even seen a coyote prowling through the parking lot, and the next day a neighbor's cat had gone missing. He didn't think it ever turned up, because the notices that had been stapled to trees and signposts remained there for weeks, until the ink had washed away in the spring rains.

But this was no raccoon or coyote. This sounded human, and right outside Connor's door. Clooney's sudden bark seemed to spook the intruder, causing him—or her—to bound down the stairs to the first floor. The motion-sensor lights had blinked on and now, as Connor yanked the door open, he saw a human form dodging around tables as it rushed toward the stairs that led down to the ground. He played the beam of his flashlight on the shadow as it took the steps two at a time, but couldn't get a good fix on who it was. Other than to be fairly certain it was a man, not a woman.

A second later he heard the slap-slap of shoes on gravel, as the trespasser hit the pavement and raced up the street. A silver moon peeked out from behind a passing cloud, but it was too little, too late. The guy was gone, and a second later Connor heard a distant car door slam and an engine roar to life.

• • •

When Connor thought back on it, he should have called the police. Definitely the intelligent thing to do, but a stubborn streak had run through him his entire life, causing him to repeat the same mistakes until a lesson finally sank in.

He stood at the railing of the drinking deck in his flip-flops, staring down at the darkened street, staring after the shadow that had just prowled his bar. And his home. Was he a burglar? Vandal? Looter? It was a reasonable question—more than one, in fact—and the intelligent thing would be to report it to Nelson Burdette. Three nights ago, he'd been lying in a bed in the ER, and the smart money said the intrusion was connected to Sunday's near-death experience. But Connor's independent streak—the same sort of go-it-alone attitude that had gotten him into trouble before—had already set in with typical stubbornness. And recklessness.

That meant no cops, at least for now.

Naturally, he couldn't sleep. The adrenaline rush had him wired, and even an hour later his eyes were wide open, staring at the dark ceiling, recycling the possible reasons someone might want to creep his place in the middle of the night. He quickly ruled out burglary, since he possessed nothing anyone would want to steal. Ditto The Sandbar, unless someone was in dire need of plastic tables and chairs, or a bottle of bourbon or rum.

Fact was, there were hundreds of McMansions all over Folly, all of them with vastly greater riches with which to abscond: jewelry, artwork, coin collections. Cash and guns. What point was there in creeping his place? He assumed thieves followed the same rule of thumb as did smart homebuyers: location, location, location.

The most plausible answer was that the gunmen who'd killed Willis Ronson had come to pay a visit. As Connor had been crouched on the ceiling of his Jeep in the runoff ditch, he'd heard his assailants as they'd poked their way through the sludge and slime. One of them had said *the others may be alive*, to which the guy who seemed to be in command had replied, *we'll deal with them later*. Breaking into the intensive care unit at MUSC would prove to be a Herculean task, but Connor was easy prey in his bachelor pad one floor above an open-air bar. If their goal was to leave no witnesses, he was the first, best target.

But if that was the case, then why didn't the shadow just point and shoot?

This entire circuit of thought cycled through Connor's brain until he eventually slipped into a roiling semi-consciousness. He kept drifting in and out of a fitful sleep, waking only when a sharp rapping downstairs yanked him out of a dream. He dragged on a pair of jeans and a T-shirt, then opened it to find Burdette standing on the top step, on the other side of the locked gate that separated it from the drinking deck.

Too early for a random visit, but at least he was honoring the boundaries Connor had set.

It was a few minutes past seven, and the new sun was casting an orange glow against the spinnaker roof. The same mourning doves were cooing in their nest in a nearby palmetto, and a persistent woodpecker hammering for grubs in a tree not far away provided a staccato cadence to the morning. A salty aroma hung in the gentle onshore breeze, and half a block up the street Gilbert was hard at work, frying bacon and brewing coffee.

"Good morning, detective," Connor called out as he trudged down the stairs to let him in. "Pretty early in the day for house calls."

"Investigator," Burdette corrected him. Again.

"I was just going to make a pot of coffee," he said. "Care for a cup?"

He did, and followed Connor back upstairs into his apartment. Not very large, barely room for two adults to turn around, so the SLED cop planted his backside on a stool and gave the place a once-over. The kitchen was little more than a fridge, oven, and sink. No dishwasher, barely enough counter space for dishes to dry. It was really just an alcove off the living room, with a separate room just large enough for a bed. Small but efficient, and all that he needed.

Connor had no idea what Burdette wanted or why he was there, especially so early on what promised to be a busy day. He left it to him to get the ball rolling, which he did just about the time the coffee began dripping through the filter into the Pyrex pot.

"You still driving that red Ford parked down below?" he asked.

"Company vehicle," Connor confirmed. "Not my first choice."

Burdette nodded at that, providing no confirmation of why he was asking. The SLED cop glanced at a page in his notebook, then said, "Where were you yesterday afternoon, around one, one-thirty?"

Now Connor understood what this was about: his drive out to Andrews. "Road trip. I couldn't get the accident out of my head, so I drove back up there to see the place."

Burdette flipped his notebook closed and drew in a breath so deep Connor could see his chest expand. "You also went to that flea-bag-motel," he said.

Busted. The desk clerk must have called him, despite the secrecy he thought he'd bought with his twenties. "After you showed me that surveillance video from the Waffle House, I wanted to check out a couple things."

"This is not your investigation, Connor. There's nothing for you to check out."

Connor handed him a mug of coffee, took a sip from his own. "It was only a quick drive-by, just to ease my curiosity."

Burdette set the mug down and stared at him from across the table. His eyes drifted to the scrap of fabric lying in a saucer on the counter, the fragment Connor had found yesterday ensnared on a clump of briars in the runoff ditch. The Dijon-colored patch that bore the logo

Ⴑ

"Where'd you get that?" he asked.

"The gully where my car plunged off the road. It was stuck on a thorn. You think it could have anything to do with the shooting?"

"At this point, everything is suspect. Were you planning on handing it over to me?"

Connor hadn't given the idea much thought but, now that Burdette was asking, the answer was a no-brainer. "I was going to call you this morning," he said. "You beat me to it."

Burdette uttered a low grunt as he took a pair of nitrile gloves out of his pocket and pulled them over his hands. He gently picked up the scrap of cloth and slipped it inside a cellophane envelope, then said, "Chain of custody on this is for shit, but we'll see what it yields."

"You think that's the number 4 or LI?" Connor asked him, indicating the logo.

"You must not buy much chicken," the SLED cop said.

"How do you mean?"

"What I mean is, it's the logo for Lomax Industries. One of the largest poultry processors in the state."

"Lomax," Connor repeated, just so he wouldn't forget it. "Never heard of it."

"Good…keep it that way," Burdette told him as he sealed the envelope. "What were these 'couple of things,' anyway? The ones that brought you all the way out to Andrews yesterday."

Connor took a sip of coffee, buying him a second or two to decide how to frame his response. And to get a handle on his own motives. This guy from SLED seemed to be a smart and competent investigator, so why did Connor feel a reluctance to back away and let him do his job? "Does the name Liz Morgan mean anything?" he asked.

Burdette gave it a few seconds' thought, but Connor couldn't read his reaction. "Should it?" he eventually asked.

"I assume you've talked with Mrs. Ronson. Willis' wife. Widow now, I guess."

A dip of his head indicated he had. Something Connor already knew, because she had told him the two of them had spoken. "It was only a few hours after she'd been notified about the accident," Burdette said.

"Thing is, she called me yesterday, said she wanted to meet with me. I'm not sure why, and she caught me off guard."

"Can't be your good looks and charm," Burdette replied. "What did she want?"

"Someone to listen to her, more than anything. But she also told me a lot more than I wanted to know."

"Like what?"

"Like this Liz Morgan," Connor said. "Seems she was someone from her husband's past, and Mrs. Ronson didn't seem happy that they'd been talking."

"News to me," Burdette replied. "Any idea why she shared this with you?"

Connor lifted his shoulder in a shrug, said, "All I know is, she seemed damned sure this Morgan woman had something to do with her husband's disappearance. And death."

"And you just felt compelled to drive up there to the no-tell motel to find out?" Sarcasm bordering on derision, with a touch of irritation thrown in. As in, *keep your fucking nose out of my investigation.*

"Playing a hunch, is all."

"And this hunch, did it pay off?" Burdette asked.

"Could be," Connor replied. "Seems Willis Ronson checked into his room with a woman, who paid up front in cash."

"Let me guess: Liz Morgan."

Connor could have answered Burdette's question in any number of ways. The easiest would have been, *I don't know.* Next up: *The desk clerk never asked for ID.* Followed by *turns out they don't keep records of that sort of thing* and *the guy wouldn't talk to me.* Or the ultimate response: *Liz Morgan's a ghost; she doesn't exist.*

"The guy behind the counter wouldn't say," was what he went with.

"When were you planning on telling me about this?" Burdette asked, the annoyance clear in his voice. And his face.

"Like I said, this morning. But I figured you would have known all this anyway, since you'd already spoken with Mrs. Ronson."

He made the same low, grunting sound, then said, "Is that all?"

"Yes, sir. That's it. If I remember anything else, I'll make sure to call you."

"You do that," Burdette said, as he made no motion to get up. He clearly had something else on his mind, and made a point of taking a long sip of his coffee.

"Did you really drop by to ask me about my car?" Connor asked, bringing it back around to what he'd said when he'd first come in. "I could have told you everything on the phone."

"I wanted to tell you again—face to face—to stay clear of my investigation. Last time you went all Rambo, you nearly got yourself killed."

Connor knew he was talking about his take-down last year of the drug czar who ran a big chunk of the meth trade across the southeast. Lots of blood had been shed, including his own, and several people ended up dead because of it. A lot of questions followed, and more than a few federal agencies made his life hell for months. For good reason.

"This is nothing like that," he insisted.

The doubt remained on Burdette's face, but eventually he set his mug down on the table and rose from his chair. "Thanks for the info," he said as he turned to go. "But not the coffee. Tastes like toilet water. And I don't mean the kind you buy your wife for her birthday."

Chapter 12

As soon as Connor heard the tires of the unmarked SLED car pull out of the gravel lot, he carried his laptop down to one of the cheap bar tables and Googled Lomax Industries. It wasn't hard to find, since the firm was one of the oldest and largest chicken producers in the South, with its headquarters upstate in a small town outside Spartanburg. Statewide, South Carolina poultry farmers raised more than two hundred million chickens for market each year, and Lomax by far was the biggest of them. It operated four processing plants and employed several hundred workers across six counties.

Colton Lomax—aka Colt—served as chairman of the public company that his grandfather founded on ten acres back in the fifties. In the early years, the company's focus was selling whole chickens and fryer parts to grocery stores around the state. When Colt assumed control in the late nineties, he expanded the firm's business model to also serve the fast-food industry. Since then, he'd increased production over a thousand percent, with plans to more than double that output over the next five years. An initial public offering had netted the company almost a quarter billion dollars when institutional investors caused the IPO price to jump forty percent the first day.

A drop-down menu under the "About Us" tab on the company's website brought Connor a link that said "Where We Are." A quick click led him to another page, this one a map of the South Carolina-North Carolina-Georgia tri-state area, marked with several dozen dots of various colors. They were spread out across the entire region, and a legend at the bottom explained what the colors meant. Red indicated farms that were actively raising poultry, blue marked the processing plans where chickens were packaged, while green revealed "sites of future expansion." The farms were scattered throughout all three states, while most of the "production for market" occurred in the upstate area around Spartanburg. Which made sense, considering that was where the firm was founded.

The green dots were what caught Connor's attention. As with the farms, most of the "future expansion" sites were dispersed across all three states, generally located within an hour of a major city. Atlanta, Augusta, Raleigh. Columbia, and Greenville. Easy access to highways and railroads, he figured, good routes to transportation hubs and the greater markets beyond.

What he found odd was that five of the dots were concentrated in a small area south of Florence and west of Georgetown. Very rural and, based on his own recent experience, nowhere near a railroad or highway adequate for a near-constant stream of eighteen-wheelers. And all of them between the small communities of Lane and Andrews.

Andrews again. *Coincidence?*

One of the programs to which Connor did not have access from his laptop was the database of county and state property records. He could try to sneak into Citadel Security's main office suite on East Bay Street and access the mainframe, but it wasn't worth the risk if he got caught. He'd been warned once before that if he tried that stunt again, it would be grounds for termination.

Instead, he scrolled through the contacts on his phone, tapped in the number for Caitlin Thomas. She was the desk jockey who supervised Citadel's digital databases, and was a master at finessing the most guarded information out of any digital drive or cloud. Or, as she had once so graphically described it, "No one is better than coaxing a weevil out of a boar's ass." In this capacity she had assisted Connor in several previous cases—both on and off the books—and seemed to savor the hunt, while thriving on danger. The more the better.

"I'm royally pissed at you," she said when she answered his call.

"What did I do now?" he asked.

"You almost got yourself killed. What sort of friend does that?"

"Definitely not my intention," Connor replied. "But thank you for caring."

"I'll let it go, this time." She let him hang there a minute, then said, "Seriously…how are you doing? You gave us all quite a scare."

"Just fine, considering the alternative." He then launched into an abridged version of the accident, much of which it appeared she already knew. As the queen of research, not one byte of data escaped her capacity to delve, probe, or pry. She regularly surfed a full spectrum of sites for the latest news and rumors, and her near-eidetic memory filled her head with trivial garbage—or, in her words again, "a useless but sizeable pile of horseshit." Whatever had been reported about the shoot-out and Willis' Ronson's death, she would have been all over it.

"What do you need?" she asked when he finished.

"Am I that transparent?"

"As a sheet of glass," she replied. "Spill it."

Connor could have been hurt, but Caitlin was telling the truth. Nine times out of ten when he called, it was because he needed her to run a search for him. The tenth time would have been when he dropped by her desk in the company cube farm to give her a rose or a Kit Kat, his way of thanking her for doing the impossible.

"I need you to do a property search," he said. "If you have time."

"Not really," she told him. "But fuck it. I'm in the car, so text me the details. When I get in, I'll see what I can do."

Connor stepped out of the shower just as his phone stopped ringing. He checked the screen, didn't recognize the number, and set it down again. He toweled off, then inspected the deep furrow on the back of his hand. Six original sutures, four remaining, neat little spiders of thread poking out from a wound that appeared to be closing up well. No redness, no infection, but the compass rose tattoo would forever be bisected by a permanent scar. He considered leaving it open to the air, but the discharge nurse had made it clear that he needed to keep it free from bacteria, so he wrapped a clean strip of gauze around it, awkwardly taping it with one hand.

As he was finishing up his phone chimed, signaling that whoever had called had left him a message. A long one, judging by the time interval. He got dressed, grabbed a banana off the counter in the kitchen, and took it out onto his landing to eat it. The tide was out, and the beach seemed to extend halfway to the horizon. In the distance he spotted a point of sail, a boat slicing southward through the open ocean rather than along the Intracoastal Waterway. Closer in, a squadron of pelicans was gliding along the water's edge, one of them occasionally breaking formation and plunging into the water with a splash.

He peeled the banana just enough to take a bite, then tapped the voicemail app. Someone nearby was power-washing a house, so the audio was hard to make out, but about two seconds into the message he realized it was Donna Ronson.

"Hey, Mr. Connor," she began. "You know, the strangest thing just happened, and for a minute I figured it was one of those scams. Assholes hacking into my phone account, or sending me a coupon for a gift card. Shit like that. Anyway, I was just going through texts on my phone…I realized I hadn't looked at them for a few days, not since, well, since the accident, and so I was scrolling through them, and I found this thing that at first I figured was more bullshit. It was from some number I didn't recognize, with a whole bunch of random letters and characters, and it seemed to me it was one of those virus things. I was getting ready to hit delete when I saw…well, there was a specific word in it that Will used to call me, a long time ago up in Florence, when we was first dating. A secret nickname kind of thing, and whenever we was on the phone and getting ready to hang up, we'd both say it. I know it sounds corny, but that's how it was. I know I'm rambling on too long, and you may not get this whole message, but the thing is, I'm positive this text came from Will. He must've sent it from someone else's phone, but it was him. I know it. And here's the thing: there was two files attached to it. Big ones I can't open, on account this phone is an old piece of crap and I don't really trust it. But I figure maybe you can do something, so I'm texting it to you. Might take a while, since they're big files, but if you get them, take a look, will you? Okay, that's it. By the way, this is Donna Ronson, if you've haven't figured it out. Bye."

Long message was right, and when it finished Connor saved it, just in case he needed to listen to it again. He checked his SMS app, saw that nothing from Mrs. Ronson had arrived yet, wondered if whatever she'd been talking about had gotten clogged coming down the 5G pipeline. He considered calling her back to let her know he'd received her voicemail, but decided to wait a few minutes, give the follow-up text time to show up.

Eventually it did.

She'd deleted whatever had been their secret word way back when, because the message contained only the two very large files she'd mentioned. Both were formatted with an extension that indicated they were videos that could be viewed on most mobile devices. Donna Ronson either didn't know this, or was rightfully suspicious that some kind of malware embedded in the text might cause permanent damage to her phone.

Connor shared the same misgivings, but figured if his phone froze up, he had the cracked device Burdette had returned to him. He briefly considered calling her back before he viewed them, but she had not actually asked him to do that. He also realized that maybe Willis Ronson had grown lustful toward his wife while he was holed up in the motel, and maybe had shot her a porno. But he ruled that out almost as quickly as it had come to him, since Mrs. Ronson had said the message had come from a phone she didn't recognize. Which possibly meant a third party was involved.

He finished off the banana, then clicked on the first file and waited while it opened a digital player on his screen.

It was, indeed, a video, and a poorly shot one. The time bar at the bottom indicated it was just under fifteen minutes in length, and for the first five or ten seconds all Connor caught was a blur of motion as the cameraman—maybe Ronson himself—seemed unable to hold the thing steady. Maybe he was trying to hide it somewhere it couldn't be detected: a buttonhole, possibly a belt buckle. Definitely an article of clothing, since the following frames were shot POV—*point of view*—as the person took a step, pivoted right and left, then took another step. A *Steadicam* it was not.

There was just enough light so Connor could see that Ronson was riding in some sort of vehicle. People seemed to be seated in front and in back of him, staring ahead or out a side window in grim silence. The lens only picked up two or three of them, mostly silhouettes in the bad lighting, no recognizable features other than beards and stringy hair and camo-patterned baseball caps. No voices, either. Evidently the camera either was not equipped with audio, or the feature hadn't been turned on.

Trees and phone poles and highway signs flashed by, along with an occasional dirt road marked by a mail box or sign post. Now and then a car would rush past in the opposite direction. Judging from the short shadows, Connor figured the video was shot in either late morning or early afternoon.

After a few minutes the image made a fast cut to another stretch of road. It appeared to be shot from inside the same vehicle, because the facial hair and ball caps appeared the same. The pines and oaks seemed to be rolling by a bit more slowly, and Connor guessed the vehicle was getting ready to exit the highway. Sure enough, it eventually turned onto another road, this one narrower and apparently unpaved, and a minute later it slowed down once more, this time almost to a complete stop.

The camera made a partial pan from left to right, and came to rest on a one-lane driveway leading away from the hard scrabble road. A metal gate stretched across the dirt lane from one concrete post to another, both of them flanked by trees and allowing no room on either side for anything other than a thin person to squeeze through. A few seconds later a man—Connor guessed it was the driver—walked into the shot as he fished a ring of keys out of his pocket. He unlocked the gate, swung it open far enough for the bus to pass through, then walked out of frame again.

The camera started moving once more, slowly, and pulled through the open gate down the road far less travelled. Connor expected it to stop again while the driver got out and re-locked the gate, but instead the video made a jerky, fast-cut forward in time.

Judging from the shadows it now seemed later in the day. Or early the following morning. No time/date stamp, so Connor couldn't tell. The quick cut now appeared to show Ronson—or whoever was holding the camera—working his way through a forest of second-growth pines and oaks and cypress. The lighting was dark, the setting gloomy, almost funereal. He didn't appear to be following any sort of trail and, at one point, he began darting from one tree to the next. As he moved, the camera would jerk, and Connor could see the barrel of what appeared to be a gun. Actually, he could swear it was an M4, just like the weapon he carried during his time in the desert.

As the camera lurched its way through the woods, it caught the motion of several other men running back and forth in front of the lens. Some appeared closer than others, and each was dressed in digital camo pants and jackets. Similar rifles were slung across their chests, ammo belts draped over their shoulders. Weighed down by helmets, goggles, and heavy boots as they humped over fallen tree trunks and slogged through mire. Still no audio, so Connor couldn't hear what was being said, but from time to time a flutter of rapid-fire flashes would burst from the barrel of a nearby gun. Which brought more jerk-action: running, stumbling, climbing, and then a bright blast directly in front of the lens. At that point the frenzied motion ceased, the camera slowly tilted up to the sky, and the picture froze on the top of a scraggly pine until it cut to black.

With the first video played out, Connor retreated to the kitchen to grab another cup of coffee. He offered a rawhide chew to Clooney, then wandered back outside and settled in to watch the second file.

As with the first recording, this one also started on a bus filled with men in military fatigues. This time, however, they were covered with mud and grime, with weary faces and downcast eyes lacking expression or enthusiasm. Almost defeated. And again, no audio.

A blur of trees and gnarled scrub flashed by outside the window until, once again, the bus slowed and turned from one road onto another. It then continued for another mile or so, hung a left, then another left before coming to a stop.

Another gate, but this time it seemed to operate automatically. The bus passed through an opening in a high hurricane fence, with razor wire spooled on top. The gate appeared to be the sort that rolled aside on tracks to one side, probably at the touch of a remote control, and the lens picked up a peek of a small sign as the bus rolled through. Whatever was written on it was obscured by shadows and the angle at which the camera was positioned.

Another minute or so of the same trees and low brush followed, but by now the road was so narrow that the branches seemed to scrape the glass. Eventually it came to an end, and the bus circled through a large field that looked as if had been bulldozed out of the woods. When it came to a stop, the lens pivoted ninety degrees, facing forward, settling on the guy slouched in the seat in front of him. Something seemed to catch the guy's attention and then, almost all at once, the tired men clad in dirty military garb rose to their feet. So did Ronson—Connor's best assumption—and they all began to move toward the front of the bus.

A lot of jostling and flaring tempers followed as the group filed down the aisle and descended a set of stairs set at the right-hand side of the vehicle. As they exited, they fell into a single line that dragged, rather than marched, toward a mound of earth near the edge of the clearing. As the line of men approached it, Connor spotted a pair of steel doors that had been swung open, revealing an expanse of darkness beyond. Uniformed guards were stationed on either side, guns held tight across their chests as the squad of soldiers entered. One of the sentries was bald, with ears that stuck out like wings, almost no chin. The other was a few inches shorter, burly almost to the point of being fat.

The camera slowly moved inside and the light shifted. The only thing that was visible was a narrow doorway, which opened into a small, darkened room. Ronson—by now Connor couldn't imagine who else it could be—took a tentative step into a tunnel of some sort. Bare bulbs in wire cages overhead barely illuminated the passageway, and another doorway in the distance had the appearance of the rusted hatchway of an old submarine.

As the lens approached it, however, Connor realized he was looking at the rear emergency exit of an old school bus. Even in the murk he could see it was painted the yellow-orange he remembered from his Michigan childhood, streaked with grime and pocked with rusty orange peel. All but the shortest of the men had to duck as they passed through the entrance and, once inside, they staggered down an aisle lined with tiers of bunks along both walls. It reminded Connor of the POW barracks in *The Great Escape*.

At the front of the bus the camera made a sharp turn where the main door appeared to have been removed. It descended yet another set of steps, then abruptly climbed back up into the rear of yet another bus. This routine was repeated for the next sixty seconds or so, as the hidden lens continued to record the tight confines of what appeared to be an underground warren of old buses. Some were lined with berths piled three high, while others were furnished with makeshift tables and cheap folding chairs. One appeared to be fitted with toilets from back to front; Connor doubted there was indoor plumbing or running water, which meant the stench had to be horrific.

What the hell was this place?

Once more, the video eventually cut to black. No warning, no more jostling of the camera. It just ended, and the time tracker at the bottom of the onscreen app said the playback was done. An icon offered him the chance to replay the silent footage if Connor chose to, but he'd seen enough.

Time to hand it over to SLED. Let Burdette figure out what it was, and what to do with it.

But not before Connor copied both files onto the hard drive of his laptop.

Chapter 13

Connor tried to motivate his legs to comply with a run on the sand, but he couldn't help but think about something that had been nibbling at the back of his brain. Now he realized what it was.

He thumbed through the image gallery on his phone, found the photo he'd snapped of the "For Rent" sign attached to the chain link at the house where Joey Barber had lived, until just a few days ago. And Willis Ronson before that, until he'd split. Time to find out where the guy known as Scissors had gone, in one hell of a hurry.

He dialed the number that was scribbled at the bottom of the sign. The phone rang three, then four times before a man with a raspy smoker's voice answered.

"Good morning," Connor said. "I drove by a house yesterday out in North Charleston that looks like it's for rent. The sign said to call someone named Gator. Is that you?"

"Yup. But you can call me John."

"Okay, John. Can you tell me if the place is still available?"

"Sure is, but it won't be for long. Got a bunch of calls on it already."

"What can you tell me about it?"

John, aka Gator, described the place as a three-bedroom, one-bath ranch built in the fifties. Two window AC units, heat pump for winter. Rent was twelve hundred a month, first and last and a five-hundred-dollar deposit. A dog was okay, with a two hundred buck fee, non-refundable.

"How long has it been vacant?" Connor asked him.

"Just a couple days. Asshole moved out, just like that."

"That sucks. You know where he went?"

"Nope, and the truth is, I'm glad to be rid of him. Sonofabitch never paid his rent on time, and the neighbors said he was doing some kind of business out of there. Lots of people coming and going, and lots of noise.

But that all stopped when he moved out. It's a good location, no crime now that he's gone. Don't need that sort of shit. You interested?"

"Might be. Let me talk to the missus."

"Yeah, well, don't wait too long. I expect to have a lease signed by the end of the day."

Another thing that had been bothering Connor since he'd first been hired to find Willis Ronson was the copper wire. According to the arrest report, the dumbass had cut several hundred pounds of it by the time the first officer on the scene had cuffed him. Ronson had driven his pick-up around to the rear of the transformer site and backed it up against a locked gate, presumably using the same bolt cutters with which he'd hacked through the fencing to open up a space large enough to stuff it through.

But then what? Did he have a source ready to offer him cash on the barrel for it? Had he done this sort of thing before, or was this his first attempt at hawking scrap metal? Connor figured a guard or inspector at the power company would quickly notice the break-in and call the police, who then would report the theft to all the local recycling centers. A massive coil of copper couldn't be as easy to fence as a Rolex watch. Or his wife's antique ring.

A quick online search of local businesses that offered cash for metal told him several were scattered around the lowcountry. He clicked on the website for the firm that appeared at the top of the list, a place called Charleston Metal Redemption that bought and sold all kinds of scrap steel, aluminum, tin, even lead. And copper, which a chart on their website indicated was selling at the market price of twenty-five cents an ounce. Four dollars a pound. About a grand, give or take, for the pile Ronson had harvested from the transformer plant before he'd been caught.

The company's number was listed at the top of the page. Connor called it, and five seconds later a live person answered, "It's a beautiful day to redeem your metal in the Lowcountry. How may I help you?"

Connor briefly explained to the woman what he was looking for, and she replied, "You'll want to speak with Mr. Grasso. Please hold."

Mr. Grasso picked up thirty seconds later, cut right to the chase. "Recycling and sales," he announced. "You buying or selling?"

"Selling," Connor replied. "Couple hundred pounds of scrap."

"Best thing to do is bring it by. We pay top dollar for steel and cast iron, lead, aluminum, brass, stainless, tin, used motors and pumps—"

"What about copper?"

"Yep, long as it's clean. No pipes with mud or gunk or sludge in 'em."

"Wire?" Connor pressed him.

"Sheathed or unsheathed?"

It was a question Connor wasn't expecting; he had no idea what sort of wire Ronson had tried to steal. "It's from a transformer station," he said. "A couple hundred pounds."

"No good," Grasso told him.

"What do you mean, 'no good'?"

"Can't take it. Dumbass punks try to boost that shit from time to time. We buy it and it turns out it's stolen, a ton of hurt comes down on us. How'd you come by this wire, anyway?"

"Actually, I'm just checking on something," Connor explained, skirting the question. "Just looking to see how someone gets rid of that much copper."

"You a reporter or a cop?" Sounding suspicious and skeptical.

"Neither. Maybe you heard about the guy a couple weeks ago who got busted trying to cut some wire from a transformer station up in North Charleston?"

"Yeah, that was right down the street from here. Like I said, we don't buy that stuff. No one does. Dumb shit."

"If you don't buy it, who would he take it to?"

"Hell if I know," Grasso said. "Someone would have to have the means to strip the sheathing and melt the metal down first, so no one would know it was wire. If this guy actually was planning to sell it by the pound, which I doubt."

"How do you mean?"

"There's a lot of uses for copper. I mean, someone could turn it into ingots and get around the theft thing, but a lot of the stuff we see these days really isn't that pure. You'd spend more money trying to melt it than you'd make on the open market. Thing is, jewelers use a lot of copper, and we're starting to see a bunch of ammo made from copper these days. No telling what your guy might have been planning."

"Wait a minute. You mean copper bullets?"

"Yeah. Some hunters swear they're more accurate and produce less kick when they're fired. Me, I prefer shooting lead all day long."

•••

Forty minutes later Connor was back in the lobby of Top Shots Sports and Armory. Once again, a signal notified someone in the back that a customer had walked in, and the same employee emerged from the back area that housed the gun range. He cocked his head as his brain went to work, then gave two thumbs up and said, "SIG P365."

"Good memory," Connor told him. "But people usually call me Connor."

The guy laughed and said, "Then I'm Garrison. You here to shoot this time?"

"Wish I could, but I've just got a quick question."

The guy named Garrison narrowed his gaze at Connor and said, "You had a bunch of those last time."

"Goes with the job. And I promise I'll be brief. You get a lot of regular customers come in here, am I right?"

"Every day 'cept Christmas and New Year's. A lot of 'em are on the buffet plan."

"What's that?" Connor asked.

"That's two questions already," Garrison said. "But since you're asking, it's one of our package deals. All you can shoot for one monthly price."

"Must get expensive, all that ammo."

"That's why we've got the fine print," Garrison said. "With some plans we supply the ordnance, some you gotta supply it yourself."

Connor glanced at the shelves lining the walls, boxes of ammo stacked on them. "You have many customers who cast their own?" he asked.

"A few of the old-timers, sure. Good way to save money, and some rifle competitions are limited to self-cast ordnance. Used to be, it was a real thing with big game hunters, who would shoot a bison or a buffalo, dig out the bullets from the carcass, and melt 'em down over a campfire. Use 'em all over again the next day."

"What about copper?" Connor asked.

"Man, you're sure asking way more than one question," Garrison replied. "But I'll bite: what about it?"

Connor let his eyes drift down the glass gun case to the corner of the room, where it cut to the right and the contents shifted from pistols to rifles. "What can you tell me about copper bullets?"

Garrison slowly drew his head left to right: not much. "Not a lot of commercial demand for them, not that I know of," he said.

"What about Tony?"

"Tony?"

"Tony Young. Last time I was in here you said if I needed clarification about anything, I should talk to Tony. The owner. Is he here?"

Garrison didn't have a quick and ready answer, which suggested the answer probably was yes. His eyes shifted downward a second, as if he were trying to find a good cover, before lifting up and looking him in the eye. "He's at lunch," he said.

Same as last time. Connor suspected the guy was lying, but for what reason he didn't know. Especially since it was Garrison who had originally advised that he speak with the guy. Who, all instincts were telling him, was somewhere on the premises.

"Well, when he comes back, please tell him I want to talk to him about these copper bullets." Connor slid a business card across the glass counter toward Garrison.

"I'll let him know."

Connor turned and made it halfway to the front door, feeling Garrison's eyes on him the entire way. When he turned and said, "By the way, do you know any place around here where you can fire an M4?"

"They're illegal, sir," Garrison told him. "But something tells me you already know that."

"Right. But I saw a training video shot somewhere around here that showed guys firing what I'm pretty sure were M4s. Same kind I shot over in Iraq. Sure would like a chance to shoot one again, if I got the chance."

"Something else to talk to Tony about," Garrison replied.

Connor could have gotten back into his car and driven out of the lot. Headed home, let it all go. Forgotten about Willis Ronson. The man was dead, SLED was investigating, and Cherine Dupree appeared to be on the mend. All those things pointed to the wise way to go.

Instead, as he stepped out into the June sun, he hooked a right and headed to the back of the building. The structure was reinforced cinder-block construction, and whatever windows had once existed had been closed over with concrete to contain any wayward ordnance. It also served to prevent anyone inside from seeing what Connor was up to.

The parking spaces out front near the street were labeled "Customers Only," but a few minutes ago when he'd pulled in, he'd noticed several vehicles parked behind the gun range. He found three trucks, two of them Fords with vinyl bedliners, one Chevy Silverado with a missing tailgate and a dented bumper. One of the Fords was a red F-250 4X4 crew cab, with sprays of mud along the fenders and matching off-road grime smeared on the windshield, where rubber blades had wiped a layer of dried dirt away. The other was a black F-150 King Ranch, all-leather, lots of chrome and side mirrors the size of small TVs screens. Top of the line, which translated to not cheap. Connor did a visual assessment only, no testing the doors to see if they were locked, then texted all three plate numbers to himself. He'd run them later, or have Caitlin do it when she was done with the other thing.

As he turned to go, a small decal on the bumper of the F-250 caught his eye. It was one of those white oval travel stickers with a black outline, the kind people place on their cars to boast about where they've been, or where they're from. OBX = Outer Banks. IOP = Isle of Palms. CHS = Charleston. That sort of thing. Except this one contained a number and two letters, printed in a stencil-type font that he had spotted just a few hours ago on the helmet of one of the guards in the video:

Chapter 15

Connor was crossing the bridge back to Folly when his phone rang. The screen said it was Caitlin Thomas, so he hit the Bluetooth speaker to talk hands-free.

"How's it coming with that info on Lomax Industries?" he asked.

"Well, howdy and a good day to you," she replied.

"Sorry…my bad. Preoccupied. How's your day been?"

"Busier than I expected, and I've really enjoyed doing all this legwork for you."

"I know, and thanks," he said, ignoring her sarcasm. Or at least he hoped that's what it was. "I can't access property records from home, and I'm sure I'd make a mess of it."

"Probably," Caitlin agreed. "Anyway, seems like your guy Lomax is undertaking a bit of corporate expansion up around Andrews."

Connor felt a tingle in his scalp; if he'd had hair, it would have been standing on end. "What'd you find?"

"The short story is, over the last two years Lomax Industries—or one of a half dozen subsidiaries and shell companies controlled by it—has made twelve purchases of land along the northern border of the national forest. All of them located on an upper estuary of the Santee River known as Wittee Branch, and all of them contiguous plots."

"How much land are we talking about?" he asked.

"They're all decent-sized parcels, and if you add them all up, it comes to sixty-five hundred acres or so. Just a little over ten square miles."

A few years back Connor had worked a case that had involved the acquisition of a number of contiguous properties as part of a covert development plan. It had involved nowhere near as much land as in this case, however, and he doubted Lomax was looking at putting in a high-end golf course or exclusive retreat. "That's one hell of a large chicken farm," he said.

"One would think," Caitlin agreed. "But I did a little more digging, and found that DNR—that's the Department of Natural Resources—has already designated most of that area as protected wetlands. No development, no cultivation, no agriculture of any kind allowed. That means no chickens, no turkeys. No houses. I'll email you the files when we hang up."

Connor thought on this for a second, then said, "Any indication if Lomax's turning it into a nature preserve of some sort, maybe some sort of tax deal?"

"Anything's possible," she allowed. "But DNR already pretty much did that, so the birds and raccoons and deer already have a pretty sweet deal. Anyway, hope this all helps in whatever you're doing."

"More than you know," he replied. "But before you go, can I ask you to look into one more thing?"

"Why did I know you were going to ask that?"

"Because you're the best at what you do."

"Flattery has no bounds. Out with it."

Connor explained about the phone number that supposedly belonged to a woman named Liz Morgan, but every attempt to track her down had failed. "She doesn't seem to exist, at least not in any human form," he said.

"The phone has to belong to a real person."

"And if anyone can trace it, it's you."

"I'm on it," she assured him, and hung up.

After being cooped up in the shade of the drinking deck for most of the afternoon, Clooney was desperate to answer the call of nature. Connor clipped a leash to the old boy's collar and they set out for a trek, winding their way through the streets of the beachfront town best described as shabby chic. Multi-million-dollar estates coexisted side-by-side with dilapidated structures that long ago lost the battle to black mold and dry rot. In the winter it was a sleepy coastal hangout far enough from civilization to seem remote, but close enough to shop at Costco and drive to a movie or doctor up in Charleston.

Summer was a different story, when thousands of tourists showed up, clogged the sidewalks and caused lines at almost every local restaurant and bar. All of it was great for the sales of fish tacos, T-shirts, and beer, but a little claustrophobic for a former veteran like Connor who continued to have issues with crowds, and the gripping social anxiety that often came with them. The daily pounding and buzzing of hammers and power saws from near-constant renovations all over town didn't help matters much.

Man and dog made it all the way to the end of the rebuilt pier and back just as Connor's foot and ankle started to seize up. The pain started with low stabbing jolts in his metatarsals as he wandered along the uneven sand, then built to hammering spasms as if Annie Wilkes was hobbling him in that Stephen King movie *Misery*. When they arrived back at The Sandbar, they both took the wheelchair ramp up to the first level, where Clooney wolfed down an early dinner while Connor opened up the bar for the night and started stocking the coolers.

It was Julie's evening off, which meant he had to manage both ends of the counter, but Wednesdays tended to be subdued and the place usually quieted down around ten. He gave last call a little after that, and thought he might be able to close up no later than eleven, when he heard a low growl behind him. He turned around and found Jimmy Brinks seated on a stool, both hands placed flat on the bar, eyes that always seemed to be as gray as a storm surge burning into him.

Turned out the growl had come from Clooney, just another one of the many souls in Folly that had no reason to trust the former felon who years ago had been part of a gang that had robbed an armored car in Phoenix. He'd fled to Belize, where local *policia* and a pair of U.S. Marshals found him hiding in a bungalow on the sand, sipping boat drinks and listening to "Margaritaville" on an iPod. He served twelve years in a federal prison, then finished out his parole before he found Folly. Or Folly found him. Rumor had it that his share of the stolen loot had never been found, but it was not a subject anyone had cause—or the nerve—to ask him about.

"Double Jack," the ex-con ordered, his voice coming out in a snarl because—as it also was rumored—one of the marshals who had dragged him off the deck of his beachfront cottage had whacked him in the throat with a length of PVC. "In my glass, not one of them cheap plastic cups."

Connor poured a healthy measure of Jack Daniels into the special tumbler he kept under the counter. Brinks knocked half of it back in one gulp—as was his custom—then pounded the rest. "One more," he said

Even though the man had to be nearing sixty he appeared to have a lot of fight in him, although it rarely manifested itself in any physical form. He seemed to get off on playing the mean dude, but he hadn't engaged in a real scuffle since a dust-up with a drunk tourist at a gas station a couple years back. The judge bought Brinks' self-defense plea, and since then he'd kept his nose out of trouble. In any event, Connor knew the guy was like a dry old-growth forest just waiting for a bolt of dry lightning to strike.

"What brings you out on such a quiet night?" he asked as he splashed another round of sour mash into Brinks' glass.

"Awww…did I spoil your plans to close up early?"

"I always look forward to taking your hard-earned money."

Brinks grunted at that, as if wondering whether Connor was hinting at the provenance of the wad of bills he always had in his pocket. "Heard you got yourself shot again," he said.

Connor had no hard evidence to confirm this, but he strongly believed he owed his life to the guy. Guns had been fired, and a man had died. The matter had come up just once in a short exchange last autumn, Brinks sitting on the same stool as he occupied tonight, but both men had spoken only in innuendo and allusion. Nothing denied, nothing confirmed.

"A habit I'm looking to break," he replied.

"You ask me, you ought to try harder."

"Thanks for the kind advice."

"You should take it this time."

Brinks knocked back the contents of his glass, smacked his lips as he slapped it down on the wooden counter. Then he dug a few bills from his pocket and tossed them on the bar as he rose from his stool. "What I hear is, they're not done with you," he said as he made his way to the exit. "Not by a long shot."

"Wait a sec—" Connor called out after him. "What the hell does that mean?"

"Nothing you don't already know," Brinks replied as he started down the stairs, leading with the leg that hadn't been shattered by two federal-issue 9 mm slugs.

Connor locked the bar down just a few minutes after eleven. After stashing the cash and credit card receipts in the floor safe in his apartment, he grabbed a beer and his laptop and sat down on his top-step landing.

He spent the next fifteen minutes feeding the numbers from the license plates of the three trucks parked behind the gun range into the DMV database. The first pick-up—the F-150 King Ranch—belonged to Anthony Young, who lived in an upscale neighborhood called Snee Farm in Mt.

Pleasant. A quick look at street view told him the house was an expansive brick colonial, white with black shutters and a couple of flowering pear trees out front. The fact that the truck was parked behind Top Shots suggested the man had been on the premises, as Connor suspected, although it was possible he'd gone to lunch in someone else's vehicle.

The Silverado with the missing tailgate was registered to a Gil Garrison. Same name as the guy Connor had spoken with, twice. He lived on James Island in a single-level ranch, with a one-car garage that appeared too small for the truck to fit. The Google image Connor pulled up on the screen actually showed the truck parked in the driveway, with the plate blurred out.

The F-250 4X4 was owned by a DBA called Mercer's Bay Outfitters LLC, based an hour up the coast outside Georgetown. A quick business search told him the company sold farm equipment and sporting goods out of a warehouse on Highway 17, a few miles south of town. Lester McIlvain, who lived in a wooded neighborhood near the Belle Isle Marina, was listed as the sole proprietor. The presence of his truck at Top Shot wasn't entirely out of place, since many gun owners by nature were wilderness enthusiasts, especially when hunting season rolled around. Maybe McIlvain had an ongoing business relationship with Tony Young, and had traveled down from the Georgetown area as part of that affiliation. Nothing suspicious, nothing nefarious.

At least for now, Connor thought as he closed his laptop and set it on the step beside him. He raised the bottle to his lips and let his gaze fall on the ribbons of moonlight shimmering on the water out beyond the sand. Thinking about how everyone on this side of the world was under the same spell of the same light from the same moon, each viewing it his or her own way. Billions of personal interpretations and experiences stitched into their private tapestry of life, one that belonged to them, and them alone.

But mostly he was thinking about Danielle, wondering if she was looking at it that very moment, too.

A little after one Connor was jolted awake by the sound of something landing on the drinking deck directly below his front door.

Clooney sprang up from where he was sleeping at the foot of the bed, confirming the noise had not just been a fragment of a fading dream. At the same time a synapse fired in Connor's memory, triggering a thought that it sounded a lot like the thud of a brick, or a grenade being hurled into a building in a burned-out neighborhood in the middle of a war.

Either way, The Sandbar was either about to blow up, or burn down.

He was on his feet in less than a second, Clooney right on his heels. He expected to see a whoosh of flames as he charged down the wooden stairs, but instead he was hit with the familiar odor of benzene, rising up from the puddle of gasoline dripping through the composite planking to the ground below. The remains of a shattered vodka bottle lay in pieces in the middle of it, and several feet away he found a charred piece of cloth he figured had been used as a makeshift fuse.

No fire, no explosion.

Connor picked the scrap of fabric up cautiously in case a few fringe threads might be smoldering, but it appeared not to have only burned briefly before sputtering out. In the distance he heard a car door slam and an engine roar to life with a throaty rumble. No flash of headlights, which was not surprising. Then the noise disappeared into the distance, and all he could hear was the blood pulsing in his brain.

"Looks like we had visitors, big guy," he said to Clooney.

Unlike the other night when he'd chased a prowler out of the bar, this time he grabbed his phone and dialed nine-one-one. Ten minutes later Sergeant Gary Booth was standing on the top step outside the drinking deck, the blue strobes of his car pulsing in the night down on the street.

"Evening, sir," the officer said, peering into the bar. "You called about a disturbance?"

Connor let him through the gate, showed him the remains of the firebomb. "Looks like someone tossed an explosive device up into the bar," he explained.

Sgt. Booth took a good look at the mess, then bent down and examined the broken liquor bottle. "Any idea who would've done this?" he asked.

"I think it's pretty clear someone's sending me a message," Connor replied, not a doubt in his mind. "Molotov cocktails aren't on our drink menu."

"Well, fortunately this one looks like it got extinguished before it had a chance to do any damage," the sergeant said. "Could have burned the whole place down, just like last year."

He was referring to the mysterious fire that had engulfed the place last summer and left nothing but a heap of smoldering embers, and the charred corpse of a suspected local drug runner.

"You think you can lift any prints from the bottle?"

"You never know," Booth replied. "We'll do everything we can to catch the bastards behind this."

"You think there's more than one?"

"Maybe, maybe not. Could be someone just out to play a prank, or someone's got a beef with you. Like whoever took a pop at you on Sunday came back to finish you off."

Those same words Connor had heard at the site of the ambush kept echoing in his head: *We'll deal with that when the time is right.* "Tying up loose ends," Connor agreed with a shrug, leaving out the part about the previous night's intruder who had fled into the darkness.

"Does that thing work?" Booth asked, gesturing toward a video camera set high up on a wall under the spinnaker roof.

"It should," Connor said. "I've got it synched to my phone so I can keep an eye on things from anywhere."

"Mind if we take a look?"

Connor opened the app and waited for the wifi to connect, then accessed the video from the cloud server. He thumbed through the footage until a shadowy figure appeared at the gate and hurled an object over the deck railing into the bar. It shattered at the edge of the frame, spewing liquid on the floor while the man—*woman?*—waited a minute, then disappeared down the stairway to the ground. A couple seconds later Connor appeared in the image, and the would-be bomber was gone.

They watched the video several more times, and at no time was the suspect's face visible to the lens. Wrong angle, and not enough light.

"Don't know if that'll help much, but can you send it to me?" the sergeant asked.

"On its way," Connor said.

Booth asked a few more questions and scribbled some notes, then gathered up the broken glass and sealed the pieces in an evidence bag. When he was finished, he took out his cell phone and busied himself taking photographs of the puddle of gasoline and the partially burned wick. Eventually he gave Connor the go-ahead to clean the mess up, said an official report would be ready by afternoon in case he needed it for insurance reasons.

"You really think you might be able to find whoever did this?" Connor asked.

"That's the public line, so I've gotta say it," the sergeant said. "But don't get your hopes up. This guy meant business, but I suspect he's in the wind."

"Unless he comes back and tries it again."

"Right. And if that happens, you might want to start sleeping with one ear open."

Connor managed little sleep the rest of the night. The firebomb—and the implication behind it—had frayed his nerves, tugging him back to those first few weeks after he'd been released from the hospital in Kuwait. He'd returned to his FOB, where he endured cold sweats and jack-hammer tremors, as every noise—every slight gust of wind—became the enemy and replayed the suicide attack fresh in his mind, again and again. The anxiety only multiplied the longer he was in-country, but he was man enough not to mention it to another soul. That sort of thing got you booted home, with a mark in your file that lasted way longer than did your ties with the Army.

But nowhere near as long as the dark dreams and night terrors.

Chapter 16

By nine o'clock the next morning Connor again was heading north on highway 41 through the Francis Marion Forest. He left Clooney back at the bar with a large bowl of water and the radio tuned to a smooth jazz station to keep him company. One of his greatest joys in life was to ride shotgun next to Connor, seat belt strapped across his chest, nose edged out the window to catch the aromas of the road. Unsafe and worthy of a citation, but the old guy refused to sit in the back, where he would start howling like his progenitor wolf ancestors.

Based on the property records Caitlin had sent him, Connor had cobbled together a rough plat depicting where the Lomax properties were located. He'd been able to overlay the specs on a Google map print-out, noticed the combined parcels included two miles on the south side of something called Santee Road, as well as several touchpoints where it intersected with the creek she had identified as Wittee Branch. He knew it was a long shot that the shredded cloth patch he'd recovered from the thorn in the ditch would connect Lomax Industries to Willis Ronson's death, but it was all he had.

Before setting out, Connor had viewed both videos twice more, this time looking for guideposts along the road. The camera had been aimed out the window a good amount of the time, mostly capturing spindly pines and second-growth saplings and wild tangles of undergrowth. Occasionally, however, a sign would flash by, usually facing the other way for traffic coming from the opposite direction, thus making it impossible to read. One of them, however, was angled just enough so he could make out the words "Church of the Nazarene 4 M." He figured if he could find that sign, he could trace the bus route in the video along the narrow, hardscrabble road and locate the turn-off that was marked by a gate, where the dirt road cut deep into the thick woods.

It took him an hour of driving one way and then the other before he matched several landmarks to screen grabs he'd saved to his phone. Next, by driving at the same approximate speed that the bus seemed to be traveling, he was able to zero-in on the location of the gate. Turned out it wasn't all that difficult to find: an eight-foot-high line of hurricane fencing with razor wire spooled on top began a half mile from the southeast corner of what he figured was the Lomax property and ran along the roadway on the far side of a shallow ditch.

A dirt road cut to the left and snaked through the pines, muddy tracks indicating that at least a few vehicles had driven through since the last rain had fallen. It was marked by a green marker on a galvanized pole, no lettering or logo, which Connor recognized from the first file. This was where the bus had pulled off the pavement and the driver had used his key to open the lock, then had proceeded through to whatever lay beyond.

Connor pulled off the road and edged up to the gate. It was clear he wasn't going to get past the fence; it was too high and the razor wire too sharp. He sat there a moment, peering through the windshield, trying to make out what was out there in the trees. His instincts, aided by GPS, had brought him out here to the distant reaches of nowhere, and there was nothing but a vast, haunting silence in all directions. Not a gust of wind, not a flicker of movement. Just an eerie, quiet stillness that had settled across the land.

Then he heard the crack of gunfire. Distant, yet distinct. A rifle, and not just any rifle. An M4. Connor recognized that sound, the same sound that filled the burned-out neighborhoods of Kirkuk with fear and dread, and continued to penetrate even the deepest of his dreams.

Another shot burst through the woods five seconds later, then another. One at a time, then in short blasts, as whoever had their fingers on triggers were getting the hang of it. Unlike the single-fire feature of the semi-automatic AR-15, the M4—when set to fully automatic fire—was capable of discharging hundreds of rounds a minute, at almost three thousand feet per second. Definitely not a hunting weapon.

The shooting continued for a good twenty, maybe thirty minutes. There were several long volleys of gunfire, then the shots would fade to nothing until there were more bursts. Connor's Google search had told him several gun ranges operated within the national forest, but they were miles away. Plus, the frenetic firing suggested these shooters were not sportsmen or hunters firing at targets, but rather amateur warriors taking random potshots.

When it was clear the shooting had ceased permanently, Connor started the engine and reversed away from the gate. He shifted into drive and bumped further up the county road until he was able to back off the blacktop into a dense thicket of undergrowth. The sun percolated through the branches overhead, the sky a brilliant blue canopy void of a single cloud, save for the thin line of a contrail forty thousand feet above. A gentle breeze was drifting in from the west, bringing with it the smell of decaying bark and moldy leaves from the soggy wetlands. Plus, the unmistakable odor of a decomposing animal somewhere in the trees, its presence confirmed by a couple of turkey vultures circling the thermals high above.

Eventually the perfect silence was displaced by the sound of an engine. Distant at first, then increasingly closer until an old box truck rumbled out of the forest and pulled up to the gate in the distance. Connor grabbed a pair of field glasses from the passenger seat and tried to get a good look at it through the brambles and scrub. He watched as the driver climbed down from the bus, unlocked the gate, drove through the fencing, then locked the gate again. By now he had a good line of sight on the vehicle, saw it was painted in standard military camo colors.

Naturally. If you're going to play army, you might as well look the part.

He keyed the engine to life as the truck edged forward and made a right turn onto the county road. He waited a good ten seconds before he pulled out from his thicket and made a broad turn that took him in the same direction. At this point the vehicle was just a speck on the road far ahead, which told him the driver would have a hard time spotting even a bright red car in the side- and rear-view mirrors.

Connor followed at a safe distance for the next fifteen miles, hanging back as it made a left turn onto Highway 41, then a quick right onto two lanes of blacktop known as Saints Delight Road. Still heading east, but now there was a little more traffic, which meant Connor was able to let an older SUV get between him and his target. It remained there, creating a visual buffer until it eventually made a right turn onto a busier road.

Then another vehicle pulled out from a church parking lot between them, providing convenient visual interference until they hit Alt-17. That was a four-lane highway with a median strip in the middle and an increased speed limit, which meant Connor needed to step on the gas if he was going to maintain visual contact.

Eventually they came to the outskirts of Georgetown, marked by gas stations and thrift shops and brightly colored shipping containers selling fireworks, since the Fourth of July was only a few weeks away. Connor was getting hungry and impatient, mostly at himself for wasting an entire morning because of a video that came from a deceased bail skip via a mysterious phone number to an estranged wife—now a widow—and possibly involved a woman who claimed to be someone she wasn't.

He was ready to give up when the driver of the box truck—now only seventy yards ahead—put on his turn signal and edged into the left lane. This was going to be tricky, since it would be obvious if Connor pulled up right behind him, so he continued driving until he reached the next left turn a few hundred yards up the road. He made a U-turn, then stayed in the slow lane until he determined that the camo vehicle had pulled into the driveway of an establishment marked by a large sign that read "Mercer's Bay Outfitters LLC."

The same business that was owned by Lester McIlvain, whose F-250 4X4 had been parked behind the Top Shot shooting range in West Ashley.

Connor found a parking space in the front lot and cut the engine. Cold air had been pouring out from the dashboard vents but now, when he opened the door to step out, a wall of heat hit him like an oven being yanked open. Instant sweat.

The box truck was not in the lot, which meant it must have pulled through an opening in the chain link fence he'd noticed around back. Anchored by the corner of the farm supply store and a detached pre-fab steel warehouse, the enclosed yard was stacked high with old wooden pallets, industrial-sized bags of fertilizer and top soil, and a full line of mowers, tractors, and front loaders. New and pre-owned. A forklift was moving a shipment of mulch, and a salesman was demonstrating the features of an all-terrain vehicle, also done up in camo. Half a dozen vehicles, mostly pickups, were parked toward the rear, and Connor figured they belonged to the employees, so paying customers could use the spaces out front.

He wiped a trickle of moisture from his forehead, then made his way toward the gate, where there was no sign telling him to *Keep Out*. Always of the belief that it was best to ask forgiveness rather than permission, he entered the compound and began wandering through the assorted machinery as if he were there to buy something. No one told him to get out, no one approached him with a marketing pitch. In fact, no one said a word until he wandered up to the box truck and ran a hand across the camouflage.

"Help you?" said a voice behind him. Terse, almost accusatory.

Connor turned and faced the voice, pretty sure it belonged to the guy he'd seen back in the woods climbing down from the cab and unlocking the gate.

"This your truck?" he asked.

"Who are you?"

"Name's Jack," Connor said. "Just admiring the paint job on your truck, here."

"Pretty sweet, huh?" the driver said, easing up on his wary approach. "Except it's vinyl, not paint. Look closer."

"For real?" Connor examined the pattern up close, ran his hand along the camo design. "You're shitting me."

"No one paints things anymore. It's all done with computers and printers these days. Takes only a day to lay it down, and it's easy to take off someday if you want to sell it. Unlike paint, which is on it for good."

"I'll be damned," Connor said. "Think they could do something like this to my RV?"

"They can do anything you want," the guy replied. "But you gotta go all the way down to Charleston to get it done. A bit of a hike, but it's worth it."

"You mind telling me who did yours?"

"Sure. Place called Lowcountry Vinyl and Tint. There's others, but those guys do great work and the price is fair. No questions asked."

Goddamn, Connor thought. *The last place Willis Ronson worked before he died.*

"And it only takes a day?"

"Yeah, but an RV might be longer. Give 'em a call, and they'll give you a quote. Tell 'em Gilbert Moore sent you."

"I'll do that," Connor said as he stored the name away and walked toward the rear of the truck. He pretended to admire the work, until his eye caught the same logo on the rear bumper as he'd seen once before:

"This 'two ayem' thing," he asked. "Does that indicate a time for something?"

A scowl formed on the face of the man named Gilbert Moore. "You ask too damned many questions," he said.

"Guess I'm a curious kind of guy. Anyway, thanks for the tip. I'll give this Lowcountry Vinyl place a call."

"You do that," Moore said. Crossing his arms, standing firm at the bumper of his truck until Connor was heading back through the gate toward his car.

Forty minutes later, just past the turnoff for McClellanville on his way back to Charleston, Caitlin Thomas called.

"I found your Liz Morgan," she told him.

"Seriously?" Connor asked, immediately humbled by her success where he had only stumbled. "I looked and looked but came up with squat."

"Well, yeah. And so did I, at first. Then I figured there had to be a reason for that, so I tried something else. After a whole lot of nothing, I found a little something that explains it. Well, sort of. And sort of not. Do you have something to write with?"

"I'm driving," he explained. "Just tell me now, and text me later?"

"Copy that," Caitlin confirmed. "Here's the thing: you're right about Liz Morgan. While it's a pretty common name, no one matches it in any of its syntactic permutations. No Elizabeth Morgan, no Eliza Morgan. No Lisa Morgan. No one with that phone number, at least not in the tri-state area."

"But you found her anyway, even though she's a ghost?"

"Thing is, Connor, she's a ghost, but her phone is very real. Not now, I mean. It's been turned off and probably fed through a stump grinder, but at some point that number existed."

"All I got was voicemail when I called it," he said.

"More than the dead air I got. But here's the thing: in order to set up a voicemail account, just about any cell phone—burner or not—has to go through a carrier. Whether you get it at Walgreens or Best Buy, there's a real-live telecommunications company providing access."

Connor was coming up behind a propane truck and instinctively slowed down. Ever since Iraq he had a phobia about following any vehicle too closely, passing one, or having one tail him too tight on his bumper. He tapped the brake, to fall back, then said, "Does that mean you were able to identify the phone company and track the usage?"

"Well, sort of, but that was the easy part," she replied. "What's more important is I was able to trace the payment method that was used to set it up."

"You mean you found the real person behind Liz Morgan?"

"Well, that's what I meant by sort of and sort of not," Caitlin explained. "Thing is, the phone appears to have been paid for with plastic. Would've been smarter to get it fully prepaid, so she wouldn't have had to go directly through the carrier. Instead, she—Liz, or whatever her name really was—linked the service to an actual credit card account."

"You mean like a Visa?" Connor asked.

"Mastercard, actually, but yeah. And I tracked it down."

"Seriously? We have the ability to do that?"

"That's another one of those 'sort of, sort of not' things," she said, a deliberate vagueness in her voice. "But in this case, what I mean is, I was able to pinpoint the account that was used to link it to the phone company."

"Are you going to tell me who it is?" he asked.

"*What*, not *who*," Caitlin replied. "Turns out Liz Morgan really is the U.S. government in drag."

"Government, like the FBI?"

"Actually, Alcohol, Tobacco, and Firearms."

"You're shitting me. Liz Morgan works for the ATF?"

"Whoever bought this phone does," she confirmed. "That's the 'sort of' part. The 'sort of not' part is that they employ over ten thousand people, and a lot of them are women. She could be any one of them."

Twenty minutes after hanging up, Connor took a backwoods detour through an area known as Cainhoy to swing by Lowcountry Vinyl.

Alex Reese was in the back of the shop, using a plastic squeegee to apply a full wrap to a cargo van owned by a local heating and air company. The tourist bus was gone, as was the orange Mustang that was getting black chrome hood stripes. Reese seemed ready to take a break and showed Connor into his office, grabbing a warm cola from a long drafting table as they passed by.

"You'd be surprised how many people come in asking for camo," he said after Connor explained why he was there again. "Camo trucks, camo Jeeps, camo ATVs. We especially get a lot of jobs for them just before hunting season."

Connor brought an image up on his cell phone, turned it to show to Reese. "How about this one?" he asked. "Guy who owns it said it was one of yours."

Reese peered at the photo, slowly nodded. "Yeah, that's our work. Company called Palmetto Nature Expeditions. We did a couple wraps for them—that truck, a few ATVs, and an old school bus. That thing shouldn't even be on the road, it's so filled with rust. Any event, I think it was Willis referred them to us. All cash job, too."

"When was this?"

"Not long before he quit. A week, maybe two. We're backed up, so it took a while to get 'em on our calendar."

Connor recalled that Reese had told him Ronson had stopped showing up for work six or eight weeks ago, so that would have pegged the job to about two months back. "You have an address for them?" he asked.

"It's in the files," Reese told him. "I'll get it."

"How 'bout that cop you were talking about, the one that made Ronson bolt?"

"No go. Guess I never made up a folder for him, and he never came back. Hang tight and I'll get that address for you."

"I'd appreciate it if you could."

The files were just that: several credenza drawers stuffed with hand-labeled manila folders. Reese dug through them, eventually pulled one out and sorted through another stack of papers jammed inside. "Someday we'll get around to computerizing all this," he said as he plucked out an invoice. "You have something to write with?"

"Just tell it to me and I'll text it to myself," Connor replied.

Reese read it off the piece of paper, including a phone number, then asked, "You think this has something to do with how Ronson died?"

"Checking every angle, is all. I really appreciate the help."

He turned to go, noticed the hood of an old truck leaning against Reese's office wall. Originally it had been white, but now it was plastered with vinyl logos from dozens of local companies. Car dealerships, plumbing firms, painting contractors, roofing companies. And in one corner, a small oval with **2AM** printed on it.

"Hey…I'm starting to see those stickers all over Charleston," Connor said, pointing at it. "Any idea what it stands for?"

"Beats me. I figure it's got to do with real early in the morning. Matter of fact, we printed and cut them for the same company that did the camo trucks. We printed too many of them, and I got stuck with the extras, if you want one."

Chapter 17

Palmetto Nature Expeditions didn't exist, not in a physical sense. Just like Liz Morgan.

The address Alex Reese had given him turned out to be a Brazilian wax parlor on Old Savannah Highway on the other side of Charleston, and when Connor pushed his way through the tinted front door it was obvious he was in the wrong place. Or, more accurately, the right place but clearly the wrong business.

"May I help you?" asked a young woman who was sprinkling flakes of food into a large glass tank that held several varieties of tropical fish. She was on the short side, maybe five-three, with black hair that was too goth to be natural. Black midriff shirt exposing plenty of belly, purple leggings, and a purple leather collar with chrome studs affixed around her neck. Brick-colored blush had been applied liberally to her cheeks, and dark mascara almost made her look as if her eyes had been gouged out.

Connor glanced from her to a menu board on the wall that listed the prices for a variety of wax services. Full leg, underarms, stomach strip, lips. And, of course, the Brazilian full monty. "Something tells me I have the wrong address," he finally said.

"Let me guess: you're looking for that nature adventure company," she replied. "We get that a lot."

"I take it they're not here?"

"Not in the six years since I signed the lease." She replaced the lid on the fish tank and set the container of food on the edge of a small file cabinet. It was her turn to study Connor, mostly the tattoo sleeves on his arms. "Hold moly, you have some seriously sweet ink going on. Did Darren do some of that?"

"Darren?" he asked.

"Darren Krider. Owns The Inkwell on James Island. Great artwork and his rates are fair. He gave me a sweet double rose with a ladybug, really delicate-like, but if I showed it to you, my boyfriend would shoot you."

"Some other time," he said with a laugh. "You say other people have come in here looking for Palmetto Expeditions?"

"Every now and then, yeah. I'd complain, but a couple of 'em ended up sticking around for a wax. We do a lot of men, you know. Mostly chest and back combos. We're running a special right now, if you're interested."

"I'll think about it," Connor told her. "Meantime, what can you tell me about these other people who came to the wrong place?"

"What's there to tell? They're all guys, looking for this company that I guess offers deep woods hunting tours. Started happening last winter, and I finally checked 'em out on the web."

"Was there anything about them that struck you as odd?"

Odd was a peculiar word, given the body wax thing. And her full-goth appearance. Still, she gave the question some genuine thought before shaking her head.

"Not really," she said. "They're mostly our age, and older. Seemed nervous to be here, too. Almost like waxing is somehow against the law, or something."

Connor considered what she was saying, realized he was feeling a little uncomfortable, too. Maybe it was the nature of the work involved, particularly the genital proximity that was involved in the Brazilian process. Along with all the razors, tweezers, and hot wax. Who knew what was going on right now behind that door, there, at the rear of the lobby?

"Maybe they're fixated on the pain, yanking out all that hair," he suggested.

"No worse than getting those," she replied, nodding at his tattoos.

"A lot of guys are wimps. That's why God doesn't allow us to give birth."

Now it was her turn to laugh. "Good point," she said. "Anyway, sorry to disappoint you about the nature expedition thing. And give some thought to our men's combo special. But not too much, 'cause it's only good through the end of the month."

On his way back to Folly Connor detoured by MUSC, where he found Cherine Dupree sitting up in her bed in the ICU. Family and friends were now being allowed into the unit on a limited basis, and he considered himself one of the latter. If only because they had shared a car ride together, as well as the same near-death experience.

Tubes and wires continued to monitor her life, but her condition had improved a bit since the last time Connor had seen her. The ceiling light was brighter, which made the room look less dismal and bleak. Several vases of flowers added a touch of color to the space, and a hard-wired phone was positioned close to her on the bedside table. He found her picking at a bowl of Jell-O with her good hand, none of it getting anywhere close to her mouth.

When Connor poked his head in, she set her spoon down and managed the slightest of smiles. "Looks like they're letting just about anyone in now," she said, working diligently to sound out every syllable.

"Good to see you, too," he replied with a grin. "How are you feeling?"

"About the same as I look, but better than the alternative."

"What are the doctors telling you?"

"That I'm one lucky woman, but nowhere near out of the woods," she explained. "Twelve broken bones, ruptured spleen, nicked radial artery, and a lead slug lodged about half a centimeter from my L5."

Connor suddenly felt guilty just for being able to stand on his own two feet, his only visible injury being the bandage on his hand. The bruises around his eyes and his jaw had faded, and he was managing to walk without a sharp pain stabbing at his ribs or ankle. There was nothing he could tell her except, "I'm so sorry about all of this."

Cherine gave a slight shake of her head, and said, "It's not your fault. No one could have known anything like this was going to happen."

Not quite true. Bounty hunting was an imprecise business, with incalculable risks and unforeseen complications. He could remind her that she wouldn't be lying in intensive care right now if he hadn't allowed her to go ride with him, but figured that probably would come across as sexist. And something she had probably figured out on her own. They could debate the causes and effects of the shootout all day long, but that would serve no purpose and resolve nothing. Or relieve her misery.

Instead, he asked, "Do your doctors have a plan to remove the bullet?"

"They're going in to get it first thing tomorrow," she told him. "Hence the Jell-O. I'm thinking maybe I could have them do a little liposuction at the same time."

Laughter is considered the best way to deal with a tough situation, and Cherine was doing her best to inject a little humor into a serious issue. "That's like giving a fish a glass of water," he replied.

"If that's a compliment, I'll take it." She studied him a moment, then added, "And don't take this the wrong way, but I get the feeling you're here for a reason. Beyond being genuinely interested in my health."

She was right, and it was complicated. Connor's immediate reason for being here, standing at her bedside and making small talk, was because he had a couple questions he wanted to ask. What she knew about Ronson and his copper theft case, what he might have told her while prepping for his preliminary hearing. And anything else of a private nature they might have discussed during subsequent conferences. Even though her client was dead, attorney-client privilege remained in effect, but he hoped she might be willing to share something that might help him make sense of what happened.

But there was another reason Connor was there in the ICU, hovering over Cherine Dupree, and it was even more complicated than the others. Maybe even counterintuitive. A few years back the love of his life had taken a bullet that had been intended for him, and she had almost died. Almost, but not quite. Her heart had stopped on the way to the hospital, and the EMTs had to use a defibrillator on her twice before they got her to the emergency room. The bullet that had ripped into her body had carved a path of destruction before exiting, and she had not been expected to live. The blood loss and serious threat of sepsis that followed had the nurses and doctors preparing for the worst, not daring to hope for the best.

Her name was Danielle, and she had pulled through. The day Connor wheeled her out of the hospital sixteen days later, she had told him she'd had a lot of time lying in her bed to reflect on her life, and decided she couldn't be around someone who continued to put his life on the line. And hers, in the process. "We only get one shot on this planet, no pun intended," she'd told him. "And I came damned near close to losing mine. I can't be with you if you insist on doing foolish shit."

Being in a hospital, whether as a visitor or a patient, caused random fragments of those days to cascade through his brain. Danielle's close call with death had devastated him, but their break-up had sent him into a tailspin. The glass of gin every night had turned into a bottle-a-day habit. Alcohol was a great way to numb the mind, and in short order it had fueled a dark depression that ultimately pushed him into a bottomless chasm of desperation. If not for the intervention of a state trooper who had peeled him out of the wreckage of his car and cared enough to see him through to VA rehab, that's where his life probably would have ended.

Seeing Cherine lying there in bed, bruised and broken with two bullet wounds—all as a result of his reckless actions—brought it all back to him.

"Did Willis Ronson ever mention someone by the name of Liz Morgan?" he asked her, pushing aside everything else that was going on in his mind.

"Who's she?" Cherine replied.

"That's what I'm trying to figure out," Connor said. "The name came up, and it may have something to do with why Ronson was at that motel."

She appeared to give the question serious thought, then said, "I don't think he ever mentioned her."

"Who didn't mention whom?" came a familiar voice from the doorway. Connor didn't need to look around to know who it was. Nelson Burdette.

"Just my doctor," Cherine covered quickly, intuitively sensing this was not something they should have been discussing. "And a med tech who was here earlier. I'm scheduled to have surgery in the morning."

The SLED investigator seemed to believe her, and Connor wondered how she intuitively knew to go into obfuscation mode. Other than the fact that she was a lawyer.

"That's what they tell me," Burdette said. "And it's why I'm here."

"Giving me one last chance to talk, just in case I don't pull through?" she asked.

"Well, that's not how I'd put it, but I do have a few more questions to run by you, if you don't mind. It won't take long."

"Define long."

"Five minutes, no more than ten," Burdette said. He drew a brief glance to Connor and added, "Just her and me."

"I was just leaving, anyway," Connor replied. He thought he caught a look in Cherine's eyes that seemed to mean *don't go*, but she said nothing as he edged toward the door and told her, "Good luck tomorrow."

It had been a long day, and Connor wasn't done yet. By the time he arrived at The Sandbar, Julie had already unlocked the booze and was standing behind the counter slicing limes. He still had a few things he wanted to check online, but that was going to have to wait until later.

"Give me five minutes to change," he told her as he headed toward the stairs that led up to his apartment.

"You're a man," she shot back. "You'll never change."

Thursdays were the start of the weekend in Folly, just like every other beach town in every other part of the world. By five o'clock a small crowd was loitering down below in the gravel lot, and as soon as Connor rang the captain's bell, they were streaming up the stairs to lay claim to a stool or a table. As with just about every afternoon, half of them were locals and the other half were tourists, either daytrippers from around the lowcountry, or out-of-towners getting an early start on the summer. There was an early run on frozen margaritas which, for some random reason, shifted to rum punches as the evening wore on.

A gentle rain moved through an hour before sunset, just enough to drive families picnicking on the beach to their cars, and those over twenty-one to the drinking deck for a beer. The shower passed as quickly as it began, but the crowd remained as the sun disappeared in the west in a brilliant palette of orange and violet. Around nine o'clock someone broke out a guitar and started strumming Jimmy Buffet tunes, with a little Kenny Chesney and Alan Jackson thrown in. The off-key, alcohol-induced crowd joined in the singing, and Connor began to fret that the cops might show up. He didn't have a license for live music, and the bar was right at the edge of a residential neighborhood with sidewalks that rolled up at sundown. It was only a matter of time before someone dialed nine-one-one.

He had just turned his back to grab a bottle of high-end Scotch from a top shelf when he caught a voice he hadn't heard in months.

"Hey, Magic Man…don't suppose you'd do that killer lime trick for me, would you?"

Man-oh-man, did that send a flush of ice water through his veins. Thinking back to last summer, when one simple magic stunt with a piece of fruit knocked down a domino line that almost got him killed in the process.

For a second he couldn't move; then he turned slowly and found himself gazing into the eyes of a distant memory. A moment frozen in time, gazing at him with eyes that sparkled like brilliant green opals, framed by hair the color of cinnamon that reached to her shoulders. Navy blue sundress with white daisies on it, white straw hat with a yellow ribbon perched at a slight angle on her head.

"Jessica Snow, as I live and breathe," he said, because he couldn't think of anything that came anywhere close to witty or clever to say.

"Mr. Jack Connor," she replied, equally adroit in her rejoinder. "How's your arm?"

She was referring to the injury he'd received last summer, when he'd taken a bullet in the middle of his black panther tattoo. An unfortunate and painful side effect of why she'd come to Folly Beach in the first place, and a good part of the reason her work partner at the time had died. All of it having to do with the wrong place and time.

"Good as new," he said. "May I buy you a drink?"

"Only if you promise to do that lime trick."

"Well, you're in luck. I just got a shipment in today. Bay breeze, right?"

Jessica removed her hat and set it upside-down on the bar. "Good memory," she said.

"How could I ever forget?" Connor asked as he poured a measure of vodka into a plastic cup. He splashed in some cranberry and pineapple juice, then added a maraschino cherry and set a plastic mermaid on the rim.

"That's a new touch," she observed as he placed the concoction on a parrot Sandbar napkin in front of her.

"Free promo from my vendor," he told her. "Really spices up a sex on the beach."

"I'll drink to that," she said.

Jessica Snow had walked into his bar just about a year ago, and then disappeared from it just as quickly. The attraction had been mutual and instant, their entanglement intense and passionate. And, regrettably, brief. Differing approaches to work and play did not bode well for the survival of a long-term liaison, and the last time they had been together was Halloween night.

Trick or treat.

"So…what brings the U.S. Marshal's Service to town, Jessie?" Connor asked.

"You do remember that my name is really Lisa King, right?"

"Maybe that's what it says on your badge, but to me you'll always be Jessica Snow."

It was four hours later, and he was no longer standing on the other side of the wooden counter, slinging drinks and making limes disappear. Instead, she was lying on her side, her face nuzzled up against his chest, their naked bodies intertwined in sheets that would need washing in the morning. He moved his head just enough so he could give her a gentle kiss on the top of her head, then softly stroked her shoulder.

"I can't just pop into town for a moment of pleasure?"

"You can, but you don't."

"You have to admit, this place is a bit off the beaten track," she replied.

"That it is. And I didn't mean for you to get your panties in a twist."

"In case you didn't notice, I'm not wearing any panties."

"My bad."

Jessica giggled, but didn't say anything for a while. Just lightly trickled the tip of her finger from his lips over his chin and over the skin of his neck, even in the darkness finding the dragon etched into his chest, following the tail all the way down to its tip.

Much, much later, she again snuggled up alongside his body and kissed him on the cheek. "In all honesty, I actually did drop by for a reason," she said, her voice little more than a purr. "In fact, there's something I want to talk to you about."

"You've always had a funny way with words," Connor replied.

Another giggle. "Body language," she told him.

"You speak it fluently."

"And you're a damned fine listener."

"I'm told it's a lost art. And since I'm so good at listening, tell me—Miss Jessica Snow aka Lisa King—what's on your mind?"

Silence again, but he sensed her studying him in the darkness. "Willis Ronson," she finally said.

That was the last thing Connor was expecting, and he lay there in the dark a moment while he tried to figure out what was going on here. Finally, he said, "He's dead."

"So I've heard."

"And you have an interest in him, why?"

"Why do you think?" Jessica countered.

Connor started to say something, but hesitated. Last summer, when she had walked into The Sandbar, she had been working undercover to bring a whistleblower into the Witness Security Program, which was a part of the U.S. Marsha's service. He hadn't known it at the time, of course, and the operation had gone downhill fast when her guy had ended up dead. So had her partner, who had turned out to be playing both sides of an elaborate cross.

She waited for him to piece together what she was saying. And, more important, what she wasn't saying.

"You were protecting him?" he finally asked.

"That was the plan," she said. "Things went awry."

"Not the first time."

Not something she needed to be reminded of, and it clearly wasn't why she was in his bed, running finger down his chest.

"So, what is it you want to talk about?" he asked.

She was gone when the divers down below on the street awakened him just before eight.

Her departure wasn't unexpected, of course, yet he was disappointed not to see her lying next there as the first rays of morning streamed through the slats in the window blinds. Lonely, too, but life goes on.

And, he hated to think so soon after her departure, she wasn't Danielle.

He snapped a leash on Clooney, who charged out the door and down the stairs to the drinking deck. He bucked and pranced to get past the gate, and when Connor opened it for him, he broke loose and shot down the ramp at a full gallop. Connor caught up with him in the gravel lot and, when he'd finished his business, they strolled up the street to Gilbert's. A fresh pot of coffee had just been brewed, and Connor ordered a large cup and an egg sandwich to go.

Clooney busied himself sniffing and snuffling at the weeds sprouting at the edge of the street while they wandered back to the bar. Connor mentally replayed the events of last night, not just the steamy interludes in the dark, but also the quiet of the night and the gentle tingling of Jessica's touch.

Back upstairs, he woke up his laptop and entered the DMV database to which he was not supposed to have access. Two minutes later he had the information he was seeking: the camo box truck he'd followed earlier in the day was registered and titled to a company doing business as Palmetto Nature Expeditions. Just as Alex Reese had told him. This time, however, the address was not for a bikini wax salon in West Ashley, but for a company located on Highway 17 up in Litchfield, which Connor knew was just a few miles south of Georgetown near Pawley's Island. A quick search on Google maps confirmed his suspicion that the address was bogus and, in fact, belonged to a franchise store that shipped packages and rented mailboxes by the month.

The nature company had a basic website and Facebook page, but no Twitter. He scrolled through a few pages that listed tour packages and personal expeditions, with accompanying photos that showed people kayaking down white-water rapids and hiking along deep-woods trails. No prices, no calendar, no way to schedule a vacation. The more he searched, the more he got the sense this was all bogus, a front for something far different from what he was looking at. The only way to contact anyone was through a number on the contacts page, but when he dialed it, he only got a voice that told him he'd dialed it in error, and please try again.

Connor then fed the company name into several other databases, but came up empty. There were no incorporation records for a company called Palmetto Nature Expeditions in South Carolina. No LLC, no S Corp. No shareholders or officers. No corporate documents, no evidence that the entity even existed.

Nada.

Eventually his train of thought circled back around to Lomax Industries, and a much broader scenario. What would a poultry empire possibly want with an expanse of second- and third-growth pines and cedars set at the edge of the swampy wetlands of a national forest? It was located nowhere near a major highway suitable for eighteen-wheelers, and the nearest railroad line was miles away. Much of the land in the area at one time had been used for agriculture, mostly rice and indigo back when slaves had worked the soil in the hot fields, then harvested the crops when the seasons rolled around. But those days were long gone, the antebellum way of life long since returned to the earth.

The land wasn't even any good for real estate development. The closest town of Andrews was about twenty miles away, population just over twenty-five hundred. Kingstree, thirty miles to the north, was only slightly larger at three thousand. Both of them too distant to build homes or commercial warehouses this far away, and any sort of exclusive golf and tennis resort was a nonstarter. Too muggy, boggy, and buggy. And, if Caitlin's research was accurate, permanently zoned against that sort of thing.

Lomax—the man and the company—had bought the property for a reason, however, and the more Connor thought about it, the more he suspected it had nothing to do with raising chickens. For starters, he was a very wealthy man. One source listed his net worth at a little more than five hundred million dollars, while another Wall Street site placed it at closer to seven hundred. Nowhere near the rarified air of the billionaire's club, but both estimates placed him among the richest people in South Carolina. Jordan James was on the same list, but much further down.

Lomax also was heavily involved in politics, both on the state and national level. He regularly contributed the individual limit to state and federal political candidates, and had personally organized several Super PACs that represented groups aligned with steadfast ideological causes. Among them: the Alliance for the Second Amendment, Don't Tread On Liberty, and something called The Patriot Front.

Despite the man's financial support for politicians, he never showed any enthusiasm for running for office himself. Not enough money in it, Connor guessed, especially when a few dollars placed here or there probably bought him the influence he craved and, at the same time, kept him out of the public eye. Over the past twenty years he'd gone from "Carolina Chickenman" to "Carolina Kingmaker," known for his exceptionally deep pockets and Machiavellian principles. Many were the craven sycophants who bowed to him and groveled at his feet, while those who refused to kiss his ring often found their careers and personal lives destroyed forever. It was rumored but never proven that his odious dirty tricks and vile whisper campaigns had gleefully destroyed more than one high-level campaign, and the man was known to stop at nothing to attain his personal objectives.

Lomax' current pet project was Garrett Tipton, senior senator from South Carolina who, just a month ago had announced his candidacy for president of the United States. The two men had been fellow cadets at The Citadel, and Lomax was a solid contributor to Tipton's Congressional campaigns. By strict coincidence, Lomax Industries saw a half dozen federal regulations ease up over the ensuing years, which resulted in higher production capacity and relaxed waste standards at his factories, drawing the wrath of neighbors and environmentalists alike.

The online version of a recent cover article published by a trusted financial magazine profiled him as a particularly boorish and ill-mannered business titan, possessed of a startling lack of ethics and scruples. Titled "The Life and Times of the Carolina Chickenman," the story recounted how Lomax was the focus of numerous legal challenges related to his strongarm coercion tactics—schemes that not only were related to his poultry farms, but also his vast real estate holdings and ties to foreign money:

> Lomax is facing no fewer than four class action lawsuits, involving contractors and employers who claim he and his company failed to pay for services rendered, withheld back wages, underpaid taxes, engaged in financial manipulation, and promoted fraudulent investment schemes.
>
> *Plaintiffs say the wealthy businessman has defaulted on loans, filed falsified tax returns, and is overextended with his lenders, both foreign and domestic. Additionally, federal investigators are looking into claims that several shell companies established by him and his associates are laundering money in an effort to fund fringe political groups engaged in vigilante justice and anti-government activities.*

Aside from his official bio on the company website, every page Connor read characterized Lomax as a hard-assed opportunist and ruthless narcissist who never took "no" for an answer. He also abhorred losing; in fact, in one pompous Q&A interview he claimed to be "a compulsive winner" who could "out-think and out-compete anyone in the business world today."

The word *pathological* easily came to mind.

A little before noon Nelson Burdette was downstairs, pounding on the gate. A solid sign that he wasn't going away until Connor opened up.

"Where the fuck were you last night?" he demanded, before Connor had a chance to even say *hello*. "Be straight with me."

"Right here," Connor replied. "I closed up at midnight."

"I assume you have witnesses?"

"Only everyone who was here. Why?"

"Don't fuck with me," the SLED cop said, jabbing a finger at Connor's chest.

"Hey…lay off," he said, brushing the hand away.

Burdette shifted his weight from one foot to the other, and a speck of certainty seemed to drain from his face. "We can check your cell phone," Burdette said. "See if it went anywhere last night."

"Knock yourself out. And like I said, what happened? Why are you at my front door giving me the third degree?"

Burdette stood there a second, then said, "Mind if I come in?"

Yes, he minded, but what choice did he have? "We don't open until five, but I can make you some coffee."

"No thanks. This'll only take a second, and your coffee tastes like chain saw oil."

"I wouldn't know," Connor replied as he unlocked the gate and waved the cop inside.

Burdette sat on a stool with his back to the shuttered bar, staring out at the beach that was quickly filling up with bikinis and board shorts. Eventually he drew his gaze back to Connor and said, "Someone broke into Ronson's room at the Starlight Motel up in Andrews last night."

That took Connor by surprise, and he let it show. "You think I had something to do with that?" he asked.

"Did you?"

"Like I told you, I was here all night."

"No, you said you closed up at midnight. What about after that?"

No need to get Jessica Snow involved. Too dicey, given her law enforcement status, and none of Burdette's business. "I was alone, but I couldn't sleep, so I watched *The Natural.*"

"Then you should know what team Robert Redford plays for in the movie?" the SLED cop asked, testing him.

"The New York Knights. Except in the beginning, he's on his way to try out for the Cubs."

"Was anyone in the room at the time?"

"What?" Burdette asked.

"At the time of the break-in."

"Oh. No. Still under official seal. And that's not how this works. I ask the questions, you answer them."

"Then ask a better one," Connor suggested, "Meanwhile, I can assure you I was nowhere near that place last night. See that camera up there?"

He cast a nod at a small device affixed to a support post, just under the spinnaker canopy that shaded the drinking deck.

"That works?"

"It should," Connor assured him. "I installed it after the place burned down last year."

Burdette gave a heavy sigh of resignation, or maybe disbelief. Then he said, "Look, Connor. I'm going to believe you, for now. I've also been more than fair with you. But if I find you've been poking around in my investigation, the hammer will come down on you swift and fierce. Job, license, everything. Got it?"

"Hundred percent," Connor replied.

"You don't happen to own a crowbar, do you?"

Connor rolled his eyes in exasperation, and said, "I did, in the back of my old Jeep. Go ahead and take a look. It's probably somewhere in your evidence shed, or wherever you guys towed it."

"I may just do that," he said as he rose from his chair and made a move toward the gate. He reached into his pocket and took out a ring of keys, one of which probably belonged to the black Yukon parked down on the street. Then he turned back and said, "There is one more thing."

"And what might that be?"

"Well, you see, Connor, *The Natural* was an okay movie, all about baseball and heartache and romance. Attempted murder and suicide, all the great elements of intrigue and mystery. But *Field of Dreams* was a much better baseball parable, in so many ways. It really could have been about any sport, because it's really not about baseball at all."

"Then what's it about?" I asked him.

"It's about the courage to dream, getting past the animosity you carry around if you don't give yourself the chance to move beyond the memories that bind you to the past. But even more than that, it's about the reconciliation between a father and his son, using the metaphor of playing catch as a means of reconnecting and finding your way home. Something I'm sure you can relate to, if you can manage to get out of your own way."

Chapter 18

Over the next week several things occurred, and/or did not occur. Nelson Burdette noticeably left Connor alone, didn't show up unannounced at the bar or accuse him of vandalizing property or interfering with his case. Likewise, Connor steered clear of anything having to do with Willis Ronson's murder, Colt Lomax and his massive business empire, and the mysterious tract of land at the edge of the national forest.

Also, Cherine Dupree was released from the hospital.

She was transferred to a place called Sea Island Rehab, and the next day Connor dropped by at her request. The last time he'd seen her in the ICU she looked like a mummy in a museum exhibit, but this morning she was seated in a wheelchair near the window, dressed in loose jeans that covered her leg cast and a turquoise turtleneck two sizes too large. She'd been cooped up forever in stuffy, antiseptic hospital rooms, no sunshine or fresh air, and a minute after he poked his head in, she asked if they could go for a stroll around the grounds. She'd been counting on hitting the beach, but that was going to have to wait until her physical therapy techs pronounced her fit enough to walk on the unstable sand.

"I'll push you," Connor said.

"I can get around just fine," she insisted. "Besides, it's part of my PT program to get my strength back."

Sea Island Rehab was a squat, one-story medical complex located in a wooded setting near the marsh in the town of Mount Pleasant. A couple centuries ago the property had been part of a rice plantation, with indigo and pecans periodically planted to vary crop output and maintain cash flow at times of drought or pestilence. Slaves worked the land until the end of the Civil War, and during the era of Reconstruction and sharecropping that followed, many of them continued to toil for the then-destitute landowners who divided their former plantations into smaller parcels that could be tended by single families. Extortionate lending practices and sheer greed ensured a system of dependence and indentured hardship, and generations of poverty among the newly freed slaves were destined to follow.

Over time the fields went untended, and a dense forest grew up where crops once had been worked. Deer and raccoons and foxes returned in numbers, and the land slowly returned to a natural state. Horse paths and levees eroded over time and makeshift cabins returned to the earth, waiting for the next epoch of human encroachment.

That came in the 1970s when the woods were bulldozed. Trees were cut down to accommodate subdivisions and golf courses and businesses, including Sea Island Rehab, which sat on ten acres of landscaped grounds. Fortunately, the architect had the foresight to preserve some of the site's natural surroundings, and had developed a paved trail that meandered through the groomed woods and wetlands.

Connor and Cherine made small talk as she wheeled herself along the neatly manicured path. Damn, was she glad to finally be out of the hospital, aching to see the ocean, counting the days until she could go home to Claire and her two Chihuahuas. Set foot inside the courthouse again, address a jury. Take a bath and eat real food.

They were slowly working their way along the bank of a small aerated pond with a fountain in the middle of it when she said, "I'm sure you're wondering why I called you this morning."

"I figured you'd get around to it when you were ready," Connor conceded.

"In the past I would have gotten around to it immediately, as soon as you walked into my room," she replied. "That's how I was: direct and to the point. But I've had a lot of time to think about things and reconnect with what really matters. Like those turtles over there." Cherine nodded at a half dozen snappers sunning themselves on the warm, grassy bank.

"Soaking up the morning rays," Connor observed. "Not a care in the world."

"Carrying their home wherever life leads, like an Airstream trailer." She hesitated a second, then said, "You know, lying in a hospital bed with wires and tubes sticking out of you gives you a new perspective on life. Makes you wonder what you're living for, who's the judge and jury. What the charges against you are, and what their verdict's going to be."

"I take it you're not a particularly religious person?"

"Actually, I was raised in a strict Seventh Day Adventist family," she replied. "My father was a deacon in the church, gave lay sermons on Wednesdays and taught us kids the lessons of the Bible on Saturdays. My mother was a librarian, and wanted me to become one, too. But I had other ideas, and I realized I was going to have to make a big break if I was going to make a break at all. But to your question…no, I'm not particularly religious, although I have great appreciation for those who are. But let's get back to the turtles."

"What about them?" Connor asked, wondering where this was going.

"For more than a week I lay motionless, just as they're doing now. And it gave me a lot of time to think about things I won't go into, and you don't need to know. But part of that time was spent thinking about Willis Ronson, and the events that led up to his being in that car that day. Getting shot."

"You, too," he said.

"Yeah, there's that," she agreed. "Thing is, he and I didn't have a lot of time together to talk as attorney and client. Mostly just a thirty-minute conference on the lead-up to his prelim. He wasn't very talkative, kept looking at his watch."

"Like he had somewhere else to be?"

"That's what I wondered. We met in a coffee shop up in North Charleston, and I got the distinct impression he didn't want to be seen with me."

She let it hang there, and Connor went for it. "Because you're Black?" he asked.

"I don't like to judge, and never want to be one," she replied. "But it's possible the Confederate flag sticker on his bumper may have had something to do with it."

A bumper on a truck that seemed to have disappeared. "Is that all?" he asked.

Connor sensed her stiffen where she was seated in the wheelchair, even though he couldn't see her face. "It's enough for me," she said.

"What I mean is, was that all there was on his bumper?"

She pivoted in her chair and looked him in the eye. "No. In fact, he was pretty much into stickers. Political, mostly, the sort of stuff I assume he thought was patriotic."

Connor pulled his wallet from his pocket, plucked out the **2AM** decal Alex Reese had given him the last time he'd visited the vinyl wrap shop. "How 'bout one of these?" he asked as he handed it to her.

She studied it a few seconds, then handed it back. "Maybe, but I can't say for sure. And I'm pretty sure I've seen it somewhere before. And that's still not why I wanted to talk to you."

"I'm all ears," Connor said.

"No, I think the tattoos beat out everything else," Cherine replied, glancing over her shoulder with a grin. "But here's the thing: Like I was saying, I spent a lot of time lying in that bed revisiting just about everything in my life. But since it was my intersection with Willis Ronson that put me there in the first place, I replayed what little I knew about him and his case.Everything he said. And there's one thing I just sort of ignored at the time."

"Which was?"

"He mentioned an old acquaintance, a guy who showed up not long after he and Mrs. Ronson moved to Charleston. Name of Scissors."

Holy shit. She was talking about Joey Barber, the man whose house Ronson had crashed at until he went missing.

"Odd name," he said, not wanting to reveal what he already knew. And didn't know.

"That's what I said, but Ronson didn't elaborate. And I didn't push it. All he said was 'I wouldn't be in this shit except for Scissors.'"

"What sort of shit?"

"That's just it. I don't know, and he didn't elaborate. And I don't have a clue who the guy might be."

Connor said nothing for a few seconds as he considered what Cherine was saying. "And Ronson didn't say anything more about him?" he finally asked.

A mullet jumped in the center of the pond, sending concentric ripples of water toward the shore. Cherine watched them until they eventually lapped at the thick grass, at which point she said, "Just that he knew him from way back when, and then he changed the subject. He wanted to know what he could expect at the hearing, how long until he went to trial, what sort of real time he might be looking at if the jury convicted him. Wrongly, he insisted."

"I bet you get a lot of that."

"All the time. Anyway, I asked him if he wanted to plead down to a lesser charge, if the DA offered one, but that just made him angry. 'No fucking way,' was his response. And we never came back around to the guy named Scissors again."

"You think he might have had a hand in whatever Ronson was up to?" Connor asked.

"Can't say, but he sure seemed to think so."

"Did you mention any of this to Burdette?"

"The cop from SLED?" Cherine shook her head, took a deep breath of coastal morning air. "As you might guess, black and blue had a distinct separation of powers in the 'hood where I grew up. Not a lot of mutual respect."

"So why are you telling me all this?" Connor wanted to know.

"Let's just say I trust my instincts. Always have, which is why I decided to become a defense attorney. Rather than go the much more lucrative corporate route."

"So you can put guilty people back on the street?"

Cherine cramped on the hand brakes and the wheelchair made an abrupt stop. She whipped her head around and glared at him. "No, Mr. Connor. It's because I feel it's my duty to fulfill the Sixth Amendment of the US Constitution, the part that says a criminal defendant has a right to a lawyer, even if he or she can't afford one."

Connor took his hands off the handles and raised them, palms outward. "No offense intended," he said. "I just want to get back to 'why me?'"

"Because instinct tells me you value the truth as much as I do," she explained.

Hard to argue with that.

Donna Ronson was ninety minutes into her ride-share shift and was up in Hannahan when Connor called her. He told her he hated to bother her and just had a quick question about her late husband, but she'd insisted she was starving and could clock out for a few minutes if he could meet her at a fast-food joint on Rivers Avenue.

She arrived first, and was already seated at a corner table overlooking the busy six-lane artery when he walked in through the side door. He stole a momentary glance at the steam trays filled with fried chicken and seasoned fries, which caused him to think of Colt Lomax and his poultry empire.

"You're not eating?" she asked as he sat down across from her.

"Late breakfast," he replied. "I appreciate you seeing me on such short notice."

"You make it sound like I squeezed you in for a root canal, or something," she said as she took a bite from a particularly juicy thigh. "You said you had a question about Will?"

"Actually, it's about one of his friends. A guy you mentioned a few weeks ago named Scissors."

A look of thorough disgust crossed Donna Ronson's face at the mere mention of the name. "Joey Barber," she grumbled as she set the piece of chicken back on her tray. She wiped her hands, then gripped the edge of the table and leaned forward. "Like I told you, bastard's a goddamned sack of shit and deserves to be where Will is."

"I guess that means you don't think too highly of him," Connor replied, going for understatement.

"Barber is no joking matter," she said. "He's a putrid blob of pus who has no business being alive. Did you know he tried to blow up a courthouse up in Columbia?"

"You mean, with a bomb?"

"Usually how it's done. Dumb shit read some sort of thing about the guy who took out that building in Oklahoma City, tried to buy some kind of explosive fertilizer from an undercover cop. Did three years for it. Why are you asking about him?"

"His name came up in connection with your late husband, and there may be reason to believe Barber was somehow involved with the thing that got him arrested."

Donna Ronson picked up a potato wedge and nibbled at the end, staring down at her tray while she seemed to ponder what Connor had told her. Eventually she glanced up and said, "I thought they were through, you know? That fucker was a bad influence, and he's one of the reasons we moved down here from Florence."

"To get away from Barber?"

"To get away from that whole crazy bunch, but yeah…mostly him. You say he might've had something to do with what got Will killed?"

"Could be," Connor replied. "They were roommates when your husband disappeared."

"That don't mean nothing."

"Maybe not. But someone mentioned that your late husband claimed he wouldn't have been arrested if it wasn't for Scissors."

"Who told you that?" Donna Ronson asked.

"Someone I believe and trust." He pointed at her fries, and she nodded a silent *help yourself*. He picked one out of the bag, bit the end. "So I'm asking you, what can you tell me about this Joey Barber?"

"Just that he's a low-life sleazebag hoodlum wannabe with his head so far up his ass he can see his tongue."

"Yeah, I've got a good grasp of that part. What I'm really asking is, do you know if your late husband could have been plotting something with him?"

"Plotting would mean thinking things through, and Will never had much skill at that." She picked up the half-eaten thigh again, took another bite. "And to tell you the truth, he didn't mention Barber, not in years. That's why I was surprised when I heard Will moved in with him. But a wife can't know everything her man is up to, and I have no idea what those two might've been thinking up. If I was you, I'd talk to him face-to-face."

"I tried that, but it seems he beat feet, too. Any idea where he might've gone?"

"Not a clue."

"What about employment?" he pressed her.

"Shithead worked as a carpenter for a while, and then as a plumber's assistant. Got fired for hawking lead from old houses they was working on. Last I heard he was a driver for a delivery company, but I have no idea what he's doing now."

"How 'bout Will? Did he keep any kind of address book?"

"Are you kidding? He maybe had a few numbers in his phone, but who knows where that went. I can check around, talk to a few people. But I wouldn't hold my breath."

"Anything you could do would be a big help," Connor assured her.

A half hour later he was back at The Sandbar. As he pulled into his space beneath the drinking deck, he noticed a car parked on the other side of the road from his house, about thirty yards up. It was a silver Dodge Charger, nowhere near new, sprays of dried mud on the fenders behind the wheel wells. Scorched paint on the trunk lid, scraped bumper. Blacked-out chrome, missing front grill.

A man was slouched in the front seat, peering over the upper arc of the steering wheel, just above the dashboard. Because of the shadows Connor couldn't see what the guy was doing, or even in which direction he was looking. But a bug was nibbling at his brain as he mounted the steps and greeted Clooney, something about this picture just not sitting right. Telling him to listen to his instincts.

The guy was probably just some schmoe grabbing a few zzzs in his car near the beach. The most likely scenario, in fact. Occam's razor at work. No harm, no foul.

Or—and this was a real possibility—Connor's PTSD was shifting into overdrive, and the recurring paranoia was beginning to kick in.

Days ago, he'd confessed to Nelson Burdette that yes, he did possess a crowbar, which now was wherever his mangled Jeep might be. Probably totaled out by the insurance company and hauled off to an automotive graveyard to be crushed into a cube of scrap metal. But he hadn't mentioned the aluminum softball bat he kept behind the bar, just in case. He'd never had to use it, although there'd been a time or two toward the end of an evening when he'd come close. Too much alcohol can flip the testosterone switch in a flash, but the sight of a dual-alloy Louisville Slugger in his hands usually put a quick stop to any sort of commotion.

After letting Clooney out for a quick whizz in the gravel lot, he set out a bowl of fresh water and grabbed the bat. Acting on equal parts adrenaline and ramped-up battlefield stress, he set off down the street. He hooked a left and then another left, making a full circuit around the block until he was approaching the Charger from behind. Connor figured the driver would be keeping an eye on The Sandbar, only occasionally glancing in his rearview mirror.

He kept his profile low, his progress slow and methodical. He didn't want any motion to distract the spotter from his surveillance—or his cat nap, if he was like many people experiencing the tedium of a stakeout. The blast furnace known as summer had already settled in, which meant the windows were up. The guy was running the AC, listening to the radio while he waited. Connor could hear Garth Brooks warbling about having friends in low places, and the driver was singing along in his own style of "carpool karaoke."

He sneaked up on the driver's side, lowering his frame as close to the pavement as possible while he crouch-walked forward, inch by inch. That way he took the guy by total surprise as he abruptly reared up and drove the metal club through the glass. Normally it would have disintegrated into thousands of shiny gems, but the dealer-installed tint held the fragments together as one big sheet that bulged inward, then collapsed into the car.

"What the Goddamned hell?" was the man's response as he bolted upright in his seat. Turning to face Connor at the same time, anger blazing in his eyes. "What the fuck—?"

Connor was in no mood for questions, especially when he spotted the handgun sitting in the center cup holder. Barrel pointing downward, butt-end sticking up. Black semi-automatic with an extended magazine, situated only a few inches from the driver's right hand.

"Don't do it," he warned the guy, meaning *don't reach for the gun*. But the shithead's reptilian brain didn't seem to register his words quickly enough, and his fingers naturally went for it.

Connor punched the business end of the bat into the guy's skull, just above the left ear. The driver let out a guttural *ooomph*! as his head cracked the steering wheel, then bounced back. A second later Connor reached through the broken window and grabbed the gun, as well as a cell phone that was sitting on the dashboard. Along with a color photograph of Connor snipped from an old newspaper article.

"Who the hell sent you?" Connor snapped at him. There was something about the guy that seemed familiar, but he was horrible at putting a face to a name. Whatever it was would come to him.

"Fug off," the guy said, blood streaming from his nose. His sunglasses had snapped from the force of the blow and were hanging at an odd angle from one ear. "Gib be by gud."

"I don't think so." Connor walked back to the rear of the Charger and used his phone to capture a picture of the license plate, then snapped one of the guy's face.

"Get the fuck out of here," he said.

"Or what?"

"You don't want to know. I said move."

"You subbitch. You dod't doe what duh fug you doig."

"What I'm doing is calling the cops if you don't get gone. And stay gone."

The driver stared at Connor, rage burning in his eyes. "You are goig to be so fuggen sorry—"

Connor didn't respond. Instead, he pretended to punch nine-one-one into his phone and waited for someone to answer. After an appropriate amount of time he said, "Yes, this is Jack Connor. There's a man with a gun parked in front of The Sandbar, and he's not with the neighborhood watch." He held for a solid a pause, then added, "Two minutes? Perfect."

"Azz-ho," the man growled. "Dis aid' ober." He cranked up the engine, touched his foot to the gas, and sped off in a blizzard of gravel.

There were no cops, of course. No need to go through the questions and the statements, especially now that the guy was gone. Only temporarily, however, since Connor had no doubt he'd be back for his gun and his phone. And, most likely, to even the score. The smart thing, of course, would be to turn them both over to Burdette, wash his hands of the entire matter. But that would mean he'd have to explain how he'd come to possess them, and the SLED investigator already had a trust issue with Connor's coloring outside the lines.

Once the silver Charger was gone, Connor stashed the Glock next to his SIG in his bedroom closet, then grabbed a sparkling water from the fridge. The spinnaker roof cast a deep shadow over the drinking deck, and he positioned a chair to take full advantage of it. The mercury had climbed into the nineties, and the misery index on his cell phone insisted the "real feel" temperature was closer to one hundred. *Horseshit*, Connor thought. *Ninety is ninety, and one hundred is one hundred. Unless you happen to be in the desert with an eighty-pound pack humped on your back, with a thirty-mile trek ahead of you. Then it's pure torture.*

Charger Man's phone was an older Android device with a cracked screen. No fingerprint ID, no password protection. Which probably meant he either couldn't afford a newer model with all the bells and whistles, or simply couldn't be bothered with the newest high-tech update.

The guy's email account revealed him to be Lyle Hicks, a name that instantly sent an icy chill through Connor's nerves. Two weeks into his gig as a bond runner, a degenerate who'd put his wife in the hospital with a tire iron had skipped out on his bail. Fifty thousand dollars, which had made Jordan James furious when he'd learned that Bucky Foster had bonded out a man like that and allowed him to be back on the street. James had a thing about domestic violence and wanted no part of anyone who raised a fist or a weapon to a woman.

Foster had gotten the message loud and clear.

When Hicks failed to show for his first court appearance, Connor had been given the job of tracking the him down. It had taken close to a week, but he finally found the slimeball holed up in a tent in the mountains near Pickens, not far from the Georgia border. He'd apparently declared himself a sovereign citizen and *Posse Comitatus*, adopting the belief that state and federal laws did not apply to him.

SLED was of a different opinion, however, and Connor's intel led to his recapture. After being held over without bail until trial, Hicks declared war on all those involved in his capture and vowed to punish them for their war crimes.

Connor included.

Which raised the question: what the hell was he doing here? The man was a sociopath and should have been behind bars, unless he'd somehow been released. Could a jury have actually acquitted him? Or maybe he escaped from whatever jail he'd been sent to? Could his wife have refused to testify against him, leading the prosecutor to drop all charges? It happened far too often, and only served to fuel the cycle of domestic violence.

"You're shitting me," Nelson Burdette said thirty seconds later, after Connor called and explained what had just gone down. "You saw him?"

"Just now, parked in front of the bar. I snapped a photo of his plate."

"Give it to me."

Connor read off the digits from the photo in his camera, deciding not to mention that he'd grabbed the bastard's phone and gun.

"Could be he borrowed the car, or stole it," Burdette said. "Either way, I'll let you know what I find out."

"That's it? You'll let me know? Sonofabitch threatened to kill me."

"I don't have access to the Department of Corrections database," Burdette explained. "Meanwhile, I'll make a few phone calls, see why the fuck this guy is on the street."

"Much appreciated," Connor said.

Appreciation didn't cut it, not when a man with a gun and a mental problem was parked across the street from his home. After he ended the call with Burdette, a quick Google search told him Hicks had been convicted four months ago on all charges: domestic violence of an aggravated nature, assault and battery in the first degree, and attempted murder. His attorney had attempted to obtain some sort of pre-trial intervention, which would have diverted him to a mental health program rather than serve time, but the prosecutor had objected and the judge overseeing the case quickly denied the motion.

There was no mention of a sentencing error or a prison break, nothing to indicate how or why the man was moving about freely. Yet the dickhead had been sitting across the street from The Sandbar just a few minutes ago, with a gun he had no business having and photos that proved he'd been following Connor. He had no question what Hicks had on his mind, wondering whether he'd been first on Hicks' revenge list, or if he'd already paid a visit to another target.

Without giving it another thought he pulled out his phone and dialed Caitlin Thomas.

Chapter 19

The next day was Saturday. It arrived with a massive storm that swept across the Lowcountry with spears of lightning and crescendos of thunder that shook the building and rattled everything that wasn't nailed down. Rain was driven sideways, hitting the windows like staccato gunfire that woke Connor from a dream in which M4s were blazing from every corner of his mind. He felt the dead weight of a buddy against him in a ditch, until he opened his eyes and realized that Clooney had jumped up on the bed and had burrowed against him as close as possible.

The tempest was so furious that he practically had to carry the old boy downstairs to do his business. Once they were back upstairs he made a pot of coffee and had just poured himself a cup when his phone rang.

It was Donna Ronson, who sounded overly animated about something, her voice bubbling like champagne. "I found him," she said.

"Found who?"

"Joey Barber. After we talked yesterday, I remembered the name of the company he used to work for. Turns out he split a couple months ago, but the guy I spoke with told me where he thought the incel fucktard is working."

"The *what*?"

"Incel," she repeated. "Stands for involuntary celibate. Total dicks who can't get laid, and are too stupid to figure out it's because they look like cavemen and smell like piss. Think women are on this planet just to give 'em sex. Anyway, this guy I talked to told me where he is."

"You have an address?"

"Not exactly, but I know where he's working. He got a temp gig at a plantation that does a lot of weddings and music festivals."

Not as definitive as Connor would have liked, but better than he had just a minute ago. "This plantation. Do you have a name for it?"

"I do, but that's not the way this is going to work."

"I just want to talk to him—"

"And I guarantee you, that's not going to happen," Mrs. Ronson assured him.

"Why is that?"

"Cuz of the way he is. I know the rat bastard, and he'd just as soon shoot you as look at you."

Her impression of Joey Barber was much different than Connor's initial take. Sure, the guy had seemed reserved and reluctant to talk, but Connor had never felt threatened. Of course, that was before Ronson had been killed, before Cherine Dupree had mentioned Barber as a possible accomplice in the attempted copper heist. The stakes had changed, and Barber had cut and run.

"I appreciate your concern, Mrs. Ronson, but I can take care of myself."

She made a noise that sounded like "huh," then said, "Just like you took care of Will?"

"I already told you, whatever your husband was up to—"

"I know," she interrupted him. "I shouldn't have said that."

"And I still want to talk to Barber."

"Which is why I'm going with you," she announced.

"What? No way—"

"Look, Jack. Hope it's okay if I call you that, 'cause I'm gonna do it anyway. I know Joey. I don't like him, but I get how he thinks. Not that he does a lot of it."

"And you think you can get him to talk just because of your intuition?" Connor asked. Leaving her obvious charm and grace out of it.

"Thing is, when Will and me was up in Florence, he was always a little sweet on me," Donna Ronson replied. "I figure if we both go pay him a visit, I can maybe get him to open up, since Will just passed and he might be feeling a little guilty, 'specially if he had anything to do with his arrest. And the bastard might figure that with Will out of the way, he might have a chance."

"A chance at what?"

"Me. Doesn't matter that Will's ashes aren't even cold yet; that's how the prick thinks. I'm telling you, he won't tell you shit without me along."

Connor didn't like what he was hearing, didn't like the idea of putting Mrs. Ronson in a spot that could turn ugly. Especially if Barber had somehow set her husband up, or gotten him into something that was way over his head.

Plus, he preferred to work alone, rely on his own instinct and aptitude and minimize the chance of anyone else getting hurt. Or becoming collateral damage, like Cherine Dupree. If she hadn't demanded on riding out to the Starlight Motel with him to pick up her client, she'd be playing with her pups on the beach right now with Claire, rather than sitting in a wheelchair recovering from her injuries. Her presence in the car hadn't been a distraction, nor had it contributed to the shooting or the subsequent accident. And he actually hadn't minded the company, despite his misgivings and her distrust of him. A loud voice in his head had kept telling him *no*, but she'd kept insisting until Connor had caved. After that, everything had gone to hell.

He didn't want the same thing to happen this time around.

"I work better when I'm on my own," was how he explained it to Mrs. Ronson.

"I figured that," she replied. "But tonight's going to be different."

"Tonight?" Connor asked her. "What are you talking about?"

"It's Saturday, and the plantation is hosting a big-ass wedding. I called, pretended I was a member of the bridal party. Champagne reception's at four, ceremony's at five. Dinner for a hundred-fifty guests immediately following in the Indigo Gardens. Joey Barber will be driving guests around the grounds in a golf cart."

"You're planning on crashing this party?"

"You and me both. Pick me up at three. And wear a jacket, if you have one."

Saturdays were the busiest night of the week at The Sandbar, but Connor had called a buddy—known to all his friends as Buddy—to come in and help Julie sling drinks until he returned. Which might happen quickly, or could be a while, depending on how things played out with Joey Barber. As it was, he promised Julie an extra night off, and gave her a gift card for a restaurant up in Charleston that someone had left as a tip and he'd never used.

Mrs. Ronson clearly didn't want Connor to see where she lived. At her insistence he picked up her up in the parking lot of a Walmart on Old Savannah Highway, where he found her done up in a silk dress, cut just above the knee, white with green leaves and a dragonfly pin on her left lapel. Matching dragonfly earrings. She still was wearing her wedding ring, which reminded Connor that he hadn't asked her about funeral arrangements or a memorial service. Not until she brought it up, which she did.

"Hard to believe the cremains of an entire person can fit into a jar that small," she said. "That's what they call them, you know. Cremains."

Yes, he did know. He'd lost far too many Iraq buddies—from war injuries over there and opiates once they were back over here—not to be familiar with the terminology.

"Willis was cremated?" was all he could think of saying.

"Is there a problem with that?"

"Not at all," Connor replied. A pop-up shower seemed to appear as if out of nowhere, and brake lights were flashing on in front of him.

"Me and him, we had our problems, and like I told you before, he'd moved out," Mrs. Ronson confided. "But that doesn't mean I didn't love him, despite his faults. Love doesn't just go away like that." She emphasized her point with a snap of her fingers.

"That's for sure."

She turned in her seat, studied him a minute. "You ever been married?" she asked.

Connor peered through the stream of water that the wipers were trying to push aside. Rain began coming down in sheets on the roof and a curtain of water seemed to have closed in around them. "Once, and they were the worst days of my life," he said. Not something he wanted to discuss right now, but also not something he ever wanted to forget.

"What happened?" Mrs. Ronson asked.

"We were too young. Didn't work out."

"And after that?"

He fell silent for a few seconds until the wipers began to slow and the shower began to ease up. "I came close again a few years ago," he confessed.

"And?"

"I put her in danger, and she got shot because of it."

"Fuck," she said. "You're saying she died?"

Connor was *really* sure he didn't want to go into any of this, not now. Not ever. But that didn't keep him from saying, "Almost. She pulled through, but we…well, I guess you could say *we* didn't survive."

"What was her name?"

"Doesn't matter," he said. "She's a veterinarian, works with large animals. Horses, zebras, rhinos. That sort of thing."

"Rhinos? Around here?"

"No, down in Orlando. Disney, in fact. And I'd really rather not go into any of that right now. Not while we're on our way to a wedding."

Donna Ronson seemed to understand, and didn't press him about it. Instead, she dug into her purse—an ivory Kate Spade knock-off with a gold chain—and pulled out a photo that was frayed around the edges. She studied it a second, then held it in front of Connor's eyes while he tried to keep them focused on the road.

"This was taken years ago up in Florence," she said. "Will with some of his biker buddies. That's him, there, with the beard and leather cap. And Joey Barber's there—" she jabbed her finger at a stocky guy with a broad face and long sideburns "—second from the right. Don't know what he looks like now. Wanna know the truth, I'm surprised he ain't pushing up daisies, on account of all the chemicals he put in him. Then again, I guess that goes for Will and me, too."

•••

Pelican Creek Plantation was exactly what the name implied: a former plantation located on the banks of one of the winding estuaries that emptied into the Edisto River.

Just under an hour south of Charleston, the antebellum homestead was established in the latter half of the eighteenth century. At the height of its prosperity in the early nineteenth century, six dozen slaves toiled in the fields, harvesting cotton before rice became the crop *du jour*. They also planted the massive "oak alley" entryway that had been featured in over a dozen movies and television shows. It occupied thirty-nine acres of lush fields and gardens, a mere fraction of its former size, and it had remained in the same family for over two hundred years. The property was distinguished by its white brick manor house and expansive floral gardens, which featured dozens of varieties of camellias, azaleas, daffodils, and roses.

The grounds were known for their exacting renovations of the original slave quarters, minus the squalid conditions that existed prior to emancipation. By contrast, the rooms in the main house had been restored to their original grandeur, furnished with early-American antiques, porcelain, quilts, and artwork that showed the opulence in which the owners had lived.

The entrance to the plantation was off a narrow two-lane trip of pavement that wound several miles from the main route that led to Edisto Beach. A brief downpour had soaked the nearby fields and woods earlier, and the Spanish moss that dripped from sweeping oaks that lined both sides of the road glistened with jewels of moisture.

Pre-wedding cocktails began precisely at four o'clock. Connor and Mrs. Ronson arrived a few minutes late and were forced to park at the fringe of a lot crowded with Cadillacs and Mercedes and BMWs. They then were hustled down a winding path to the carriage house via a golf cart decked out with flowers and white taffeta.

Joey Barber was not the driver.

"Looks like the reception's in there," she said. "Let's get a drink and blend in, look around for Joey."

Connor didn't care much for weddings in general, and large crowds of people made him nervous. *Any one of these people could be wearing a suicide vest.*

No one seemed to be checking a guest list. Mrs. Ronson headed directly for the open bar, where she ordered a Moscow mule that came in a hammered copper mug. Since Connor was the designated driver and needed to maintain his senses, he went for a tonic and lime. Neither of them knew anyone in the oversized room, which was just fine with him.

Doors at both ends of the room had been opened to allow a gentle breeze to drift in from the creek. A quartet was set up in one corner playing Carolina beach music, a popular favorite in the Lowcountry closely associated with the style of swing known as the shag. A few couples were out on the polished wood floor, most of them dancing poorly, and not seeming to give a damn. *Dance as if no one is watching* appearing to be their collective mantra.

Ten minutes before five the guests were herded outside to a massive expanse of lawn edged with pink and white tea roses. Rows and rows of chairs had been set up to face a latticework altar that featured the creek and marsh as a backdrop. White carnations and more roses spilled from silver urns as if pouring forth from fountains, which Connor figured a wedding planner had pitched as a symbol of eternal love and happiness.

Fortunately, the rain from earlier had passed through, and someone had thoughtfully wiped every folding seat with a towel.

The ceremony was short. The self-written vows seemed heartfelt and not too sappy, the first kiss an honest one. There were none of the usual overplayed or clichéd songs, no surprise flash mob. And, best of all, the new couple seemed genuinely happy and in love. There were a lot of camera clicks, birdseed was tossed, and someone released a kaleidoscope of monarch butterflies into the crowd. Pure magic, without any lime tricks.

While family and friends were bustling about, congratulating the happy new couple and snapping photographs, Connor called The Sandbar. Just to check in, he assured Julie, who told him things were busy but running as smooth as the Irish cream she was mixing into a frozen Mudslide.

"I'm hoping to get back before last call," he said.

"No rush," she replied. "We're doing just fine."

A half dozen golf carts were waiting to transports those guests who chose not to walk from the wedding to the reception. Connor and Donna Ronson slowly edged past them, eyeing each driver as they passed. At one point she nudged him in the ribs and whispered, "That's him."

"You're sure?"

"Older and flabbier, no beard. But yeah, I'm sure of it. What now?"

"Get in," Connor said.

"What? We can't just—"

But Connor was already sliding into the seat behind the driver. He moved over to the other side, and Mrs. Ronson reluctantly got in beside him. "Normally we'd walk," he said to the driver. "But I just had a bad accident and my leg's not quite right."

"No problem, sir. I'll have you and the missus to the gardens in under a minute."

"Awesome."

The driver stepped on the accelerator and they glided along a pebbly path for a good thirty seconds. Then Connor said, "You know, you look familiar."

"I don't think so," the driver said, facing forward.

"Yeah, I'm sure of it. I ran into you when I was with a friend of mine. You're Joey—" he hesitated, as if trying to think of his last name "—Joey Barber, right?"

The guy seemed to stiffen, but didn't turn around. "Who wants to know?"

"Jack Connor," he said. No point in giving him the runaround. "You're buddies with Willis Ronson."

"Ronson's dead."

"Yeah, I know. The accident I mentioned…I was driving the car when he was killed."

Connor sneaked a glance at Donna, who was doing an Oscar-worthy performance of not letting her anger and grief collide in a nuclear cataclysm.

"What the fuck do you want?" Joey Barber asked.

There was no need to work around the edges and prolong things. Donna had mentioned he had the temper of Vesuvius, and could erupt at any moment.

"You see, Joey. I'm a bounty hunter. Willis and I got to be friends when I was driving him back to county, after he skipped bail. We talked about a lot of things, and one of those things was how he wouldn't have been in this shit except for Scissors. That's you."

They were nearing the section of the plantation known as Indigo Gardens, and the golf cart began to slow down. Barber glanced up at the rearview mirror, said, "Fuck…you're Will's old skank. Donna Allen."

"Ronson now, from one skank to another," she replied. "How you been, Jo-Jo?"

"Get out."

"That's no way to treat friends of the groom," Connor said.

"Bullshit," Barber snapped. "You're just here to harass me. Runnin' some sort of play, is that it?"

"You and Will, you planned the whole thing," Donna told him. "The theft at the power plant. What I want to know is why? *Copper wire*? Who does that?"

"Get the fuck out of my cart," Barber said, more threatening this time.

"Or what?" Connor asked.

"You don't want to find out."

Connor lashed out a hand and grabbed Barber by the back of the neck. He sank his thumb and forefinger into flesh and applied pressure at just the right points, as he'd been taught.

"You're messing with the wrong guy, asshole," he growled in Barber's ear. "And if you take your hands off that wheel, you're gonna be teething on it with your gums."

"Shit, man. Let go."

"Don't try anything dumb."

He didn't. He pivoted his head left to right, and there was an audible crack. Then he said, "You a cop?"

"I told you, bounty hunter. What did you plan on doing with the copper?"

"Fuck you."

Joey Barber clearly had a short memory, which Connor quickly rectified with his grip of steel. Firmer this time, more pressure. "I'm going to ask you again: what were you going to do with the copper?"

There was no immediate answer, so Connor tightened his hold. Eventually Barber succumbed and said, "Ordnance."

"Ordnance, like in bullets?" Connor asked, easing his grip a notch. "Why?"

Barber lowered his head in an agonized nod, said, "Cuz it's harder and penetrates better than lead. Lot less fragmentation, too. Makes it hard to trace."

"Ronson had two hundred pounds of it ready to go," Connor said. "That's a shit ton of bullets."

"You think?" Barber replied. Then, without warning, he wriggled free from Connor's grip and pushed his way out of the cart. A second later he was running across the grass.

Connor had anticipated him bolting and chased after him, but his ankle was throbbing and his ribs were screaming with pain. He figured Barber was making a break for his car and, despite the guy's girth, he raced down a dirt path toward a barn and what appeared to be the employees' parking lot. Loaded with pick-ups and old sedans, and a few SUVs. Nothing like the luxury cars out front.

Barber lumbered toward an old Toyota Tundra with a tailgate slathered with bumper stickers. He jumped in through the unlocked door, keyed the engine, then hit the gas and jolted forward. He cranked the wheel hard and tires spun on loose gravel, the slick rubber kicking up a cloud of dust as he fishtailed down the dirt drive that wound through a stand of pines.

Connor watched as the Tundra disappeared around the bend, then limped back to where he'd left Donna Ronson. He found her leaning against the front of the golf cart, slowly cleaning dirt from under her fingernails. A thick mist had begun to roll in from the creek, odd for late May, but Connor had given up trying to understand the Lowcountry weather. He was out of breath from his chase, reminding him that as soon as his injuries were mended, he needed to resurrect his morning runs on the beach.

"Well?" she asked as he approached.

"He got away," Connor told her. "But you heard him. He pretty much admitted he was involved with what got your husband arrested."

"But *copper bullets*?"

"I'll check it out. Meanwhile, do you know if Willis was into shooting guns? Or maybe was friends with people who did?"

Donna Ronson nodded, pushed off the small hood of the cart. "Half the guys he hung out with up in Florence probably owned 'em," she said. "But because of the felony he couldn't get one himself, and he knew if he was caught anywhere near one, he'd be back in Tyger River faster than a bullet out of a barrel."

She clearly didn't know about her husband's visits to Top Shot shooting range, and there was no need to bring it up. "Well, someone he knew was planning on making his own ammo, and lots of it," Connor pointed out. "Any idea who?"

"This is all news to me," she said. "What now?"

"Head home?"

She considered it, shook her head. "We're already here, and that bartender makes a mean Moscow mule. What d'you say we have one for the road?"

Connor was anxious to get back to The Sandbar, but Mrs. Ronson clearly was not. One drink turned out to be two, then three. The same quartet was playing the same beach music, old standards from The Drifters and The Tams and Chairmen of the Board. For a woman who was within the accepted range of mourning, she loosened up quickly and actually danced a couple numbers with one of the guests. A guy who claimed he was an old boyfriend of the bride, and insisted he had no intention of causing any trouble. He didn't, and was enough of a gentleman not to make a scene when Connor eventually coaxed her back to the car.

Moments later they were heading back down the infamous oak alley toward the main road. The mist that had seeped in earlier had now turned to a fog almost as thick as the veil that covered the bride's face earlier. It hung close to the ground, a gray shroud of billowy swirls obscuring all but the glow of his low beams, an occasional billowing shadow in the night beyond.

As he slowed and made the turn onto the narrow county road that led back to civilization, the shroud only seemed to get thicker. They crawled along just fast enough to keep the needle above zero, just in case raccoons or deer were about. Fog like this in the Carolina Lowcountry was the result of warm, wet air from the south moving up over the colder water. Usually in winter, but this was June. Unseasonably odd.

Then the tire pressure light blinked on, while at the same time Connor felt the steering wheel pull hard to the right. A second later there seemed to be a pronounced sound of rubber scrunching on gravel, and he said, "Fuck."

Up to that point Mrs. Ronson had been gazing into the misty wall ahead, but she turned to him and said, "What is it?"

"I think we have a flat."

"You're kidding, right?"

"Not about something like this," Connor said, shaking his head. "Fuck."

By now the mist was so thick, so dense, he could barely see whatever might be lurking in the gloom as he gently eased the car onto the shoulder. No trees, no fence. No ditch. All good. He pulled off the road as far as he could, until he felt the gravel turn to grass. The fog seemed thicker here than it had been all night, and he wanted to be well off the pavement in case another car happened along.

"Please tell me you have a spare," Mrs. Ronson said, glancing at the clock.

"I think so," Connor replied as he opened his door. "Hopefully this won't take long."

He stepped out into the night and immediately sensed a cloying unease. Visibility was no more than a couple yards, and his mind went to Joey Barber. It had been almost an hour since their verbal altercation, and the dumbass should have put a lot of gone between them by now. But what if he had turned around, came back to settle a score with a gun—the kind of incident that makes the evening news?

As Connor made his way around the car to the rear, he perceived someone—*something*—directly beyond the gray veil, checking him out. He glanced around but saw nothing, heard nothing. The hairs on his neck and arms stood at attention as he popped the hatch and removed the carpeted cover that hid the tire compartment. He was relieved to find a small jack assembly, along with a fully inflated donut spare.

He hoisted it out and started to set it down on the ground, when he felt something firm and hard press into his spine, just between his shoulder blades.

Chapter 20

Connor's brain immediately went to *gun*, because that's what the thing felt like. He let go of the tire, waited for someone—most likely the scruffy incel named Scissors—to either pull a trigger, or order him to put his hands up. Which he did anyway, just to be on the safe side.

But no one said a word, and after a couple seconds the pressure on his back eased up. No shots fired, at least not yet.

Then he heard a snuffle. Then another and another, further behind him, followed by a slightly different sound that a childhood memory told him was a *nicker*.

Keeping his hands up out of an abundance of caution, Connor slowly turned and found himself staring into the eyes of a magnificent horse. Chestnut and black, sweeping mane that glistened with droplets of moisture. He—maybe she—was sizing him up at a distance of about twelve inches, eyeing him with a curious interest that served to settle its nerves. Connor lowered his arms to show he was not a threat, then slowly reached out and allowed the animal to sniff his hand. It let out a low snuffle—*acceptance?*—and then glanced backward, raising and lowering its head several times.

As if on cue, more shadows slowly began to emerge from the mist. Connor almost bolted, calculating the number of seconds it would take him to jump back into the car and lock the door. But the shadows turned into horses, and within seconds he was surrounded by at least a dozen of them. All sizes and breeds and colors, nosing around him with the same curiosity as the first, which now was nosing his bare scalp.

He heard the passenger door open, and Donna Ronson climbed out. "What are you doing out here…*oh my frigging word—*"

"Have you ever seen anything like it?" he asked her.

"How…where did they come from?"

"Horses in the mist," was all he said.

She cautiously came around the side of the car to where Connor was standing. The ponies didn't seem to be shy at all as they kept approaching, certainly not wild and definitely not hostile. Just curious and, most likely, lost.

"They must belong to someone," she said as she reached out and allowed one of them to sniff her hand. Reddish-brown, same large, wondrous eyes.

"Probably one of the farms around here," Connor replied. "On a night like this they really risk getting hit by a car."

"You think we should call someone?"

"Who?"

Neither of them had an answer for that. They didn't live anywhere near there, didn't know anyone who did. Didn't even know the name of the road they were on. "Maybe someone at the plantation knows someone," she suggested.

"Not a bad idea," Connor agreed. "See if you can find a number."

At that moment the faint glow of headlights pierced through the fog, heading toward them. A vehicle was traveling slowly, only a couple miles an hour through the murk, the spread of its beams covering the roadway from one side to the other. Eventually they illuminated the silhouettes of several animals that were standing at the edge of the road, and pulled across the pavement onto the wet grass in front of them, moving off the asphalt as far as it could.

It was a white GMC pick-up, and as it came to a full stop, Connor noticed lettering on the door that read:

Gregorian Chants Ranch
Giving Animals A Second Chance At Life

If Connor had hair on his head, it would have tingled and stood at full attention. As it was, an Arctic rush swept through him as a voice was telling him, *No fucking way…it can't be.*

A few of the horses appeared to recognize the truck, because they started moving toward it. It seemed they were almost relieved to see something familiar and, as the driver's door opened, several of them let out eager snorts of reassurance.

A woman stepped down from the cab, and immediately the entire team of animals hurried toward her. They definitely recognized her, nuzzling up to her as she gently caressed them on their noses with encouragement and relief. She was dressed in jeans and a light blue long-sleeve T-shirt with a logo from the Kingdom of Disney, pink baseball cap tugged down over a ponytail.

She spent a full thirty seconds petting and loving them, making sure she gave every creature a round of affection before turning her attention to Connor and Mrs. Ronson. "Thank you for finding my ponies," she said, and then her jaw dropped.

"It's more like they found us," Mrs. Ronson replied.

But Connor just stared at the woman from the truck. She stared back. Finally he said, "Danielle?"

"Connor." Using his last name, as she always had. "What the hell are you doing way out here?"

"Wedding," was all he could say.

"Yours?"

Connor glanced from her to Donna Ronson, then back. "What? Oh, no. Nothing like that. I was just…well, it's a work thing."

"You're a wedding singer now?"

"No. I mean, there was someone I needed to talk to, and he was at the plantation down the road. It's connected to something I'm doing and, well, you know—"

"Mr. Connor is trying to find whoever it was killed my husband," Mrs. Ronson said. Then she said to Connor, "Are you going to introduce us?"

"Uh, yeah, sure. This is Danielle Simmons. Danielle, meet Donna Ronson. Like she said, I'm looking into the death of her husband."

"You're still doing that sort of thing?" Danielle asked, running a hand softly through the mane of the chestnut.

"No. I mean sort of. Mr. James gave me a job as a bond runner for his bail company. I was escorting Mr. Ronson back to jail when…well, it's a long story."

"They were shot at and run off the road," Mrs. Ronson finished for him.

"Long story, same plot," Danielle replied with a sigh. There was a long, awkward silence, and then she said, "Anyway, thank you for finding my horses. The gate to their paddock somehow was left open, and they got out."

"For what it's worth, I'm glad you took the job," Connor told her, glancing at the sign on the truck door.

"Me too," she said as she gave the horse a kiss on the nose.

"You look good."

"You, too."

"Your injuries heal up?"

"I feel a sharp pain now and then, but the doctors say it's just a phantom thing." She pulled a phone out of her pocket and said, "I have to make a call, get these animals rounded up."

"Beautiful creatures," Connor said.

"Yes, they are."

"Mind if I call you sometime?"

"Probably not a good idea," Danielle said, then turned around and punched a number into her cell.

It was well past midnight when Connor dropped Mrs. Ronson at her car in the Walmart parking lot. He was still reeling from his random meeting with Danielle, his brain swallowed up by the chance encounter in the fog.

She was the flame that continued to burn, the woman he'd loved and had planned on spending the rest of his life with. The only woman he'd ever given a real damn about, and who had almost died because of his reckless mistakes. A woman who had made it clear—more than once— that she never wanted to have anything to do with him again.

Julie had already given last call and told Buddy he could go home when Connor parked his car below the drinking deck and trudged up the stairs. Clooney glanced up when he entered the bar and offered a wag of his tail, then lowered his head back onto his crossed paws. A half dozen customers were still perched on stools at the counter, nursing beers and boat drinks, while a young couple occupied a shadowy corner, pushing the outer boundaries of decency. The popcorn machine had long ago burst its last kernel, and the Seeburg was scratching out a record: Buster Poindexter proclaiming it was "hot-hot-hot."

"I was beginning to think you may have gone with the new bride and groom on their honeymoon," Julie greeted him as she ran a damp rag over the polished bar.

"Bad fog and a flat tire," he said.

"That sucks," she replied, a hint of doubt in her voice.

He ducked down under the wooden counter and began dumping maraschino cherries from the garnish tray back into a jar. "How did it go tonight?" he asked.

"Busy, but we managed," she replied, tucking a wisp of hair behind an ear. "Receipts are already in the safe."

Connor tried to figure out whether she was tired, or simply annoyed by his last-minute plan to leave her in charge on a Saturday night while he went off on some half-cocked quest that had nothing to do with business. He'd never had much luck trying to read her, but knew she'd let him know if she was hanging on to any resentment. She seemed good at that.

"Anyway, thank you for holding down the fort," he told her. "I owe you."

"I know. And just so you know, Jimmy Brinks—the armored car guy—was in here earlier, looking for you. What a creepoid."

"He say what he wanted?"

"Just to let you know he stopped by."

What the fuck does he want? Connor wondered as he tucked the jar of cherries into the beer fridge. "Thank you, I think. Now get out of here. I can close up the rest of the way. It's the least I can do."

She nodded and folded her rag on the counter. "'Night," she said as she collected her backpack and disappeared into the night.

Connor awakened the next morning to the diver alarm. Eight o'clock sharp. He could set his watch to their clanging tanks and weight belts if he ever needed to.

After taking care of his and Clooney's morning ablutions, Connor brought his laptop down to the drinking deck while Clooney attacked a bowl of kibble and salmon. He spent the next five minutes going through emails, most of them spam or marketing promos from suppliers. That's how he came upon a message from Caitlin Thomas that had arrived a little after ten the night before, just about the time he was driving home from the wedding and experiencing the horses in the mist.

The email contained a brief note that read:

> I did a little digging, as you asked, and found a few things about Hicks you need to know. As I tell a lot of my women friends, not the sort of dude I'd hitch my wagon to.

The attached files contained standard information: date of birth, South Carolina driver's license, and current address, which was a street in Hannahan. Google street view showed it was a three-level brick apartment not far from the noxious paper plant, dirty beige paint with streaks of mold on it. The landscaping was hard-packed dirt where grass had once been, crepe myrtle trees with bad haircuts and a lone river birch drooping at a precarious angle.

Hicks had worked upstate as a deputy with the Oconee County Sheriff's Department, from which he resigned under a dark cloud that hinted of improper use of force. A divorce was pending, not surprising considering the circumstances of his domestic abuse arrest. No children, which was a good thing. He had a license to carry a concealed weapon, most likely the Glock Connor had lifted out of the center console, as well as other weapons he imagined were stashed around his house. Maybe in his car, which he assumed the cops were looking for, and which he again told himself was none of his concern.

Hicks had a sealed record from when he was in high school, something that must have been minor enough not to hinder his ambition to become an officer of the law. Connor guessed vandalism, or maybe theft that did not involve a firearm. Expunged, and a moot point now. One year of college, at Appalachian State in North Carolina, no declared major and no sports. A string of jobs followed him for the next seven or eight years, until he moved to Oconee and joined the long arm of the law.

Even though it was Sunday, Connor called Nelson Burdette. Church was several hours away and, if the man had a family, he'd probably be planning something fun with them later on. Maybe a weekend visit to the beach or the aquarium. Connor had only one question, which he asked despite the fact that the SLED investigator sounded peeved to be interrupted on his day off.

"Just wanted to know if you've found Lyle Hicks," he said.

"It's Sunday, Connor. I'm having breakfast with my wife and kids."

"And I have an escaped convict stalking me."

Burdette exhaled an audible sigh and said, "The short answer is no."

"And the long answer?"

"Same thing. State and local cops are out looking for him, knocking on doors. I'll let you know the second I know anything. As I've told you before, stay out of this. Goodbye."

Another half-dozen questions were spinning in Connor's head, but Burdette was gone before he got a chance to ask even one of them. He knew he could be as irritating as a skin rash, and he'd intruded on the guy's day off. Couldn't really blame him for his brusque attitude.

He hadn't even put his phone down when the screen lit up with another incoming call. Caitlin Thomas. He'd been planning on calling her, but not until after he'd finished reading her report.

"Did you get my email?" she asked, direct and abrupt.

"The bar gets loud on Saturday nights," he said, not wanting to get into his trip to the wedding the night before. "Didn't know you'd sent me anything until just now."

"Well, as you can see, there's not a whole lot that tells you much about Mr. Hicks," Caitlin said. "Former cop, now doing time for beating up his wife. Except he somehow got out and seems to be circling back to a few folks he blames for his hard luck. Including you. Which is why I'm calling you so early on a Sunday morning."

"Go on."

"Thing is, I tapped another database for law enforcement records, and found that, while your guy Hicks was working for the Sheriff's Department, a few reprimands were placed in his file."

"Reprimands for what?"

"It seems your friend is a little prone to violence."

Just as he'd figured. "How violent?" he asked.

"The man goes from zero to sixty faster than a Tesla. Not long after he became a deputy, he pulled over a car outside of Clemson, no license plate light. A physical altercation ensured, and the driver ended up in the hospital for close to a week."

"Let me guess: the guy was Black."

"In fact, he was. But the next one wasn't. A kid stumbled out of a roadhouse up in Seneca, made it halfway to his car when he encountered Hicks. Ended up needing dental implants. Lawyers got involved, money changed hands. The sheriff stood up for him, but a third strike two months later—something about a bartender ending up with a detached retina—got him the boot."

"Sounds like a real boy scout," Connor said. "And I appreciate your concern, but I'm not planning on going anywhere near this guy."

"You might not have a choice, if he comes looking for you."

Connor waited out the Sunday lunch crowd before wandering up the street to his favorite taco joint.

The sky was a brilliant blue with soft strokes of white painted across it. A gentle breeze was drifting in from the beach just a couple blocks south, rattling the fronds of the palmetto trees. The kitchen grill was pumping out a savory mix of carne asada, barbacoa, and shrimp, blended with rich salsa and cilantro. Connor was sitting at the outdoor patio bar, nursing a bloody Mary far too early in the day than was prudent, considering his history. A ball cap protected his bare head, and dark lenses shaded his eyes.

The restaurant was a pet-friendly joint, so Clooney was lying in the shade of Connor's stool, his tongue drooping on the tile floor. When the server arrived with a plate of fish tacos and a side of black beans, Connor plucked a morsel of mahi from one of the folded tortillas and slipped it to him. Clooney, not the waiter.

He had just taken his first bite when his phone rang. The screen told him it was Jordan James, which was odd for a weekend. Even odder because James had been mostly hands-off since Connor had begun work at Citadel Bail Bonds, except to pick him up from the hospital in Kingstree.

"I heard what happened," the seventh-richest man in Charleston said.

"And what was that?"

"Lyle Hicks. That wife-beater you tracked down last fall. I heard he dropped by The Sandbar the other day to even the score."

"We don't know for a fact that's why he was there," Connor said. "Could have been any number of reasons."

"Get real, Jack. They found his attorney an hour ago. Most of him, at least."

Chapter 21

Connor said nothing for a second, wondering where the man got his intel. A few hours ago Nelson Burdette had assured him there was no update on Hicks' whereabouts but, if Jordan James was right, the escaped asswipe had just killed his lawyer. Which meant he probably still had Connor in his sights.

"Where did you hear that?" he finally asked as he rubbed Clooney behind the ears.

"Never mind about that. The thing is, you need 'round-the-clock security until this guy's caught."

"I *am* security, remember? I'm on your payroll."

"I'm talking cops, Jack. State, county, local…whatever it takes to keep you safe."

Connor had been thinking the same thing, but didn't want to get into it. Not with Jordan James, not right now. He had two guns—his own Sig P365 and the Glock he'd lifted out of Lyle Hicks' car—and he'd earned more than a few shooting commendations during his training in the U.S. Army. Not that any of that would protect him from a psycho dirtbag who had tried to beat his wife to a pulp and, it seemed, had brutally killed the attorney who had represented him at trial.

"What do you mean, they found most of him?" he said.

"Details are sketchy. All I know is there was a lot of blood, and maybe a missing body part or two."

Connor gave an involuntary shudder as he wondered which parts. He thought back to the intruder he'd chased away a few nights back, and the failed firebomb that had been tossed into the bar. At the time he'd mentally written both incidents off to the ambush out on Indigo Road, the two would-be assailants back to settle the score. Now he wasn't so sure.

"Anyway, that's not why I called you," James continued. "I know it's very last-minute, but I was hoping I could buy you a cocktail."

Connor could think of a dozen ways he'd rather spend his Sunday afternoon, but he knew from past experience that his boss never took "no" for an answer. Instead, he asked, "At your place on Murray Street?" *Place* being a euphemism for one of the largest, most opulent waterfront mansions on the entire Charleston peninsula.

"Actually, I'm up in Summerville today," James replied.

Connor couldn't see Jordan James having too many reasons to ever go to Summerville, other than to visit one of the many businesses he owned around the greater Charleston area. Especially on a beautiful Sunday afternoon in June.

"What time, and where?" he asked, possibly sealing his fate for the rest of the day.

"Two-thirty, Sunshine Bowl-A-Rama."

"That's where we did the exchange," Connor said. He was referring to the "grand reveal" several years back when he'd refurbished Eddie James' sixty-seven Camaro, fitted it with handicap controls so the injured vet would be able to drive it himself again. The exchange had been a major deal, and was even featured on a TV talk show that had provided the funding to make it all happen.

"Exactly," James replied. "At the time I didn't see a bowling alley as a long-term enterprise, but it pays for itself and the bartender makes a mean martini. See you there."

• • •

As soon as he finished his tacos and bloody Mary, Connor returned to The Sandbar and loaded Clooney into his car. While the Lyle Hicks matter didn't involve Cherine Dupree, he realized she remained at risk until Burdette and the SLED team apprehended the two goons who had shot her and killed Willis Ronson. His own experience with in-patient rehabilitation told him security was lax, even at a VA facility where just about everyone—patients and administrators—had been taught how to shoot a gun.

Thirty minutes later he pulled into the lot at Sea Island Rehab and parked in the shade of a large, sweeping willow. Inside, he asked to speak with the security manager, and a couple minutes later he was greeted by a man named Quinn. He didn't say if that was his first or last name; just Quinn. The plastic tag pinned to his collar was equally ambiguous. A laminated ID card hung from a lanyard draped around his neck, but it was flipped around backwards so Connor couldn't read what it said.

"There's only two ways into this place," Quinn assured him. "Front door you came through just now, and one around back. And we have measures in place to prevent against unlawful entry."

"You mean locks?"

"I'm not at liberty to reveal exactly what they are, because doing so would constitute a violation of the system itself."

Locks, Connor mentally confirmed.

"You are aware that one of your residents was shot in a high-profile murder case, right?" Connor pressed. "And whoever did it very well might come back to finish the job."

"Relax, Mr. Connor. No one is going to get in here. I assure you, every one of our residents is one hundred percent safe with us."

"All I'm asking is you keep an eye on her, watch for anyone who shouldn't be here," Connor said.

"We have a strict sign-in policy for visitors. No one gets through the door without proper credentials."

"What about after hours?"

"No one gets in, period."

"And if they're armed?"

Quinn said nothing, just tapped the butt of a gun holstered to his belt. The gesture did little to ease Connor's concerns.

He knew Quinn was trying to sound helpful, but protocols were made to be violated. "I just want to make sure Ms. Dupree is safe," he said. "Maybe you can move her to another room?"

"We did that this morning, at the recommendation of a cop from SLED," Quinn replied. "I assure you, she's safer here than she is at her own home."

Seemed Nelson Burdette wasn't taking any chances, either.

"As long as I'm here, do you mind if I look in on her?" Connor asked.

"No problem," the security manager said. "Visiting hours are nine to six."

Cherine turned out to be in a physical therapy session in the workout room at the far end of the building, and couldn't be disturbed. A nurse politely explained that Connor could hang around until she was finished, but he didn't want to lie about why he'd dropped by, or give her any reason to think she might be in any danger. He elected not to stay, or even leave a message. If Burdette was satisfied with her security, he should be, too.

•••

Creature of habit that he was, Jordan James was sitting at the bar inside Sunshine Bowl-A-Rama when Connor arrived.

The place was vintage Americana, a low-slung cinder block building with chipped paint at the rear of a moonscape parking lot. A full wall of plate glass covered with peeling mirrored vinyl reflected the harsh glare of the bright June sun. At night, an animated neon sign out at the street depicted bowling pins being knocked over by a ball, but by day it just looked desolate and lonely, scarred by dust and time. A few cars and trucks indicated the place was busy, but not packed. One of the vehicles was a midnight blue Bentley with loads of chrome that glimmered in the afternoon sun.

Connor opened the glass door for Clooney, who immediately began following a trail of something particularly odorous around the carpeted lobby. The scent eventually led to a cocktail lounge set off to one side, where a handful of patrons seemed to be glued to a NASCAR race on TV. The bar was called The Gutter, and James was already seated on a stool, nursing a martini and chatting up the bartender. She appeared to be about Connor's age and in serious competition with him in terms of body ink, mostly butterflies and roses and characters from an Asian language he couldn't identify. She also had a colorful Indian mandala on her neck, a design he knew was designed to focus a person's spirituality and emotional center. Or something like that. Her hair was an unnatural shade of red, like magenta printer ink, black roots showing through and a silver ring embedded in her nose. Constellations of tiny studs were punched into the upper cartilage of both ears.

Clooney nosed up to James and came dangerously close to sniffing his crotch before Connor called him off. "Down," he ordered, and within seconds the chocolate lab was lying on the floor, his head resting on an outstretched paw.

Jordan James pivoted on his stool and said, "Howdy, Jack. Wherever that dog is, I know you're close behind. Make yourself comfortable and say 'hi' to Teena."

"Hi, Teena," he greeted her. "You've got some serious street art going on, there."

"Likewise, Mr. Jack." She let her eyes linger on whatever ink was visible, glanced at Mr. James and then back to Connor. As if thinking, *what are these two dudes doing, hanging together*? Yin and yang. Mutt and Jeff. "You drinking, or just here to bowl a few frames?"

"He's having what I'm having," Jordan James said, settling the question before Connor had a chance to respond. "And make me another, while you're at it."

"It's a little early in the day, sir," Connor said, tapping the face of his watch. "And a long drive home."

"No worries, son. I own a taxi company and a towing service, so you and your car will make it back just fine. Now sit your tats down and make yourself comfortable."

"It's not me I'm worried about," Mr. James. "How long have you been here?"

"Long enough to know when to hold 'em, and when to fold 'em."

Connor wasn't certain what his boss was getting at, except that the words sounded better coming from Kenny Rogers. And that the seventh-richest man in Charleston was well on his way to getting crocked, if he wasn't there already. He knew he should bundle James into his car right now and drive him home, but instead Connor did what the Army told him to do: obey the orders of his superiors. That in mind, he slid up onto the stool and studied the martini glass sitting on the bar. Empty, except for a pimiento-stuffed olive in the bottom, which James fished out with one finger and popped into his mouth.

"One is my limit," Connor said.

"Suit yourself," James replied. "We should be done by then."

"Done with what?"

"What I called you all the way out here for."

Connor studied the red lines in James' eyes, pondered whether they'd become a permanent marker of his fondness for gin. "Yeah, I was wondering about that."

"Shake 'em nice and good," James advised Teena, ostensibly talking about their martinis, although he could have been alluding to something anatomical, as well. Then to Connor he said, "All in good time, soon as we have a toast."

"A toast to what?"

"Patience, young man. I'll get to that."

He did, only after Teena set their chilled cocktails in front of them, on napkins that duplicated the toppling pins on the neon sign outside. He touched his glass to Connor's and said, "Here's to always holding family and friends close to your heart, and gin and vermouth inside your gut."

Connor took a modest sip, then another as he had to admit it tasted good going down. The bloody Mary he'd consumed earlier had already laid the groundwork for the alcohol, but he knew he had to keep his intake to just one martini. Definitely no more than two. He had a long Sunday night behind the bar ahead of him, and a history with gin that followed him like a shadow.

"So…what's up?" he asked.

"Actually, it's Eddie," Jordan James said. Eddie James was his only son by his first ex-wife and the buddy whose life Connor had saved in Iraq that, in turn, had led to his serial employment gigs with one or the other of Jordan James' companies. "His doctors are worried that his *arcuate fasciculus* may not be functioning as well as it was."

Along with losing his arm at the elbow during the suicide blast, Eddie had suffered damage to several parts of his frontal cortex, leaving him with multiple physical impairments, and barely able to speak. "I'm not sure I know what that is," Connor said.

"Me neither, until his doctors explained it to me. The *arcuate fasciculus* is a band of nerves that connects two sections of the brain: Broca's area, which helps you turn your ideas and thoughts into actual spoken words, and Wernicke's area, which is involved in the understanding and processing of speech and written language. The *AE*, as his doctors call it, bridges the two functions so you can form words and speak clearly."

Connor nodded; the bomb blast had clearly robbed Eddie not only of his ability to speak, but also to process some of the simplest of concepts—many of them having to do with functions of daily living.

"I am so sorry, sir," he said. "I swear, if I'd seen that van coming at us, none of this would have ever happened."

Jordan James raised a hand to that, like running back stiff-arming a tackle. "We've had that discussion a thousand times, Jack. It's not your fault. Eddie did what he thought was the right thing at the time, signing up for God and country. What's done is done, and he has to live with the consequences."

"We all do," Connor replied. "From the time you sign up you know there's this dark side of war, and there's a chance you won't make it through the day. Thing is, you're never ready for it when it happens."

"Same thing goes for being a parent." James took a long, slow sip of gin, then let out a deep breath. "And that's all behind us now. The point is, his doctors tell us that the VA has a new experimental treatment for patients suffering from the same kind of brain trauma that Eddie has. In fact, they tell us he's a perfect candidate."

"What kind of treatment?"

"Experimental," James repeated. "That's all we really know, except that they appear to be having a solid success rate with it."

"Outpatient or residential?" Connor had experienced both types of therapies for issues related to his own PTSD, and knew each carried its own risks of letdowns along with the chance for improvement.

"This particular program is a long-term-care thing, up in Richmond. Six months to two years. It'll be hard to have him gone for so long, but… well, we're all for it if it helps him get better. God knows, Shirl's done all she can up to this point."

Shirl was Eddie's mother, and had been caring for him ever since he'd been discharged from Walter Reed up in Bethesda years ago. It was a fulltime job from the start, and Connor figured it had evolved into an overwhelming task.

"Sounds like it's the best thing all around," he replied.

"We think so." James raised his glass and took a robust sip, then said, "We're going to have a big send-off for him when final approval comes through, and I'd like you to be there."

"Wouldn't miss it for the world," Connor told him as he finished off his drink. He set his glass on the counter and started to get up from his stool, but James put a hand on his shoulder and gently pushed him back down.

"That's still not why I invited you here." He glanced at Teena, who was wiping down the far end of the counter, and signaled for her to fix another round.

"Mr. James…I really don't think—"

"Humor me, Jack. One for the road."

"It's the road that I'm worrying about," Connor said.

"Like I said, I'll make sure you and your car get home safe and sound," James insisted. "And incidentally, that's why I asked you to meet me here."

Connor had grown accustomed to James' habit of speaking in riddles, particularly when he'd been drinking. Which seemed to be most of the time these days. Hard to imagine how he could consume so much gin and expect his brain to fire on just a single cylinder or two.

"Well, here I am, sir," he said. "What's this all about?"

"Well, you kind of hit it on the head earlier, when you mentioned this was where you returned Isabella to my son." Isabella was the name Eddie had given his prize sixty-seven Camaro, vivid orange with a convertible top and a hungry 396 V-8 under the hood. "He hasn't really taken her for a spin since you had her up-fitted for him to drive, and it's time to pay it forward to someone who can appreciate her quirks and idiosyncrasies."

"What are you saying?" Connor asked him.

James dug into his pocket and produced a ring of keys. "I'm saying she's yours again," he replied, setting them on the bar in front of him.

Connor stared at him, waited to speak until Teena had deposited their new drinks and walked back to the other end of the bar. "Mr. James...I really don't—"

"I can't think of anyone who's more deserving," James interrupted. "And it's what Eddie wants. He can't speak very well, but he can listen and nod."

"Sir, I know you mean well, but I can't accept this."

"You can, and you will. She was yours once, and now she is again. End of discussion."

Usually when Jordan James said a conversation was done, it was done. No argument, no debate. But not this time. Connor had fallen in love with Isabella the moment he'd seen her parked in the driveway, keys dangling from the ignition. Her power and speed made the vehicle a true joy to drive, particularly on a top-down morning when the sun wasn't too hot and a slight breeze was drifting in from the ocean. She had been an unexpected gift he never felt he deserved, and had worked with a veterans' charity to make her street legal so Eddie could handle the controls. It was a well-intentioned endeavor, but the poor guy had taken her out no more than a half dozen times since then. Never by himself, and always just a quick tool up Palm Boulevard and back.

Even if he couldn't drive it anymore, there was no way on earth Connor could ever take her back.

"I have a different idea," he said.

"A different idea about what?" Mr. James asked, picking up his martini glass.

"Just hear me out," Connor said, looking him square in the eye. "There's an organization I learned about at when I was at the program down in Georgia that helps vets like Eddie get back on their feet. Sometimes literally, sometimes just in their heads. Anything that works. The people who work there take guys out on boats to go fishing, or hiking up in the mountains, or maybe just up in the air so they can get free of gravity for a few hours. They also take 'em out for road trips, even let them drive a bit, if they're able to. Sure, I love that car, and I appreciate you thinking of me. But she's a real special piece of machinery, and she needs to go where she can do the most good. And maybe change the lives of other veterans just like Eddie. I think you should give her to them."

While Connor had been talking, Jordan James hadn't sipped his gin. Hadn't said a word. Now he set his glass down on the bar, picked up the soggy napkin with the bowling pins printed on it and touched it to one eye, then the other. Eventually he said, "That is the most generous thing I believe I've ever seen anyone do, Jack."

"Just paying it forward, like you said."

Mr. James nodded—no argument—as he picked up the keys and slipped them back into his coat pocket. "To Isabella," he said. "Far may she roam."

They sat there in an awkward silence for a few seconds, staring at their respective glasses, taking almost identical sips. The gliding of balls on polished hardwood, then knocking into pins, created a steady thrum in the place, while cheering, cursing, and laughing brought it to life. Connor would have liked to have polished off his drink and fled out into the sunlight, but he couldn't just pound the gin and flee. Not with James sitting beside him, slinging martinis down his throat.

Eventually he turned to him and said, "Mind of I ask you a question, sir?"

"Anything you want."

"It has nothing to do with Eddie or Camaros—"

"So much the better," James said.

"Well, the thing is, I was wondering if you've ever had the opportunity to deal with a man named Colt Lomax. From what I hear he's a dark money man and power broker—"

At that point James raised his hand and said, "Don't go there."

"Excuse me?"

He regarded Connor with rheumy eyes, then shook his head. "You don't want to be anywhere near that sonofabitch, Jack. What's this about, anyway?"

"I've been looking into something that isn't making much sense, and I need to talk to someone who might know him. Not just the sort of thing you can find on the internet, either. The stuff that goes on behind the scenes."

"I can tell you the bastard owns the chicken market in this state, has his hands on both supply and demand. Which really screws with my restaurant business."

"I was thinking more along the lines of power and politics," Connor explained.

James picked up his glass by the stem and swirled the contents, but did not drink. Not right away. "You haven't lived in this state long enough to know this, Jack, but every election there's always some sort of scandal gets cooked up. A war hero running for president secretly fathered a secret love child with a black woman. A former governor cheated with a campaign staffer in a motel room in Utah, or somewhere. All of it's bullshit. Politics has become a shady business in this country of ours, but downright amateurish compared to what goes on here in South Carolina."

"Who would I talk to for a personal perspective?" Connor asked.

He finally took that sip of gun, long and slow, appearing to think about Connor's question. Eventually he said, "If you're really hell-bent on this, try Byram Higgins."

"Who's he?"

"Someone you might call a facilitator. Made things happen, back in the day. If anyone can tell you about Colt Lomax, it's him."

"Is he still around?" Connor asked.

"Far as I know. He was on the news about a month ago, calling Garrett Tipton a snake and a thief and a scum-sucking con artist."

Connor recalled that Tipton was the South Carolina senator who had just tossed his hat into the presidential melee. Colt Lomax's fellow cadet at The Citadel and, he suspected, a willing puppet on a string.

"You know where Mr. Higgins lives?"

"Don't know, don't care," Jordan James told him. "You're going to have to find the answer to that one yourself."

"Well, anyway, thanks for the name. Much appreciated."

"Not if you know what's good for you. You start asking around about the Carolina Chickenman, you stand every chance to get fried."

Chapter 22

Before Connor left the Bowl-A-Rama he made absolutely sure Jordan James could operate his Bentley without endangering himself or others. Not convinced, he followed the man back to Charleston, hanging back a hundred yards until he pulled into his driveway and made it through the gate that led to the carriage house in back. Convinced he was safe—and other drivers were safe from him—Connor headed home to Folly, staying in the right lane and keeping both eyes open for unmarked cop cars.

Nelson Burdette called him just as he was pulling into his space beneath the drinking deck. He cut the engine and got out, answering his phone as he juggled his keys.

"I thought you were spending the day with your wife and kids," Connor said.

"We stopped for ice cream on the way home, and I don't want it to drip all over the car," the SLED cop replied. "Plus, I didn't want them to hear what I'm about to tell you."

"You mean that Lyle Hicks killed his lawyer?"

"Dammit, Connor. Where did you hear that?"

"Bad news travels fast. I assume it's true?"

Burdette hesitated a second, probably figuring the best way to play this. Then he said, "That's the going theory, yes. We're looking at surveillance footage from his doorbell, and the house across the street. Seems Hicks wasn't worried about being sloppy."

"I take it he's still on the loose?"

"We have a bulletin out for his arrest, but wherever he is at present is anyone's guess."

Connor checked his watch, saw it was already half past four. He could see Julie upstairs at the bar, getting ready for another long evening, and he needed to join her. "What about his wife?" he asked.

"She's safe."

"Good to know. And I hate to do this, but I'm late for work."

"The limes and olives can wait a second," Burdette said. "You need to know that Hicks is in possession of a firearm. A Glock, to be precise."

Not exactly, Connor thought. Unless the guy had two of them. "Is that how he killed his lawyer?" he asked.

"You know I can't comment on that. But you need to be careful until we have this shit-for-brains in custody. You scared him off once, but he'll be back."

"I can take care of myself," Connor assured him.

"You can until you can't," Burdette countered. "Which is why you may see a car rolling by your place every now and then."

"You're providing me security?"

"Such as it is. Meanwhile, promise to let me know if you see anything suspicious."

"After nine-one-one, you're first on my list," Connor said.

Connor had just settled in behind the bar and was mixing a couple margaritas when a low-pressure system announced itself with spears of lightning and rolls of thunder in the distance.

Rain pummeled the sand in large, hard drops, and the wind swirled through the palmettos and oaks and sweet gums lining the road. The deluge continued for a good part of the evening. Sundays typically produced a steady stream of patrons, but the beach emptied out early and only a few die-hard locals ventured out into the night for a cold beer or a margarita.

One of these was Jimmy Brinks, who showed up around ten o'clock. Connor caught sight of him trudging up the wheelchair ramp, threads of water dripping from his scraggly hair and a soaked T-shirt plastered to his skin. By the time the erstwhile thief had planted his ass on a stool, Connor had poured a couple fingers of Jack Daniels into his special glass tumbler and set it on the bar in front of him.

Brinks picked it up and knocked half of it back, then set the glass back on the counter. "You are one dumb sumbitch," he said, smacking his lips.

"You're the one out in the rain tonight," Connor replied.

"And you're standing behind that counter, in full view of anyone might just be passing by on the street."

"Meaning?"

"Meaning, you got a big bullseye painted on you."

Connor ran his rag over the counter, even though there was nothing to wipe. "Where'd you hear that?" he asked.

"Never mind that. Fact is, there's a mean motherfucker on your ass, already capped his lawyer. Word is, you're next on his list."

"Yeah, I heard," Connor said, thinking where the hell does Brinks get his information.

"Yet there you stand, doing shit while he could be lining you up right now." He knocked back the rest of his sour mash, indicated he wanted a refill.

Connor splashed another measure into the glass, set the bottle on the bar. "Wouldn't be the first time," he said.

"Don't say I didn't warn you," Brinks replied, downing the amber liquid in one gulp and rising from the stool. He dropped a wad of bills down, gently tapped the bar before he turned to go. "Then again, it didn't save your ass last time, did it?"

Ten seconds later he blended into the rain and the night and was gone.

Connor closed the place down before midnight. The lightning and thunder had faded, the low front had retreated out to sea, and Julie had gone home early. No need to make her hang around when business was so slow. No boogeymen showed up, no shots were fired. A black SUV with *government* written all over it rolled past The Sandbar a few times, but there was no sign of Lyle Hicks. Which didn't mean he wasn't out there in the darkness, keeping an eye on things.

Waiting for the right moment to strike.

The next morning, Connor Googled Byram Higgins while he wolfed down a toaster waffle. First off, the man was alive. That was good. Eighty-five years old, maybe not so good. Memories start to be unreliable around that age, and Connor wanted to know whatever Higgins could tell him about Colt Lomax. Or at least what the old man cared to tell him.

Several websites listed him as *senior partner emeritus* at his former law firm, which meant he was still on the letterhead but not the payroll. He was the former member of a dozen local boards and community organizations, but none now. A blurb from ten years ago mentioned a wife named Helen, but no word about children or grandchildren. Connor assumed there had to be several. Offspring, not wives. Maybe wives, as well.

At one time he'd lived in the toney South of Broad area of Charleston, a couple blocks from Jordan James' waterfront mansion on Murray Boulevard. Now he owned a house on Kiawah Island, not far from the beach, which suggested he'd done well in his law career, but not quite well enough to own a place directly on the sand. Connor obtained the address from another proprietary database, but the Google camera apparently was not allowed past the twenty-four-hour guarded gatehouse. Hence no street view. He also got a phone number, which—given Higgins' age—he figured was probably a landline. Maybe an old one, maybe disconnected. Maybe only hooked up to a fax machine. Whatever it was connected to, he dialed it.

Four rings later, a voice answered, "Higgins residence. How may I help you?" Southern accent, smooth and silky. Female. Polite, yet suspicious at the same time.

"May I please speak with Byram Higgins?" Connor asked.

"Who's calling?"

At least the number was correct, and the aging lawyer probably was there. "Please tell him it's Jack Connor, from Citadel Security."

"You're calling from The Citadel?" Confusion and wariness in her voice.

"No, Citadel Security." Not quite a lie, since the bail bonds company was a subsidiary of Jordan James' security firm.

"What's this regarding?" she asked.

He could give her all sorts of subterfuge, try to mislead her about why he was calling, what he wanted. But there was no point, since she clearly was the gatekeeper and Connor needed to get past her. "I'm doing some research for a project, and I'd like to get his thoughts on state politics."

"He gets exhausted easily," the woman replied.

"All I need is ten minutes. I promise I won't tire him out."

His request drew a moment of silence as she gave it some thought. Then she said, "Can you be here at one? He'll have finished his lunch by then, and won't have started his occupational therapy yet. The intellectual stimulation will be good for him."

Known for its sun-washed days and star-studded skies, Kiawah Island was named for the tribe that had lived there prior to the arrival of English settlers in the sixteen-hundreds. As new arrivals always seem wont to do, they pushed out the indigenous people and seized the land. In this case it was passed down for centuries until, in the early 1950s, when a lumberman from Georgia purchased it and began building a modest community near the shore. Following his death, his heirs sold the entire parcel to a firm of wealthy Kuwaiti investors, who subsequently developed the place as a world-class resort.

Famous for its lush maritime forests, brackish ponds, and salt marshes, the barrier island was home to several dozen varieties of mammals and hundreds of species of resident and migratory birds. The most notable inhabitants, however, were the rich and near-rich who built massive estates tucked in amongst the live oaks and pines and palmettos, monuments to excess that could only be seen by visitors who were granted access past the twenty-four-hour manned gatehouse.

The Higgins house was one of these. A southern colonial with symmetrical double-stacked porches, it was set on a quiet lagoon at the edge of a golf course. Accessed by a circular driveway and a central stairway that led up to the front veranda, it was shaded by sweetgums and poplars and tupelos. The siding was forest green shingles, and a van was parked in front of one of the wood-grained carriage doors, its roof clearance too high for it to fit into the garage space beneath the elevated house. The vehicle's side windows were all tinted dark, and a collapsible lift was attached to the passenger-side sliding door.

Connor pulled in behind the van a few minutes before the appointed hour. He studied the handicap lift, figured there had to be an elevator somewhere in the bowels of the garage, but he opted for the stairs that took him up to the first-floor porch. When he rang the bell, a blue light indicated that a camera had been activated, and someone deep within the dwelling muttered something inaudible to him. Thirty seconds later there was movement behind the sheer drape that covered the glass, followed by a series of clicks. Then the door opened, and a woman poked her head out.

"Mr. Connor?" she asked in the same smooth, southern voice of earlier that morning. She was wearing white jeans and a pale top the color of key lime pie, silver sand dollar earrings. No name badge, no sign of her being a professional caregiver. A daughter or niece, maybe? Certainly not Higgins' wife.

Then again, one never knew.

"Sorry if I'm a bit early," he said. "It's always hard to second-guess the traffic coming down here."

"Especially during beach season," she concurred. "Follow me."

She walked him through a living room that could have been featured in *Coastal Living*, furniture color-coordinated in light blues and grays, nautical motif and shell patterns throughout. There was a broad view across the lagoon to the ocean, which this morning looked like a sheet of tin foil glimmering in the sun.

They continued down a hallway fitted with an Oriental carpet runner, and finally stopped at a closed pocket door. "He's just had a bowl of shrimp and grits, so he may be a little lethargic," she said. "And cranky."

"Who wouldn't be?"

"This is his library. He spends most of his day in here, including his naps. You have fifteen minutes."

That was five more than he'd asked for, but much less than he thought he might need. She slid the door open halfway and he edged inside. Higgins was slumped in a battery-powered chair, fitted with a keypad and a joystick, staring out the window of a room that looked more like an art gallery than a library. Not many books, just a lot of photos and maps on the walls and a large flat-screen TV tuned to a cable channel Connor never watched. The volume was muted, but the news ticker running across the bottom provided an update on the news of the day. Or at least a politicized version of it.

"There's a button on his armrest if he needs me," the woman informed him. She stood there, as if thinking of anything else to say, then abruptly turned and left. He heard the pocket door roll closed behind him, then moved into Higgins' line of sight.

"Good morning, sir," he said to the man huddled in the chair. "I'm Jack Connor. Thank you for agreeing to meet with me."

"When did I do that?" Higgins asked.

"I called this morning. The woman who answered the phone said to come by at one."

"That woman is my daughter, so don't go getting any ideas."

Daughter. That explained the relationship, as well as her protective approach to her old man. And, it seemed, vice versa.

"No, sir. My ideas are strictly professional."

"Especially with all those the tattoos," Higgins continued, as if he hadn't heard Connor's reply. "When I was your age that meant you either spent time in the military or grew up on the wrong side of the tracks."

Correct on both counts, sir, Connor thought. "I like to think of them as an art collection I can take wherever I go," he said instead.

"As long as you don't sell it for an arm and a leg," Higgins replied, chuckling at his attempt at humor. "Then again, I'm stuck in this damned chair. Stroke screwed up my whole right side. Doctors called it an aneurysmal dilatation, but I know what it was. Fingers on my left side can work a keyboard, so I Googled it."

"Well, I do appreciate you agreeing to see me on such short notice," Connor replied, not sure that the man had actually agreed to any such thing. Nor was he convinced this meeting would be at all productive.

Higgins didn't respond right away as he appeared to be running a search function in his brain. Then his eyes lit up in an *a-ha* moment and he said, "You're the one Adrienne said was interested in this state's bullshit politics, and such."

"That's right," Connor said, figuring Adrienne and the daughter were one and the same. "But mostly I want to ask you what you know about a man name of Colt Lomax."

For a man who'd had an aneurysmal dilatation, Higgins' brain seemed to function just fine. At the mention of Lomax's name his eyes blinked to high alert, and he said, "The chicken man? Yeah, I know the prick. Why do you ask?"

"Something I'm looking into," Connor replied, keeping his words nebulous and his purpose vague.

"Well, don't."

He cocked his head at the abrupt answer and said, "Sir?"

"He's not a man to mess with. Not in politics or anything."

"That's what I've heard. Tell me why they call him the Carolina Kingmaker."

"They call him a lot of things," Higgins said with a wheeze. "And whoever *they* are, they're right. No one goes through the meatgrinder in this state without going up against Lomax, since there's no going around him."

They were both talking in generalities, and Connor had gone there looking for specifics. "I'm told he can be a real sonofabitch," he observed.

"You're being way too kind," Higgins said with what could only be described as a chortle. "That motherfucker likes to think he hit a home run in business, but he forgets he was born on third base."

"Because his father started the company?"

"Well, sure, there's that, and he did turn it around when he got control of it. But his momma was the one brought money into that family. Tobacco heiress whose lucre goes way back."

"You don't see that mentioned in his bio," Connor agreed.

"Not something he likes to admit. 'Self-made' has a better ring to it, and he likes people to think he's a real King Midas. The man with the golden touch, and if anything—anyone—ever got in his way, he'd just buy himself a new loophole or kill off a pesky law. Or a lawmaker."

"Seriously?" Connor asked.

"Figuratively," the old man replied with a nod and a shrug at the same time. "But maybe literally, too. Nothing in this state is sacred. Or as it seems. Politics has always been about the flow of money, and Lomax is a master at controlling the spigot. And I can tell you, no other bastard has killed more political ambitions in this state, destroyed the lives of a lot of good men. A few women, too. Rumors, innuendoes, lies—they're all his power tools, and he wields them like a pro."

"How does Garrett Tipton fit in?"

"Tipton's nothing more than his chew toy *du jour*, a means to an end," Higgins observed. "Fact is, Lomax's all about power, always has been. *Quid pro quo*. This for that. If Garrett gets to the White House, Colt will have the douchebag's testicles in a vice."

Connor winced at the mental image, said, "Sounds painful."

"It will be, and Garrett knows it. Or should. Problem is, he's so blinded by ambition he can't see the train coming at him. And by the time he does, it might be too late."

"Too late for what?"

"To avoid the chaos Lomax's capable of," Higgins explained. His right hand lay motionless on the armrest of his chair, but his left was trembling like a dog that had just been rescued from a frozen pond. "Between you and me, the guy misplaced his marbles years ago. Four of his staffers who were caught up in that January sixth thing, and he paid their lawyer's fees. Word is, he's funding some of the dark groups that are calling for blood in the streets."

"You mean, like civil war?"

"Lomax craves power the way a heroin addict craves his next high," Higgins said. "I believe he's working his way toward a major overdose."

Too many of Connor's buddies had travelled that very path with opioids, and had hit that point of no return. A few were lucky to find their way back, but most had been buried by wives or mothers or fathers who were left behind to try to make sense of it all.

"And when that happens?" he asked.

"I hope the good Lord takes me before it does."

"A minute ago you said there's no going around Lomax," Connor said, attempting to steer him back on track. "What do you think he's capable of if someone did?"

The old lawyer fell quiet for a moment, as if he was giving the question some serious thought. Then he asked, "You've already come up against him, haven't you?"

"Indirectly," Connor said.

"And that's the real reason you're here."

"The real reason is that several people are dead, and I think Lomax's hands have blood on them."

Higgins stared at Connor with his steel-blue eyes, partially obscured by a fold of skin shadowing his brow. "Here's the deal…what did you say your name was, Mr.—?"

"Connor."

"Right. Connor. So, Mr. Connor…I'm going to tell you what you really came here to learn. Although you may not have realized it. Whoever it was told you to talk to me, probably told you I ran a lot of campaigns in my day. State level, although a couple were national. Anyway, there was this one fellow—I'm not going to tell you his name—who ran for a state senate seat. Special election, and he beat out five other candidates. Then he won again, with almost two-thirds of the vote. Now, this guy didn't get elected on account of his good looks, or because he was a great campaigner. Hell, he wasn't even a *good* campaigner. But he had me, and I got him to Columbia."

"The man behind the scenes pulling the strings," Connor said.

"Well, I never looked at myself as a puppet master, but essentially you're right. Some of these assholes who run for office don't know squat about shooting their mouths off, or keeping their peckers in their pants. But that's not the end of the story. You see, this guy—a two-term senator—got a little power hungry and decided he'd make a good lieutenant governor. Which, as everyone in this state will tell you, is just one small step away from the top job. He had experienced people in place, and enough money to make a good run at it. Plus he was ahead in the polls right up to a week before the primary, and then—*wham*! He was blindsided."

Connor was worried Byram Higgins might be experiencing another aneurism. His skin had grown pale and his left hand—the good one—was now shaking almost violently on the arm rest of the wheelchair. But he let the man continue, because he knew he had about four minutes to go, and daughter Adrienne was sure to appear right on schedule.

"All of a sudden a story hit the news cycle about how Mr. Senator had used money from an escrow account at his law firm to pay off gambling debts."

"And these rumors were lies, I assume?" Connor asked.

"There was no evidence at all, no witnesses who would talk on the record," Higgins replied. "Just 'he said,' 'she said' bullshit that mysteriously went away the day after he lost. Nothing more than a Goddamned whisper campaign."

"And Colt Lomax ties in to all this how?" Connor asked, bringing him back around to the reason he was there.

"He ties in because Mr. Senator wouldn't support a bill that would relax the regulations covering the processing of waste from poultry farms. Lomax was just cutting his teeth on strong-arming elected officials, and he'd offered a comfortable cash infusion to the campaign. Under the table, all hush-hush. When my guy declined, Colt threatened to have him thrown off the committee that was considering the bill. Didn't budge an inch, and five days later the article ran in the paper. His opponent went on to win the election, and the following spring South Carolina got a new law that allowed raw chicken sludge to be dumped into open holding ponds no matter how close they were to rivers or homes."

"Empires are built upon the backs of the people you defeat on your way to the top," Connor pointed out.

"Precisely, and Lomax is more twisted and evil than Mephistopheles on his darkest day," Higgins agreed. "Capable of anything if he believes he's been crossed."

"Extortion and corruption?"

"Without a doubt."

"What about murder?" Connor asked.

Again, Higgins seemed to give considerable thought to the question before answering. "Let me put it this way," he finally said. "Six weeks after my senator lost, he and his wife were driving home from a Christmas concert in Columbia. A car ran them off the road and both of them were killed. Left behind a son and a daughter, who had to be raised by grandparents."

"And the driver of the other car?"

"Never caught," Higgins said. "And I'll just leave it at that."

Chapter 23

More than two weeks after the shooting, SLED still had no solid leads. Or at least nothing Burdette had shared with Connor, other than the basics about Lyle Hicks. Willis Ronson had already been cremated, and Cherine Dupree was set to be released from rehab in just a few days. Jimmy Brinks hadn't made another cryptic appearance at the bar, and Clooney maintained his habit of lying in the corner of the drinking deck, watching lizards scurry across the floorboards.

On a Tuesday afternoon Connor was using the dumbwaiter to haul cases of beer upstairs from the street-level storage room when his phone rang. It was Caitlin Thomas, who said, "You still looking into the Willis Ronson hit?"

Truth was, with Lyle Hicks on the loose, Connor's priorities had shifted. And multiplied. Yes, the gunmen who had killed Ronson remained in the wind, and he considered them a very real threat. But Hicks had made a grisly statement by murdering his former attorney and making threats against his wife. Given Connor's unprovoked attack on him, a return visit was only a matter of time.

"Among other things," he said.

"Things like Liz Morgan?"

"I'm thinking she's probably a dead end," he told her.

"You might want to think again," Caitlin said. "I've been doing a little more digging and came up with something."

"Something like what?" he asked.

"A real name, for starters. I can't prove it, but I think she's actually an ATF agent named Brenda Buckner working out of the field office in Columbia."

"Seriously?" he said. "You've spoken with her?"

"Not directly. But someone who shouldn't have been talking to me said Ms. Buckner had been working undercover on the theft of weapons from

Camp Lejeune north of Wilmington. Thing is, she hasn't been seen or heard from in weeks—not since around the time Ronson was killed—and a lot of people are getting nervous."

"Brenda Buckner," Connor said, running the name through his brain so he wouldn't forget it. "Have you tried finding her?"

"Please," Caitlin replied, in such a way that he could sense her rolling her eyes. "I've already located her house up in Chapin, ran what I could of her credit records, checked the DMV database. Found an email address and two phone numbers, but when I called them all I got was squat."

"You think Willis Ronson was in cahoots with her?" he asked.

"Makes more sense than an old flame trying to hop in the sack with him. Did Mrs. Ronson say when they met?"

Connor thought back to what Donna had mentioned, something about how Liz Morgan —possibly Brenda Buckner—had written to Willis when he was doing time in Bennettsville. Six, seven years ago. *A sicko inmate pen pal thing*, was how she'd described it.

"The first time he was in prison," Connor said. "Two years for B and E, sentence chopped almost in half."

"Think Buckner could've dangled a carrot, convinced him to become a confidential informant?"

"It's as good a theory as any," he replied. "If we can find her, we also might find out why she squirreled him away to that motel up in Andrews."

Caitlin nodded slowly, then frowned as a look of confusion crept into her eyes. "You know what I don't get?"

"No, but I'm sure you're going to tell me."

"Wise-ass." She made the sound of someone passing gas, then said, "The thing is, if Ronson was working with the ATF on something, and it meant he had to jump bail, why didn't this Buckner woman work with his lawyer and the judge to get his court date postponed? That way he wouldn't have violated the terms of his bail, could have saved a lot of time and effort. And he might be alive today."

"Good point," Connor agreed. He was almost one hundred percent certain Liz Morgan had paid for Ronson's motel room, and had ordered mushrooms on her half of the take-out pizza. If Ronson had been working as a C.I. for the feds, was the attempted theft of copper wire from the transformer plant part of the original play? What role did Joey Barber have in the set-up, if anything? And, as Caitlin had suggested, why had the judge in the case not been informed of what the ATF was up to so he—or she—could issue a postponement?

"Don't suppose you can find out who presided over the case," he said.

"It's all public records," Caitlin replied. "You'll know as soon as I do."

The judge's name turned out to be Charles Huger, pronounced the Charleston way: *You-gee*.

Since it was a Tuesday, he was holding court at the J. Waties Waring Judicial Center in downtown Charleston. The building was named for the son of a Confederate soldier and early hero of the civil rights movement, a federal judge who'd had the audacity to denounce segregation as an "evil that must be eradicated." His strident—and unexpected—views helped pave the way years later for Brown v. Board of Education, a perspective that didn't go over very well with much of the local populace. Years later, however, when state lawmakers realized desegregation had become a *de facto* part of American life, the building was named in his honor. Much to the dismay of a full coterie of voters who remained torn by the rocks and bottles they and their parents has hurled at Black kids whose only sin was to try to get a good education.

Judge Huger was overseeing jury selection for a criminal trial, and was not available for a quick conversation. Not today and, as a bailiff made clear, he likely wouldn't be available tomorrow, either. Not until the case was over and done, and probably not even then. Connor was certainly welcome to come back any day—the courtroom was a public venue, and anyone could watch a trial from the gallery—but the odds of him getting a word with the Honorable Charles Huger were slim to none.

Connor considered waiting the judge out, maybe try to catch him in the hallway, but eventually figured it would be a waste of time. Ronson must have been one of dozens of cases on Huger's docket at the time, and it wasn't his job to keep track of each and every defendant. That's what court clerks and prosecutors were for, and if Ronson had been a no-show because he was involved with some sort of government sting, that was his problem, not the judge's. It was a loose end Connor couldn't ignore, like something stuck between his teeth that he just couldn't get at.

On the way home he called Cherine Dupree at Sea Island Rehab. She was making a remarkable recovery, and hoped to be home by the end of the week. No complications from the surgery, and her occupational therapy was progressing as well as could be hoped.

"I feel like a new woman, except I have the same old bills to pay," she'd told him. "What's up?"

"What can you tell me about the judge who presided over the Ronson matter?" Connor asked her, getting right to it.

She hesitated a second, then said, "Remind me who it was?"

"Charles Huger."

"Good 'ol Dixie boy and a real windbag," she said. "Why do you want to know?"

"Because something came up that doesn't make sense." He explained about Liz Morgan/Brenda Buckner's involvement with the ATF, and the theory that Ronson may have been a CI in some sort of government operation. "I thought maybe you had a line on Huger, might know something that could explain why he didn't postpone Ronson's hearing."

"Wait...back up a sec. You're saying my client was working with the feds?"

"Looks that way," Connor replied.

There was a stunned silence, and then Cherine started giggling. "Well, if that don't beat all," she said. "Willis Ronson, a jailhouse snitch. Just doesn't seem the type."

"You had no idea?"

"Like every other client, he got dropped in my lap," Cherine replied. "Luck of the draw. And he never said a word to me, not about that. But it could explain a lot of things, including the ambush."

"You think someone found out he was a C.I. and went gunning for him?"

"All of us," she reminded him. "But yeah...it's as good an explanation as any. Any idea what they had him working on?"

"No, and it's just conjecture at this point. But I suspect it could lead back to your guy, Joey Barber."

Cherine fell silent again, and Connor figured she was thinking this through, trying to make sense of what he was telling her. Eventually she said, "I can't help but think there's more to this than a stupid attempt to steal copper wire. That was just the tip of something a lot bigger."

Connor was already way out ahead of her, but kept his thoughts to himself. Instead, he said, "If Ronson was a snitch, wouldn't someone have alerted the judge on the down-low that he wasn't going to be able to make his court date?"

"One would think. Seems to me, someone dropped the ball."

The evening started off fast, especially for a Tuesday, but hit a lull a little after ten. Connor closed the bar not long after midnight, and was in bed an hour later.

The night was unseasonably chilly, with a steady wind from the southeast and low humidity. Perfect sleeping weather, so he left the windows open to let the cool breeze in. Clooney had no trouble quickly dropping into dreamland, but there were too many random anxieties colliding in Connor's head for him to do the same.

They began with the old chestnut: who shot Willis Ronson? Followed closely by, what had Liz Morgan/Brenda Buckner gotten him involved with? What was Joey Barber's involvement, and how did he fit in with the copper theft? Was it all part of a munitions operation, making homegrown bullets that couldn't be traced? Also, what was up with Barber's copycat plot to blow up a federal building? How did that play into this, if at all?

Topped off with, where the hell was Lyle Hicks?

All intertwined with misty images of Danielle Simmons, lovingly caressing her horses in a billowing swirl of a thick lowcountry fog.

Sleep eventually came, but it was fitful and fleeting, involving much tossing and turning and crazy visions that caused Connor's brain to come to a rolling boil. But sleep was sleep, and he took what he could get, until his phone abruptly rang on the nightstand beside the bed. His first thought was that good news never called at 2:47 in the morning, which was what the clock was signaling. Nor did he recognize the out-of-state number on the screen.

"What's wrong?" were the first words out of his mouth.

"Mr. Connor? This is Claire Windham. I'm Cherine's wife—"

Connor blinked the last thread of a dream from his brain and thought, *where did she get my number*? "Oh, yeah…I remember," he said. "What's up?"

"Well, the thing is, I'm out of town," Claire replied. He sensed her trembling, a thick fear in her voice. "Down in Birmingham, working on a Law Center thing. I just got a call from Cherie, and she said something was going on."

"What do you mean, going on?"

"At the rehab place. Loud noises, fighting down the hall. Alarms ringing, that sort of thing. She's afraid. Scared for her life."

"She told you that?"

"She didn't have to; I heard it in her voice. Look, if I were home, I'd drive over there, see what was going on. But I'm stuck down here—"

"Don't worry about it," Connor said. "I'll get over there as soon as I can."

"I hate to call you like this—"

"No worries," he told her. "I'm on my way, and I'll call you when I find out something."

"I…I thank you so much, Mr. Connor. I know it's late—"

"Right. And I need to hang up now so I can throw some clothes on."

"Got it. Please hurry."

"On my way."

There was no traffic and Connor drove as fast as he could, figuring the only cops on duty at this hour would be booking the drunk drivers they'd pulled over earlier. But there were no cop cars lying in wait for him, although he did pass one just as it was leaving Sea Island Rehab thirty minutes later as he was pulling in. Definitely an indication there'd been some kind of commotion that, whatever it was, appeared to have been subdued. He pulled into a parking space near the front entrance and cut the engine, then hobbled toward the front door.

He leaned on the buzzer, kept his finger pressed to it until a man in a guard's uniform eventually came lumbering around the corner into the lobby. He waved his arms at Connor as he approached, indicating he couldn't come in.

"No visitors," he said into a speaker mounted just inside the door. He was white, a little under six feet, buzz-cut with gray eyes and King Charles ears. Not the guy named Quinn, with whom he'd spoken a couple days before. "Come back in the morning."

"A friend of mine is a patient here," Connor said into a pinhole microphone on his side of the glass. "She called me, said there was a brawl." A bit of a stretch, but the guard didn't need to know about Claire Windham.

"Nothing to worry about, sir," the guard tried to convince him.

It didn't work. "The police were called. I just saw them leave. So I'll ask again: what's going on?"

"I'm not at liberty to say. Like I said, come back in the morning."

"It *is* the morning," Connor pointed out, gesturing toward an analog clock with hands on the lobby wall. Three-twenty-two.

"Just a misunderstanding, is all," the guard insisted. "Rest assured, the place is secure."

"Secure from what?"

"Everyone. Now go home."

Connor stood there, powerless to do anything, not sure there was anything to be done. The grounds around Sea Island Rehab appeared to be quiet. No police, not now. No one trying to get in, no one causing a commotion. Whatever Cherine Dupree had called Claire about seemed to either have subsided, or had been a non-starter.

"I'm on my way," he told the guard. "Appreciate your help."

He slowly trudged back to his car, where he keyed the engine to life. In the rearview mirror he saw the sentry studying him through the glass, before eventually retreating further inside the building. Once Connor was sure he was no longer watching, he pulled through the parking space as if he were leaving.

Instead of driving home, however, he circled through the lot, then backed to the far edge of the parking lot and slipped into a dark space beneath the weeping branches of a willow. Same one as the other day when he visited the security manager named Quinn. If he was lucky, the rest of the night would remain quiet and he might be able to snag a few hours of much-needed sleep before the sun began filtering through the surrounding pines a couple hours from now.

He tilted his seat back until he could barely see over the dashboard, then hit the redial function on his phone. Claire Windham picked it up on the first ring and said, "Mr. Connor… what's the word?"

"Nothing, at least not now," he told her. "The cops were here earlier, but they're all gone. Everything seems nice and quiet."

"Where are you?"

"Parked under a tree, keeping an eye on things. Just in case."

"Just in case of what?"

"I don't know. Whatever. You want me to call Cherine, tell her everything's okay?"

"No…let me do that," Claire said.

"She doesn't know you called me, does she?"

"I didn't know what else to do. I asked her for your number, but didn't tell her why I wanted it. How long are you going to stay parked under that tree?"

"As long as I have to."

"Okay. Good. And thanks. I wasn't too sure about you, first time we met."

"And now?"

"First impressions are made to be changed."

About thirty minutes later Connor was awakened from a light sleep when a vehicle thumped over a speed bump at the street entrance, its headlights suspiciously off. It slowly cruised on a lazy arc through the lot, past the cluster of cars belonging to the skeleton crew. It was a pick-up truck, make and model not immediately discernible in the night, but as it circled around toward the double doors, he recognized the ribbed tailgate of a newer model Ford F-150.

It slowed to a halt just shy of the portico roof that protected visitors from the weather, and sat there with its engine running. Tinted glass and the prevailing darkness obscured whoever was inside, and the angle at which Connor had parked his car eliminated any chance of making out even a single digit of the license number. He'd planned on sleep, not surveillance.

The truck—black or dark gray—sat there for a good five minutes, not moving. Then it began to inch forward, through the *porte cochere*, and made an abrupt turn that, if it kept moving, would bring it within a few yards of where Connor was hunkered down. He lowered himself even further in his seat and studied the pick-up as it slowly edged past, and this time he could see the silhouette of a man in the truck cab. The guy was facing forward, keeping one hand on the wheel while glancing at something that seemed to glow in the other.

A cellphone.

He didn't appear to notice Connor as he rolled toward the exit. Still no lights, but just before he disappeared from view the moon peeked through a gap in the clouds, casting a sliver of light across the tailgate. Not sufficient to give him anything from the license plate, but more than enough to illuminate the vinyl sticker affixed to the bumper:

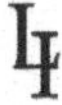

Same logo as on the ragged patch Connor had found at the crash site out on Indigo Road, same as on every page of the Lomax Industries website. Every package of Lomax chicken that rolled off the production line. And now here, on a truck prowling through the dark parking lot at the rehab facility where Willis Ronson's attorney was recovering from a gunshot that had almost killed her.

Right above another sticker with the now-familiar black oval outline:

Chapter 24

Chalk it up to impulse, a reckless streak, or the lingering effects of the gin he'd had earlier, there was no hesitation. No second-guessing. Not a doubt in his mind.

Connor followed it.

He gave the truck a good fifty yards before he fell in behind it. Lights off, not an issue at this early hour as both vehicles moved past the oaks and sweet gum until they hit a two-lane road that bisected the old maritime forest. The pick-up came to a rolling stop at the intersection, then turned right at the same instant its blue halogens flashed on. Connor hung back a few seconds, figuring at this late hour it couldn't be too difficult to keep tabs on a single set of taillights a couple hundred yards ahead of him. His real problem was when to turn on his own beams which, with the lack of traffic, would immediately appear suspicious in the F-150's rearview mirror.

He elected to keep them off until they came to the next major intersection. Following another rolling stop, the truck made a left turn onto another road that would take it toward the junction with Highway 17, the major north-south route through coastal Carolina. At that point the driver would either be forced to pull straight ahead into a residential neighborhood, or turn left or right. If he chose the latter, Connor would have a good idea where he was headed.

He did.

The traffic light turned red before Connor got there. He looked both ways, then blew through it, finally switching his headlights on as he completed the turn. Up ahead at the next intersection, the truck edged into the left lane and turned onto Highway 41, and once again Connor followed. For the next thirty minutes both vehicles cut through the darkness of the national forest, Connor taking care to hang back as far as possible until they got a few miles past the Jamestown crossroads. At that point he flicked off his lights again and inched up behind the F-150, waiting for it to make the turn off the main drag onto the county road he knew eventually would lead to the expansive tract of land owned by Lomax Industries.

The truck continued along the narrow blacktop a couple more miles. Then the brake lights blinked on as it swung onto a dirt track that cut off to the left and snaked through the pines. Muddy tracks indicated that several vehicles had driven through since the last rain had fallen, and even in the pre-dawn darkness Connor recognized it from his own excursion out here.

He drove right past, found the same hiding spot as last time on the other side of the road, and backed into the trees as far as his vehicle would go. By now he'd had close to an hour to sort through all the reasons why a Lomax pick-up had come to Sea Island Rehab in the middle of the night. Each time he concluded there was only one: to get to Cherine Dupree. Killing her in the hospital downtown might have proven to be difficult, but penetrating security at a small facility out in the middle of the boondocks? Not so much.

Which begged a further question: what was the commotion that had caused her to call Claire, who then had called Connor? Why had the cops been summoned? Had the man in the truck tried to gain entry earlier but maybe panicked, decided to make another attempt later, after the police were gone? And then got spooked, made a phone call, and drove all the way back out here?

Too many questions, and not enough answers. Certainly not one that would even come close to explaining what Connor was doing out here, and what he was about to do next.

The engine ticked as it cooled in the evening chill. Connor climbed out of the SUV, then gently nudged the door closed with his hip. He would have preferred to have locked it, but was concerned that the automatic chirp might pierce the silence of the woods. He moved as fast and stealthily as his swollen ankle and sprained ribs would allow, his eyes set on the gate where the F-150 had passed through just a moment before. He imagined the eyes of bears, coyotes, bobcats, even alligators fixed on him as he slipped across the roadway, nothing but a vast, haunting silence in all directions. Not a gust of wind, or a flicker of movement. Just an eerie, quiet stillness that had settled across the land.

He approached the gate, saw it was constructed of eight-foot hurricane fencing with a spool of razor wire coiled on top. Impossible to get over without a ladder or a length of rope, but boot camp had prepared him for such things. He looked left and right, arbitrarily settled on the latter and picked his way through the thick underbrush along the chain link until he eventually came to a water oak with a low limb that arced upwards and over the concertina wire. Even with his ankle throbbing he was up and over in under thirty seconds, easing himself to the forest floor with nothing more than a quiet rustle of leaves.

Once again Connor found himself crawling through briars and vines as he inched his way back toward the dirt road. He was just about to emerge from the brush when the scraping of boots alerted him to a sentry walking toward him. One slow step in front of the other, the glare of his cellphone illuminating his face. Paying no attention to his surroundings, working on a text to his girlfriend, or maybe playing *Call of Duty*.

Connor waited until the guy was a good fifty yards up the road, then followed along behind, keeping his profile low and muffling his footfalls. He kept close to the thick scrub in case he needed to make a quick retreat, but figured the guard was either too bored or too tired to spot him. Probably both.

He moved along the edge of the dirt track a yard at a time, keeping both ears tuned for the sound of voices or more footfalls. Twice he thought he heard the guard returning, causing him to duck into the underbrush, but both times turned out to be false alarms.

Eventually the trees gave way to a clearing about the size of four football fields. He crouched down as low as he could and tried to figure out what he was looking at: no lights, no trucks, no structures. Just acres and acres of unmown grass, and an array of earth mounds situated in a rough circle about a hundred yards across. The lack of light made it difficult to determine their size, but they appeared to be maybe fifteen feet high and twice that from one end to the other.

By now Connor was a good hundred yards inside the fence, thankful the clouds were cooperating but worried that first light might appear soon. His watch told him it was a little after five, and this time of year sunrise came before six. Maybe his eyes were playing tricks on him, but he was beginning to detect a subtle definition to the trees in the east.

The air was cool and quiet. No crickets, no wind. Dark enough for the grackles and crows to be asleep, no food yet to be scrounged. Not even the murmuring of voices from the armed guards he suspected were in the compound with him. He hoped to hell they weren't equipped with night vision glasses.

Connor slowly creeped his way toward the nearest of the earthen mounds, remaining as close to the ground as possible. His earlier height estimate turned out to be accurate, as it sloped gently upwards to a crest of about five yards at the summit. He edged around the low knoll, obviously manmade, spotted several trucks parked near a similar mound on the other side of the flat field. Including, it appeared, the F-150 Connor had followed from Sea Island rehab. There was no sign of movement, no lights, no odor of smoke that would suggest a fire or cookstove. Or cigarettes.

He retreated back to the far side of the mound and slipped into a tangle of brush and briars, just enough not to be detected by a passing guard. Something was gnawing at the back of his brain, something that reminded him of his FOB outside Kirkuk.

A few minutes later the sky to the east began to take on a lighter hue, and Connor heard the first stirrings of human life. A truck door slammed, and sixty seconds later a vehicle rolled around the edge of the encampment and pulled onto the dirt track that led back through the trees to the razor-wire gate out by the county road.

Connor didn't know what he was seeing, and he realized it was pointless to hang around. He had sworn off this reckless craziness, yet he continued to place himself in situations that were beyond his control. He also seemed to have an angel sitting on his shoulder, watching out for him when he got tangled up in shit that wasn't his. Problem was, he knew that someday that angel would give up on him and seek a more responsible subject.

He was just getting ready to pack up and go home when he heard another rumbling. This one was different: louder and throatier and smellier, as the first hint of diesel fumes hit his nose. He remained in the scrub, hunched as low as he could as it got closer and closer. Eventually the source of it came into view, and it was nothing that he'd been expecting.

It was a full-sized passenger bus, white with red and gold graphics on the side, large block lettering that read "American Trail Tours." All but the front windows were covered with a material that Alex Reeves had described as vinyl perf, a material honeycombed with holes that adhered to glass so passengers could see out, but no one on the outside could see in. As it pulled close, he was convinced it was the same bus he'd seen being wrapped when Connor had swung by the vinyl shop over a week ago.

What was it doing here? Dropping off new recruits, or picking up trained soldiers?

The bus followed the ill-defined dirt road out of the trees and into the compound, bouncing over the hardened ruts toward the complex of mounds. Connor instinctively decided to follow it, moving along behind in a low crouch until it made a gentle turn and headed toward the clearing in the center of the complex. At that point he ducked in behind a cluster of fuel drums, spray-painted in military camo, providing good cover from which to observe whatever was about to go down.

The vehicle made a broad turn through the compound and eventually slowed to a stop in front of one of the mounds. Dawn was close enough to yield enough light for Connor to make out a set of steel doors, not unlike those of a metal shipping container, that seemed to open out from the large hillock. A few seconds later, two men dressed in camo fatigues climbed out of a matching SUV and approached the bus. The side door swung open with a hiss, and one of the men appeared to have a few words with the driver. The bus then pulled around the compound in a tighter circle, then backed it up until it was just a couple yards from the earthen bunker.

Connor expected to see passengers either emerge from the bus or file into it, but neither of those things happened. Instead, the vehicle idled there for a few minutes until the men opened the double steel doors, exposing a large storage area set into the side of the manmade hill. Someone flicked a switch and the interior was bathed in a low glow, revealing row upon row of stacked blue storage drums.

The driver climbed down from the bus, and soon all three men were using hand trucks to move the containers from the underground depot to a ramp that had been extended up through the front doorway into the bus. They maneuvered them one at the time into the darkness, until all of them had been moved inside. Sixty-four, at Connor's count.

What the hell? he thought, and then his mind went back to what he'd read about Joey Barber's fascination with Timothy McVeigh. The barrels of highly explosive ammonium nitrate fertilizer, and the manifesto he'd downloaded from the dark web. All apparently part of a thwarted plot to blow up a courthouse up in Columbia.

Connor had seen enough. If luck was with him, there was some sort of cell signal out here in the middle of bumfuck nowhere. If he could make it back to the trees and dial nine-one-one. He was just starting to turn around to make his exit, when something hard came down on the back of his head, sucking his brain into a dark, black hole.

Chapter 25

Not once in his entire time in the U.S. Army had Connor been in the brig. Never had seen it, nor had he ever experienced the inside of a jail until he'd been falsely accused of receiving a quarter pound of weed via Fed Ex a few years back. Set up by an arrogant thug whose ego he'd damaged, and then was summarily released as soon as the matter had been cleared up and dismissed by the magistrate. With a little persuasion on the part of Jordan James.

In any event, the hole he now was in was far worse than what he'd ever envisioned a brig to be. Cold, damp, dark, except for a dim bulb glowing from an overhead socket. Mold growing on the walls, moisture seeping through seams in the ceiling where sheets of sheet metal had been riveted together. Dripping on his head, cold rivulets of water trickling through his hair and down his neck. It reminded him of an old cistern he'd been trapped in once, nothing but darkness and water up to his knees and living creatures slithering in the darkness that turned out to be frogs.

Whatever this shit box was, Connor felt a steady pounding at the base of his skull where he'd been cold-cocked with what felt like a tire iron. He couldn't tell if he was bleeding, because his hands were bound together with zip-ties. Same thing with his ankles. And something sticky—he presumed it was duct tape—was pressed across his mouth.

His eyes had difficulty adjusting as he began to come around. Everything was fuzzy and out of focus, which he connected to the blow to his head. Or maybe some kind of drug he'd been given to keep him sedated. He kept blinking, hoping that maybe the flutter of his eyelids would reboot his vision, but it didn't work.

His nose did, however, and it told him that wherever he was being held prisoner, sewage was nearby. His cell reeked of it. Urine and feces, enough to make him gag if his mouth hadn't been taped shut.

He had no idea how long he'd been lying there. His watch had been stripped from his wrist, and he couldn't feel his phone in his pocket. Same as the two guns he'd taken from his bedroom closet before leaving home. The only source of light was the overhead bulb, low wattage flickering as if it might change its mind and go dark any second.

Eventually Connor's eyesight began to adjust, and he started to soak in some elements of his surroundings. First, he was in a bunk. Steel frame, thin mattress, soiled and thick with body odor. Another bunk was above him and, judging from his distance to the floor, one more was beneath him. A square of sheet metal had been welded to the wall next to him, and across a narrow aisle were three more bunks, and more steel.

As his throbbing brain processed these disparate elements, he began to realize where he was: An abandoned bus, stripped and refitted, just as he'd seen in the video Donna Ronson had sent him. Probably located in one of the earthen mounds where he'd been watching the workers load those large drums into the tour bus, just before someone had come up from behind and shellacked him. It wasn't the first time he'd been attacked from behind and tossed in a dungeon, and he figured the odds of escaping this place were mind-bogglingly slim.

Someone notable—Connor couldn't remember who—once said the baseline of optimism is sheer terror. Now, as he lay there on that stinky mattress in a bus that smelled like a pit toilet, every worst torture scene in every movie he'd ever seen came back all at once. So did memories from high school history involving Nazis and demented doctors experimenting on prisoners. None of those images imparted a sense of confidence, and when thoughts of Dr. Mengele began flashing through his mind, he knew he had to get out of there.

The big question was *how*?

Connor closed his eyes, tried to slow his breathing to a relaxed rate, as he'd learned to do during meditation classes at the VA. Hard to do, considering the spasms of pain ricocheting through his head. After a few minutes the pounding began to subside, and a comforting feeling of calm settled over him. So far so good, except part of his brain knew he was working against time. Whoever had brought him here and tied him up would be coming back, either hours from now or in mere seconds.

Keeping his respiration even and steady, he allowed his mind to drift to one of the hundreds of random YouTube videos he habitually wasted far too much time with. Clips that depicted everything from amazing football plays to scenes from *The Sopranos* to road rage drivers. One of them featured a young woman who had escaped from zip-cuffs after a stranger snatched her from the street and stashed her in a basement, presumably to be sexually assaulted. It was a real-time re-enactment that showed how she had removed a shoelace from one of her sneakers, then used her mouth to slip it around the tie that bound her wrist. After that she pulled it back and forth quickly, creating enough friction to soften the plastic. The strategy worked because her shoes had been left on her feet, and her hands hadn't been bound to a pipe or a headboard.

Connor's captors clearly hadn't watched the video.

It took him several minutes to contort his twisted body far enough to remove a lace through the eyelets of his left shoe. Two more to then work it through the zip-tie that bound his wrists, then pull it back and forth quickly to create enough heat. Once his hands were clear it was easier to free his ankles and pull the tape from his mouth, but the clock was ticking. He had no idea how much time he had until his captors returned, and it didn't take much imagination to figure out that, when they did, he wasn't going to get out of there alive.

When he was done, he quickly re-laced his shoe, then pushed off the bunk and stood up on wobbly legs. His head was pounding, and a lump the size and texture of a peach had formed at the base of his skull, causing him to wince when he touched it. Lesson: don't touch it. His vision had gradually returned, and now it was the vile stench that dominated his senses as he glanced around the bus.

"Holy Christ," he swore, trying not to gag. "What the fuck is this place?"

When he'd watched the second of Ronson's videos, he'd seen the men enter through the rear emergency exit, then shuffle up the aisle and exit through the right front door. He had no idea how many buses might be entangled in this underground warren, but logic suggested the way out was via the rear, through whatever rusted vehicles were connected behind it.

He started to move in that direction, when he heard a feeble voice call out. Tired, scared, and seemingly at death's doorstep. A woman's voice, the thinnest thread of hope seeming to separate her from life and whatever was on the other side.

"Please...help me—"

It was coming from the other direction, probably the next bus forward in this crazy underground labyrinth. Connor's impulse was to get out of there before his captors returned, but his instinct told him to help whoever was crying out to him. He also intuitively suspected who it was before he was able to get to her.

He followed her cries and found her at the front of the next bus, bound in the fetal position in the space where the driver's seat should have been. It had been removed, as were the gas and brake pedals, and two sets of heavy-duty rings had been bolted to the steel frame. A withered and terrified woman was shackled to them, her wrists and ankles raw from where she had pulled and strained against tempered chains secured with padlocks. She shrank back when she saw him, eyes wide with fear, not knowing if Connor was friend or foe.

"Don't be afraid," he assured her. "I'm here to help you."

She didn't say a word, her body shaking as if she were experiencing a seizure.

"Hang in there," he told her. "I'm going to get you out of here."

She stared at Connor as if death were just seconds away. Her face was battered and bruised, and blood had dried where it had streamed from her nose and mouth. A large welt had been opened up along her cheek, and she had a pair of black contusions, one under each eye. Even in her cramped position he could see that one of her ankles was twisted into a pretzel position, and several of her fingers appeared to be dislocated.

"Liz Morgan?" he asked her. "Or should I say, Brenda Buckner?"

She dropped her head in the slightest of nods, then whispered, "They're going to kill me."

"Who has the key?" he asked as he knelt down beside her. His head was thumping like a jackhammer, but he knew her own pain had to be considerably worse.

"Guards."

"Let me see those locks," Connor said.

All she could do was tremble as he leaned forward to see what kind of security he was up against. Not good news. They both said Arbus Titanium, which meant they would hold tight against anything except the proper key. Definitely not a bolt-cutter or hacksaw, neither of which just happened to be lying around, anyway.

Connor grabbed one of the steel rings, taking care not to twist her bloodied wrist any more than it already was. He gave it a firm pull, felt not a micron of give. He tried the same thing with her ankle shackles, this time felt a little more play. They were fastened tight, but enough strength and patience might give him a shot at working them free from the wall.

But that was going to have to wait, because just then he heard a faint clang echo through the maze of buses, near where he imagined the exit to be.

"Gotta go," he told her. "I'll be back to get you when I can."

Not something she wanted to hear. "Don't leave me—"

"Just stay quiet," he said, keeping his voice to a whisper.

"But—"

He touched a finger to her scabbed lips and said, "Shhh." Then he hobbled back the way he'd come, pulling himself back up onto his bunk just seconds before a guard burst through the rear exit and climbed up into the bus.

Connor had stretched out in the same position as when he'd awakened a few minutes ago, his hands and feet positioned as if the zip-cuffs still tightly bound them. He closed his eyes, pretending to be asleep, but cracked one slightly as he sensed the man coming closer.

"Wakey-wakey," the approaching guard taunted him. Camo jeans, camo T-shirt, military grade cap embroidered with the **2AM** emblem. "Time for a little fun."

Connor remained silent and mentally assessed his situation. He was no former Navy SEAL, no boxing champ, no barroom brawler. It had been years since he'd been in a real fight, and even longer since his hand-to-hand combat training in boot camp. Over the last few years, he'd let a lot of his muscle mass go slack, although on a good day he could pound out three miles on the sand with little effort. Five, if he really pushed it.

Trouble was, this was not a good day. He'd just been beat to shit and bound to a bunk. Every inch of his body ached, and his head was jackhammering. He was at a clear disadvantage, and had no idea what this ass-wipe had in mind—at least not until he noticed the electric chainsaw in his left hand.

"That's right, fucker," the guy said, a broad grin showing a mouthful of crooked teeth. "Time to lose a few pounds the quick way."

With that he flicked the button that started the motor. It came to life with an unnerving whir, not the loud roar Connor remembered from the Texas massacre movies. Then, from one bus over, Brenda Buckner screamed, "No—"

Her voice could barely be heard over the noise of the electric motor, but that single word probably saved Connor's life. The guard instinctively glanced in the direction of the noise and, as he did, Connor shot out a foot that struck him in the chest. Not particularly hard, just enough to catch him by surprise. He momentarily lost his balance and the hand holding the saw swung up, the chain clattering off a metal support for one of the bunks. In the same instant his finger slipped off the throttle, and the engine cut out.

Connor leaped out of the bunk as fast as he could, catching the guy in the chin with his other foot. Again, not a hard kick, but it caused the guy to crack his head on the bunk behind him. For a second he was stunned, and Connor slammed him with the full force of his body. The bus aisle was narrow, no more than eighteen inches across, not enough space to get in more than a couple quick rabbit punches. He went for his nose, while the guard aimed a bit lower and tried to land a blow to Connor's gut. His fist flailed wide, and Connor followed through with an uppercut to the chin. He felt the wound on the back of his right hand rip open, but he could deal with that later.

If there was a later.

The guard was in much better physical condition, but Connor had the element of surprise on his side. He landed another right and a left, and the guard did the same in return. Connor rammed his head into the guy's skull, then spun around with as much of a roundhouse as he could manage. It landed squarely on the guy's ear and he yelped, so Connor did it again, then pivoted and cracked him with an elbow in the nose. Blood erupted from both nostrils, spraying across the bus wall and the nearby bunks. Connor took the opportunity to seize the guy's head in both hands and crunch it against the bunk frame. Hard.

The guard sank to his knees, whereupon Connor kicked him in the teeth. His head flew back, causing him to crumple to the floor. Connor kicked him one more time in the jaw, then rummaged through the guy's pockets, where he found a small ring of keys—including one that read *Arbus*. He also confiscated a cell phone and a pistol that said Ruger on the grip. Then he grabbed the chainsaw and made his way back to where Liz Morgan—Brenda Buckner—was huddled against the bus wall, wrists and ankles strained against her shackles.

He had her loose in thirty seconds, but her trouble didn't end there. She'd been bound in that position for so long—evidently set free only long enough to eat and to use the compost toilet—that her arms and legs were stiff and weak. She could barely move when he released her, and it took most of a minute just to get her on her feet.

"I don't think I can do this," she said at one point.

"You can't *not* do this," Connor urged her. He pulled one of her arms around his shoulder and gently hoisted her up, then grabbed the electric saw and slowly assisted her down the aisle to the rear exit.

In the next bus the security guard was blinking his eyes open. Connor took care of that with another vicious kick, then tore a length of sheet from one of the bunks and hogtied him. He wrapped another length around his own hand to stanch the blood. "Time to go," he said.

"Nazi pigs," Brenda said, getting her own feeble kick in, as well.

Turned out there were four buses between them and the start of the maze, where a doorway led to what Connor presumed was the opening in the mound he'd seen in the video. "This way," he said.

"How do you know?" she asked as they climbed out of the last bus through the rear exit.

"Later."

"At least tell me who you are—"

"Jack Connor."

She shook her head; the name meant nothing to her.

"I'm the bond runner who tracked down Willis Ronson," he explained. "I was transporting him back to jail when we were ambushed."

She pinched her eyes shut for a moment; when she opened them she said, "Oh my God. How is he?"

"Dead. Never had a chance."

"Oh, Christ. I had no idea—"

"Like I said, later," Connor interrupted her.

"Shit." She clamped her eyes shut, either from pain or anguish. When she opened them again she said, "He was down here…he shot video—"

"I know. What is this place, anyway?"

"Pure hell. I think it's where they keep the numb nuts who lose during their daily battlefield drills. They're pretty beat up when they get back. And angry."

Connor thought on that, said, "We really need to move."

"They're heavily armed out there—"

"That's how I ended up down here."

Liz Morgan looked momentarily confused, then said, "I don't think there's any cavalry coming."

"I was the cavalry."

"So what are you doing in here?" she asked him.

"I could ask you the same thing," Connor replied.

"They were waiting for me when I went to see Willis."

"At the motel?"

"Nearby," Buckner/Morgan replied.

"He was your C.I.?"

"Something like that. But can we do this later, like you said?"

"Sure." Connor peered through the doorway, saw it opened onto what appeared to be a large metal room. A box of some kind, with corrugated walls. Then it hit him: a shipping container, illuminated at the ceiling by yet another single bulb in a cage. "Looks like we're almost there."

"Where?" she wanted to know.

"Out of here."

"Then what?"

Good question. He edged into the metal box ahead of her, the Ruger in one hand, the chain saw in the other. The wood floor was smeared with muddy footprints and droplets of what appeared to be blood. The air was stagnant and quiet, and Connor helped ease the ATF agent against the wall as her lungs struggled for air.

The steel door that led outdoors was ajar, just enough to let in a line of sunlight from floor to ceiling. Which made sense if the guard had let himself in. Connor tried to sneak a peek through the crack, but didn't dare push it open any further. He had no idea what awaited them out there, although he suspected he was at the entrance of one of the half-dozen mounds he'd spotted earlier. Beyond that stretched a good hundred yards of clearing, all enclosed by a hurricane fence with razor wire on top, and patrolled by armed guards. How many of them, he didn't know, nor did he want to find out the hard way.

An image of Steve McQueen jumping a prison camp fence on a motorcycle flashed through his head.

"How are you holding up?" he asked Brenda.

"I need about a hundred Advil," she said. "Or a bottle of Scotch."

"As soon as we're out of here."

"Then what are we waiting for?"

Not to die, was the first quip that came to mind. But it actually was a good question, since someone else eventually would come to check on where his buddy was. They could wait here for that to happen, and Connor actually considered that option, figuring he could pick them off one by one as they entered. At some point, however, someone would get wise, and then the troops would converge in force.

Or he would run out of bullets.

He didn't answer her question, instead pushed the door just enough until the thin slice of light had expanded to about an inch. The narrow angle limited his field of vision, although he knew there had to be several guards patrolling the premises. Possibly one positioned just outside the door. He had no idea what time it was, or how many hours had passed since he'd been tossed in the hole. Nor did he hear any voices, although a dozen armed men were probably out there, wandering the perimeter or watching from some sort of guard post he hadn't noticed last night.

"You're sure you're up for this?" he asked Morgan/Buckner.

"Define *this*," she replied.

"We stay as calm—and low—as possible, and go for the trees."

"Then what?" she asked.

"Ask me when we get there."

He slowly pushed the door open a few more inches, and immediately caught movement to his left. A guard was approaching, just twenty yards away, wandering across the compound while staring at his phone. Probably not the same dumbass who'd been patrolling the perimeter last night, but it suggested these guys were bored. Nothing ever happened here, so they played games or chatted with girlfriends. Which this one seemed to be doing, until he got to the door and found it unlocked.

Connor gently pulled it closed, then moved Brenda as far to one side of it as he could. He didn't know what the security protocol in this camp was, hoped maybe the guy would just assume the other guard had left it unlocked when he'd entered a few minutes ago. Or maybe wondered why he hadn't already dragged Connor out in pieces.

Either way, the guy pulled the door open and called out "Earl," providing a name to the shit-kicked guard deep within the bowels of the bus maze. "You in there?"

When he got no response, he hesitated. The warren of buses didn't allow sound to carry very far, and he had no idea where Earl might be in the depths below. Maybe using his chainsaw on their new prisoner, or torturing the ATF bitch. Connor saw the fear in her eyes, and again touched a finger to her lips. She responded with a slight nod, but her entire body was trembling.

The guard did what any guard would do. He stepped into the steel container, far enough for Connor to see him. Far enough for him to see Connor, too, and in that instant he drew his gun.

But Connor already had Earl's Ruger out, and had the drop on him. He'd killed two men in Iraq, and had dispatched a few more in self-defense here at home. He tightened his finger across the trigger and gave it a firm pull.

The guard was blown back against the steel wall, then slid to the floor. Brenda screamed. Connor hesitated just a second, then approached the dead guard and bent down into a crouch. Felt for a nonexistent pulse, then shifted his gaze and looked him square in the eyes.

"Holy shit," he said.

"What?"

"I know this guy. Name's Joey Barber."

"Seriously?" Morgan said. "He's the sonofabitch who set up Willis Ronson, got him into Two A.M."

That caught Connor's attention and he asked, "Two A.M.? What do you know about that?"

"More than I'd like to," she replied. "Stands for Second Amendment Militia. Some homegrown terrorist group trying to liberate America from tyranny and remake it in their own sorry-ass image."

"That's what this is all about?" Connor asked.

"Yeah. Mass casualties and blood in the streets. They've been stealing weapons from military bases all over, and we've been trying to nail 'em for months."

"Well, it looks like we found them." Connor picked up Barber's gun—well-scuffed, with the word Springfield on the side—and wedged it into his waistband.

"Someone had to have heard the shot," she said, when she regained her composure.

"Probably."

"Think they'll come for us?"

"No doubt."

"Can I have a gun?"

"Can you shoot?"

She cast him a peculiar look and said, "I'm fucking ATF. What do you think?"

Chapter 26

They waited a good thirty seconds, but no one came. Then Connor heard a staccato volley of gunfire coming from the Joey Barber's pocket, sounding almost like the finale from *Scarface*. He fished out the dead man's phone and answered the call, cutting off the ringtone.

"Yo," he said.

"What the hell was that, Scissors?"

Confirmation of what he already knew. "Misfire," he answered, holding his hand over the pinhole microphone to muffle his voice. "Dropped my damned gun."

"Jesus fuck," was the response. "You okay?"

"Just pissed that I wasted a round."

"Yeah, well, be careful. You checking on Earl?"

"Heading in now." Trying to keep his words short and sweet. The fewer he uttered, the better.

"Okay. Just watch the trigger."

"You got it," Connor said, ending the call.

"What now?" Morgan/Buckner wanted to know. Still shivering as if in a deep freeze. "Maybe we can call nine-one-one?"

Not a bad thought, and he tapped in the digits before the screen went dark. Waited a couple seconds, then heard a three-toned signal, followed by a computer that said, "Your call cannot be completed as dialed."

"Shit," he said, trying it again. Same response.

"What?"

"Damned call won't go through."

Morgan/Buckner said nothing, just stole a quick glance at Joey Barber. Blood was pooling under his head, which caused her to quickly turn away.

The rising temperature inside the metal box indicated it was early afternoon. Sooner or later there the day's losers would be returning to the brig, and Connor wanted to be miles away before that happened.

"All right," he finally said. "Time to make our move."

"What's our plan?"

"How do you feel about running?"

"Better than dying."

Connor hadn't thought to take the camo jeans and T-shirt off Earl down below, only his gun and phone. But Scissors, who was lying just inside the closed door, was a different story. Even though half of Barber's face was gone, he quickly stripped him of his **2AM** clothing and insisted the ATF agent change into it.

"You've got to be kidding me," she said.

"I'll turn my back until you're done," he assured her.

"But—"

"Trust me," he assured her.

Morgan/Buckner realized any objection would be fruitless, so she worked quickly, then stuffed her hair up under the baseball cap that was gooey from all that blood. She shuddered as she tugged it on, but didn't say a word. Too much was at stake to complain.

"You're sure you can do this?" Connor asked her as he pulled the bill a little further over her eyes, in case someone might have a rifle scope trained on the front door as they exited.

"Not if we keep talking about it," she said. "Let's go."

They went.

He opened the door and they both slipped out into the steaming Carolina sun. The ATF agent had been cooped up underground for so long she was momentarily blinded and disoriented by the glare. She had no sense of where she'd been held, or what the terrain outside looked like. Connor had briefed her about the large clearing with the earthen mounds, the razor wire, and the approximate location of the gate, but she needed time to adjust herself to her surroundings.

"This way," he urged her, nodding in the direction where he hoped the narrow road led from the clearing through the woods toward the gate. "Fast, but not too fast."

She did a good job pretending to lead him away from the compound and across the field, as a guard might do. They managed about thirty yards before a voice on a bullhorn called out, "Barber? That you?"

Morgan raised her hand in recognition as they continued their steady march toward the tree line, which was about fifty yards ahead.

"Stop right there," the voice called out.

"Get ready to move," Connor whispered to her.

"Just say the word," she said.

It wasn't a word that it did; it was the crack of a gun that kicked them into gear. They both lurched forward, then to the left, then right, just as they'd planned before leaving the underground container. Harder to track them and target center mass if they were moving in a zig-zag pattern. Another shot rang out, and Connor spotted a sentry about a hundred yards to their left sighting down a rifle barrel at them. They kept charging through the tall grass, Brenda staggering more than running as they neared the woods. Thirty yards, twenty-five, twenty.

They had the weapons Connor had lifted off Earl and Barber, but there was no point in wasting ammo. Their assailants were well out of range of a handgun, and it was best to save their fire for when it was most needed. Which turned out to be a lot sooner than Connor had figured on.

When they got within fifteen yards of the woods a man stepped out from behind a large oak and shouted, "Hands up. Now."

They both froze as if they'd entered a mine field. Morgan had been leaning against Connor for support, and he felt her body tense from fear. She'd already confided that she could not go back down in that hole again, not under any circumstances. Now they were facing that very real prospect, which meant the next few seconds were critical.

"I said, hands in the air."

Not happening.

"Down," Connor whispered as he yanked her arm and tugged her to the ground.

She made an *oomph* sound as she dropped alongside him. An instant later there was another shot, this one coming from the man dead ahead of them.

"Don't move," he yelled.

"Stay down," Connor said as he sighted down the barrel of Earl's Ruger. The guard was too far away for him to aim with any accuracy, but he pulled the trigger anyway.

Twice.

The guard wasn't expecting return fire, and the blast forced him back into the trees. At the same time, another rifle crack came from behind them, and a puff of dirt kicked up through the grass a few feet away.

Rapid-fire gunfire after that, shots coming from the front, the rear, and both flanks. Connor felt something whiz over his head, hoped it was only a bumblebee or a dragonfly. Because they were lying prone in the grass, they were difficult marks to hit, but the bastards kept trying. And kept closing.

"Give it up," came the same voice over the bullhorn, which Connor sensed was coming closer across the field. "Hands in the air."

Neither of them was about to do that, but they'd run out of options. Connor wasn't sure if his life was starting to flash before his eyes, but his brain turned to Danielle, how he'd royally fucked things up by getting into situations just like this one. Death was coming at him from all sides, and all the mindless bravado and courage that had brought him to this point was nothing but horseshit. All that mattered now was a chance to say goodbye to the people he'd loved, but he'd gambled away every chip he'd ever had.

To prove what?

His thoughts went full circle back to Danielle again, and then another round of gunfire opened up. More bullets flew over their heads, keeping them pinned down. They couldn't move, dared not speak. Barely breathed.

"You have ten seconds to give yourselves up," came the bullhorn again, and the shooting ceased. Temporarily.

Bonnie and Clyde joined Butch and Sundance in Connor's mind.

Then another voice boomed across the field, this one through a much more powerful bullhorn. "Weapons down. Everyone on the ground. Now!"

Authority and power, no bullshit. No fucking around.

No one moved or spoke for a good ten seconds. Then a barrage of gunshots erupted from all directions, rapid bursts coming from the clearing on either side, some from the compound behind them, even more from the woods in front of them.

"Federal agents," boomed the amplifier. "Put your weapons down and place your hands on your heads. Immediately."

Federal agents? What the fuck?

A few more scattered shots were fired, followed by a period of confusion. Neither Connor nor Morgan could see what was happening, but a wild card had just been tossed on the table.

"Do. It. Now."

But the 2AM dumb-fucks didn't do it, instead deciding to engage in a full-on attack. Automatic rifles fired, magazines emptied, and a couple grenades were lobbed at nothing in particular.

Connor was convinced they were going to die. Liz/Brenda murmured words that sounded Biblical, something about the valley of the shadow of death. Then he realized the shooting from their left flank had stopped, and a few seconds later the right side fell eerily silent. The entire field did, except for the megaphone that said, "If you're anywhere out there, Jack Connor, get up on your Goddamned feet up and reach for the sky."

Nelson Burdette was beyond furious. Beyond apoplectic. Connor had crawled around behind his back, stepped all over his murder case. He'd caused the SLED investigator to put himself in harm's away, along with an untold number of federal law enforcement agents who could have lost their lives.

He demonstrated just how damned pissed he was by slapping cuffs on Connor's wrists and locking them as tight as he could. Then he sat him down hard in the field and began reading from a card, "You have the right to remain silent. Anything you say can and will be used against you in a court of law—"

Meanwhile a team of EMTs scrambled out of the woods and tended to Morgan/Buckner, who appeared to have passed out. They loaded her onto a stretcher and rushed her to an ambulance that had pulled in through the gate, waiting behind a line of black SUVs.

"You are in so much fucking trouble, Connor," Burdette snarled when he'd finished reading the Miranda card. "I'm going to throw so many books at you, it's going to feel like the entire Library of Congress fell on you."

"I guess saying I'm sorry won't cut it," Connor replied.

"It's your Goddamned guessing that almost got you killed. And a lot of good men."

"I know. The stupidest thing I've ever done."

"Stupid doesn't even come close. You're a goddamned moron."

"At least Liz Morgan is alive," he pointed out.

And there it was. Burdette couldn't deny that Connor had probably saved her life, even while he'd endangered many others. In fact, the ATF team probably had given her up for dead.

"Don't count on it being your 'get out of jail free' card."

"I'm not counting on anything," Connor said. "How'd you know where I was, anyway?"

"Because I knew you wouldn't stay out of this."

"What does that mean?"

Burdette glanced around, as if trying to make sure no one was within earshot. Then he leaned in close and said, "It means I put a GPS tracker on your vehicle."

"When?"

"After you went back to the motel. And it was legal. I just knew that sooner or later you'd do something totally dumbass, and I wanted to know where you were when you were doing it."

Connor had nothing of substance to say. He'd violated Burdette's trust, probably obstructed justice, and lied to him outright. Like a teenager caught in a grand deception, he deserved no leniency. No mercy. But he was curious about something, so he said, "Took you long enough to find us."

"You're damned lucky we're here at all," Burdette bristled. "Someone else got to your car first."

"Meaning?"

"Your friends here torched it."

Shit. Connor thought he'd been clever, backing it far off the highway so no one would find it. But that was last night—this morning—in the depths of darkness, in the middle of the woods. At that point he hadn't intended to be here in the heat of day. Hadn't planned anything.

"How bad?" he wanted to know.

"Do the words 'totally incinerated' mean anything?"

The car ultimately belonged to Jordan James, but Connor would have to pay the deductible, as well as anything his own insurance wouldn't cover.

"I need to tell you something else," he said. "It's important."

"Save it."

"I'm serious," Connor insisted. "There's a bus. A big one, the kind that drives tourists up and down the coast. I saw them load a bunch of barrels into it."

"So the fuck what?"

"I think it was ammonium nitrate."

"How would you know?"

"Big blue containers, maybe a hundred pounds each."

"Shit," Burdette said, glancing up at a turkey vulture circling high overhead. "When the hell was this?"

"What day is it?"

"Wednesday."

Good; Connor had only been unconscious for a few hours. "Just before dawn. I know I fucked up big time, but I think these shitheads are planning something epic."

"Why should I believe anything you have to say?"

"You have good reason not to. But these 2AM assholes are experienced in explosives—"

"Wait. Two AM?"

"Second Amendment Militia," Connor explained. "And if that bus is a rolling bomb… well, you've got to find it."

Burdette stared at him for a good ten seconds, then retreated back across the field to consult with a couple of dark suits with the letters FBI on their vests. They spoke for maybe a minute, then Burdette marched back to where Connor was sitting in the grass.

"You and I are going for a ride," he said. Matter of fact, no emotion or affect.

"Where to?"

"You'll find out when we get there."

Chapter 27

Connor rode in the back of Burdette's GMC Yukon—cuffs off but doors automatically locked—to the Williamsburg County Law Enforcement Center in Kingstree.

It was a single-story building with almost no glass, red aluminum roof, and a windowless annex off to one side. Scraggly elms and oaks and tupelos shaded a fenced parking area that was set back from the street, not enough cover to protect against the large plops of rain from a passing shower. A pair of huddled cops lowered their voices as he was led past them through a side entrance, and lots of eyes stared as they passed by.

Uniformed deputies and civilians wandered the halls, where everyone seemed to know everyone else. Burdette escorted Connor to the equivalent of an interrogation room, but it wasn't like anything he'd seen on television. No table and chairs bolted to the floor, no steel rings for wrist and ankle manacles. No two-way mirror with visitors standing behind it, watching every gesture and facial tic. He did notice a camera in a corner of the ceiling, but there was no flashing red light, so he couldn't tell whether it was operational or not.

Still no handcuffs, which he considered a good sign.

He sat there alone for a good thirty minutes before a woman unlocked the door and came inside. She was a little on the heavy side, with rosy cheeks and an eyelid that seemed to droop. Short hair, no discernible make-up. No uniform, either, just black jeans and blue polo shirt, which indicated she wasn't a cop. Unless she was plainclothes, since hers couldn't look any plainer. Connor didn't catch the name that was printed on a plastic badge pinned to her shirt, and got the feeling that was her intention.

She set a bag of KFC take-out on the table and said, "Someone figured you probably hadn't eaten in a while. Put the bones back in the sack when you're done."

Chicken. How appropriate.

Eventually Burdette wandered in, preceding another man who also was not wearing a uniform. They both looked angry, neither of them appearing ready to cut Connor any slack. This was going to be a bad-cop, bad-cop routine. The new guy seemed out of place in gray slacks and a long-sleeve blue shirt, no tie, probably had a matching jacket draped over a chair somewhere else in the building. He carried a notebook with loose pages stuffed inside, while Burdette held a cup of coffee Connor knew was not meant for him.

They both sat down across the table, four menacing eyes glaring at him as if they were trying to bore into his psyche. Then Burdette said, "Connor, this is Deputy Director Leland Emery from Homeland Security. Office of Operations Coordination."

Homeland Security? Connor wondered. *What the hell is he doing here?*

"Glad to know you," he replied.

"You won't be," the Homeland guy said. "You stepped in big shit."

"Not my intention. And I have to make a phone call."

"You will when I say you will."

"I need to get someone to let my dog out," Connor said.

"Should've thought of that earlier," Emery told him.

"I didn't expect to be gone this long."

"Did you expect to fuck up a major federal operation?"

"I sure as hell didn't expect to find out that Colt Lomax is funding a terrorist militia group that's training for all-out civil war," Connor replied.

Emery shot a look at Burdette, who shook his head with a look that implied *I didn't tell him a thing.*

The Homeland agent's irritation level ratcheted up, but he wasn't going to get bogged down by trifles. He placed both palms flat on the table in front of him and glared at Connor, then said, "Do you have any idea how much you screwed things up?"

"Two weeks ago someone shot up my car and tried to kill everyone in it, sir," Connor replied. "I have reason to believe whoever it was came at me after that. What was your federal operation doing about that?"

"You're in no position to be acting like an asshole," Emery said. "Do you really want to spend the next ten years in federal prison?"

Connor hoped Emery's question was rhetorical, but now seemed not the time to spar with a government suit—*sans* jacket—who clearly held the better cards. The only way out of this "big shit" into which he'd stepped was to fess up to what he'd done, and what he knew. That meant admitting to his earlier visit to the Lomax property and his trek last night into the woods and the compound of earthen mounds. He took a deep breath, then launched into a story about the shooting range, the camo truck he'd tailed to a farm supply store outside Georgetown, and Joey Barber's involvement with Willis Ronson's attempted theft of copper.

His tale took a good forty minutes, with plenty of questions and interruptions from Deputy Director Emery. It was clear that he'd viewed both of the clandestine videos, and he pressed Connor about their provenance. "Just how did you come to possess those files?" he asked.

"Mrs. Ronson sent them to me," he replied.

"Why you?"

"You'll have to ask her," Connor said. "And for the record, when I got them, I passed them on to Burdette."

"After you watched them?"

"Of course. I had no idea what they were until I did."

"Then you know what we're dealing with out there."

"What we're dealing with is a bunch of sickos who are itching for a bloody war." Connor drew his gaze to Burdette and asked, "Have you located the bus I told you about?"

At that point Emery gave a sharp glance at the SLED investigator and said, "Outside."

They both stepped out into the hallway and closed the door, presumably for some sort of powwow. Connor heard a lot of shouting, wall-pounding, and door-slamming, followed by a long silence. The two men returned a half hour later and sat down, both of them glaring at him again. Since this had started out as a state investigation into a homicide but had evolved into interference with a federal operation, Connor suspected Emery was in the catbird seat.

He was right.

"It appears we have a jurisdictional dispute, and a broad difference of opinion," the Homeland guy said. "Burdette wants to keep you here in South Carolina, while I want nothing more than to lock you up and throw away the key. I hear Leavenworth is really nice this time of year."

Connor nodded but said nothing.

"You compromised a federal operation, interfered with law enforcement, and obstructed justice," Emery continued.

"Again, that was not my intention," he replied. "I was just following up on a report that someone was trying to break into a rehab facility and kill Ronson's public defender."

"And you almost got yourself killed in the process. Almost got *my men* killed. Now we're scrambling to pick up the pieces of a case that has crumbled under the weight of your careless—and possibly criminal—interference. Understand what I'm telling you?"

"Yes, sir," Connor said. If there ever was a time for contrition, it was now.

"If it were my decision, I'd hang your ass out to dry."

Connor glanced at Burdette, who just shrugged.

"Like I said, you stepped in some big shit," Emery continued. "You disrupted a long-term, multi-million-dollar investigation, and also killed a man—"

"Self-defense—"

"That remains to be seen."

Connor shifted uncomfortably in his chair and said, "I also saved a woman—*a federal agent*—who had been tortured and was probably hours away from dying."

"A woman who *also* stepped in big shit. But yes, you saved her life. Which Burdette, here, so kindly reminded me of just now. So, against my better judgment, I'm going to make an arrangement with you. An arrangement, not a deal. And certainly not a promise, which he also tells me you're not that good at keeping."

No argument from Connor.

"Thing is, if I drag your ass back to D.C., I'll have to write up a dozen Goddamned reports detailing how I allowed some washed-up bounty hunter with a history of booze and PTSD to step all over my investigation and *ruin it*. That wouldn't look good. Not for me, and not for my boss. Or her boss. Instead, I'm going to let you be Burdette's problem, at least for now.

"Yes, sir."

"And don't think for one second that you're off the hook," Emery continued. "You're going to have to go through interviews and depositions, get strapped in for polygraphs, maybe get your ass hauled up in a federal sling. But for now, you're an albatross I don't want, and don't need. In fact, I'm out of here."

With that, the Deputy Director pushed back from the table and stood up. He glared at both of them, then did a one-eighty pivot and crossed the tiny room to the door. As he yanked it open, he focused on Connor and said, "You'll be hearing from me, I shit you not."

Then he left.

Burdette and Connor sat there for what seemed like forever, but probably no more than ten seconds. Connor was waiting for him to speak, figured the investigator was giving Emery enough time to leave the building. Or at least exit the hallway.

Eventually Burdette scratched a fleck of dry skin off the tip of his nose with his thumbnail and said, "What Mr. Homeland didn't mention just now is that the Virginia state police stopped your bus about an hour ago, about two hours south of D.C.," he said. "The driver didn't go down easy, and was critically injured during a brief gunfight."

"What about the containers I saw them load inside?"

"Field analysis indicates it's ammonium nitrate, like you said," Burdette confirmed. "About five tons of it. To put it in perspective, it's more than twice what McVeigh used to blow up the Murrah building in Oklahoma City."

"Shit…those guys meant business," Connor said. "Any idea where it was headed?"

Burdette appeared indecisive about how much to reveal, considering the deep shit Connor was in. He'd already told him way too much, given Connor's track record. But in the end he threw up his hands and said, "Screw it. The driver had a destination plugged into GPS on his phone. Ninth Street and Pennsylvania Avenue."

Connor shook his head; the address meant nothing to him. "Where's that?" he asked.

"U.S. Justice Department. Across the street from the FBI building."

"Damn."

The two men sat in the interrogation room a few more seconds, silence between them. Finally, Burdette said, "Can I offer you a ride somewhere?"

"Excuse me?"

"A ride. I'm driving back to Charleston in about five minutes."

"What about…all this?" Connor glanced around the interrogation room to indicate what he meant by *this*.

"Don't be fooled by my pleasant demeanor," he said. "*This* isn't going anywhere. You've been a royal pain in the ass and you're looking at all sorts of charges. But you saved the life of a federal agent, and might have saved many more. And you don't have a car."

There had to be a catch, especially after all Connor had done, and hadn't done. And Burdette certainly had no good reason to want to help him. It sounded more like a set-up, a plot to get him alone and then transport him to some secret SLED holding tank where a federal judge would arraign him on any number of felony charges.

"In exchange for what?" he asked.

"Nothing, at least not tonight. Take it or leave it, but the way I see it, you really don't have a choice. Or much time to make it."

He was right. Connor's burned-out Ford was likely on its way either to an impound yard or an evidence garage, where it would be torn apart by forensics experts searching for any kind of clues related to the fire. Insurance would cover most of Connor's liability, but he'd have a lot of explaining to do before Jordan James bought him another one. And *that* wouldn't happen until he was able to get another phone, since his captors had seized his and he had no idea what they'd done with it. It would probably show up at some point, but once again it would be appropriated as evidence in a crime. A shit ton of them, most likely.

"Act quick, before I change my mind," Burdette said as he stood up to go.

The last thing Connor wanted was to spend the next hour and half with a SLED agent whom he had repeatedly deceived, circumvented, and lied to. Burdette had every reason to lock him up for a host of flagrant crimes, and then destroy the key. But he wasn't threatening to do that, at least not at the moment, and Connor took that as a good sign. So was allowing him to ride in the front seat of his GMC Yukon, rather than cuffed in the back.

Burdette stashed his service gun in the glove box, then started the engine and slowly eased out of the lot. Neither of them said anything for the first five minutes of the ride, Connor sagging low in his seat as he watched the trees flash by in the twilight. The dashboard clock indicated it was almost nine p.m. They were heading south on a two-lane stretch of state highway, through some swampy woods flooded with runoff reflecting the last of a blood orange sunset painted across the cloudless sky in the west. Not much different from the evening he'd been driving Ronson back to jail, after collecting his drunk ass from a motel not too far from here and loading him into the rear seat of his Cherokee.

Burdette had been kind enough to loan Connor his phone so he could call Julie and let her know what happened. She'd already figured something was wrong, since Clooney had been trapped on the drinking deck, where Connor had left him before heading out the night before.

"Arrested?" she asked after he'd filled her in. "Shit, Jack…what the hell is going on?"

"I'll explain when I get there. I should be back before last call."

"They released you?"

"It's complicated," he said.

She grunted something else into the phone, and then he heard someone order a rum punch and a G and T, and she hung up.

He and Burdette rode in silence a while after that, which allowed Connor to close his eyes. He'd been awake for most of the last thirty-six hours, and what little sleep he'd managed had come as the result of a probable concussion. It wasn't long before his head was lolling against the side window and his brain had dropped into a deep, slow-wave sleep.

Then Burdette punched him on the shoulder and said, "You are one lucky sonofabitch."

Connor couldn't tell if he was referring to the fact that he was alive, or not locked up in jail. Or maybe just because he was getting a free lift home. "I know an apology won't cut it, but for what it's worth, I know I totally screwed the pooch," he said.

Burdette shot him a quick glance, said, "You're right, on both counts. And don't get any idea that you're in the clear, because you're not. But what I mean is, you're lucky that Homeland shit-for-brains didn't haul you off with him. Otherwise, you'd be lost in the system. The American equivalent of Siberia."

"I was wondering about that. How did you pull that off?"

"Let's just say I owe him one. Which means you owe me."

"I'm aware of that," Connor said. "It's what worries me."

"It should."

Connor hated being indebted to anyone, or anything. He held no mortgage, had no car payment, and managed to pay off his credit card every month. "That's why I'm here with you, and not Emery?" he asked.

Burdette ignored the question, instead asked one of his own. "How did you manage to find that place? Homeland spent weeks sending up drone after drone, but they never came close to finding it."

"It was that patch I found at the crash site," he said. "The one with the Lomax logo on it, remember? A property search showed me that Colt Lomax had bought up thousands of acres of worthless property around there, and when I drove up to take a look, it kind of matched what I'd seen in the videos. And before you beat me up over it, yeah, I should have told you what I'd found."

"If you had, none of this would have happened," Burdette said, gesturing with his hands to mean everything he'd fucked up over the last twenty-four hours.

"What are you talking about?" Connor asked.

"The night of the attempted break-in at the motel in Andrews, remember?"

"I told you, I had nothing to do with that—"

"I know what you told me," Burdette said, glancing over at him. "But when I showed up at your door the next morning you said you'd been home all night, watching *The Natural*. I had the good sense not to believe you, so I got a warrant that allowed me to place that tracker on your car. I knew sooner or later you'd pull some stupid move, and I wanted to know what you were up to when you did. Good thing, too."

Connor didn't say anything for a while as he considered the corner into which he'd painted himself. Finally, he replied, "Well, you're wrong about one thing."

"Is that so?"

"You said *Field of Dreams* was a better movie than *The Natural*, but c'mon…what dad ever said to his son, 'do you want to *have* a catch?'"

Burdette actually considered what he said, and Connor could swear he saw him try to hold back a grin. Then he said, "Let's get back to Willis Ronson. Poor bastard had been murdered, and his lawyer was severely injured. You were one lucky sonofabitch to escape with only a few scrapes. All you needed to do was let me do my thing and stay the fuck out. What in God's name were you thinking?"

Connor had no answer for him. He was treading water here, not convinced Burdette wasn't going to throw him in a cell at the end of the ride, just to cause him to sweat. And think. Something he clearly hadn't been doing up till now.

"Did you know about Lomax, and what he was involved with?" he asked.

"Emery wasn't exactly forthcoming with facts," Burdette admitted. "Just played the federal card when I turned the videos over to him."

"What does that mean?"

"It means I told him you'd driven out to that area well over a week ago. Emery was convinced you were wrong, that nothing was going on there. GPS said your car was around the place early this morning but, since it's only accurate to a hundred yards or so, we didn't know exactly where you'd gone. We came out and looked around, trying to figure out what you were up to."

"So, what happens to Colt Lomax?" Connor asked. "He's a dangerous and powerful man with friends in high places."

"That's for people higher up the food chain to—"

Burdette never finished his sentence. At that moment the rear window of the Yukon exploded in a rapid burst of gunfire. A half dozen rounds at least, then several more as he lost control and the SUV veered off the road. It ripped through a stand of second-growth saplings as it pitched and rolled through the woods, bouncing off trees and rotting dead fall. Finally coming to a rest upside down, headlights casting a ghostly glow through a thick curtain of briars and vines.

Déjà vu all over again, as someone once said.

Chapter 28

The Yukon had barely come to a rest in the trees when a pair of lights pulled off on the grassy shoulder back up at the road. Blue halogens, just like the F-150 Connor had seen lurking outside Sea Island Rehab last night.

But there was no time to determine if it was the same truck. Not with Burdette hanging upside down from his seat belt, his face looking like a side of beef that had just gone ten rounds with Rocky in a meat locker. Air bags sometimes were worse than the accident itself.

A flicker in his eyes indicated he was alive, and so was Connor, although he felt as if his shoulder had been dislocated and his nose pulverized. But he pushed aside the pain, since they were like ducks on a pond for anyone with a gun. And that included whoever was in the vehicle that had pulled off the road behind them.

Just like last time.

"Help me out of this," Burdette groaned, meaning his seat belt. Connor fumbled with the plastic release and, when it unlatched, he tumbled down onto the upturned ceiling of the Yukon. Then he said, "Glovebox."

Connor had seen him stash his gun in there when they left the Williamsburg Sheriff's headquarters, and he worked the latch until the door popped open. Since the vehicle was upside down it didn't flop down, and he had to snake his hand up inside until he felt the metal barrel.

"Give it to me," Burdette said.

There were two more quick shots outside, and Connor realized they weren't coming from a mere pistol. Something more on the order of an AR-15, sounding just like the type of weapon that was used to kill Ronson and critically injure Cherine Dupree.

"They're coming to finish us off," he whispered to Burdette.

"You think?"

Whoever was driving the truck left the headlights on, the final streaks of sunset now completely folded into night. Connor estimated the Yukon had careened about thirty yards off the road, leaving a path of splintered trees and uprooted creepers in its wake. It would be slow going, but eventually the gunmen—he assumed there were at least two of them—would be on them.

"Can you squeeze through there?" Burdette asked.

He was referring to the passenger window that had shattered during the crash. It hung like a warped sheet of diamonds from the steel frame, and Connor kicked at it with his heel. Lots of pain, and he realized he'd either broken or badly re-sprained his ankle.

The pulverized glass fell away, leaving an opening just barely large enough for Connor to slide his feet through. He peered through the rear of the Yukon and saw two elongated shadows backlit by the halogen headlamps, now about twenty yards distant. Approaching on Burdette's side, at an angle where they wouldn't see Connor if he slithered out.

"They're coming up on your left," he said.

"Thanks. Now get out."

"But—"

"That's an order."

Connor saw he was serious, realized there was nothing he could do if he remained inside the upturned Yukon. As he began to wriggle legs-first through the jagged window, he detected the odor of gasoline. The fuel tank must have been punctured during the crash, and there was a good chance it could blow any second. He hated leaving Burdette behind, but the SLED cop had a gun and Connor didn't.

"Blow 'em to fuckin' hell," a voice called from the other side of the Yukon, now just fifteen yards away.

"Quiet…there's a house back there on the road," was the response. It sounded like it was coming through a gob of chewing tobacco. "We got to be discreet."

"Like last time?"

"We didn't know that bitch was with him. Be patient."

That bitch he was referring to was Cherine Dupree, and Connor felt his blood begin to boil. These had to be the same bastards who had forced him off the road and had killed Willis Ronson. If he'd had a gun, he would have taken them both out right then. Or so he tried to convince himself, as he slipped the rest of the way through the window.

He couldn't see what Burdette was doing inside the Yukon. He clearly was in a worse position than Connor was, hunkered down on the ceiling, his vision obscured by airbags that had inflated and then gone soft. He was bleeding and probably suffering from internal injuries, maybe some broken bones. Connor couldn't shake the idea that this was all his fault, that the SLED investigator might die because of reckless impulses he had difficulty controlling.

He pulled himself into a low crouch, making himself as small as possible as he tried to figure out his next move. The two shooters were gaining ground, one cautious step at a time, and he managed to peer over the up-turned wreckage to get a fix on where they were. Closing quickly on Burdette's flank maybe ten yards away. Guns drawn, aimed forward.

"Hold your fire," cautioned the one who again seemed to be in charge.

"This time we shoot on sight."

"When I say so."

If Connor could hear what they were saying, he figured Burdette heard them, as well. He was probably prepping himself inside, getting ready for a firefight, while Connor was out in the trees doing nothing. They were seconds away from acting, and he felt he had to do something.

He raised his head just enough to peek over the mangled wreckage of the up-turned wheel well. As he did, his hand touched something hard, a little smaller than a baseball. A rock, maybe a chunk of crumbled asphalt that had been dragged through the trees. He didn't have time to study it, just enough to grip it and hurl it into the brush on the other side of the Yukon.

"Fuck…what was that?" the trigger-happy gunman said as he squeezed off several random shots into the woods, beyond the glow of the headlights.

"I said, hold your fire," the leader snapped.

"Someone's out there—"

"Distraction, you dumb shit—"

His words were met with yet another blast, this one more muffled than the others. A smaller gun, accompanied by a flash inside the SUV. Burdette must have lined up a shot from inside the cab.

"Goddamn—" Trigger yelped as he dropped to the forest floor.

"Shit…guy in the car's got a gun," Leader cursed, then released a burst of fire on the Yukon like a summer hailstorm.

Connor hated to think what Burdette was going through in there, knew he had to do something. He felt around for another rock, instead found a length of sapling that had snapped off as the vehicle had come to a rest in the trees. About the length and weight of his Louisville Slugger back at the bar. Without thinking, he rose to his feet and unleashed a wild sidewinder over the upside-down SUV.

The man with the gun didn't see it coming. The spinning club whacked him in the side of his head with full blunt force. The impact compressed his jaw and cheek and crushed his nose, flinging a spray of blood in the glow of the headlights.

It wasn't enough to kill him but, as he spun around, Burdette took care of that with two quick shots to the chest.

Connor waited a few seconds to make sure no more gunfire was coming. Then he crouched down to the shattered window and said, "You okay in there?"

"I'm hit," was Burdette's reply.

"Where's your phone?"

"Fuck if I know."

Trusting that the two shooters were permanently down, Connor crawled back into the Yukon and searched for the device. It took a while, but he finally found it wedged against the folded-up sun visor. Burdette was moaning in pain, blood seeping from an open wound in his arm.

Connor activated the phone, found it was protected with fingerprint security.

"Give me your hand," he said.

Burdette had to shift his body a bit to extend his gun hand, his index finger still wrapped across the trigger of his Glock. Connor managed to touch his thumb to the screen, and it unlocked. He dialed 911, and a few seconds later the call connected to a dispatch center somewhere. In as few words as possible Connor managed to explain what was going on, told them a SLED officer was down and two suspects were wounded, maybe killed.

He was still wearing the shirt he'd slipped on the night before when Claire had called him in a panic. Now he pulled it off, gave it a massive rip, and tightened it around Burdette's arm above where it was bleeding.

"Where else are you hit?" he asked when he was done.

"Ear, I think." Burdette managed to pivot his neck just enough for Connor to see where a bullet had taken off a chunk of cartilage. Nothing too deep, just a trickle of blood.

"Not life-threatening, but it's gonna leave one helluva a scar."

Connor sat with him until the first flashes of blue appeared through the trees. The scene of the crash was easy to find, since the gunmen had left their truck up on the shoulder with their headlights on. Within seconds the first state trooper was hurriedly clawing his way through the trail of snapped trees and mangled briars.

"In here," Connor called out to him.

"Keep it down," Burdette said. "My head's ringing like a sonofabitch."

EMTs treated his injuries at the scene, then loaded him into the back of an ambulance and rushed him to the hospital in Georgetown. Connor remained at the crash site while the sheriff and a posse of deputies scoured the perimeter. An hour after that two of Burdette's SLED partners showed up to assume control of the investigation, and to get his story. They already knew he'd obstructed an inter-agency op and thus was responsible for what had happened, and they treated him like a suspect. Which was on the order of dirt, and something he figured he deserved.

They hammered him with questions and accusations about the ambush on the road, and the events that occurred in the woods. Connor answered them truthfully, explaining that Burdette had acted heroically in taking down both suspects and saving their lives. Sure, Connor had unleashed the likes of a baseball bat at one of them, but Burdette had finished him off with the kill shot. Connor was just along for the ride.

It was after midnight before he finally was told he could go home. No cuffs, no ride back to the interrogation room. No jail cell. When Connor explained that his car had been torched and Burdette had been driving him home, he was told, "Figure it out."

Burdette's phone had ridden with him in the ambulance, and no one seemed very quick to lend him one. Not after the events of the day, and Connor's complicity in all of it. By now Julie would have locked up the bar and gone home, once again figuring his word was no good or he was spiraling into another post-traumatic meltdown. Wouldn't be the first time. He had no close buddies to call, definitely no girlfriend who would come and fetch him in the middle of the night. There was always Jordan James, but he'd probably be either three sheets to the wind, or sleeping off a major bender.

At one point he managed to get close enough to the suspects' truck to see a red plastic gas can in the bed, along with an empty vodka bottle of the same cheap brand that Connor had found in pieces on the drinking deck a few nights back. Along with a ripped T-shirt, same color and texture as the wick that had been lit, but fizzled out before it had a chance to ignite the propellant and burn The Sandbar down.

He glanced around for a forensic tech who might listen to him, check out the potential evidence in the back of the pick-up. Everyone was too busy to give him the time of day, however, and he gave up just around the same moment a bright yellow BMW convertible sports coupe came racing up in the northbound lane. It made a quick U-turn across the roadway and lurched to a halt on the grassy shoulder, heading the other way.

A moment later a woman wearing a baseball cap over her ginger hair opened the door and unfolded from the front seat. She glanced around the accident site, wandered over to where Burdette's Yukon had been winched out of the trees, and was waiting on the side of the road for a truck vehicle to haul it away. Probably to the same evidence barn where Connor's burned-out Ford had been taken earlier in the day.

Eventually the woman spotted Connor in the glare of a fire truck's headlights. She flexed her shoulders and sauntered over as if she had not a care in the world. Then a big smile formed on her lips and she said, "Hey, Magic Man…don't suppose you'd do that killer lime trick for me, would you?"

Sonofabitch. What in Holy Hell was Jessica Snow doing here? Lisa King. *Whatever.*

He looked deep into her green eyes and said, "Is this where you tell me you were just in the neighborhood, thought you'd drop in?"

"What in God's name happened here?" she wanted to know, ignoring his question as she stared at the mangled SUV. "Whose car is that?"

"Investigator Burdette's," Connor told her. An EMT had wrapped a blanket around him because he'd used his shirt to tie off Burdette's arm, and he was shivering.

"He'd be the SLED guy, right?"

"You know him?"

Jessica Snow shook her head as she gazed about at the shredded trees, the tire tracks, and the gouged earth. Then she glanced back at Connor and noticed the bandages on his forehead and chin, courtesy of the med techs who had worked on Burdette and eventually carted him off.

"Jesus…you're bleeding—"

"Scratches, mostly. And I re-sprained my ankle."

"Were you in…that?" she asked, indicating the wrecked Yukon.

Connor nodded, said, "Airbags come at you fast."

"Follow me," she said, taking his hand in hers.

"Where are we going?"

"I'm taking you home."

They walked back to the yellow two-seater, a dozen questions spinning through Connor's mind. When they got to her car, she unlatched the front door and opened it for him. "I heard you found Brenda Buckner," she said.

"Otherwise known as Liz Morgan. Seems all you fed types have more than one name, Ms. King."

She didn't respond to that, just added, "I also heard you saved her life."

"It wasn't quite that dramatic," he replied.

"Well, get in the car. You can tell me what the fuck happened on the way back."

He felt too wiped out to talk, too exhausted to protest. Too drained to do anything but go along with what she was saying. Sixty seconds later they were back on the road, the Bavarian three-liter engine whining as she opened it up along the straight stretches and leaned into tight turns through the trees. The waning moon was rising in the east, its brilliant luminescence casting arthritic shadows of pine and oak limbs across the pavement.

"I assume you know her?" he asked, once they were well on their way. "Brenda Buckner."

"We took a couple training classes together," Jessica said. "Georgia and New Mexico."

"But you're a U.S. Marshal and she's ATF—"

"All under the same DOJ umbrella," she explained.

"It can't be coincidence you were just driving along, happened to stop to give me a ride home."

Even in the dark Connor saw Jessica wink at him. "Coincidence is God's way of remaining anonymous," she said.

"Is that why you're here? Because of her?"

She thought on that a moment, then said, "You know the other night, we talked about Willis Ronson?"

"We talked about a lot of things, but yeah, I remember," Connor replied. "You said you were protecting him."

"That was the plan," she confirmed. "Brenda had contacted me a few weeks earlier, said she had a C.I. who was going to blow the lid off something big. She needed me to get him into the witness program."

"And then things went off the rails," he reminded her.

She fell silent for a bit after that, fiddled with the car stereo for a few seconds as a distraction, but eventually turned it off. Then she said, "Big time."

Neither of them said anything for a while after that, not until after they were well into the darkness of the Francis Marion Forest. Occasionally a racoon or a skunk waddled across the path of her headlights; otherwise, everything was silent and black. Eventually she gave him a sideways glance and said, "The other evening, I wasn't sure whether I could trust you."

He let her words sink in a moment before he said, "Wait a second… you thought I had something to do with Ronson's death?"

"I don't know what I thought. But he was the second witness who had come into contact with you and got killed while I was trying to bring him in."

"And both times I could have been killed, too."

"You're still stuck on that thing from last summer?"

"Your plan put everyone in my bar at risk," he reminded her.

"That's what I wanted to talk to you about the other evening, before you fell asleep."

"I was tired, and you were gone when I woke up," he reminded her.

"I promise not to make a habit of it. And that's what I wanted to talk about."

"Habits or promises?" he asked her.

A deer bounded across the roadway a hundred yards up the road, and she eased off the gas until it disappeared into the trees. Where there was one, there might be more. Then she said, "Have you ever been to Fairbanks?"

"As in Alaska?"

"Only Fairbanks I know," she replied. He glanced at her, kept his eyes on her dim silhouette but said nothing. Eventually she got the hint and said, "It's where I'm going, day after tomorrow."

"I hear it's nice this time of year," Connor observed, not quite sure where she was going with this. "All day, no night."

"It's the other way around that's got me worried. Winter's going to be a bitch. No limes…and, I hear, not a whole lot of magic."

"If you're trying to tell me something, you're doing a horrible job at it."

"What I'm trying to tell you is…well, I've been given a long-term assignment."

"You're hiding witnesses all the way up in Fairbanks?"

"More like they're hiding me," she said.

He stared at her while he made sense of what she was telling him. Then: "You're being transferred? Because of Willis Ronson?"

"That and a few other supposed transgressions they found in my file."

"Can they do that?"

"Of course they can. They're the government."

She dropped him off a little before two. They'd made small talk the rest of the way, when they'd talked at all. She stopped the car in the gravel lot below the drinking deck and leaned over, gave him a peck on the cheek. She didn't ask to come up, and he didn't extend the invitation. Long day, exhaustion, dehydration. All of it. He felt his heart tighten as he got out, and gently closed the door behind him.

"Enjoy the northern lights," he told her.

"I'm told they put on quite a show. And by the way, of all the gin joints in all the world, you'll never know how much I enjoyed walking into yours."

Clooney was waiting for him at the top of the stairs. He seemed anxious and wired about something, and Connor let him out for a much-needed nature break. While he was waiting for the old guy to return, he found the note Julie had left for him.

"We need to talk," was all it said.

The phrase *habits and promises* ran through his mind as he trudged up the stairs to his attic apartment. He needed to address both concepts, along with trust, or he was going to lose the best employee he'd ever had. And a true friend.

Clooney followed right behind, tentative and uncertain, the way he was whenever Jimmy Brinks showed up and ordered a double Jack. When they got to the top landing Connor started to insert his key into the deadbolt, but found the door unlocked. In fact, it was open a crack, and when he gave it a gentle nudge it swung inward on silent hinges.

Not all the way, but enough for him to see a man seated in a chair in his living room, a gun aimed directly at his chest.

Chapter 29

"Don't you move a Goddamned muscle," the gunman said.

"Who the fuck are you?"

"I don't want to shoot you, but I will without hesitation or grievance."

The only light in the place came from the recessed cans in the kitchen ceiling, dimmed to cut the glare. Just enough illumination for Connor to see the guy's round head and thick neck, and a black T-shirt that exposed banded muscles and old prison tats that had mostly gone to black. Or maybe had started out that way. He was about the same height and weight as Connor, but probably much better shape.

Connor didn't want to be shot, either, but he was damned sure the guy wouldn't hesitate if he didn't do as ordered. "Whatever you want, take it," he said.

"Dumb bastard. You just don't know when to stay out of business that isn't yours."

These words came from another man, who stepped out of the bedroom on the other side of the living room.

"Who the fuck are you?" Connor asked.

"Take your time…it'll come to you."

Connor didn't need more than a second before he recognized the guy from a half dozen online photos he'd Googled over the last few days. Same thick gray hair, square jaw and teeth that looked too perfect not to be implants. Dressed as if he had a tee time at the country club: green-and blue plaid trousers, yellow shirt, visor advertising a brand of golf ball pulled down over his fleshy brow. Strange attire for two in the morning.

"You're Colt Lomax," he said. "What the hell are you doing in my house?"

The man with the gun made a motion to use it, but Lomax waved him off. Then he said, "You have no idea how much trouble you've caused me, you prying little prick."

Connor felt the first flickers of fury building inside him, but he tamped it back down. The words of Dr. Pinch, his old shrink at the VA, played through his brain: *For everything there is a season, and a time for every purpose under heaven.* In other words, play it smart.

"How did you get in?"

"That's immaterial. Fact is, I'm here, and you're in deep shit."

"I know your type, Lomax," Connor said, calculating how long it would take to get to the guy with the gun. *Too long,* he told himself. *Be cool.*

"What are you talking about? What type?"

"You're a predator. A vindictive thug with neither conscience nor courage. You've spent your entire life hiding behind threats of violence—" he glanced at the man holding the pistol "—and surrounded yourself with obedient foot soldiers that line up to lick your boots."

Lomax let out a noise that would best be described as a chortle, then said, "Don't fool yourself into thinking I take offense at your words, Mr. Connor. What you don't seem to realize is that, while this is your home, you are not in charge here." He pulled a chair out from under the small kitchen table and pivoted it around with one hand. "Sit the fuck down."

The man with the gun gestured with it, emphasizing what Lomax had ordered. Connor crossed the room and lowered himself into it, but Clooney remained in the doorway. He let out a low growl, but also seemed a bit guilty.

"How'd you get past my dog?" Connor asked.

Lomax cracked a thin smile and said, "Nothing that a raw chuck roast can't fix."

"Then tell me what you came for, and get the hell out."

"I came for silence."

"It's a little late for that, wouldn't you say?" Connor replied. "The feds have pretty much shut down your weekend warrior sandbox."

"A minor inconvenience," Lomax said, waving his words off like a housefly. "Thing is, I know all about you, Connor. You got your little niece killed, your family blamed you, and you joined the Army to escape the guilt. One of your buddies got himself killed on your watch, and another lost his arm and his brain. You've got a death wish, and you can't hang on to a woman because of it. And you go around sticking your fucking nose where it doesn't belong. Fact is, you are becoming one major pain in my ass."

"Is there a point to all your blather?"

Lomax let out a snort, took a step closer. "The point is, keep your mouth shut."

"Yeah, I kinda got that part."

He glared at Connor, then glanced over at his armed sidekick. Finger on the trigger, more than eager to pull it. "I'm here to tell you that our illegitimate government has convened a secret grand jury to persecute me. Don't ask how I've come to know this fact; I just do. I've also heard that you're going to be called to testify, sometime soon. Whole thing is being fast-tracked on account of you and your meddling. Goddamned political witch hunt, is all it is. Deep State doing what it does best."

"You think maybe it has to do with the Second Amendment Militia you were funding, pushing for a bloody civil war?"

"I said, keep your Goddamned mouth shut," Lomax snapped.

"The bus attack was stopped, you know," Connor went on, ignoring him. "No blowing up anything in Washington today."

He caught a flash of rage in Lomax's eyes, apparently he hadn't heard the news, and didn't sit well with him. "Just a small blip in a grander plan," he said with a snarl. "And that includes you shutting your goddamned mouth when you're summoned to appear."

"You want me to clam up in front of this grand jury," Connor said.

"If I hear you said a fucking word—and believe me, such information will get back to me—I will personally put a gun in your mouth and take an inordinate amount of glee when I pull the trigger."

The darkness in his eyes indicated he would do exactly as he'd just said, and would enjoy every minute of it.

"I have no knowledge of anything that directly leads back to you or your company," Connor assured him.

"Then we have an understanding?"

"It appears so. Now get out."

Colt Lomax stood there a moment longer, not moving. Not saying anything. Then he motioned to his wingman that it was time to go, and opened the front door. He turned back and shot one last glance at Connor as if this were his big Oscar moment, and said, "Remember: all that lives must die, passing through nature to eternity."

"Some rise by sin, and some by virtue fall," Connor replied. He'd learned a little Shakespeare, too, by way of community college.

Chapter 30

Two days later Connor was greeted at his front door by a sheriff's deputy, who handed him a summons ordering him to appear before the grand jury Colt Lomax had told him about.

Because of the secrecy involved, he was only given a few hours' notice. The deputy duly explained that the proceedings would be led by a federal prosecutor for the U.S. District covering the state of South Carolina. No judge would be present in the room. No lawyers, either. The subject of the inquiry—Colt Lomax—had no legal standing and, in this particular case, had not been informed that evidence was being collected, or testimony heard by jurors. Hence the word "secret." Connor was not entitled to have an attorney at his side, and no one but the jurors, a bailiff, a court reporter, and the prosecutor would be in the room. Furthermore, any transcript of his testimony would be sealed.

All of which, if Lomax truly had someone on the inside, didn't mean shit.

"It's all pretty regular," the deputy assured him. He was a large Black man named Clyde Silver, early forties with a bald head and dark eyes, large hands that tightened like vice grips when he introduced himself to Connor. "The Supreme Court ruled years ago that these things need to be secret in order to get witnesses to tell the truth without fear of reprisal," he explained.

"How secret is secret?"

"Like Las Vegas. Whatever happens there, stays there."

"I've been to Vegas, and it's not like that at all."

"What are you saying?"

"The grand jury has been compromised," Connor informed him.

"Now, hold on a second—"

But Connor didn't let the deputy finish. Instead, he explained how the Carolina Kingmaker paid him a visit the morning before last with an armed goon and had threatened him to keep his mouth shut. He didn't get into Lomax's exact words about taking glee when putting the gun in his mouth and pulling the trigger, but his story was pretty convincing.

"You're sure of this?" Silver asked when he was done.

"I wouldn't be risking my life telling you about it if I wasn't."

Connor could see the deputy's brain working on what he'd just told him, figuring how to proceed next. Then he said, "Do you have any proof of what you're telling me?"

"In fact, I do."

After the mysterious fire the previous summer, Jordan James had installed a pair of security cameras down on the drinking deck, where they could catch the comings and goings of anyone suspicious. Connor had taken it one step further by concealing a mini-spy device in the ceiling AC vent in his apartment. It had taken him less than ten minutes to set it up and, when he was finished, it was invisible, unless someone was looking for such a thing. He'd also paid the ten dollars a month for unlimited twenty-four/seven cloud storage. Video and audio.

His problem—and it was a big one—was that he had no idea whom he could trust. Including Deputy Silver, who had just randomly shown up at his door with a grand jury summons. Was he on the level, or could be he a snitch? Maybe even one of Lomax's lackeys? What about the prosecutor, or someone on the government's legal staff? Or perhaps one of the jurors? Or the court reporter? Whoever it was, the kingmaker had claimed to have an inside source, and Connor could trust no one.

After Lomax departed, Connor downloaded the video file onto his laptop and ran through it at least a dozen times. When he was convinced beyond all doubt that the Chickenman had admitted his complicity in the planned attack in the nation's capital—and also had threatened him with his life—he copied the entire thing onto a USB drive. He used a file-share platform to send it to himself, then hid the original in a can of screws he kept under the kitchen sink.

"I need to talk to whoever's in charge, and no one else," he now explained to the deputy.

If Silver had been on Lomax's payroll, Connor would probably be dead within seconds. Instead, the deputy acted as if he'd experienced this sort of thing before with grand jury witnesses, and said, "I'll make a call."

An hour later Connor found himself being transported to what turned out to be a renovated building off Morrison Avenue in Charleston, less than a mile from the foot of the Ravenel Bridge. One exterior wall of the structure was encased in scaffolding, and a team of masons was busily laying a façade of bricks. As with most of the Charleston neighborhood known as Upper King, it was in an area that was undergoing frenzied regentrification. New condos and office structures were sprouting like weeds on lots where old laundromats, gas stations, and run-down corner taverns once had stood.

Deputy Silver had called ahead as they were crossing the bridge and, when they pulled around to the rear entrance, they were met by two additional deputies who shielded Connor from any possible threat. It appeared there were no assailants on the ground, no buildings high or near enough for a sniper to get a good line of sight through a rifle scope. No unmarked vans lingering out on the street.

His new guards escorted him to a stuffy room designed to seat a dozen people around a massive table. In the center was a digital console about the size of a dictionary, as well as a tablet device that Connor figured operated the large screen at one end of the room. No windows, and the only door was the one through which he had entered. He accepted the bottle of water he was offered and sat in a chair positioned at the far end.

A few minutes later the door opened and two more people entered. One was Deputy Silver, who stationed himself just inside, arms crossed, gun within easy reach. The other was a woman Connor had not seen before, and she carried an imposing presence as she stepped inside and proceeded to come around to the end of the table where he was seated. She was Asian with soft, bronze skin, short black hair with threads of gray in it. Dark eyes that seemed to catch everything in the room almost instantly. Navy blue skirt and white blouse, with a lace RBG collar buttoned tightly at her throat. Despite her height—maybe five-five—she stood with a commanding posture that gave no doubt she was in charge.

"I'm Susan Kim, U.S. attorney for the District of South Carolina," she introduced herself. "You have no idea how pleased I am to meet you, Mr. Connor."

"Me as well," he replied. "I think."

"Please rest assured, you can trust me," she said as they shook hands. "And I want to tell you how much I appreciate your coming forward today.

It's not an easy choice for anyone to make, when someone makes a threat against you or your family."

She patiently and thoroughly explained that she was the prosecutor overseeing the secret grand jury that had been convened in the Colt Lomax matter. She'd made a series of phone calls following the one Deputy Silver had made from Connor's apartment, and insisted on seeing him right away. Hence the hasty trip to this building, whatever it appeared to be, and the security detail that accompanied him inside.

"What choice?" Connor asked. "Lomax made it pretty clear what he was capable of."

The prosecutor nodded at what he was saying. "Yet here you are," she observed. "Deputy Silver said you have evidence. Did you bring it?"

"Yes, ma'am. And I hate to do this to you, but how do I know you are who you say you are, and Lomax isn't waiting for me in the next room?"

Kim offered a broad grin and nodded in understanding. She opened the dark briefcase clenched in her hand and took out a leatherette folder, which displayed a half dozen cards, badges, and credentials. They all confirmed her identity and her position within the federal government.

"Impressive," he said. "If they're real."

"Trust is something we're just going to have to build," she replied as she tucked the portfolio back inside the briefcase. Then she sat down in the chair next to him diagonally, and folded her hands on the table. No recording device, no pad of paper on which to take notes. "So…Colton Lomax threatened to kill you?"

"He did. No doubt in my mind. Or yours, when you play the video."

"You recorded this exchange in your home?"

"On a security camera in a ceiling vent."

Susan Kim glanced over at Deputy Silver, who confirmed what he'd said with a single dip of his chin. "Did you bring the recording?" she asked.

"A copy, one of several." Connor removed a flash drive from his pocket and set it on the table. Then he glanced at the screen on the wall and asked, "Is that connected to a computer?"

"It was the last time I checked."

She picked up the memory device and inserted it into the console in the center of the table. Then she picked up the tablet and powered up the flatscreen monitor on the wall. She typed in a few commands, and said, "Okay…let's see what you've got here."

The prosecutor didn't say a word as the digital file played, and when it finished seven minutes later with Colt Lomax making his exit, she froze the footage on one final image. She sat there for a moment, staring at the screen, not saying a word. Jaw set, her mind furiously at work.

Eventually she said, "Thank you, Mr. Connor. This piece of evidence significantly changes the complexion of our investigation. We're still going to want your testimony for the grand jury, but not today." Then she took a cell phone out of her attaché case and scrolled through her contacts. Finally settling on one, she tapped the name and waited impatiently for the call to be connected.

"Judge McEvoy?" she said when it finally rang through. "U.S. Attorney Susan Kim here. I'm going to need you to sign a warrant."

The person on the other end—Connor assumed it was a judge named McEvoy—asked her something, to which she replied, "Yes, for the arrest of Colton Lomax. Yes, your honor. *That* Colton Lomax."

Judge McEvoy peppered her with a few more questions Connor couldn't hear, and then Ms. Kim said, "Of course I have evidence. The sort of smoking gun you always dream of but never get."

She waited for the judge's response, then told him, "I'll be sending a sheriff's deputy over for your signature as soon as it's drawn up."

Chapter 31

Investigator Burdette was discharged from the hospital that same afternoon. His injuries included a concussion, subarachnoid hemorrhage, fracture of occipital condyle, skull fracture, laceration, several hematomas, and traumatic shock.

He called Connor the following morning to let him know he was not off the hook, even if he'd helped save his life.

"Just so we're clear, this does not absolve you in any way," was how he put it.

"I wouldn't expect it to," Connor said.

"Also, I'm sure you'd like to know that Brenda Buckner is expected to recover fully. Physically, at least. Mentally, she's got a long road ahead of her."

She and Connor hadn't discussed what she'd had to endure down in the dungeon, but he'd assumed there was a lot of physical and psychological torture involved. Sexual assault, too, but she hadn't brought it up and he didn't want to raise the issue with Burdette. The woman had suffered enough, and her life as she knew it was changed forever. Personal experience told him that PTSD came at you from out of nowhere, at the slightest of provocations, as she was probably just now beginning to realize.

"Did she mention anything about Ronson being a confidential informant, or what he was doing for her out at the motel in Andrews?"

"You know I can't talk about that," the SLED cop reminded him.

"Can't or won't?" Connor asked.

Burdette remained silent for a good five seconds, then ten. Finally, he yielded and said, "Okay, she said a lot of things and covered a lot of ground, most of which is sealed. But yeah, Buckner was looking into widescale theft of weapons from Camp Lejune up in North Carolina, apparently tracked it back to this paramilitary group called Two A.M. You were right about that."

"What about Judge Huger, who was overseeing Ronson's case?"

"What about him?"

"He had to have known that Ronson was helping the feds," Connor pointed out.

"One would think," the SLED cop said.

"Then why didn't he postpone the hearing so Ronson could continue to do whatever he was doing?"

"Buckner didn't say, and I didn't ask."

Burdette went on to explain that the two gunmen who had opened fire on his Yukon had been identified. Both were deceased, and both had been employed by the company that provided security to Lomax's poultry empire. Hence the ripped patch Connor had found ensnared on the brambles at the site of the initial ambush. Furthermore, the SLED ballistics lab had conclusively connected an AR-15 that belonged to one of the suspects to the bullet that had been removed from Cherine Dupree's spine.

"We believe they were the same shitheads who killed Ronson and ran you off the road," he said. "No one likes a snitch."

None of this surprised Connor, since he'd seen the empty vodka bottles in the back of the suspect's truck. Plus, the torn T-shirt that had been used to fashion the makeshift fuse that had sputtered out when it was tossed onto the drinking deck at The Sandbar.

"Coincidentally—or maybe not—a Glock that was found in the dead gunmen's truck was registered to Lyle Hicks," he said.

"Sonofabitch," Connor said, realizing that if the SLED techs dusted the gun for prints, they'd find his all over it. That could pose a problem that he couldn't easily wriggle his way out of. "You going to tell me the guy's name?"

"No, I am not. He's deceased, and the weapon is evidence in an ongoing investigation. You are done with all this."

Truth. Connor *was* done with it. Done with terrorist militias and underground school bus mazes and enough explosives to blow a large crater in the Department of Justice building. Or the FBI headquarters, depending on which side of the street the tourist bus would have parked.

After Burdette hung up, he dug deep into a law enforcement database and found the name of the dead gunman who had shot Alisha Dupree and killed Willis Ronson:

Caleb Elkins and *Mitchell Shaw.*

Finally putting names to the shooters who had started all this.

Cherine Dupree was released from Sea Island rehab just before noon the same day. Claire picked her up and took her to the beach, where Cherine texted Connor a picture of her two Chihuahuas sniffing a curl of foam at the edge of the sand. The accompanying message read:

> Finally made it to the shore. So glad to be back on my feet. I owe you.

To which he replied:

> Sorry to have put you through all that. I think we're even.

Her response:

> Never in a million years. I hope you never get locked up, but if you ever need a defense attorney, give me a call. Pro bono.

To which Connor shot back:

> Done deal.

He had barely put the phone down when it rang again: Mrs. Ronson.

"Jesus Horatio Christ…they ambushed you all over again?" she asked. Three days after the fact, but better late than never.

"At least this time I wasn't driving," he said.

"Those bastards just don't give up."

"They will now that they're dead."

"Seriously?" she asked. "For real?"

"Looks like," he replied. No need for details.

There was a gasp on the other end, followed by a long silence as she processed what he'd just told her. Eventually she asked him, "You're sure of this?"

"Same guns, same guys," he said.

"Do these guys have names?"

"And toe tags," Connor confirmed. And then, because he hadn't gotten any of it from Burdette, filled her in about the dead man who had murdered her husband in cold blood.

That same afternoon he received a call from Jordan James. They hadn't spoken since before the "Shootout in the Woods," as the local media had dubbed it, for which Connor had been placed on paid leave. An arrangement he knew could only last so long.

"Meet me at three o'clock," James told him. It was more of a command than a request, which didn't bode well.

"Give me the address and I'll be there," Connor said, since he didn't have much else going on in his life.

There turned out to be a tract of a couple hundred acres known as the Sol Legare Country Club—Legare being pronounced *Le-gree*—located along the edge of a pristine saltwater marsh and an estuary of the Stono River. Sometime around the turn of the millennium, a cadre of developers had envisioned a world-class facility with perilous water hazards and treacherous bunkers, and large lots featuring architectural wonders. Perhaps even an occasional stop on the PGA tour.

None of that had come to pass except for eighteen holes of poorly planted fairways and greens that were covered with nutsedge and dove weed. Great for geese to nibble, but impossible to putt on because of their excrement.

Jordan James was seated behind the wheel of a golf cart pimped out with polished chrome wheels and tinted windshield. Purple body with an orange roof, the colors of Clemson. He was discussing something on his cell phone when Connor walked up.

"Three o'clock, right on the dot," he said. "Punctuality is a solid trait in a man. Courteous and respectful."

"Yes, sir," Connor said.

"Well, don't just stand there. Hop in."

"Where we going?"

James plucked a can of orange soda out of a dash-mounted cup holder and took a sip, then said, "For a ride."

Three in the afternoon and no martini? Connor thought, knowing enough not to say anything. "Where to?" he asked instead.

"The best journeys in life begin with no known destination."

"If you say so."

"Grab a beverage…there's a cooler behind you."

Connor wasn't particularly thirsty, but he grabbed a can of lime fizzy water and popped the top. He took a sip, then sat down in the passenger seat and said, "To wherever we're going, then."

They rode in silence for most of a full minute, James keeping the cart on a path that had been graded at the edge of the fairway but never paved. They bounced over rocks and through eroded run-off troughs, and eventually the old man said, "You're probably wondering why I invited you here."

"I figured you'd get to it in your own time," he replied. "Meanwhile, it's a beautiful view."

"Wait till we get to the fourth tee. It's right at the edge of the marsh, and you won't believe the egrets and herons. But you're right, I did invite you here for a specific purpose."

Connor cast him a wary glance and said, "Please don't tell me you're thinking of making me a groundskeeper here—"

James chuckled but didn't answer right away, instead steering the cart across the nonexistent fairway to a line of trees on the other side. "They relocated a couple of live oaks over there," he explained as they jounced across the brown field. "Cost twenty grand apiece to carry them in a sling under a Chinook. I want to see how they're doing."

They seemed to be doing just fine, and a minute later the cart was heading back toward the path. "Anyway, the answer is no," James assured him. "I'm not going to transfer you here. Not a good fit if you don't play golf. Plus, you're doing fine at The Sandbar. Expenses are under control, and profit margins are solidly black year-over-year. But the thing is, you can't keep working at Citadel. That stunt with those militia dickwads caused me to get a bunch of calls from folks in DC who aren't too happy. Columbia, too. Turns out there's more than a few clauses in my contracts that you unwittingly violated."

"I apologize for that, sir. Whatever you need to do, I understand."

"I also got a notice that SLED is revoking your bond runner's license."

Connor had been waiting for that shoe to drop, but had not yet received his own notification from the state. "Not surprised," he said.

"The thing is, something happened the other day that changed my perspective on a few things. Gave me a new priority or two, you could say."

"I'm not sure I understand," Connor said.

"I think you do," Jordan James said. "I caught you looking at my can of soda just now when you arrived. And I know what you were thinking."

"You have to admit, you usually have a martini in your hand this time of day." *Or any time of day.*

"Precisely. And what I need to tell you is, the other day I was driving over the Ravenel Bridge when all of a sudden I saw some blue lights flashing in my rearview mirror. Seems my car couldn't decide which lane it wanted to be in, so it was going back and forth."

"Uh-oh."

"Not the words I used, but yeah. I spent the next sixteen hours sitting in jail until my lawyer got me bailed out. God, I had no idea how bad the toilets were in that place. Food, too. Anyway, it gave me a lot of time to do some thinking, about a lot of things. And one of them was drinking and driving."

"That would be two things," Connor said.

"Smartass. Anyway, it wasn't my first time. And George—he's my lawyer—said I needed to make a sincere effort to change my ways if I'm going to convince a judge to let me off with just a wrist slap. Hence the soda."

"Smart move," Connor said. "I'm sure your liver will thank you."

"Definitely an added incentive," James replied, nodding in agreement. "But that's not the only thing, and also not why I asked you out here. Fact is, as part of those sixteen hours I had a lot of time to reflect on things, particularly Eddie. And how I've been trying to drown my mistakes with him by trying to do right by you."

Connor tried to read his eyes, but the glare of the sun wouldn't allow it. "Sir?" he said.

"You see, when Eddie was just a boy, he and I were best buds. I had a lot more time back then, and he was such a bundle of energy. Like that rabbit with the drum on TV. We played catch, I taught him tee-ball, we flew kites. Rode bikes. That sort of thing. Later we rebuilt a car together, his first wheels. An old AMC Javelin, mostly yellow with a gray hood."

"My uncle had one of those," Connor said. "Sounds like a sweet ride."

"It was," Jordan James agreed. "But as he got older, he tried to do what all kids do, and that is to leave the nest. Sprout wings and fly. We had words more times than I can count, and he would storm out. I wasn't prepared for that, so I tried to hold on tighter."

"My old man and I were a lot like that."

"Then you know what I'm talking about." They were back on the path now, the cart veering back and forth. This time Connor couldn't blame it on the gin. "The point of all this is, the harder I tried to hang on, the harder

Eddie pushed back. Which is why he joined the Army and ended up over there in that Hummer that day."

"You can't blame yourself for things that were beyond your control," Connor told him. "It was his life, his choices."

"I know that now. That was part of those sixteen hours of reflection. But please…hear me out. Since I blamed myself for what happened, and because you saved him that day, I latched on to you almost as another son. I felt it was my responsibility to bring you under my wing, give you a job. Keep you close. I gave you Isabella to drive, made sure you were part of the family. And you always will be, no matter what."

The *no matter what* part was what Connor had been patiently waiting for.

"The thing is, it's time that I cut you loose," Jordan James explained. "Let you sprout your own wings and take flight, if you will."

"Yessir, and I completely agree." As much as he had appreciated Jordan James' generosity and attention over the years, many times he'd felt smothered by the man. And had made more than one attempt to put some space between them.

"Of course you do. But don't worry, I'm not going to boot your ass to the curb. Like I said, you're doing fine at The Sandbar, and you never mess with a good thing. It was your decision to go to Iraq, but it's my fault you put your life on the line when you got back. I messed up with you, just like I messed up with my own son."

"You didn't mess up, Mr. James. You just cared for Eddie more than he felt he needed at the time. It happens."

On any other day that would have caused his soon-to-be ex-boss to take a long sip from a martini glass; today it was just a swig of orange soda from a can. "Well, in any event, I've decided to make a couple changes in my life."

Connor said nothing, just cast a suspicious glance his way.

"Number one, I've decided to cut alcohol out of my diet. My lawyer and my doctor both insist it's for the better, although I can't deny I get cravings from time to time. And number two, just in case number one falls short occasionally, I'm hiring myself a full-time driver."

"Mr. James. If you think I'm going to—"

"No, I don't mean you," James cut him off. "You may not know it, but I happen to own a livery company that has a small fleet of Lincoln town cars. I rather like the way they handle on the uneven streets of this city, and I can do business out of the backseat."

"You and the Lincoln lawyer," Connor quipped.

"That's where I got the idea," James said. "But it leaves me with one small problem, which is the disposition of my Bentley."

At that moment they arrived at the fourth tee, and Jordan James veered over to a small rivulet that gurgled under a stone bridge and emptied into the marsh. A great blue heron was standing in the pluff mud at the edge of the grass, staring intently at the water.

"I'm sure you can just fold it into your limo company," Connor suggested.

"Not a good fit," James explained. "It's just Lincolns, mostly for executive trips to and from the airport. And now me, of course."

"Well, I'm sure it won't be hard to sell."

"But then I wouldn't know what kind of home it was going to. This way, I do."

He steered the cart toward the bridge, pulled to the top of the gentle arc, and braked to a halt. Then he reached into his pocket and took out a set of keys, which he handed to Connor.

"What's this?" Connor asked.

"Whatever you want it to be," James answered. "You could give it to that charity down in Georgia, like you suggested I do with Isabella. Or maybe put some money in the bank if you decide to part with it. Or you can get a chauffeur's license and go into business. Hire yourself out for weddings, birthdays, proms…that sort of thing. Whatever you decide to do."

"There's no way I can accept this, sir. It's way too much."

"Too late, Jack. Since you already turned down the Camaro, I went ahead and transferred the title into your name." James checked the time on the Rolex on his left wrist and added, "Right about now it's being parked in the shade under The Sandbar."

"But—"

"It's a gift, Jack. Treat it as such. You'll figure out what to do with it."

Connor didn't say anything for a moment, just gazed out at the water glimmering beyond the marsh. Then he turned and said, "Don't take this wrong, sir, but I don't think a British luxury car is going to cure whatever ails me. We both know the snakes of war are with me pretty much twenty-four-seven, and I'm meeting with my old shrink to help me deal with that. I also have to do something that makes a difference to those who are going through the same sort of shit." James was studying Connor, listening to him carefully. Taking in every word he was saying. "Any ideas what that might be?"

"In fact, I spoke with a guy down in Georgia at that VA charity, as you called it. They have a slot for someone who's been through the same shit as a lot of the guys in the program. I think I can do some good there, and no one in the program gets anywhere close to being shot at."

"That's a noble thing to do," Jordan James said. "This guy you talked to…what did he tell you?"

"I have the job if I want one," Connor told him.

"What about The Sandbar?"

"That's the toughest part. If I decide to go, I'd have to give that up."

Mr. James massaged the back of his neck and stared out at the water beyond the marsh. Then he turned to Connor and said, "When do they want an answer?"

"Next few days. If I say yes, they'd want me to start two weeks after I turn in my resignation."

"Well, think carefully," James said. "Do whatever you feel you need to do. And whatever you decide, I request just one thing."

"Whatever you want, sir."

"I want you to join us for a celebration for Eddie tomorrow night, at the new pier. A space finally opened up in that rehab program up in Richmond, and he's leaving Monday."

"Wouldn't miss it for the world," Connor told him.

Chapter 32

On the drive back to the bar, U.S. Attorney Susan Kim called to let Connor know that a team of federal marshals had tracked Colton Lomax to a private airfield outside Spartanburg in the upstate. Agents from Homeland and ATF surprised him on the tarmac as he was trying to board a Citation he'd leased through a shell corporation, a tax arrangement he'd probably believed was far below the feds' radar.

His bodyguard had acted impulsively and pulled a weapon, a reactive move that resulted in an exchange of gunfire that did not go well for either the Chickenman or his armed wingman. Connor wondered if the guy might have been the same toady who had confronted him in his attic apartment a few nights before. No matter, the guy was shot multiple times and died at the scene.

During the shootout Lomax had tried to flee across the taxiway. He'd apparently made it about fifty yards before at least one bullet brought him down, and EMTs pronounced him dead on the way to the hospital. Interestingly, four passports and an unspecified amount of cash was found in his luggage.

Kim also explained that state and federal examiners had excavated the underground dungeon in which Connor and Brenda Buckner had been held captive. Replicating the efforts of a Canadian survivalist, Lomax had ordered the woods to be bulldozed to create the maze of buses, then backfilled the entire complex with concrete and dirt. Viewed from a plane, drone, or any passing satellite it just looked like a fenced field with a few gentle rises in the middle of it.

One more detail: Judge Charles Huger, the magistrate overseeing Willis Ronson's attempted theft case, had been apprehended that same morning in his chambers at the courthouse in downtown Charleston. Turned out the feds had been watching him, too, mostly for the legal assistance he'd provided for his employees who had been apprehend for their part in the insurrection at the Capitol. The fact that there appeared to be no record of payment—or taxes—for those services suggested an arrangement that violated the law, one that also caused Huger to look the other way when Brenda Buckner notified him that Willis Ronson was involved in a government op. And then contacted the Second Amendment Militia to have him ambushed.

That night The Sandbar had an inexplicable run on painkillers. Not the sort dispensed from bottles with child-proof caps, but the liquid kind concocted from five types of specialty rum, pineapple and coconut, and a dusting of nutmeg. A favorite down in the islands, *mon*, but only two other joints in Folly served them—and nothing came close to what Connor served up at The Sandbar. They were smooth, creamy, and just as tropical as a smear of cocoa butter.

The downside was, they could knock your socks off. Great quantities of rum had that effect on most folks, something most rookies discovered too late. Order one, you were putting yourself at risk. Ask for another and the world might start spinning. Top that off with a third, and the road became a hazard for others—which easily could turn into a liability issue for Jordan James, since his name was on the business license.

The result was always the same: unhappy customers who believed their rights were being trampled on when Connor cut them off. When that happened, slurred voices grew loud as the offended party protested the violation of his or her due process, and a god-given right to party. A gentle reminder that the police were just a phone call away usually returned order to the moment.

A little after seven o'clock the cocktail *du jour* switched to salty dogs at his end of the bar, while white Russians were favored in Julie's corner. Go figure. By nine most of the tourists had wandered back to their hotels and VRBOs, and the locals began to drift in. The popcorn machine went into high gear, while the jukebox shifted from oldies to classic rock and started competing with the clubs a couple blocks over on the main drag. Connor ran through two rounds of stupid bar tricks, almost cutting up the wrong credit card in the process. The bar ran through two kegs of draught beer in short order, and the third was running on empty by the time Connor was able to duck downstairs to the locked store room and load a new cask of IPA into the dumbwaiter.

It landed in the steel lift with a loud clang, just as he felt something hard press against his neck, at the base of his skull.

This time he knew it wasn't wild horses. No mist, no nickers. No nuzzling.

"On your knees, fuck face," a voice snarled behind him. Low and breathy, with the odor of Slim Jims.

"What the hell—?"

"Shut up and do it," the voice said again, and in that moment, Connor was able to place it.

"Lyle Hicks," he said.

"I said, shut the fuck up. Get on your knees."

Connor raised his hands up and outward, to show he meant no harm. No sudden moves. He bent his knees and began to do as he was told. Knowing as soon as he was down, this asshole with the gun wouldn't think twice about pulling the trigger.

"You don't have to do this—"

"You messed with the wrong man, dipshit."

"A real man doesn't beat up his wife," Connor said.

"You don't get it, do you?" Hicks replied with a snarl. "This is the end of the line."

"There's eyes everywhere. Upstairs, across the road—"

"Fuck if I care. In the dirt. Now."

Connor lowered himself further, the next moment coming in small fragments as his mind ran through a sizzle reel of his life: Jumping his bike over a ditch when he was eight, hitting his first jump shot in a junior high round robin. His niece getting shot, a carton of moose tracks ice cream clutched in her hands. Pumping a round into the young kid in the grocery store in Kirkuk, and the suicide van that took off Eddie James' arm. Danielle almost dying, and then running into her just a week ago in a veil of fog. Finding Clooney at the side of the road in the hurricane a couple years back…

Hicks pressed the barrel of the gun harder into his neck, and Connor sensed his finger tightening on the trigger. This was it, the moment his clock ran out. His time to die. To the tune of the Rolling Stones' "Out Of Time" playing on the old Seeburg one floor up.

Then two things happened that created a wrinkle in the fabric of time, or at least his little fragment of it.

A dark, shadowy mass lunged from the darkness and jolted Lyle Hicks, just as a round exploded from his gun. Later, Connor would swear he heard the chunk of lead whiz by his ear, but that was probably just his imagination due to the music, the yelp, and Clooney's vicious snarl as he sank his teeth into Hicks' bare ankle.

At the same time, another blast erupted from further away. A few yards, to Connor's left, from the darkness between the wooden pilings on the other side of the storeroom. A fraction of a second later he felt something warm and wet spray the side of his face, and Hicks crumpled to the ground.

The forward motion drove Connor into the dirt. He caught a mouthful of gravel that tasted of motor oil and salt. And blood, which he now realized was the stuff he'd felt spatter him just a second or two before. Not his own, since he was feeling no pain except for where he'd bitten his tongue when he made contact with the earth.

"Connor," a voice called out, from the same direction of the second gunshot. Followed by a mad scrambling sound that included a car door being flung open. "You hit?"

At that point he felt something completely different, like a piece of flank steak being drawn repeatedly across the side of his face. It was Clooney, lapping his massive tongue at Lyle Hicks' blood. Connor rolled to one side and brought himself up into a crouch, gently nudging the old chocolate lab away.

"That you, Burdette?" he called out.

"Yeah, and almost too late," the SLED cop replied. "They pulled my patrol guys off you, so I figured I'd make a drive-by to make sure you were okay."

"Sonofabitch," was all Connor could say.

The arrival of police for some reason chased all but the die-hards away. No one was a witness to Lyle Hicks' shooting, but most customers paid up and shuffled off toward the exit as fast as their flip-flops would carry them. Before long there were just a few old souls propped up at the bar, and Julie volunteered to take care of them while Connor dealt with the authorities. That included Burdette, two local officers, and a small squadron of investigators from the sheriff's office. Plus, a forensics team that stayed on-site until well past closing, taking photos and collecting casings and making casts of shoe prints in the dirt.

Burdette was in no condition to be out, much less behind the wheel. Or firing a gun. But he'd heard a report on the radio that Hicks had been sighted outside his ex-wife's house, possibly armed and dangerous. A neighbor had called nine-one-one, but the fugitive had sped off before anyone arrived on the scene. That's when Burdette had learned that no one was assigned to watch The Sandbar, and he'd taken it upon himself to haul his ass all the way down to Folly Beach to check in. Sub-rosa, of course. Off the books.

"You did that for me?" Connor asked him.

"If you'd died, that would have been it," Burdette explained. A third of his head was wrapped in gauze, and he had difficulty speaking because of the hairline fracture in his jaw. "I wasn't going to let you off the hook that easy."

Beach Music

The send-off for Eddie James was neither private nor an exclusive affair.

Every Saturday night during the summer, the town of Folly Beach scheduled a Shaggin' on the Shore dance shindig at the end of the reconstructed pier that extended a thousand feet into the surf. Jordan James had piggy-backed his son's going-away party onto the festivities, which was the proper thing to do since almost everyone in town knew Eddie's story. And because… well, why not?

Several local bands rotated performances throughout the summer, and this night it was a quartet that billed themselves as The Bonefish Boogie Band. Connor had heard them a couple times at various clubs back when he had played congas in the Bob Marley tribute band, and their set list was mostly the classic beach music that was part of South Carolina's cultural DNA. Connor had tried it once with Danielle, who had explained that songs with a four/four "blues shuffle" rhythm and moderate-to-fast tempo were most suitable, although at the time he had no idea what she was talking about.

Nor had it mattered.

He and Julie opened The Sandbar as usual at five o'clock, and then Buddy filled in for him a little after eight. Because it was a farewell to Eddie James, neither had a problem with him being gone for the rest of the evening, although Julie did add it to the rapidly expanding IOU list. Connor arrived at the party a few minutes late, and by the time he reached the end of the pier, the celebration was in full swing.

Jordan James was standing near the rail with his current and fourth wife Lynette, a can of soda in his hand. A good sign. Eddie was seated in a motorized chair next to him, and on the other side was Shirley, who was James' first ex and Eddie's mother. The last time Connor had seen Eddie was at an event at Shirley's home on Isle of Palms last March, and he'd been zipping around the massive back patio in his new wheels as if he was doing laps at Darlington Motor Speedway.

He seemed more subdued tonight, although his wrist was cranking the joystick back and forth, causing the chair to pitch forward and then roll backwards. As if waiting for a flag to be dropped so a race could start.

The band was playing a cover of Alabama's "Dancin', Shaggin' on the Boulevard," and Connor watched as a dozen couples slow-danced in what seemed to be one fluid motion. The distant lights of Charleston lit up the sky, casting just a faint glow along the bellies of a few clouds to the west.

And there, in the middle of the dance floor, Danielle Simmons was dancing with a man Connor did not know. Following his lead, holding his hand, shuffling through a few simple steps, swinging into an over-the-shoulder twirl. He felt the blood drain from his head as he floated back to the first time he'd set eyes on her six, maybe seven years ago. She'd knocked on his front door unannounced and, when he'd casually opened it, she had hit him square in the face with a heavy shot of pepper spray.

Seriously: *Danielle Simmons*? Shagging with a stranger on the old pier here in Folly Beach? *What were the odds*?

At that same moment Jordan James touched him on the shoulder and said, "Isn't that your girl out there?"

"Huh?" Connor replied, the old high school heartache known as jealousy causing the synapses in his brain to misfire as she seemed to move about comfortably with some douche bag he didn't know. Wearing a crisply ironed aloha shirt and creased white shorts, Tevas with socks.

"Danielle. Right over there."

"Yeah…looks like."

"Wonder what she's doing here," James continued.

The song was coming to an end, and Connor knew one of several things would happen next. Danielle and the guy would stay out there and go for another dance. They'd drift to the edge of the dance floor and he'd offer to buy her a drink. Or they'd walk arm in arm off into the night, and he'd never see her again.

Then James dug his elbow into Connor's ribs and said, "Go out there and cut in."

"What? I can't do that—"

"You have to. It's kismet."

"What?"

"Fate. Your destiny. Don't let it slip away."

"But she's with a someone," Connor protested.

"Hell with that, Jack. Just do it."

Connor knew the song, knew there were only a few bars left, and his moment was either now or never. An entire lifetime sometimes hinged on a mere fraction of a moment, and he was on the verge of losing this one. Maybe forever.

He glanced back at Mr. James, who had a knowing glint in his eyes, then felt a surge of courage he hadn't experienced since Iraq. Probably not even since junior high, when he had marched up to Marcia Finch in the school cafeteria and asked her to the eighth-grade dance.

He slipped out of the crowd and edged up to Danielle just as the band played its final note. Without knowing what the next song was going to be, he leaned in and said to her, "May I have the next dance?"

If she was surprised to see him, she didn't show it. In fact, a twinkle flashed in her eye and he sensed the faintest hint of a grin on her lips. Then she took his hand and said, "Why yes, Connor, that would be lovely."

Connor. Just as she'd always called him. Never Jack.

Then she gave her partner a nod and he slipped away, and Connor was left with the distinct feeling he'd just been hosed.

The next song turned out to be a cover of the Zac Brown Band's "Toes," a little more up-tempo than he'd anticipated, but Danielle swung him right into it. It took him a moment to get the metre right, and he made a great show of pretending he was leading her, rather than the other way around. But then they fell into the old rhythm that had been a part of their lives, before events had turned deadly and ripped them apart.

At some point Connor murmured the words "I'm sorry" into her ear, which caused her to touch a finger to his lips.

"Just dance," she said.

They danced.

The song ended, and they danced again. Connor neither knew nor cared what the song was, the only important thing being that they were there together, enveloped in each other's arms at the end of the pier, a quarter of a mile out in the middle of the ocean. The glow of Charleston in the distance, the universe winking its approval at them overhead. Everything in that moment seemed as perfect as perfect could get, their tempo precise as they both seemed as young and innocent as they'd ever been.

Danielle spent the night at Connor's place above the bar. They sat up talking for hours, Connor once more apologizing for almost getting her killed and promising never to put her life in danger ever again. She said she accepted his apology and believed she could trust him to keep his word, but Connor knew the proof would be in his future actions. And he would *not* get another chance.

They were seated on the couch in his cramped living room, Clooney draped across their feet. Danielle gently rubbed his ears, and he responded by letting his tongue hang out, dribbling long strings of drool to the floor. Clooney, not Connor.

"I'm so glad this old guy is still here with you," she said.

"I'm glad you're here with me," he replied. His teeth were still sore from where he'd tasted gravel the night before, and he tried not to wince when he spoke. "I can get used to this."

"One step at a time."

"I'm good with that." They both fell silent for a bit, and then a bit more. Then Connor said, "Everything about tonight was a set-up, wasn't it? You being there, and all."

"I've never stopped thinking about you," was her response. "About us."

Could have fooled me, he felt like saying but didn't. "How did you pull it off?" he asked instead. "I mean, how did you know about tonight?"

She flashed him a smile, then gave him a gentle kiss on his right eye. "After I saw you that night with the horses…well, I realized I was jealous, you being with that woman, and all."

"That woman really was the widow of a man who was shot while I was transporting him back to jail," Connor insisted.

"I know. Mr. James explained all that to me, later. But at the time… well, I know I'd told you that I never wanted to see you again, after I almost died—"

"Because of me," he interrupted.

"Yes, because of you. I did my best trying to forget you, hoped that I'd never run into you. Because I knew that would expose the lie I'd been living all this time."

"What lie was that?" he wanted to know.

"I'd convinced myself that I didn't love you anymore," Danielle confessed. "Then I saw on the news that a bunch of paramilitary shitkickers had almost killed you."

"Proving once again that my word is worth shit," Connor said. "I broke a lot of promises to a lot of people."

"Something you really need to work on. But it was then that I realized you could have died without me telling you how much I loved you, and needed you in my life."

"Even though I'd been stupid and almost got myself killed."

"Even more so, oddly enough. Anyway, I did a little checking, found you were still working for Jordan James, so I gave him a call."

"When was this?" Connor asked.

"Just in the nick of time," she said. "By the way, why is his Bentley parked downstairs?"

Connor still couldn't accept that the luxury motorcar was his, nor did he know what he was going to do with it. He didn't even know how much gas was in the tank. He'd walked the six blocks to the dance party, and Danielle had driven them back after they'd said their goodbyes.

"It's a gift," he replied.

"What? *He gave that thing to you?*"

"Dropped it off yesterday while I was out," he said. "Paid a full year's taxes and insurance on it, too."

"But what are you going to do with a *Bentley*? Don't take this the wrong way, but it's so…not you."

"You're right, and I really haven't had time to figure that out. In fact, I've already been offered a job at a place that works with disabled veterans outside Athens."

"Athens, Georgia, or Athens, Greece?"

"Georgia," Connor said. "Until tonight, when I saw you out there dancing with that schmo in that goofy shirt."

Danielle giggled nervously as she squeezed his hand, then said, "That was Mr. James' idea. Mason's a carpet installer who works at a flooring company he owns, asked him if he could come to the thing tonight."

"Part of the whole set-up?"

"His idea," she admitted. "But I have a much better one."

"And what's that?"

"Come work with me."

"Do what?"

"Work with me," Danielle repeated. "I'm setting up my own mobile vet service, working with farms down in the Edisto area. I need someone who isn't afraid of large animals, and you did great with my ponies that night."

"What about the rescue ranch?" Connor asked.

"I'll continue to do that," she replied. "But there's a real need for a vet who can work with cows and goats and pigs."

"And horses."

"Exactly. Anyway, that's my idea. Just think about it, will you?"

"Say please—"

"Don't push it, Connor."

"You know something, Connor?" she said much later as they lay there in the darkness of the room. The sun was about an hour away from slipping through the slats in the window blinds, but neither of them cared. Right now, day was night and night was day.

"What's that?"

"I think this is the first time we've ever slept together that we didn't, well, actually *sleep together*."

Not necessarily his idea, but he'd honored her wish to take things *slowly*. To be sure things were *right*. "Does that make us old?" he asked.

"No," she said. "It makes us…*us*."

"What does that mean?" he asked, propping his head up on his elbow. It was a rhetorical question and he suspected he knew what she meant, but he wanted to hear her explanation. Reassurance from her that what he was feeling was *us*, too.

"More than just steam and sex between the sheets," she said with a giggle.

"I like steam and sex between the sheets."

"Me too," she replied. "But sometimes inaction speaks louder than action."

"Well, if you say so, who am I to argue?"

She giggled at that and pecked his cheek, then said, "You really are the last true gentleman in Charleston." An old reference to an earlier time, before the twists and snags of life made things complicated.

Sometime after that she drifted off to sleep. Connor lay there in the dark, staring at the ceiling, for the first time in a long while feeling at ease and safe in his world. No midnight triggers that jolted him from his sleep and caused him to jump at every noise outside in the dark. No blasts of phantom grenades in his ears, no screams of dying men toggling his brain. He thought back to that English class he'd taken in community college so many years ago, recalled the words of a poet whose name he couldn't recall: "The past is a bucket of ashes, so live not in your yesterdays, nor just for tomorrow, but in the here and now." He was pretty sure the same poet also had said, "Come clean with a child heart. Laugh as peaches in the summer wind, let rain on a house roof be a song. Let the writing on your face be a smell of apple orchards in late June."

As he lay there, Danielle snuggled warm and hard against his side, he breathed in all those things, inhaled all those senses. Content, at ease, in the cradle of peace for the first time in a very long time. Grateful for all those who had come into his life, determined to keep them there. Safe and secure.

As long as forever lasted, coming at him one day at a time.

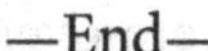

—End—

Author's Notes

Readers who might draw parallels between the entirely fictional Colt Lomax and any contemporary politicians or kingmakers are on the right track, up to the point. The character is, in fact, loosely based on a real powerbroker and financier, but one would have to go back to the mid-south in the 1960s and '70s to identify the exact person (now deceased). Due to that person's imperious and exacting nature and the long arm of retribution, however, his name is known only to me.

While the "bus maze" may seem overly fantastical it is, in fact, based on the doomsday bunker built by a retired couple outside Toronto. Using 42 decommissioned school buses encased in concrete and buried 15 feet underground, they created a 10,000-square-foot survival shelter capable of accommodating 500 people for several months.

The "horses in the mist scene" actually occurred, after my wife and I left a wedding in New Hampshire a few years ago and punctured a tire. There was no Danielle Simmons to show up in a pick-up truck, but we were treated to over an hour of equine enchantment in thick fog until a mechanic arrived with a spare.

To those who were wondering (or checking their trivia skills), the poet mentioned at the end of the final chapter is Carl Sandburg. One of my all-time favorites.

A big shout-out to Frank Metzger, owner of Lowcountry Wraps in Charleston, for teaching me every aspect of the business of wrapping vehicles in vinyl. Also, many thanks to Thomas Sinkler, who made certain I got my facts straight about bond runners and bounty hunters in the state of South Carolina. I also extend my appreciation to the Charleston County Public Defender's Office for their input on courtroom logistics and legal hearings. Any errors I might have made are entirely on me.

As always, I want to thank Jennifer McCord, Phil Garrett, and the rest of the team at Coffeetown Press/Epicenter Press for believing in Jack, and for all they do to provide him a warm and caring home.

I extend boundless gratitude to my amazing and tireless agent, Kimberley Cameron, for her continued career maintenance, and her input in shepherding the entire Jack Connor crime series through to publication.

Last, and in no way least, I thank my incredible wife Diana for her continued love, inspiration, and support for (and of) this odd thing I do that's known as writing. Without your patience and understanding none of this would be possible, and certainly not practical. As I've always said, we're in this bold and dashing adventure together.

About the Author

Reed Bunzel is the author of a half dozen crime novels and thrillers, as well as several nonfiction books. He also is the author of *BunzelGram*, a weekly newsletter that focuses on mysteries and thrillers both in print and on the screen.

A former media industry executive, Bunzel was editor-in-chief for United News and Media's San Francisco publishing operations, overseeing the weekly publication of *The Gavin Report* and *Gavin.com*.

Earlier in his career he was editor-in-chief of Streamline Publishing's *Radio Ink* and *Streaming* magazines, as well as an editor at *Radio & Records* and *Broadcasting* magazine. Additionally, he served in an executive capacity at both the National Association of Broadcasters and the Radio Advertising Bureau.

A graduate of Bowdoin College in Brunswick, Maine, Bunzel holds a Bachelor of Science degree in Anthropology, *cum laude*. A native of the San Francisco Bay Area, he resides with his wife Diana in Charleston, South Carolina.